Never Volunteer

William Alan Larsh

First published in 2023 by Blossom Spring Publishing
Never Volunteer Copyright © 2023 William Alan Larsh
ISBN 978-1-7392955-2-3
E: admin@blossomspringpublishing.com
W: www.blossomspringpublishing.com
Published in the United Kingdom. All rights reserved under
International Copyright Law. Contents and/or cover may not
be reproduced in whole or in part
without the express written consent of the publisher.
Names, characters, places and incidents are either
products of the author's imagination
or are used fictitiously.

Dedicated to my granddaughter, Lucy, whose mere presence brings absolute joy.

Chapter One

Remembering Pearl Harbor

As the years pass me by, I find myself reminiscing more and more about the good old days. I miss them like I miss an old friend. Everybody I know, it seems, says they miss the good old days, but what they really mean is that they miss their younger days. My younger days began February 21, 1925, when I was born. My formative years were interrupted by the Great Depression. Most people would probably agree that it doesn't make a great deal of sense that the worst economic times in American history were the good old days, but they were for me.

This wonderful and memorable time in my life transpired, oddly enough, not only during the Great Depression but during World War II, as well. It would be difficult for many to concede that the good old days coincided with this tumultuous point in history, but they most certainly did. The biggest irony was that they occurred during one of the most devastating times on earth when the ambitions of the most evil and wicked men in all of human history sought to overtake the world. Surprisingly, I had many more friends in those days and was far more socially active than I would ever be again. More significantly, I met and fell in love with the sweetest, most adorable girl in the entire world. In any event, these were without a doubt the good old days, at least in my own little universe.

I had a grand time during the late 1930s and early 1940s. Grand, now there's a word that nobody uses anymore. Back in those good old days, we had many a grand time at parties, dances, and nights out on the town with friends. My youthful exuberance and my love for a girl may have contributed to this being the most enjoyable time of my life. As I reflect on the past, it's hard to believe life was ever so much fun, fulfilling, and meaningful. Who would have thought I could have experienced so much joy in such a short period of time in a world so turbulent and volatile? My buddies and I tended to say with frequency that we had a grand time, as did all the girls we knew. Most guys and girls of that era also described a happy person or event as gay. Nowadays, it would just confuse people to say we had a gay time, but everybody said it back in my day. It could have been that this word was later appropriated because women seemed to have used it more often, but I certainly don't know. I still miss the gay times we had in those days, and it's a shame no one from my generation can describe it in that way any longer.

Back then, my friends and I were all tough guys, and if a guy didn't measure up to being tough or masculine, then we called him a big sis, as in sissy, but never gay. My friends and I frequently hung out on the street corner, usually at the intersection of Federal and Aisquith Streets in Baltimore City. We referred to ourselves as fellas. All of us smoked, drank, cursed, shot craps, participated in stupid arguments, and occasionally engaged in fisticuffs with one another. More importantly, our favorite topic of discussion was girls. The fellas were my friends and there were no sissies among us.

I began smoking cigarettes at the age of sixteen. The brand I preferred was Chesterfield. Unfortunately for my health, I genuinely enjoyed smoking. I smoked two packs of filterless cigarettes a day for the next thirty-seven years, even after filters were introduced in the 1960s. Nearly everyone smoked in those days. Nobody ever told us it would kill us until decades later. By the time I reached middle age, I was so addicted to nicotine that I would become quite irritable and downright surly without ingesting two packs of Chesterfields each and every day. I recall one Thanksgiving during the 1970s when I had run out of cigarettes. As a result, I had been out of sorts the entire morning. My wife and the five kids were really plucking my fragile nerves, and I let them know it. It was the usual noisy and boisterous crowd in the Culpepper household.

"Hells bells! Will you people keep it down?" I implored in an angry, agitated tone, shortly before dinner started at about two in the afternoon.

"Geesh, Dad," my eldest daughter exclaimed. "You need to lighten up, it's Thanksgiving."

"You're all too damn loud," I shouted, having no self-awareness regarding my own decibel level.

They had done nothing to deserve my wrath other than being in my presence. I suffered through dinner with every member of the family grating on my last nerve. Finally, after dinner, my wife pleaded, "Monty, please do everybody a favor and go out and get some cigarettes."

I jumped up from the dining room table and made a beeline for the front door. I said nothing to anyone. I drove my 1968 Delta 88 Oldsmobile like Mario Andretti to Read's drugstore located in the Perry Hall Shopping Center less than a mile away. I purchased a carton of Chesterfields and ripped open the box as I exited the store. I lit up a cigarette right there on the sidewalk in front of Read's. I felt like a junkie getting his fix for the day. I returned to the house a changed man to enjoy the rest of Thanksgiving with my family.

Sorry, I digressed. Let me get back to the grand times with me and the fellas on the street corner in 1941. At times, however, grand times turned into trouble, as in physical fights. We generally argued without resorting to violence, but sometimes situations just deteriorated. The battles my friends and I got into typically were not all-out brawls, but minor disagreements settled with the occasional fistfight. The worst fight I ever got into in my life, oddly enough, was with one of my best friends, Moe Moran, and it had nothing to do with any personal quarrel. It came about following the Joe Louis-Billy Conn fight for the world heavyweight championship. Billy Conn was the light heavyweight champion, but he had tried his hand unsuccessfully in the heavyweight division against the best heavyweight fighter of all time, Joe Louis. The fellas and I would often watch highlights of Joe Louis' bouts when they appeared in the newsreels at the movie theatre, but we normally listened to his fights on the radio live. Joe Louis was unequivocally the greatest fighter I had ever seen. Many people later said Cassius Clay, oh excuse me, I guess he was Muhammad Ali, was the greatest of all time, but let me tell you, Joe Louis would have wiped the floor with him. Nobody punched as hard as the Brown Bomber. In my opinion, if Joe Louis and Muhammad Ali had fought in the same era and their prime, Joe would have murdered him.

Back to my own personal greatest fight. I had just seen the newsreel of the Louis-Conn fight at the Hippodrome Theatre downtown. I was describing every detail of the fight, round by round, to Moe and the fellas, as was highlighted in the newsreel. I demonstrated Joe Louis' moves and combination punches. Louis knocked out Conn in the thirteenth round, which I expertly reenacted. I played Louis while Moe stood there as Conn. In doing so, I accidentally hit Moe in the face with a right cross, the punch in which Louis finished off Conn. Well, holy cow, all hell broke loose. Moe went absolutely bananas. He was beyond thoroughly incensed.

I had seen Moe get mad before, but never with this degree of rage. His face went blood red, and he came at me like a wild animal. It felt as though we fought fifteen rounds for the heavyweight championship of the world right then and there on the street corner, except, unfortunately, there were no breaks between rounds, and we were not wearing boxing gloves. Regrettably, too, I was no Joe Louis. We were closer in size to two Billy Conns, although not nearly as big, but as evenly matched as could be, at least physically. We were both athletic, and with all due humility, very coordinated as well. Both of us were about average height with slim builds, five feet ten inches tall, weighing a hundred and fifty pounds, tops. It was more of a welterweight fight really.

At any rate, we threw left jabs continuously, and more right crosses than I ever imagined. We were each landing shots to each other's heads and many to the rib cage. It was brutal. I felt as though I was fighting for my life. If ever there was a time to keep your guard up, literally, this was it. Luckily, we eventually stopped brawling, mainly due to our arm weariness and overall fatigue. Moe was as exhausted as I was, without a doubt. Thankfully, the other fellas watching this extraordinary bout called it a draw and encouraged us to quit. Without much hesitation, both Moe and I immediately stopped fighting. After all, it was getting late, and we had school the next day. Breathing heavily, Moe and I shook hands, smiled at each other, and headed home. We remained good friends and never bore any animosity toward one another following this memorable, long-drawn, dragged-out, almost historic fight.

As I stated previously, I was born on February 21, 1925, which was a bitter cold Saturday winter night in Baltimore City. I was delivered by a midwife who weighed me on a meat scale in the kitchen at a whopping twelve pounds. This might well be the primary reason my mother never liked me. My life began right dab in the middle of the Roaring Twenties. Calvin Coolidge was the President of the United States at the time, governing over a nation during a period of great economic prosperity. Coolidge's reputation was renowned for being a man of few words. Once at a White House function, a woman told the President she made a bet that she could get him to say more than two words during the evening. Coolidge famously responded, "You lose."

During these thriving times, my family lived comfortably in the rowhouse where I was born at 1103 East Federal Street, located a mile or so northeast of downtown Baltimore. It looked very much like most all the other rowhouses in the city with its three stories, marble steps, and an alley out back. About fifty years later after playing a round of golf at Clifton Park with my thirteen-year-old son, John, I decided to drive the short distance from the golf course to show him my birthplace. I had been feeling a bit nostalgic. I lived there until I was twenty-one years old. When we arrived at the 1100 block of East Federal Street, I saw nothing. My boyhood home was no longer there. Not only was my house not there, but the entire block of rowhouses was gone too. In their place was a parking lot. It gave me such a melancholy feeling. Only my memories remained of the place where I grew up.

"Aww, it's a parking lot," I said disappointingly to my son.

It bothered me on a much deeper level than I let on. I had a wonderful childhood there, despite the fact that my family provided me with a minimum amount of love and affection. I had not recognized their lack of feeling at the time, probably because I had great friends and experienced grand times growing up in the neighborhood. It really made me depressed, though, to see that the house and the entire neighborhood had disappeared. The good old days of my youth on Federal Street had literally been leveled flat.

I was the third child of Montgomery and Jessie Culpepper. I had two older sisters, Margaret, who was three years older, and Edith, who was fourteen months older than me. As children, Edith was my nemesis. The sibling rivalry was constant, plus she was just plain nasty. My mother favored the girls. I believed my mother never wanted a boy. In fact, no one in my family ever called me by my given name. I was nicknamed Boy. For my entire life, even as an old man, everybody in my family continued calling me Boy. Even my nieces and nephews called me Uncle Boy. My family was not all bad as families went, but thinking back on it, they were not all that great either. Despite my mother and sister, I enjoyed my childhood.

"December 7th, 1941, a day which will live in infamy," President Franklin Delano Roosevelt declared to Congress after the Japs attacked Pearl Harbor. President Roosevelt's words described this horrific day in history perfectly, but it was a horrendous day for me personally for an entirely different reason. I was a junior in high school at the time. I attended the Baltimore Polytechnic Institute, colloquially referred to as Poly. The boys in Baltimore who excelled in mathematics normally attended Poly, as it was a technical engineering school. It was also an all-boys school. The guys who did not excel in mathematics generally went to the less prestigious high school, Baltimore City College. I hate to be a braggart, but I was a wizard when it came to mathematics. It came naturally to me. When I took algebra in the eighth and ninth grades, my friends struggled to figure it out, but I took to it like riding a bicycle.

In the tenth grade, I conquered geometry. I never missed a single geometry question the entire semester, not one. The geometry teacher gave me a ninety-nine percent grade at the end of the semester and told me, "Monty, you're my best student and I know you've never missed a question on any test during the semester, but I am only giving you ninety-nine percent for your final grade because nobody is perfect."

As a fifteen-year-old, I was a little put off with the geometry teacher. I certainly believed I deserved a one hundred percent grade. After all, as the teacher said himself, I had not missed a single question on any test. It was just common sense that I deserved to receive the grade I truly had. I thought, "How dare he deprive me of a perfect grade when I earned it?"

As I grew older, however, it occurred to me that maybe the teacher was right. I came to the realization after years of facing the trials and tribulations of life that my tenth-grade geometry teacher actually had made a rather profound remark. I grew to appreciate that he must have possessed a certain amount of wisdom; way beyond what my young and inexperienced mind could have comprehended. After all, no one was indeed perfect, least of all, me.

I had another teacher, Mr. Eisenberg, back in grade school, who taught me something even more valuable. Mr. Eisenberg had been a veteran of the Great War, having served in the United States Navy. He told us once in class to never draw on ourselves. The smartest kid in the class, and my good friend, David Collins, said with a certain degree of irony, "But Mr. Eisenberg, you have a tattoo of an anchor on your forearm."

"That was when I was young and foolish," Mr. Eisenberg glibly responded without hesitation.

In the years that followed, when I served in the United States Navy, the sailors going ashore were all getting tattoos. I recalled Mr. Eisenberg's words and refrained from the tattoo ritual with my friends. However, this was not the greatest lesson he taught me. Mr. Eisenberg actually educated me on two things I would never forget throughout my life. The second lesson he instilled in me occurred after he told a story to the class about an experience he had in the First World War. He recited what I thought was a tall tale to the class, concerning gold coins falling from an airplane being retrieved by the infantry on the ground.

As I sat listening to Mr. Eisenberg's story, I whispered to David Collins seated next to me, "He's lying, he's lying, he's lying."

David was often amused by my flippant remarks, and I really only said them for David's benefit to entertain him. I truly believed, however, that Mr. Eisenberg was telling an outlandish story. I never intended for anyone to hear me other than David. Unfortunately, Mr. Eisenberg overheard me. He immediately grabbed me by the arm and dragged me out of the classroom and into the hallway.

"Boy, you never call anyone a liar," he said sternly. "Even if you think that person is lying, under no circumstances do you ever call them a liar. You might not believe their story or what they are saying, but never call them a liar. Do you understand?"

"Yes sir," I answered immediately. "I understand."

For the rest of my life, I heeded Mr. Eisenberg's advice. I never called anyone a liar, even when I knew they were lying. I often told individuals who obviously were lying that they must be mistaken, or that they were not making sense, or even that they must have possibly heard wrong, but I never accused anyone of lying. Furthermore, I never drew anything on myself and never, ever, even remotely considered getting a tattoo, either while in the Navy or at any point thereafter, thanks solely to Mr. Eisenberg.

Now, we were discussing one of the worst days in American history, December 7, 1941. As I stated previously, it was not such a great day for me, either. It started out all right. My father generously allowed me to borrow his car, a 1940 Buick. Sunday was Pop's day of rest, but not for any religious reasons. My family had not been to any kind of church service since I was five years old. I recall my parents taking my sisters and me to the Presbyterian Church. I think my mother was raised Presbyterian back in Scotland where she grew up, but she was not very religious, and neither was my Pop. For whatever reason, my family stopped going to church when I was little.

Pop was a lather by trade. A lather was not a guy making soap suds, mind you. In the old days, a lather was a guy who worked in construction making sure the wiring and pipes and everything in the ceilings were in place by installing insulation and plaster in the ceiling. At least that was what Pop told me and I worked as a lather myself after the war for a short time. I hated it. It was hard work and physically exhausting. Pop was a member of the Baltimore Lathers' Union as far back as I could remember. He became the President of the Union in his later years. Pop worked with his hands above his head all day long for over forty years. If anybody thought that didn't keep a fellow in great physical shape, they should try it sometime. My Pop was in top form his entire life, always very lean and muscular. He only developed a very slight paunch after he retired at the age of seventy.

Pop was slender, but he was a strong, wiry fellow. Until he retired, his belly was as tight as a steel drum, and although his arms were not particularly big, the definition of muscle in his forearms and biceps was pronounced, kind of like Popeye's, but not quite that large. When I was a boy, I saw Pop flatten a guy in the city with a quick right cross. I have no idea what the beef between my father and the man was, but I witnessed him deck this guy in an instant. I was quite impressed. The image stuck with me my entire life. I realized from a very young age that Pop was as tough as nails and not a person to be trifled with. I knew he was out of work for a time during the Depression. When I was very young, I remembered once we went through a soup line because we were so poor. Pop loved President Roosevelt, or FDR as Pop always referred to him. He said that thanks to FDR, the New Deal, and the Works Progress Administration, he finally got steady work, which kept us out of the poor house.

My Pop worked ten hours a day and came home dead tired. He had a routine where he came through the front door every evening at six o'clock, took a shower, and headed to bed for a two-hour nap. He never ate dinner with the family. Mom normally fixed dinner before he got home. After we ate, she saved his meal to heat up later when he woke up in the evening at eight or so. My family was a strange bunch. I never really interacted much with Pop, and unfortunately, I saw too much of Mom.

My sisters were a mixed bag. My oldest sister, Margaret, was a sweetheart. She was tall, good-looking, and a fine person. In fact, sometimes I think some high-class family must have raised her and transplanted her into our household. She had such poise and refinement that I honestly wondered where she could have come from. It was not as if my parents had no class or anything like that, but Margaret seemed so different. Mom and Pop were not ignoramuses, for Pete's sake, but they just happened to be normal working-class folks. Pop had no illusions about his lot in life. I doubt if he ever even gave it a second thought. I would describe Pop as the most pragmatic man I ever knew.

I knew Pop lost a lot of money in 1929 when the stock market crashed, and the banks closed. I heard him complain about it numerous times growing up. What really got his goat was the banks. Boy, did he ever hate banks. His life savings, a considerable amount of money from the way he described it, was lost when his bank went under following the crash. He never put another dime in the bank for the remainder of his life. I suspected he stashed his money somewhere in the house, but the hiding place was some sort of state secret. I never knew where it was, nor did anyone else. Of course, I was fairly certain he never had too much money to hide anyway.

I was always under the impression that my mother liked to think she was high-class, but she wasn't. If she actually believed she was, then she was delusional. Her father had been a police constable in Inverness, Scotland, where she was raised. She came from a large family, one brother and the rest were girls, five sisters in all, I think. She often spoke of the small stone house they lived in at 26 Tomnahurich Street near the River Ness, a few blocks from downtown Inverness in the Highlands of Scotland. She did not come from the upper crust of society. Mom dressed impeccably though, and always had perfectly coiffed hair. She always endeavored to look her best. One might have even described her as attractive. I would not say she was movie star attractive, but her appearance was more fashionable than most other kids' mothers in my neighborhood. She wore stylish new dresses, while everyone else wore more plain-looking outfits. Her hair was always fixed up nicely while everybody else's appeared ordinary. But neither Mom nor Pop could ever be mistaken for being anything other than just regular people.

My oldest sister, Margaret, on the other hand,

possessed this rare quality of beauty, sophistication, self-assurance, and intelligence. The splendor of Margaret was that she had no air of pretension or any hint that she was at all taken with herself when she easily could have. She was one of the sweetest, kindest people I ever knew with absolutely no malice in her heart.

My other sister, Edith, however, was the Anti-Christ. I would have to say that she was jealous, spiteful, and just plain nasty, particularly to me. When I was twelve, I told her to go soak her head during an argument we were having. I have no memory of what it was all about, but it was a dandy. She became infuriated at my remarks.

"You can't talk to me like that," she said.

My father's hammer was nearby, unfortunately. My skinny little sister grabbed the hammer and came up behind me, whacking me on the back of the head. I never felt such pain before. I collapsed face down onto the floor. I had no idea how long I lay there. I remembered trying to clear my head. What a headache I had! I placed the palm of my hand on the back of my head and felt a large bump, tender and painful to the touch. Luckily, she was not very strong. I think she hit me with the side of the hammer. Had she hit me straight on with that hammer like hitting a nail, she probably would have killed me, or at least have caused a permanent indentation in my skull, if not brain damage.

Throughout my years growing up with Edith, I described her in only one way. She was "the quintessential bitch." Well, I guess she could be described in two ways. I forgot, she was the Anti-Christ, too. My mother spoiled her rotten. As far back as I could remember, I had been excluded from every trip my mother and sisters had gone on. Before I was born, I was told Mom took them back to see her parents in Inverness. Mom had subsequently taken Margaret and Edith to New

York, Boston, Philadelphia, Atlantic City, Ocean City, and a number of other places on day trips or overnight trips on the train or bus. She had never once taken me along. My father never went because he had to work, although he had no interest in going anywhere anyway. I became accustomed to being left out, but I never forgot it. It irked me my whole life because they never stopped excluding me, even after we were all grown up and married with children.

After the war and nearly every year for the next two or three decades, my mother vacationed at the beach in Ocean City with Edith's and Margaret's families. Without fail, my crazy mother said to me following every one of these vacations, "Boy, you should have been with us at the shore last week, we had a great time!" Maybe she was totally unaware of how insulting she was, but it was infuriating, nonetheless.

She never invited me once, not once. I went one time with all of them in 1968 with my wife and five children, only because I found out they were going, and I invited myself. It turned out to be a mistake. Everybody generally had a good time, but by that stage in my life, I didn't fit in. It was slightly uncomfortable knowing that Mom, Margaret, and Edith had planned the trip and I just horned in on it. I never went again, and I was never asked either.

It was not as if my parents were mean to me when I was young. They usually let me do whatever I wanted, well, except for going to the pool hall. My mother thought that every degenerate in the world hung out at the pool hall. I went there all the time, as did my friends. We never considered ourselves degenerates. I loved shooting pool and I was not bad at it either. I liked betting with the fellas. We never played for much money, typically only two bits a game. I enjoyed the competition and more often than not, I came out a winner.

I loved the fact in pool that nobody ever said, "good shot." Instead, the acknowledgment of a good shot was banging the bottom of the pool cue on the floor, as if clapping. I relished the whole atmosphere of the pool hall, the comradery with the fellas, the competition, the smoking, the cursing, and, of course, the betting.

As much as I loved the gambling aspect, I was never stupid enough to get suckered in by any pool sharks. Pool sharks were the really exceptional players who conned guys by letting them win a few games before they suggested playing for money. Then they played just well enough to win. I knew who those guys were. I generally just competed with the fellas. My problem with my mother was that I always forgot to wash my hands after leaving the pool hall and heading home. On occasion when my mother caught me coming through the door, she would grab my hands to see if I had any chalk on them. When she saw pool chalk, watch out. Many a time I got slapped upside the head entering the house because I forgot to wash my hands.

"I told you not to go to the pool hall," she yelled at me. "Only criminals and troublemakers frequent pool halls."

"Oh, Mom!" I responded. "My friends all go and they're not criminals. They're good guys."

"They might be good people, but the rest of the people in there are no good itinerant criminals," she roared back at me.

"I give up," I said to her, hurrying to my bedroom to get away from her. My mother had an extremely violent temper. Honestly, I thought the woman was crazy. Half of the time, I never knew what the hell she was talking about. Itinerant criminals? What the hell was that?

I came to accept the fact that my mother preferred my

sisters over me. Heck, they all referred to me as Boy, even my Pop. I mean nobody in my family ever called me by my given name, Montgomery. Of course, nobody in the world called me Montgomery anyway. My friends all called me Monty. My mother even had a female friend my age who she preferred over me. Her name was Jane Hasslinger. Jane's father owned a very successful seafood restaurant in Baltimore somewhere, but I had never been there.

Jane was nice enough, but her constant presence in the house was annoying and disruptive. She was always hanging around. She was not the most attractive girl either. I had never seen her in a dress. She always wore slacks. Her hair was cropped short, and she was a little chubby. I gave her some credit for at least having an amiable personality. She was very vivacious and always seemed to be enjoying herself. She continually appeared happy and content. I never saw her depressed or in a bad mood. My mother adored her. I guess Jane didn't get enough attention at home or something, I really never knew. All I knew was that she got way more attention from my mother than I had gotten from her my entire life. I guess that was the real reason why I found Jane so objectionable.

When I think about it, I didn't get too much attention from anybody in my family. Pop worked all the time and normally took a nap when he got home from work, so consequently, I didn't talk to him very much. He was a good guy and all, but he wasn't exactly an attention-giving kind of guy. In my entire life, he never really said a helluva whole lot to me, although he never treated me badly either. It was just that he never went out of his way to show any affection toward me. The best thing I could say about Pop was that he would generally let me use the family car. On Sundays, he usually didn't go anywhere.

He never attended church or really did anything else, except relax at home, have a few beers or some whiskey, and listen to the ball game on the radio.

On Sunday, December 7, 1941, when I was sixteen years old, I asked Pop if I could take the Buick and drive the fellas over to Clifton Park to play football.

"Sure," Pop said.

"Thanks, Pop," I said. "You're the greatest."

Clifton Park was less than a mile from our house. My best friend, Bill Rowley, lived two doors down at 1107 East Federal Street in a three-story rowhouse identical to ours. Everybody called him by his last name, Rowley. My other friends, Moe Moran and Joe Albrecht, lived a few blocks away on Aisquith Street. After Rowley and I picked up Moe and Joe, we swung by Ed "Irish" Clark's house on Biddle Street to pick him up. We all lived in rowhouses. Baltimore was packed with rowhouses, one looking very similar to the next.

As we made our way toward Clifton Park, Irish suggested we get some ice cream first before playing football. It was funny how everybody called him Irish. Irish lived in the middle of the Tenth Ward in Baltimore. I think everybody in the Tenth Ward, apart from my family, was of Irish descent. It seemed nutty that my friend was called Irish rather than his given name. Everybody's nickname in the entire Tenth Ward could have been Irish. Anyway, Irish was always hungry and on this particular day, a rather cold one, Irish desired ice cream before partaking in a collegial game of football.

We drove north on Gay Street which turned into Belair Road before making a left, heading west onto the winding roads through Clifton Park. We passed by several holes on the golf course, the clay tennis courts, the Clifton Park clubhouse, which formerly had been Johns Hopkins' summer home the previous century, and past the baseball fields. There was nary a person in sight playing any sport. We then turned right onto Harford Road heading north to the ice cream shop a couple of miles up the road. Personally, I didn't want any ice cream. It was too cold outside. I was only interested in playing football, but Irish was such a baby if he didn't get his way. Upon turning onto Harford Road, I accelerated rather quickly. I guess I was showing off a bit with the fellas. As I raced down Harford Road, either Moe or Joe said, "You're going a little fast, aren't you, Monty?"

Upon hearing this subtle critique of my driving, I hit the gas a little more. After all, I was a sixteen-year-old kid. I was like most guys that age. If a buddy told you to slow down, of course you were going to go faster. Who was driving this Buick anyway? I wasn't going to listen to any backseat drivers. No sooner had I accelerated when I noticed a car entering the intersection to my right from Erdman Avenue. By this time, my speed was up to sixty-five miles per hour.

The putting green for the first hole at the Clifton Park golf course was on the south side of Erdman Avenue, as well as Mother's Garden, a picturesque part of Clifton Park with a stone pavilion and bridge. A large sedan suddenly turned right onto Harford Road from Erdman Avenue directly in front of me. I reacted by slamming on the brakes and turning the steering wheel sharply to the left to avoid colliding with the vehicle. I hit the brakes with such force that I thought my feet would go through the floorboard. The result of turning the steering wheel and hitting the brakes simultaneously while driving roughly sixty-five miles an hour was that the car went airborne and flipped over several times as it propelled down Harford Road.

The good news was that I missed the vehicle that turned in front of me and no other cars were traveling south on Harford Road in the other direction. The bad news was that my passengers and I were thrown around the inside of the vehicle like laundry in a spin dryer. Moe broke his arm and Joe bashed his head and was bleeding. They were both taken to the hospital in an ambulance. Luckily, Rowley, Irish, and I walked away with just a few bruises. The Buick, however, was totaled. It no longer even resembled a drivable vehicle. It was so banged up and dented that it went straight to the junkyard.

The police arrived and questioned me regarding the accident. I told the officer that the other car turned right in front of me from Erdman Avenue.

"Son, were you speeding?" the policeman asked.

I knew damn well that I was speeding, but I answered, "I didn't think so."

The police could always tell how fast a car was going by the length of the skid marks on the road. They could make some computation and figure out that if you made some ten-foot skid before you stopped, then you were going a hundred and fifty miles an hour or something. My skid mark must have been no more than a foot since I immediately went airborne. The police officer's computation measuring the short skid mark indicated erroneously that I was traveling under the speed limit. Had he figured into his computation that I went airborne, I might have been in big trouble. I was not aware of the police having any equations for a vehicle becoming airborne, but the bottom line was that he never cited me or fined me for speeding or reckless driving or anything. In fact, he faulted the person driving the other vehicle who turned onto Harford Road in front of me. The driver of that vehicle never even saw me coming since I was traveling practically at the speed of light.

"There was really nothing you could do," the police

officer told me. "You clearly had the right of way."

Holy crap, what a stroke of luck! Apparently, nobody saw me flying down Harford Road. Fortunately, the golf course was void of any golfers on such a cold day. If anybody had been playing golf on the first hole, they surely would have seen me speeding. The only witnesses to my reckless driving were my best friends, and they wouldn't have ratted me out in a million years.

After the police completed their incredible accident investigation, Rowley, Irish, and I walked to Union Memorial Hospital several blocks away at the intersection of 33rd Street and Guilford Avenue, where an ambulance had taken Moe and Joe. We found Moe with his arm set in a cast and Joe with stitches in his forehead. The five of us then walked home. It was about seven o'clock in the evening when I finally arrived home. I dreaded having to tell my father I wrecked his car. I was fully expecting Pop to murder me. As I entered through the front door, my whole family was gathered around the radio in the parlor. Margaret and Edith glanced at me with very worried looks as I walked into the parlor. Both immediately turned back to give their full attention to the announcer on the radio. Mom and Pop were listening so intently to the news reports that they weren't even aware I came into the room. The radio was broadcasting the news about the Japanese bombing of Pearl Harbor.

None of us had ever even heard of Pearl Harbor except for Pop. He was the only one who knew where Pearl Harbor was. Pop had served in the United States Navy for over seven years. He enlisted when he was eighteen years old in 1913 and served through the First World War before being discharged in 1920. On the evening of December 7, 1941, as the family was gathered around the radio, Pop explained how he was assigned as a Gunner's First Mate aboard the *U.S.S. Oklahoma*, which docked at

Pearl Harbor for two weeks back in 1915. He had shore leave in Honolulu for forty-eight hours. Pop reminisced fondly all evening about his younger days serving in the Navy as a deep-sea diver and how he met Mom in Inverness, Scotland after the Great War ended when he was dismantling mines in the Cromarty Firth, a bay located north of Inverness. The mines were initially placed there during the war to prevent German boats from attacking the north of Scotland. I finally interrupted Pop while he was telling his war stories to tell him about the accident.

"Pop, I've got some bad news," I blurted out. "I had an accident this afternoon in the Buick."

"What happened?" Pop asked as he turned from the radio looking straight at me.

"Well," I said. "The fellas and I were heading up Harford Road when a car pulled out right in front of me from Erdman Avenue. I hit the brakes and turned away from the guy real sharply, but the car flipped over. The car's wrecked beyond repair. Moe and Joe went to the hospital. Moe broke his arm and Joe got stitches in his forehead, but the rest of us are okay."

"Don't worry, Boy, it's all right," Pop said to my complete surprise. "Accidents happen. Let's just be thankful nobody was hurt bad, or worse yet, killed."

"Yes sir," I responded in disbelief.

"Boy, the important thing was that nobody was seriously hurt," Mom chimed in. "Your father can replace the car. Isn't that right, Monty?"

"You're right, Jessie," Pop said as he nodded in agreement with Mom. "Don't worry about the car, Boy. We can get another one."

I really thought I was in the deepest trouble I had ever been in. I conveniently left out the part of the story that I was going sixty-five miles an hour. I was lucky Pop was in the strangest and most benevolent mood that night. Thank heavens for that! Who would have thought that an attack on Pearl Harbor would have saved my neck?

The next day, Rowley and I caught the trolley to go to school. Rowley was my closest friend at Poly. David Collins was on the trolley too. He attended Poly as well. It was always awkward running into David because he had been one of my best friends from grade school. David lived only a block down the street from me on Federal Street, but he never hung out with me and the fellas. Sadly, the fellas generally didn't care for him. David once asked me why they didn't like him. I told him I had no idea. I sort of knew, but I never wanted to hurt his feelings. I surmised that David was a bit too strait-laced for the rest of the fellas. He neither smoked, drank, gambled, nor cursed, so he never quite fit in.

I always liked him, but we just sort of went our separate ways. I had classes with him at Poly and I always said hello to him. David's father was a very nice man, too. He was very tall like David, but he always struck me as a bit of a big sis. Rowley just plain never liked David. Maybe Rowley thought David was a big sis, too, but I never really knew the reason why, and I never asked Rowley or the fellas about it. The other fellas never did anything malicious or mean to David, they were just completely indifferent toward him. In a way, it was mean. Irish, Moe, and Joe went to City College, so they rarely ran into him. Anyhow, as we rode to school on the trolley, Rowley and I both wondered if Moe and Joe made it to school after suffering their injuries from the car wreck on Sunday.

"I bet they're okay today," I told Rowley. "Heck, they walked miles to get home last night. It's not like they're in wheelchairs or anything."

"Yeah, I guess you're right. They were fine," Rowley

said. "So, how'd it go when you got home last night? I bet you got hell from your old man for wrecking his car!"

"You wouldn't have believed it," I said. "He was so caught up with the Pearl Harbor attack; he was just thankful nobody got hurt in the accident. I thought I was in some kind of dream. First, the cop thought the accident was unavoidable, and then Pop let me off the hook for the whole mess, Scot-free. I think maybe I should get into some kind of high stakes craps game or a raffle or something tonight."

"Wow, you are pretty damn lucky, Monty," Rowley retorted.

"It gets better," I continued. "My mother practically ordered Pop to get a new car and fast."

"What the hell?" Rowley said. "She doesn't even drive, does she?"

"No, she doesn't," I responded. "Do you remember earlier this year in school when I was so tired because I had to pick up my mother at one in the morning downtown at those dance contests?"

"Oh yeah, I remember," Rowley said. "She really loves going out dancing, doesn't she?"

"Yeah, she's nuts," I said.

"But why can't she get home?" Rowley asked.

"I don't know," I answered. "I think maybe the trolley service stops at midnight or at one or something. Or maybe she doesn't want to go home alone."

"How come your father doesn't go with her?" Rowley asked curiously.

"He works every day," I said. "And besides, he doesn't dance."

"Who's she dancing with?" Rowley probed.

"Well, she mostly goes with Pop's best friend," I answered. "You know him, John Battaglia. He owns the barbershop."

"Oh yeah, the bookie," Rowley said.

"Yeah, he's good to Pop," I said. "He's been friends with Mom and Pop forever. John and his wife don't have any kids. So anyhow, Mom wants this car so she can continue to go out. It's good for me because Pop lets me use the car. The only downside is I'll have to pick up Mom downtown in the middle of the night."

"How come John doesn't take her home?" Rowley asked.

"I don't know," I responded. "He just doesn't. I guess he has to get home. Besides, she doesn't always go with him. Sometimes she goes alone and participates in those stupid dance contests."

"That's weird," Rowley said.

"Yeah, my mom is weird," I shot back, completely unembarrassed. "She's a screwball!"

Rowley and I were so consumed with the car accident that we nearly forgot about the country being at war. Every boy at school that week was full of excitement. They talked of nothing but going to war. Germany declared war on us after the Pearl Harbor attack. The United States declared war on Germany and Japan. The world had gone insane. I never saw so much anxiety amongst my classmates. The rumors were running rampant, including that the Japs had bombed California. Then the gossip was that they invaded the west coast and that the Nazis would invade the east coast. Of course, none of it was true. My eager classmates and I, though, were all making plans on signing up to fight as soon as we graduated. The problem was that we were only juniors in high school. Graduation for my class was still a year and a half away, but that was soon to change.

After a couple of weeks, we were off from school for the Christmas break. It was a good thing, too. The guys at school really needed to calm down. Nobody was able to concentrate on school with all the talk of war. Despite the apprehension concerning our future, the fellas and I had a great time over the Christmas break. I played a lot of football with my buddies, minus Moe, of course, who was still nursing his broken arm from the car accident. The guys frequented the Alcazar Ballroom on Friday and Saturday nights during the winter break. The Alcazar was a nice hotel in Mount Vernon on Cathedral Street about a mile or so from my house. Mount Vernon was a very nice neighborhood in Baltimore and was mostly known for having the first monument ever erected to George Washington. The swingingest bands played at the Alcazar. Of course, they never had big-name bands such as the likes of Tommy Dorsey, Artie Shaw, Bennie Goodman, or Glenn Miller, but they had some damn good ones, despite being local, small-time orchestras. My Pop never danced to my knowledge, but I could really cut a rug. I was not the best jitterbug partner in the joint, but I held my own. I had some decent moves and could really bop with the beat. I never tried any acrobatic moves like some of those real swinging cats did. Some of those guys, and the girls too, looked like they should have been in the movies dancing. I was respectable, but I was not as good as some. At any rate, I liked it, and it was a good way to meet girls.

At the time, I dated a few girls, and I liked girls generally, but I wasn't really interested in getting too serious with any one girl. I took pleasure in dancing and maybe getting a kiss now and then, but I wasn't looking for any steady girlfriend. Most of the girls I knew actually annoyed me, particularly in the phony manner in which they talked and walked. They all seemed to be putting on an act as far as I was concerned, but I relished dancing, especially with a good-looking girl. I had a wonderful time during the winter break dancing at the

Alcazar, playing football at the park, and shooting pool with the fellas, as well as ice skating, another activity I found entertaining. It all took my mind off the war, too.

The real surprise that winter was what I learned about my parents from my spinster aunt, Isabelle Macintosh from Inverness, who came to live with us the previous summer. She occupied the bedroom that my grandparents formerly inhabited. Pop's parents, Leonard and Amanda Culpepper, lived with us since I was a little boy until they died. Grandpa died when I was thirteen years old. He was much like Pop. He never said a whole helluva lot either. I remembered very little about him except that I was a little afraid of him. He was a tall man with gray hair and a huge, gray bushy mustache. I imagined he was not really a bad guy, but I never truly knew him. He just seemed so elderly, and he smelled funny too, like an old person. He always had a cigarette hanging from his lips, as if it were stuck there with glue. He worked as a lather his whole life, like Pop. He evidently did not have enough money to be able to afford his own place in his old age. Nobody got Social Security checks in those days, so when Grandpa got too old to work, he and Grandma had to move in with us.

The only thing Grandpa left Pop after he died was his lucky 1881 five-dollar gold piece he carried with him his entire adult life. Pop told me once why it was so lucky. The details were a bit sketchy, but it had something to do with him being paid with the five-dollar gold coin by his employer back in his hometown in Des Moines, Iowa. The story was that when Grandpa was a young man, he was standing inside a place of business in Des Moines in front of a large pane glass, store-front type of window while waiting to be paid for his services. His employer evidently tried to hand him a five-dollar gold piece as payment, but the coin dropped to the floor. Apparently, at the very moment Grandpa bent over to pick it up, a stray bullet came crashing through the front window, whizzing over Grandpa's head, and striking his employer square in the chest, killing him instantly. Had he been standing, the story went, the bullet would have surely hit Grandpa, and not his poor, unfortunate employer.

Grandpa reportedly said, "It sure was lucky I dropped that coin. I'd have been dead for sure, and that boss man would have been walking around alive five dollars richer instead of me. That there is the luckiest five-dollar gold piece on the face of this earth." Grandpa never spent the five-dollar gold coin and instead carried it with him for the rest of his life. Pop inherited the lucky coin and Pop said I would get it after he died.

Grandma died two years before Grandpa when I was eleven. She was certainly old, too. My recollection was that she was always a bit grumpier than Grandpa. She had a perennial sourpuss face. All I knew about her was that she came from Sweden when she was young. She was Grandpa's second wife. His first wife died young. We had a photograph of Grandma hanging in the house she had taken when she was about twenty years old shortly after she arrived in the United States. She was very good-looking in the portrait, but in her old age, she hardly even resembled her former self. Pop had one brother and four sisters. My Uncle Lincoln, who lived in Baltimore somewhere, was deaf and dumb. He would visit the house occasionally, but it was awkward since he could not communicate well. They told me he worked at a bakery somewhere across town.

Pop's oldest sister, my Aunt Edith, who my sister was named after, lived nearby around the corner so we saw her and her family regularly. They could all hear and speak so communication was a bit easier than with Uncle Lincoln. Aunt Edith was married to George Mowery, but poor Uncle George died young, about the same time Grandpa died. They had two kids, Evelyn, and George Ellsworth Mowery, but they were a bit older than me and my sisters. My cousin George went by his middle name, Ellsworth, for some odd reason. I guessed it was because Ellsworth was Grandpa's middle name. Ellsworth was at least ten years older than me. I never saw him as much as Aunt Edith and Evelyn. I didn't like that name, Ellsworth. It sounded so hoity-toity. However, I never knew Ellsworth well enough to make a judgment regarding his possible snobbishness or lack thereof. I didn't know which was worse, being called Ellsworth or Boy.

His sister, Evelyn, was always around our house when I was little. She never bothered with me, though. She loved Margaret and Edith and acted as if she was their big sister or something. I never got the time of day from her, but I never really cared. I was not interested in playing with girls. I was about thirteen when Uncle George died suddenly. It must have been from a heart attack. I just remembered him being there one day, and then he was gone. I never saw my cousin Evelyn much after that. She stopped coming over. Margaret and Edith were getting too big anyway for Evelyn's sisterly protection. Pop had another sister, Lula, who visited our house when Grandma and Grandpa were alive, but she stopped coming around after they died. Pop had two other sisters, but I had no recollection of them ever visiting us nor of Pop saying much about them.

In fact, my parents spoke very little about their family histories. They provided little detail about how they came to meet, except that Pop said he met Mom in Inverness when he was in the Navy. I knew Pop was born in Chicago, Illinois, and Grandpa was born in Des Moines, Iowa. Grandma came from Sweden, but that was basically all I knew. Grandma and Grandpa were buried together in a beautiful cemetery on Taylor Avenue on the outskirts of the city. We rarely went to visit their graves though. The last time we visited the cemetery was one Sunday afternoon a few months after Grandpa died. There were no headstones on their graves. I guess nobody had enough money to pay for them. Pop said later that there was no point in visiting anymore since the grass had grown in over their plots and he wouldn't be able to find exactly where they were buried anymore, so we never went again.

Chapter Two

Alpine

My mother's sister from Scotland, Aunt Isabelle, came to live with us on Federal Street when I was sixteen. Only one of my mother's sisters, Charlotte, had married. Charlotte had two children, Betty and James Fraser, the only cousins I had in Scotland. Her other two sisters were apparently spinsters, too. Aunt Isabelle stayed in Grandpa's and Grandma's former bedroom which had been vacant for years after they died. My knowledge of Mom's family in Scotland increased substantially over the winter break, thanks to Aunt Isabelle. I never really talked to her at great length before, but for some reason, we began talking in the parlor late one night after everybody else went to bed.

"Boy," she said. "Do you know the story of how your parents met?"

She referred to me as Boy, since every other person in the household called me that. I had no problem being called Boy. It was the only name I was ever called by my family. I think if they suddenly called me Monty or Montgomery, I would have dropped over dead.

"No, Aunt Isabelle," I answered. "I have no idea how they met. No one has ever told me."

Aunt Isabelle then began to enthusiastically tell the story. I was all ears. I couldn't have been more intrigued. The only thing I knew about my parents was that they met in Scotland while my father was assigned there during the Great War. Incidentally, I was named after my father, who was also Montgomery Culpepper. However, I was not a junior. My father had no middle name, so my mother wanted to name me after her father's given name,

Alpin. I wouldn't have minded the name except for the fact that she named me Alpine instead. My own mother misspelled her father's name and gave me the middle name of Alpine. I think maybe she was drunk or something at the time of my birth. My full name appearing on my birth certificate was Montgomery Alpine Culpepper. Montgomery was bad enough, but Alpine? Come on! During my entire childhood, I hadn't told a single soul what my middle name was. In school, I was listed on the rolls as Montgomery A. Culpepper. I lived with this deep, dark secret during the entirety of my youth and beyond; pretty much all my life.

Aunt Isabelle started describing my parents' courtship in critical detail that night.

"Your mother was the youngest of five girls," she began. "I was the second youngest. We all had red hair. Father was a police constable in Inverness. I had an older brother, Duncan, but he married against my father's wishes when I was a little girl. I'm not sure what happened to Duncan. We never saw or heard from Duncan again after he married, and my parents never spoke of him again. It was as if he never existed. It was very sad. I had heard rumors years later that Duncan and his wife went to Canada. Your mother and I were very close, since we were only a year apart, and she confided in me about her relationship with your father."

"Really!" I exclaimed, as I sat there, listening intently.

She continued her story without missing a beat, "During the Great War, your father was stationed at the United States Naval Base in Inverness as a mine inspector or diver or something. Mines had been installed in the waters around Inverness, mostly in the Cromarty Firth, about ten miles north of the city. After the war ended, the Navy had to remove the mines. Monty, your father, remained stationed in Inverness for months after the war ended."

"No kidding," I said.

"Jessie was such a good-looking, spirited, strong-willed, young girl," Aunt Isabelle continued. "She was only sixteen when Monty first took notice of her. Jessie was the glamorous one of the family. Her appearance was always impeccable. She wore nothing but new, stylish dresses. Her hair was always done up, too. When she walked down the street, men took notice. Your father first saw her after having dinner one Saturday evening in downtown Inverness during the spring of 1918, about six months before the war ended."

"Wow!" I said to her, leaning my chin on my two hands listening attentively. Aunt Isabelle spoke in a Scottish brogue that entranced me. Mom had no trace of an accent when she spoke. No one would have ever believed Mom was born in Inverness. She sounded like everybody else.

"Your father was pursuing Jessie," Aunt Isabelle explained. "Jessie saw him, she had told me later. She was walking from downtown and over the bridge across the River Ness. Upon crossing the bridge, she made her way home a short distance away to our stone house at 26 Tomnahurich Street. Monty saw my sister make her way to our house on the corner. He later told Jessie he was mesmerized at the sight of her, not realizing she was only a girl of sixteen. A week later, your father had dinner at the same restaurant, hoping to see her again. Your father was really quite a shy, quiet man, but thoughtful, and possessing a deep intensity. He was determined to meet and speak with her. He stood outside the restaurant on the street for about twenty minutes, smoking a cigarette, when he saw her coming from town on the other side of the street. She stuck out in the crowd, as she always did, looking very smart. Her bright red hair was high on her head, and she wore a similar dress to the one she had worn the week before. He made his way across the street, timing it to intersect with her as she walked by. He was dressed in his sailor suit and made for a dashing figure himself. Jessie said she immediately took notice of the handsome, lean military man."

"This is incredible," I said.

Aunt Isabelle continued to tell the story to me with such precision that it almost sounded as if she was the third wheel in this whirlwind romance.

"As Jessie glanced at Monty, he boldly asked her if he could walk her home. Jessie was slightly taken aback, but then gave him a wry smile. He told her his name was Monty Culpepper. He said he noticed her walking down the same street the previous Saturday and he'd be happy to accompany her home. Jessie told him she wouldn't mind, but that if her father saw them, he'd have a fit. Jessie explained that her father was very particular about the boys with whom his daughters socialized."

"Sorry to interrupt, Aunt Isabelle, but are you sure you're talking about Mom and Pop?" I asked.

"Well, of course I am, Boy," she answered in a very serious tone.

"If you say so," I responded, somewhat flippantly.

"Monty told Jessie that he thought Father would approve of him since their two countries were Allies in the war," Aunt Isabelle continued. "Jessie explained that Father would definitely not approve of him because sailors had bad reputations, particularly American ones! Monty thought that if Father met him, he would approve. Jessie enlightened Monty that he did not know Father. Monty tried to make clear to her that she was the first Scottish girl he'd spoken to since being stationed there for months. Monty was convinced he could make Father understand his good intentions, but Jessie was not having it. She parted with Monty after telling him it had been a pleasure meeting him. She instructed him to stop accompanying her after the two of them crossed over the bridge just a block from our house. He obliged her request and stopped. Jessie continued on, but she couldn't help herself and glanced back in a flirtatious manner, smiled, and said goodbye."

"I still can't believe you're talking about Mom and Pop," I said, skeptically.

"Monty then yelled to her that he didn't know her name," Aunt Isabelle said, ignoring my interruptions. "Jessie loved the attention and told him her name as she continued smiling at him. She looked back one more time and waved before going inside the house. Monty was encouraged and waved to her with a big smile. I was spying through the window from the house and witnessed all of it. I saw your father turn and with a bounce in his step, make his way back across the bridge over the River Ness and into downtown."

I tried not to interrupt her inconceivable story again.

"Monty later told Jessie that he did nothing but think of her as he worked day in and day out in the mine shop on the base and while diving in the deep waters of the Cromarty Firth, installing and repairing mines," she continued. "He was smitten and could not wait to see her again. He returned to the restaurant on Saturday for dinner in hopes of running into her. He ate dinner quickly so he wouldn't miss her walking down the street. As he waited outside, he saw her coming down High Street in downtown Inverness sporting another pretty dress looking like some famous actress from the stage. As I said, Jessie really was the glamorous one of the family."

I couldn't help but think Aunt Isabelle was talking about someone else. Never in my life did I ever think of my mother as glamorous. Of course, I never saw my mother when she was young. She could have looked like a movie star way back then, for all I knew. As a middle-aged woman though, I couldn't picture her as even remotely glamorous. Movie actresses such as Carole Lombard or Ginger Rogers, or even Sylvia Sydney I could see as glamorous, but definitely not Mom.

Aunt Isabelle carried on with her story, reciting it like a novel.

"Monty hurried across the street and made his way toward her. She stopped this time as he approached and told him she thought she might see him again. Monty said he was looking for her and hoped he'd see her downtown. Jessie did enjoy shopping and never missed a Saturday afternoon browsing through the stores. She loved nothing more than buying a new hat or dress. So, Monty asked her if he could accompany her on her Saturday afternoon shopping outings to which Jessie supposedly replied, 'If you're there, then I guess you can't help but accompany me.' Father would have confined her to the house, had he known. Monty, on the other hand, was thrilled at this response. He not only met her in town on Saturdays but later convinced her to meet him for strolls on Sunday afternoons along the River Ness. Jessie met him on the sly each time, not revealing to the family, except for me, their clandestine meetings. Jessie enjoyed being pursued and reveled in the secrecy of it all. Although she revealed to Monty after several months that she was actually still only a schoolgirl, this disclosure did not deter Monty in the least. He was utterly smitten with her. He told her that he wanted to marry her when she was of age."

"How old was she anyway?" I asked.

"You're not listening, Boy," Aunt Isabelle answered, somewhat annoyed. "I already told you. She was only sixteen; seventeen by the spring of 1919, now hush, Monty."

"Sorry, Aunt Isabelle," I said, sheepishly.

"He, meaning your father, said that when the war was over, they would get married. Jessie repeatedly told Monty that Father would never approve of her marrying an American sailor. She explained to Monty the story of how Father did not like the family of the woman my brother, Duncan, chose to be his wife because the girl's uncle was a criminal of some sort. My father arrested the man twenty years before when he was a constable in Inverness. Monty did not like being compared to a criminal. He said he was a fine, upstanding man and a dedicated sailor who fought for his country and hers, and that Father should appreciate that. Jessie told Monty that although she was certain Father would respect his patriotism and sense of duty, he would nevertheless disapprove of a marriage to an American and never give consent due to her age. Monty became even more emphatic in his desire to marry her. He said he would wait until 1920 when his reenlistment was up, and she turned eighteen. He told her they could marry as soon as he got out of the service, and she'd be of age then. Jessie said, 'Aye, she would be of age, however, Father would still not approve.' Regardless, Monty was persistent in his quest to marry your mother and continually said how much he loved her and how they could live in America."

What the hell? I couldn't help but think Aunt Isabelle must have been talking about somebody other than Pop. I never heard Pop say I love you to Mom or to anybody else for that matter. I have never heard him utter the word love in my entire life. This story was incredible, but it was a good one. I was still not sure Aunt Isabelle had the right two people, but I had never been more fascinated. Aunt Isabelle kept on with her story.

"Jessie found it all very exciting. Monty and Jessie continued seeing each other in secret for the next several months. The Armistice was signed on November 11, 1918, officially ending the war. Monty remained stationed in Inverness through the winter of 1918 and into 1919. He was transferred back to the states in early 1919 and reported for assignment aboard a ship in San Diego, California. By the summer of 1920, Monty received an honorable discharge from the United States Navy and returned home to his parents' house in Baltimore City. Just prior to leaving the Navy, he had written Jessie and told her he had made a small fortune gambling aboard ship. I recall he won somewhere in the vicinity of $2,000 from his fellow sailors in one night, a tidy sum of money for a young single man."

I had previously heard all about Pop's crap game aboard the ship before he left the Navy. This was the one story Pop spoke of on more than one occasion, as he was quite proud of his gambling accomplishment. Prior to Pop's discharge from the Navy, he participated in a crap game aboard the *U.S.S. Melville* that, he said, surpassed every other game he had ever played. He played in hundreds of crap games during his time in the Navy, he had told me. He loved gambling and had always been lucky rolling the dice. During his seven years in the service and just prior to his last game on the *U.S.S. Melville*, he estimated he had come out ahead by more than $1,000. His roll of the dice that night on the *U.S.S. Melville* two weeks before he left the Navy, however, was like a dream, he said. Every time his turn came, he would roll a string of sevens on his first roll. His luck continued as he made point number after point number before finally rolling craps.

Craps was a simple game and very popular not only among sailors but among a significant portion of men on street corners and in bars all across America in the first half of the twentieth century. I personally loved shooting craps and did so quite frequently. It was a fast-moving game involving a lot of betting. The first roll of the dice required a seven or eleven to win. If a two, three, or twelve was rolled, it was a loser. If a four, five, six, eight, nine, or ten was rolled, then that became the point number. The bet then became whether the shooter rolled the point number before rolling a seven. If the shooter made his point number, he won. If he rolled seven before rolling the point number, he lost. If the dice roller made the point number, he won his bet and the game started over. After each point number was made, a seven or eleven on the next roll became a winner again. Pop said he rolled so many sevens and elevens on his first rolls and so many point numbers that evening that he came away from the game over $2,000 ahead. In all his years shooting craps, never had he had a winning streak like this one, he boasted. He came home from the service with a total of more than $3,000 from his gambling winnings.

"Monty was twenty-five years old when he left the Navy," Aunt Isabelle stated. "He was still pining for Jessie. He had corresponded with her in letters since he left Scotland. He professed his love for her and his intention to marry her in every letter. Her letters reciprocated love for him, but she seemed skeptical with regard to Monty actually returning to Scotland. For Jessie, it seemed to be a fairytale that might never come true."

"Monty went home to Baltimore City after leaving the Navy," Aunt Isabelle continued. "He lived with his parents and a younger brother and sister, who were both of adult age, as I recall. His siblings worked. Monty apparently went to work with his father on construction sites. Both men were lathers. Monty told Jessie he worked as a lather prior to his military service and resumed his former occupation, even though he had come home with a considerable amount of money derived from his winnings after gambling aboard ship."

"Monty had only one thing on his mind after returning home," Aunt Isabelle said. "His desire was to return to Scotland, marry Jessie, and bring her back to America. They corresponded for two years after Monty left. Jessie, however, would not commit to Monty's proposals of marriage. She knew that Father would never approve of the marriage. She loved Monty and was excited with the idea of him coming to sweep her off her feet, but she did not believe deep down that he would actually come for her. She was, after all, a young, attractive girl of eighteen, with many suitors. One young man, a solicitor in Inverness, was smitten with Jessie. His name was Hugh MacKaye. Father knew the MacKaye family well. When Father had been a Constable, he had dealt with Hugh's father often. The law firm of MacDougal and MacKaye had been in existence for more than fifty years. When the young Hugh MacKaye came to ask Father for his permission to marry Jessie, Father had no reservations at all concerning the union. He was relieved that Jessie would be marrying a highly successful and upstanding citizen of Inverness from a well-respected family."

"Gee whiz, what a soap opera," I said.

"It was not a soap opera, Monty, just real life," Aunt Isabelle said. "Although Jessie agreed to marry Hugh, she never stopped thinking of Monty. I'm not sure Jessie really loved Hugh, but he was pleasant and treated her very well. At the beginning of 1921, she received another letter from Monty. Monty told her he was coming to Scotland in the spring to marry her. Jessie was thrilled at the thought of marrying Monty. She truly loved Monty and felt passion for him, unlike any feelings she ever had for any other man. She certainly did not have the same feelings for Hugh. It seemed she was merely settling for him. Jessie knew Father would never approve of Monty. If Monty actually came to marry her, they would have to elope. The prospect of this scenario delighted Jessie. She began to imagine running off with Monty to America. It all seemed so romantic and exciting."

Aunt Isabelle said that my mother left a note with the family before eloping with my father, which read, "By the time you read this letter, I will already be married and on a ship for America."

Although it was hard to imagine for me now that my parents were ever this romantic and adventurous, their courtship stirred something inside of me. My interest in girls increased considerably after hearing this incredible and inspiring love story.

Just by coincidence, I went to the Alcazar Ballroom with Irish and Rowley the next Saturday night, just five days before New Year's Day. A real cool hep band was playing. I was thoroughly enjoying the music. I asked a couple of girls to dance and was having a good time. Then I saw a girl on the dance floor who would change my life forever. She was the cutest little bundle of joy I had ever seen. I was mesmerized at the sight of her. She was maybe five foot tall, if that, but what a figure. I didn't really like those tall, slender, long-legged gals who looked like a tall drink of water. I liked curves on a girl, but not too much. I definitely didn't like them plump. This girl was just right. She had curves but was perfectly proportioned.

I think my love of geometry came into play with my critique of the shape of a girl. My geometry teacher would only have given her figure a ninety-nine percent grade, but I gave her a hundred. Perfect! Her face was her best feature. She had big brown eyes, rosy cheeks with pronounced dimples, a cute little nose, and the most beautiful smile this side of paradise. Her hair was brown, thick, and wavy. It was combed and all, but not overly coiffed like most of the girls. I hated the way they piled it on the top of their heads trying to look so debonair. This girl's hair looked totally natural, but beautiful.

The most attractive thing about her was her humility. Although guys were falling all over themselves to get to her to dance, she didn't seem to realize how popular she was. She appeared as genuine and nice as any pretty girl I had ever seen. Most of these good-looking girls pretty much made me sick. If guys fawned all over them, they usually ate it up with a spoon and then acted in a phony or uppity fashion. I could see that this girl was nothing like that type. She just came across like she was having fun, with no pretensions or airs at all about her. I am not sure she was even remotely aware of all the attention she was getting. It obviously was not going to her head, which made her even more appealing. I would love to have danced with her, but I couldn't navigate through the crowd. I grabbed Irish, who was standing near me, to get his attention.

"Hey Irish, who is that cute little brown-haired girl over there with the boys mobbing her?" I asked as I pointed across the dance floor.

"She lives down the street from me, Mary Lucille Flanagan, the cutest little Irish girl in the entire Tenth Ward!" Irish responded. "She goes by Lucille. I can't believe you don't know her. I've been in love with her my whole life, but I've been too afraid to ask her out. She's way out of my league, but she's the sweetest girl you'd ever want to meet. Completely down to earth. She has no idea how beautiful she is."

"How is it I've never seen her before?" I asked.

"I don't know, Monty, maybe you ain't been looking in the right places," Irish continued. "Maybe you're just blind!"

"I think I might be in love," I blurted out. I immediately felt embarrassed by expressing my inner feelings. I was not even kidding though.

"You and every other red-blooded American boy in the Tenth Ward, my friend," Irish said flippantly.

Irish was always a real card. He was not the most handsome fellow, but he had a quick, acerbic wit. He was a little on the heavy side. His face was slightly pudgy, and he had an unusually small mouth, but with buck teeth. Irish had a bad habit of hanging his mouth open, probably due to his rather large front teeth. I heard a girl once refer to him as a ferret-face. Luckily, Irish was not in earshot of her callous remark. Honestly, I don't even know what a ferret looks like, but judging by the way the girl said it, I knew it could not have been attractive.

"Would you like to meet her?" Irish asked. "I see her all the time. Her house is right on the corner of Biddle Street and Nursery Place. Her parents, brothers and sisters, and aunts and uncles and cousins all live upstairs and next door."

"She lives only a few blocks from here, then," I said to Irish. "I don't want to meet her right now. Maybe another time. There are too many guys here tonight."

I did not dance with Lucille or even speak to her, but I could not take my eyes off her the remainder of the evening. I arrived home that night and went to bed just before midnight. I was unable to sleep, though. All I could do was lie there and think about that cute little Lucille Flanagan. I made up my mind that I would return to the Alcazar next Saturday night. I would have to get there early, so I could be the first to ask her to dance. I spent all week playing football, ice skating, shooting pool, hanging out with the guys, and thinking about Lucille.

Finally, it was Saturday night again. I arrived at the

Alcazar at about eight in the evening with Irish, Rowley, and Joe. Moe still had his arm in a sling and didn't want to come. He said he would feel like an idiot trying to dance one-armed. As we entered the ballroom, the band was just warming up. I scanned every corner of the ballroom. No sign of Lucille. Irish saw me with my searching eyes.

"She ain't here yet," Irish advised. "She told me she's coming with a couple of her girlfriends a little later."

"You didn't tell her about me?" I asked excitedly.

"Well, sure I did," Irish said nonchalantly.

"What the hell, Irish?" I said, a bit angrily. "I didn't want you to say anything to her. I wanted to meet her naturally with no preconceived notions."

"Don't worry, chum, I did you a huge favor," Irish responded. "It turns out after I let the beans spill that a certain someone named Monty Culpepper was eyeing her up last Saturday night, another certain little cute as a button someone tells me she's had a bit of a crush on the handsome Monty Culpepper ever since she saw you when she was only fourteen, two years ago. So, you can just thank me now!"

"No kidding, she said I was handsome?" I asked skeptically.

"That's right, genius," Irish shot back with his normal acid tongue. "Thanks to your old buddy, Irish, the wheel has been greased."

"I hope so," I said, still somewhat embarrassed by Irish's proclamation to Lucille about me.

Just then, I saw Lucille and her two friends entering the ballroom. The band started playing the Benny Goodman number, *Sing, Sing, Sing*. I loved that tune; it had a great beat, perfect for a jitterbug. Lucille was still with her girlfriends, chatting it up on the other side of the dance floor. Hardly anybody was dancing, as most of the crowd had not yet arrived. The place pretty much did not get packed until about nine. This was a golden opportunity to dance with her and maybe talk before her mob of suitors showed up. I hurriedly made my way across the dance floor, which was easy, since only a few couples were dancing. Her back was to me as she was speaking to her friends. I tapped her on the shoulder. She turned around and seemed a bit surprised to see me. She raised her eyebrows giving her a slightly startled look, but then she flashed her sweet smile, which made my heart melt.

"How 'bout this dance?" I asked.

"Sure," she said.

I grabbed her hand, pulling her onto the dance floor. We both got right into the beat of the song. She was a great dancer. She moved so naturally and effortlessly. She had no inhibitions when it came to dancing. Boy, was I having a blast. She had a big, gorgeous smile and danced with real joy without overdoing it. We went together like two peas in a pod, it seemed to me, at least on the dance floor.

When the song ended, Lucille exclaimed, "Whew, that was a fast one!"

The band then began playing *All or Nothing at All*, a slow one. Frank Sinatra usually sang this one on the radio with the Harry James Band, but the band at the Alcazar had no vocalists. They always played instrumentals. I motioned to Lucille to dance, and she moved in real close. I thought I had died and gone to heaven. Her hair was soft and silky against my cheek. I knew nothing about perfume, but she evidently had on just a touch. I thought I detected a lilac scent. It was not overwhelming, just enough to make me imagine I was on a picnic with Lucille in springtime. My mind was racing as we danced. I wanted nothing more than to have this girl in my arms forever. It never felt so right. I had danced with plenty of girls, but I never had the feeling I didn't want the dance to end. And there it was, the trumpet sound holding the long, sustained note to end the song. We both stepped back and clapped for the band as we looked to the stage.

"Thanks for the dance, Lucille," I said. "I'm Monty."

"Yes, I know," she said. "I'm glad to meet you, Monty. I'd better get back to my girlfriends over there." She glanced over to her friends, both of whom were looking our way. "Would you like to meet my friends?"

"I'd be happy to," I said.

However, at that moment, I really did not care about her friends. My innate manly instincts were telling me that I wanted to go off somewhere and be alone with her. Lucille had me absolutely mesmerized. I could barely concentrate on anything else. I followed her off the dance floor to her friends who seemed giddy watching us approach.

"Monty, these are my two good friends, Cuddles and Fran," Lucille said.

"How do you do? I'm Monty Culpepper," I said, as I nodded to them.

"Our pleasure, Monty," the mousey blonde on the left said. "I'm Cuddles."

"I'm Fran," the other girl said.

Franny Driscoll was her full name. She was a tad chunky and very bubbly. Cuddles was on the skinny side. Her real name was Mary Cuddy. Her chin was a bit weak, and her face was thin. Her nose stuck out of her face like a mouse, hence the mousey reference. They both seemed nice enough, but everything out of their mouths seemed unnatural to me. They were typical of the girls I knew. They always tried to act or talk in a certain way. I guessed it came from insecurity or something; however, I really didn't know. The only thing I knew was that

Lucille was not anything like that. She seemed to be so at ease with herself that nothing she said came out phony or sounding insincere.

"So where do you go to school?" Cuddles asked.

"I go to Poly," I replied.

"We all go to Seton," Cuddles said.

"You know, the all-girls Catholic school," Fran chimed in.

"Yes, I'm aware," I retorted.

This small talk with Frick and Frack was starting to get on my nerves. I wished Irish and Rowley would have gotten their asses over here and taken these two other girls away somewhere, as in far away, for the rest of the night. I wished, too, that I was Lucille's steady. I was standing there imagining myself as some hip cat, grabbing Lucille by the hand, telling her, "Come on Baby, let's blow this joint," and Lucille would follow without hesitation. Oh my gosh, snap out of it, stupid. I wanted so badly to make an impression on Lucille.

"We're all seniors," Cuddles proclaimed. "What year are you in?"

Oh shit, was Cuddles talking again? I was ignoring her and focusing on Lucille. What the hell was she talking about anyway? School, I think. Oh, yeah.

"I'm a junior," I answered. "Have you been enjoying the Christmas break?"

"Yeah," Cuddles replied. "We've been having a ball. Too bad school starts on Monday."

"Everybody at school was so anxious before the break," Lucille chimed in. "All the talk was about the war and invasions. It's all so troubling."

"Yeah, it was the same way at Poly," I said. "The rumors were running rampant. All the guys are talking about signing up as soon as they graduate."

"But you don't graduate for another year and a half,"

Lucille said.

"We heard some rumors that they might move up graduation," I said. "Most of the boys are chomping at the bit to go anyway."

"Oh, that's awful," Lucille said. "I hate to think of all the boys going off to war. My older brother's in the seminary and he wants to quit to join the war."

"You mean he's studying to be a priest?" I asked.

Secretly, I immediately thought he didn't like girls and must be some kind of big sis. My mind was full of a million other questions about her brother, but I was not about to risk asking her anything more. The last thing I wanted to do was to offend her in any way. I could tell by her serious tone that she really admired her brother.

"Yes," she said. "He's been in the St. Charles Seminary since he was thirteen. Seven years, and now he wants to quit because he feels it's his duty to go fight. My mother is worried sick."

"He sounds pretty close to becoming a priest," I said.

"He would still have some years to go before getting ordained, though," she said. "He's a wonderful guy. I hope you get to meet him sometime."

I could not believe my ears. Does she want to see me again? Maybe at her house? Where else would I get to meet her wonderful big brother? I needed to calm down. I had to be smooth here. I didn't want to blow it with this dream girl right out of the box. Careful, boy!

"I hope I do get to meet him," I said intently. "If he's anything like you, he must be a great guy."

"Thanks, Monty," she said. "You're very kind."

"Maybe next Saturday I can pick you up at your house for a movie and then dancing at the Alcazar," I said boldly.

"That would be great," she said smiling.

"How about I meet you at your house at seven-thirty

and we can take the trolley downtown to the Earle Theatre for the eight o'clock picture show? Then after the movie on the way back, we can stop here for some dancing."

"Sounds like a date," she said, still smiling with those adorable dimples on that heavenly face.

I was on cloud nine. "I'll see you then," I said, trying to hide my jubilation. I thought I might bust right then and there. Just then, a crowd of guys moved toward Lucille. The next thing I knew, she was on the dance floor with some other fellow. There were plenty more in line waiting for her. This was not my scene. I was not going to fight for her attention. I had my date next Saturday and I was not only satisfied but elated. I certainly didn't want to be stuck there talking to Cuddles and Fran, either. I went back across the dance floor to the other side of the ballroom after spotting Irish and Rowley.

"Hey, Irish," I said. "Guess who I'm going out with next Saturday night."

"Don't tell me, the skinny blonde mouse I saw you talking with across the dance floor earlier?" he asked in his usual sarcastic manner.

"No, smartass," I responded. "You know who I got a date with and she's no mouse."

"Oh, so you like 'em a little plump then?" he continued. "You must have a date with Franny Driscoll."

"Wrong again, funny man," I said. "You know, maybe you should be on the stage with all your jokes. I got a date with Lucille."

"Well, good for you, Monty," Irish said, sounding a bit jealous.

"Yeah, Monty, congratulations," Rowley said, after listening to our back-and-forth banter. "Lucille is a real looker. I wouldn't mind going out with her either."

"Yeah, well, truth be told, I'd like to go out with her, too," Irish said, getting serious for a change. "After all, I've known her forever. I'm actually friends with her."

"Irish, you'll never be more than friends with her," Rowley added. "She's way out of your league anyway."

"Hey, boys, go get your own girl," I said protectively. "Lucille's mine."

"I don't think so Monty," Rowley retorted. "One planned date don't make her yours."

"That's right," Irish said. "She's fair game. I might make some progress with her beyond being just friends. Besides, she thinks I'm hysterical. She said so once."

"Really, Irish?" Rowley questioned. "Did she tell you this in grade school?"

"Very funny," Irish said indignantly. "I think you're the one who should be on stage."

"Okay, fellows," I said. "Let's get serious. I feel like dancing."

I danced with a few girls, but it was not quite the same experience as with Lucille, not even in the same ballpark. However, I had fun. I kept my eye on Lucille most of the evening. She was extremely popular. She danced with at least two dozen different boys throughout the evening. The other girls all liked Lucille, too. I saw her in conversation with scads of other girls besides Cuddles and Fran. I could not wait until next Saturday night. I loved looking forward to things, particularly fun and exciting ones. Meeting Lucille was undeniably the most fun and exciting event of my life, and if December 7, 1941, was the day which would live in infamy, then January 3, 1942, was the day for me which would live in my heart with love and affection for Lucille forever.

I started back at school on the following Monday. It sure had been a fantastic Christmas and New Year's break. The rumors at school had not died down any. All the boys were still talking about a possible Jap invasion on the west coast. Most of the guys didn't think we would finish high school because the country would need every able-bodied man to defend it. There was talk that the Nazis might bomb New York or Washington or even invade. It was hard to concentrate on schoolwork with the constant talk of war. I was not so much fixated on the war, as much as I was on Lucille. Saturday night could not come fast enough.

I still worked diligently at school, as I was always very grade conscious. My toughest class was trigonometry, but the truth was, mathematics had always come easy for me. I was determined, however, to be well-rounded. I had made a concerted effort to understand the English language as well as I understood math. Most of my friends studied English and did well, but they did not put into practice what they learned. It must have been something about where we lived.

For instance, everybody in this town pronounced Baltimore as if it were spelled differently than it was. I swear I have never heard a soul in this city enunciate the "T" in the word Baltimore. For some odd reason, the "T" has always been substituted with a "D", so it came out "Baldimore." Hell, most people dropped the "ore" for an "er" and it came out sounding like "Baldimer." A lot of folks just said "Ballmore" or even "Ballmer." I would be damned if I ever said it that way. Saying Baldimore was bad enough, but Ballmer? My distaste of the pronunciation of my hometown sounded as if I was getting a bit snobbish or full of myself, but I really was not. I merely believed that all words in the English language should be pronounced properly and correctly.

I made one exception for myself, however, in speaking proper English. A common colloquial expression in Baltimore involved a person's intention to go to one's home or the beach. Most people in Baltimore expressed traveling to Ocean City, for example, as "I'm going down the shore this weekend" instead of "I'm going down to the shore or vacationing at the shore." Baltimoreans also routinely said, "I'm coming down your house" as opposed to "I'm coming down to your house." I was no different.

My favorite actor when I was young, and for all time, was Ronald Colman. Now there was a guy who I thought spoke perfect English, at least on screen in the movies. His speech was nothing short of magnificent. I loved how intelligent he sounded. I never tried to speak exactly like Ronald Colman, but I strove for better enunciation and proper English. For Pete's sake, I would have sounded like a nut if I had spoken like he did. I loved repeating one of his most famous lines from his movie, Charles Dickens' *A Tale of Two Cities,* in his inimitable style, "It's a far, far better thing I do than I have ever done. It's a far, far better rest I go to than I have ever known."

Of course, it was all in good fun, imitating him to my friends. I could always count on amusing them. Nevertheless, I equated speaking English correctly with solving complicated mathematical problems. I never understood how one could be so adept at math, but then have no idea whatsoever in speaking correct English. I was certainly not going to solve a math equation by getting it only partially correct. I saw the difference between mathematics and English though. People understood English even when it was not proper English. I merely believed that speaking English should have been as precise as mathematics.

I noticed when speaking with Lucille that her grammar was impeccable. I immediately deduced that her attention to proper English was probably a result of her Catholic education from the nuns at Seton High School. It was always my understanding that teaching proper grammar was of paramount importance in Catholic schools. She didn't sound as if she would have ever said "Baldimer." If she said "Baldimore," I would have probably let that slide. School flew by that week in anticipation of my date with Lucille.

Pop had not gotten another car a month after I wrecked the Buick. He would have never let me use it on a Saturday night anyway. He generally went out Saturday nights with Mom, John Battaglia, and Mrs. Battaglia. They usually ended up at the saloon. Sometimes they went dancing, even though Pop did not dance. Mom always danced with John. I heard her complain a thousand times how Pop would not dance, but John would always dance with her. At least I didn't have to pick her up. The only downside of Pop finally getting a new car would be that I would be back on taxi duty picking up Mom in the middle of the night on a weekday. I was not looking forward to being her chauffeur again.

I had to walk to Lucille's to pick her up for our date. The trolley line did not go from my house to hers. It was about a ten-block walk, but at least the trolley line was nearby her house to get downtown to the Earle Theatre. Lucille lived more directly north of downtown. My house was northeast, so it was a bit of a walk to catch the trolley. The trolley was a very convenient and inexpensive way to get around town if you did not have a car.

I arrived at 615 East Biddle Street at about twenty-five after seven. I was walking at a quick pace. It was a rather mild night for the second week of January. It was not freezing. The temperature was in the low forties, really quite a beautiful winter evening. All the stars were shining and twinkling in the sky. I arrived at her rowhouse on the end of the block where "615" was printed above the front door. I walked up the three shiny marble steps and rang the bell. A short, portly woman with partially gray, curly, thick hair answered the door. She smiled and said, "You must be Lucille's date."

"Yes ma'am, I am," I said as politely as I could. "My name is Monty Culpepper."

"I'm Lucille's mother," she said. "Have a seat in the parlor and make yourself comfortable. Let me get Lucille. I think she's still getting ready."

Mrs. Flanagan disappeared from the room, and I could hear her climbing steps. I was a little surprised that Mrs. Flanagan looked nothing like her daughter. I did instantly recognize that they both had the same sweet dispositions. I wasn't at all accustomed to people with delightful personalities, with the exception of my eldest sister, Margaret. My mother's disposition could never be described as sweet. I wouldn't say that my mother had a bitter nature, but she was a person with a hard exterior. I would describe my mother as a temperamental type of woman. Her temper could go off at any time, and often did. Her pleasant moments were few and far between. She liked to do things her way and my Pop usually let her. I have witnessed her temper tantrums and I mean nobody, but nobody would ever have wanted to invite her wrath. It was just a quick, first impression, but my guess was that Mrs. Flanagan appeared to be the antithesis of my mother.

After sitting in the parlor for less than a minute, a kid strolled through the room. "Who are you?" he asked.

"I'm Monty," I said. "I'm waiting for Lucille."

"How come?"

"We're going to the picture show," I said.

"Oh, like a date, I get it," he said, proudly. "Lucille has lots of fellas waiting for her in the parlor before they go to a picture show."

"Indeed! When was the last fellow here?" I inquired.

"Oh, I don't know, maybe before Christmas," he said.

"Do you live here?" I asked.

"Sure, I do," he answered. "Lucille's my sister. I'm Charlie."

"What grade are you in Charlie?" I asked. "You look like a big boy."

"I'm not so big for the sixth grade," he said. "Plenty of kids are bigger than me in my class, even some of the girls."

"Where do you go?" I asked as I waited for Lucille to come downstairs.

"St. John's," he answered. "I'm an uncle. I'm the only kid in school who's an uncle already."

"How's that?" I asked curiously.

"My oldest sister, Esther, and her husband, Gordon, have a baby named Donny," Charlie said smugly. "He's two and he's my nephew. I've been an uncle since I was nine. Nobody else in school is an uncle. They live upstairs on the third floor."

As he finished telling me about his greatest achievement in life, being the youngest uncle in the city, Lucille suddenly appeared in the parlor. I did not even hear her coming down the steps.

"Wow, you look snazzy," I exclaimed. Lucille was wearing a cute blue dress and her hair was fixed the same way it was last Saturday night. Boy was she a knockout!

"Thanks, Monty," she said.

"Are you ready to head downtown?" I asked. "We should make it in time for the eight o'clock show."

"Yes, let's go," she eagerly said.

I escorted her to the door and helped her with her coat on. Charlie was watching us leave. "Nice talking to you, Charlie," I said. "See you again some time, I hope."

"Maybe, bye," he replied.

As we walked out the door and down the marble steps, Lucille exclaimed, "So you met my little brother?"

"Yes, he's quite the little man, isn't he," I said.

"Well, he's something," she said. "He's a good boy, though."

We caught the trolley about a block and a half away and headed downtown. We arrived at the Earle Theatre about two minutes before eight. I was glad we were not late. I liked to see the newsreels before the picture started. The movie title on the marquee was *Sullivan's Travels*. It starred Joel McCrea and Veronica Lake. I never heard of the movie, but I was familiar with the children's story, *Gulliver's Travels,* by Jonathan Swift, about a guy from a shipwreck washing up on shore in a land of little people. For some odd reason, I had it in my head that this movie was going to be similar to the Jonathan Swift story. I bought a large bucket of popcorn and two Cokes. Lucille and I sat in the back of the theatre, as it was already quite crowded.

The newsreel was just starting as we sat down. They showed President Roosevelt addressing Congress the day after Pearl Harbor and then gave a whole rundown on what the Japs and the Nazis were up to. The Japs were pretty much running the show in their part of the world. They seemed to be winning in the South Pacific, China, and Indochina. The Germans were not doing too badly, either. They had control over Europe and North Africa and were bombing London to hell. It sounded as if they would take over Russia, too. The President's remarks and the war news certainly made everybody feel patriotic and eager to join the fight. The whole thing just looked like once we got into the fight, it would be the end of the Japs and the Germans. It sure got me in the fighting spirit. If I hadn't had a year and a half left of school, I would have joined right then and there.

I was a bit disappointed in the movie, *Sullivan's Travels*. Joel McCrea never washed up on shore in the land of the little people as I was expecting. Instead, he played a movie director posing as a hobo in America to learn about life. I didn't care for it that much, but I never admitted to Lucille that I thought it was going to be the Jonathan Swift story. I felt a bit dumb after the movie started and it was clear the story didn't even remotely resemble Jonathan Swift's *Gulliver's Travels*. Sometimes I could be such a dope. I still had a great time being with Lucille, just to sit with her and share popcorn made me feel like a lucky man. Afterward, we caught the trolley to Mount Vernon Square. We danced together for the next two hours at the Alcazar Ballroom, jitterbugging, taking breaks to have a Coke, and slow dancing to romantic songs. At about midnight, the band played its last number and started packing up. I walked her home the few blocks from Mount Vernon.

When we got to her doorstep, I told her, "Lucille, I never had a better time in my life. Can we do it again next Saturday night?"

"Sure, Monty," Lucille said. "I had a great time, too."

"I'll call you next week," I said as I put my hands on her shoulders leaning in to kiss her on the lips. She closed her eyes and kissed me for several seconds.

"Thank you, Lucille," I said after our kiss. "I had a grand evening. See you next week. I'll call you. Good night."

"I had a nice time, too, Monty," she responded. "Good night."

I left Lucille walking down the street like I was on cloud nine. I was so smitten. In my mind, Lucille was without a doubt the perfect girl.

"Boy, I love that girl," I said to myself out loud walking home.

I spent the next day ice skating with the fellas, but I was not engaged with them at all. In fact, I said very little all day to anyone, as my thoughts were consumed with Lucille.

Chapter Three

Celibacy

For the next several months, I had a standing date on Saturday night with Lucille. We would go to the movies, dance at the Alcazar, go ice skating or roller skating, attend parties with the kids from school, walk arm in arm through the park or just stroll the downtown streets looking at the store window displays. We always ended up back at Lu's house in her parlor. I loved the name, Lucille, but soon I got in the habit of calling her "Lu" for short. Everybody in her family, however, called her Lucille.

After spending so much time in her home and interacting with her family, I could clearly see she was her father's favorite. Lucille was the second youngest of five siblings. Her two sisters, Esther and Nancy, were eight and six years older, respectively. Her brother, John, who had been away attending the St. Charles seminary since Lu was about ten years old, was three years older. Charlie was the youngest of the brood, five years younger than Lu. I became certain Lu was her father's favorite of the five for a few reasons. First of all, I could see with my own eyes how he visibly showed her the most affection. Her sisters were extremely nice, but they lacked Lu's natural sweet disposition. Esther displayed a very tough exterior and was obviously a no-nonsense type of person. She was married to a fellow named Gordon, a true tough guy who appropriately worked as a guard at the city jail. They had a two-year-old boy named Donny. They lived on the third floor. Nancy, who was single, was very pleasant and good-looking, but she was a bit flighty.

When Lu was just five years old, she suffered from

scarlet fever and nearly died. The doctors removed her infected mastoid bone because of the fever. Consequently, she lost her hearing in her right ear. Lu told me that her father was deeply shaken by the fact she nearly succumbed to the disease, thus he became very protective of her. Her dad was a great guy. He was extremely personable and had so much kindness in his heart. I think Mr. Flanagan talked to me more that spring than my own father had my entire life. Their family seemed to possess more love and affection than mine ever did. I would talk to Lu's brother, John, periodically, when he came home from the seminary. My first impression of John was that he seemed like a great guy, too, like his dad. I believed he would have made the perfect priest, not that I really had any clue what kind of person would make a suitable priest. I had always heard that a fellow would get the calling, but I had no idea what that really meant. I presumed that God somehow spoke to the person. I never asked John about it though. Regardless, John always seemed to be in a great mood. Personally, I found it hard to imagine that anybody could be that happy all the time.

At any rate, John was very personable and outgoing, as was everyone in the Flanagan family. He appeared to be a solid, upstanding guy, but honestly, from the day I met him, I always thought he was a little odd, despite his good nature. He was about three years older than me, but he was not the type of guy who could hang out on the corner with the fellas. He never smoked, gambled, or drank. I certainly never heard him uttering any curse words. I doubt he had ever been in a fistfight in his entire life. The problem with John was that he was just a bit too holier than thou for me and my friends. He was not what you would call "a regular guy." He never fit in, partly, I surmised, because he spent seven years in the seminary from the age of thirteen, training to become a priest. In fact, in the spring of 1942, he quit the seminary with only one year left to go to enlist in the United States Navy.

Lu told me her parents were extremely disappointed when John left the seminary, especially Mrs. Flanagan. Mr. and Mrs. Flanagan had a unique marital situation. Mr. Flanagan was an Irish Catholic while Mrs. Flanagan was of Jewish heritage. Mrs. Flanagan was born and raised Jewish, but then converted to Catholicism when she married Mr. Flanagan. Lu told me that the Jewish side of the family, the Horwitzes, disowned her mother for marrying a Catholic. The Horwitzes all lived in west Baltimore near Pimlico, a primarily Jewish section of the city. Mrs. Flanagan had not seen her parents or siblings in over twenty-five years. Lu never met her mother's side of the family. The Horwitzes immigrated to America from Russia in 1889 with their eldest child, Ida, when Ida was just two years old. Mrs. Flanagan and the rest of her siblings were all born in Baltimore. Lu's grandmother, Sarah Horwitz, died years before in the mid-1920s. Mrs. Flanagan apparently was not welcome at her own mother's funeral. Lu's grandfather, Louis Horwitz, was still alive, residing in west Baltimore but had nothing to do with his daughter, Dora Flanagan, or any of her family.

Strangely, Mrs. Flanagan became one of the most devout Catholics in the entire Tenth Ward; a section of the city filled predominantly with Irish Catholics. Mrs. Flanagan even volunteered to do the laundry for the priests at the rectory at St. John's Church. I think she wanted to prove that she was a devoted Catholic. A lot of the Irish in the neighborhood looked down on her because she was Jewish. I never heard anybody say anything prejudiced against her, but my friends told me there had been talk. She was the sweetest woman, too.

She had a tough life having been disowned by her family for marrying an Irish Catholic, and then the Irish Catholics never fully accepted her because she was Jewish. What a cruel world it was. She just couldn't win for losing.

When John announced his intentions to leave the seminary, Lu's mother, not surprisingly, took it harder than the rest of the family. A large part of her distress was her fear of John joining the service and being in danger, but another aspect of her anxiety was her fervent desire for John to become a priest, proving to everyone in the neighborhood once and for all how dedicated she and her family were to Catholicism. It was silly really because she didn't have to prove anything at all. She was a wonderful, kind-hearted, benevolent woman who loved everyone and who everyone loved dearly in return. Sadly, poor Mrs. Flanagan was one of the worst chronic worriers I had ever come across. She was always asking me where I was taking Lu and when she could expect us to come home. She forever told us to be careful and to watch our step getting on and off the trolley cars and to look both ways for automobiles. If she read about an accident about someone getting hit by the trolley or falling from a trolley car, she would always read us the newspaper story and then reiterate for us to be extra careful.

Lu said her mother worried about everything and everybody. Her mother had told Lu the story many times about how Lu's Uncle Harry Horwitz had died in a car accident when he was only nineteen and what a tragedy it was for his life to be cut so short. Mrs. Flanagan said Harry was the oldest son and had so much promise. It devastated her entire family. Mrs. Flanagan never got over his tragic death and was forever worried for her loved ones' safety. When John said he was joining the service to do his part in the war effort, this almost ruined poor Mrs. Flanagan. The thought of her eldest son in harm's way frightened her to death. John explained to his mother that he didn't feel right studying to be a priest, safely hidden away in the seminary while other young men went off to war. He also explained to his mother that he liked girls and hoped to fall in love someday.

Now I always thought John was a bit of an oddball, but I had to admire him for at least not wanting to be celibate for the rest of his life. I thought it was an admirable thing to become a priest and to give oneself to God, but swearing off women, I thought, was unnatural. Despite being a square, John was a handsome, athletic guy with a great smile, while possessing a charming, outgoing personality. I was sure women found him attractive and I respected him for his seemingly difficult choice.

Mr. Flanagan asked me that spring to take John out with my friends. John had been so sheltered at the seminary that he had no group of friends in the neighborhood like everybody else had. John had spent his teenaged years either at the seminary or at St. John's Church. He was a great tenor and sang in the choir. He volunteered all his time to the church. I asked John if he wanted to go out with me and my friends, as Mr. Flanagan had requested, and John said he would be delighted. John's presence that night hanging out with the fellas was the worst. It was such an awkward evening. John and the fellas went together like oil and water.

First, we went to the pool hall downtown. The fellas and I all smoked. John did not. The pool hall was an invariable cloud of smoke. John complained about it the whole time. My friends and I were all fairly decent pool players, too; of course, John was not. John had never picked up a pool cue in his entire life. He was not that bad, but he was not in the same league as we were. Also, he never gambled. We had bets on every game.

"I don't gamble," John said awkwardly to the fellas. It was a smart move on his part, since he would have lost his shirt had he bet on any game.

Then there was the cursing and the occasional Lord's name taken in vain. Every time Moe missed a shot, he said, "goddamn." Moe's cast had been off for months, but he was still a little out of practice at pool. John's face grimaced every time Moe blasphemed. Poor John was completely out of his comfort zone and clearly was not having a good time.

We left the pool hall and caught the trolley back to the Tenth Ward. We ended up hanging out on the corner just shootin' the breeze. It was me, Irish, Rowley, Moe, Joe, another buddy, Harry Strawbridge, and John. We talked about the war, graduating from high school, joining the service, girls, and a bunch of things. We smoked cigarettes, cursed, and even got a crap game going. John didn't say very much except to add that he was joining the Navy in June. He excused himself when we started shooting craps and said he had to get home. After he left, Rowley said, "John's a nice enough guy, but he's a bit of a goody two-shoes, isn't he?"

"Isn't that the truth?" I agreed. Rowley pretty much summed it up about John.

Lu and I continued going out nearly every Saturday night through the spring. I spent a lot of time at her house after our dates, sitting with her in the parlor, listening to music on the radio. We were rarely ever alone. Her little brother, Charlie, seemed to be around all the time. He could be so obnoxious at times, a typical twelve-year-old. I generally bribed Charlie with a nickel to scram. Nancy always had a date and was rarely there. Mr. and Mrs. Flanagan liked drinking beer and spent nearly every Saturday night at the saloon. Esther and Gordon and the baby were on the third floor, so occasionally I saw them coming or going. John spent a lot of time at St. John's. Mr. Flanagan's older sisters, Nan and Nellie, lived next door at 613 Biddle Street. Her Aunt Nan was married to Thomas Digelman. Tom was a taxicab driver just like Mr. Flanagan. Her Aunt Nellie was married to Frank Harris. He worked at the paper factory. Aunt Nan and Uncle Tom had no children. Nellie and Frank had a son and a daughter, Tom and Francis, both in their early twenties. I rarely ever saw them.

I really loved Lu's close-knit family, though. Lu told me that her grandmother, Mr. Flanagan's mother, had lived with them when she was little. She often spoke of how affectionate she was, even though she died when Lu was only eight or nine years old. I had no such memories of my grandparents showing any affection toward me or to anyone else for that matter. It was heart-warming to see how nice Lu's family all were. You could sense the love in those two households, unlike anything I had ever experienced in my home. They were all hard-working people, good Catholics, and decent folks, but they also were a fun bunch who liked to enjoy themselves, with the exception of maybe John. Well, perhaps this was unfair to John. I guess John enjoyed himself in his own way, but he was definitely different. He was a very upbeat guy and always positive, but, as I said, a little too positive for me. He was always stating, "Isn't it a beautiful day" or "It's great to be alive" or some other nauseating comment. It could be a cold, dark, dank day outside and John would find something good to say about it. Nobody could be that happy.

Lu and I became very close in the months leading up to her high school graduation. We spent so much time together. I loved her dearly and thought of her all the time. I was not interested in any other girls, but Lu occasionally dated other boys. She told me she was very fond of me, but she thought we were too young to get too serious. She was only sixteen years old, and I was seventeen. We spoke often about the war and how I would eventually enlist or be drafted. She graduated from Seton High School in June. She would not turn seventeen until August. She had skipped a grade in grammar school. I was only a junior, but Poly instituted a plan for my class to graduate in an accelerated senior year over the summer. The country needed soldiers to fight the Japs and the Nazis. I was very excited about it and anxious to join the fight. Rowley and I decided to join the Marines with a couple of other classmates after graduating from the Poly War Class at the end of August. I was very busy that summer studying in what amounted to cramming my entire senior year of high school into three months.

After I graduated, my mother had a cookout for me in our backyard. It was just my folks, the Battaglias, and my sisters in a small celebration. I invited Lu, as she had not yet met my family. Lu showed up dressed in the cutest outfit I ever saw. She wore a short-sleeved striped summer knit shirt and a short white skirt. Her thick, brown wavy hair looked so natural blowing in the breeze. She had the cutest little nose, dimples in both cheeks and her chin, and her smile was infectious. She possessed the most beautiful white teeth that beamed with every smile and laugh, which occurred quite frequently with her sunny and affable disposition. My parents liked her immediately, as did my sisters. Lu could get along with anybody.

Lu and her girlfriends joined the United Services Organization, popularly known as the USO, that summer and spent a lot of time attending dances downtown and taking the bus to Fort Meade to attend USO functions. She met a lot of servicemen throughout the entirety of the war, many of whom she really liked. The USO was founded in 1941 to provide recreation for United States military personnel on leave. The USO recreational clubs supplied a place for everything from dancing, movies, and live entertainment to a quiet place to talk or write letters. During World War II, more than one million volunteers operated more than three thousand recreational clubs which were established wherever they could find room.

At the end of the summer following my graduation, she got a job as a secretary at the United States Army Curtis Bay Ordinance Depot in south Baltimore, which stored ammunition and shipped it off to the troops. She was the secretary to the Colonel, the Major, the Lieutenant, and the Administrative Officer, all of whom were in the front office at the installation. It was really quite impressive that a young girl attained such an important position, but nothing surprised me about Lu. She was not only adorable, but she was intelligent, personable, mature, and down to earth. Everybody liked her. She was also an outstanding typist and stenographer.

Rowley and I fully intended to join the United States Marine Corps upon graduation, along with two classmates, Jack Burke, and Bill Cox. However, we didn't anticipate that we would need our fathers' permission since we were underage. Jack and Bill's fathers signed their papers, but our fathers balked. I didn't know why Rowley's father refused, maybe it was because he thought he was too young, but my father was never going to sign unless I joined the Navy. When I found out Rowley was not joining either the Marines or the Navy, I wasn't going to enlist in the Navy alone. Rowley was deeply discouraged about the whole debacle. All summer long, we had been talking about joining the Marines. We were both bitterly disappointed.

"The hell with it, Monty," Rowley finally said. "My father just told me to wait until I got drafted."

"My Pop said he's not signing unless I join the Navy," I told Rowley. "I'm not joining the Navy all by myself. I may as well go to college. Pop said he'd pay for me to go to the University of Maryland at College Park. It's either that or I'll have to go to work as a lather. I think I'd prefer to go to college for now."

"Yeah, why not?" Rowley said. "We're going to get drafted anyhow. My father says not to be in such a great hurry."

"He's right," I said. "We'll have our chance soon enough, I guess."

"What the hell am I going to do?" Rowley asked. "I don't turn eighteen until next January."

"That's not so long," I told him. "My birthday isn't until the end of February. I'll have to wait six months. Your birthday is the beginning of January, so you'll only have to wait five months."

"Yeah, I'll turn eighteen on January 7th," Rowley said. "I guess it won't be that long for us to wait to get into the fight."

"Why don't you go to college with me?" I asked.

"My father can't afford it," Rowley said with a hint of embarrassment. "I wish I could. That would be great, but it'll never happen. Maybe I'll just wait to get drafted after I turn eighteen like my father said. I don't know."

"I don't know, either," I said. "But maybe we could join the Marines together after I turn eighteen."

"Maybe," Rowley said, still dejected about the whole situation. "I'm gonna head home, Monty. I'll see ya."

"See ya later, Rowley," I said. "I'll call you to go swimming or something."

"Okay," he said.

A couple of days later, I had a date with Lu. We went

to the movies and saw *Talk of the Town*, starring Cary Grant, Jean Arthur, and Ronald Colman. As I stated previously, I loved that guy. His speech was such a contrast to how everybody in Baltimore talked. Hardly anybody I knew even made an effort to speak proper English. Part of the reason I loved talking to Lu was the educated way in which she spoke. Thank you, Seton nuns!

One of my biggest pet peeves was with people who ended sentences with a preposition. When I hung out on the corner with the fellas, they would invariably ask, "Where's Rowley at?" or "Where's Moe at?" I never corrected them, but it drove me crazy. One thing a person could never do was correct someone else's grammar. It was a sure way to lose friends. If I ever wanted to be known as a real uppity pompous ass, that was all I needed to do.

I never corrected anyone, but every time one of the fellas said, "Where's he at?" I responded without fail, "Yes, where is he?"

Sometimes I would even sing, "Where is he? Where is he? Where is this beautiful boy?" The actual words in the song referred to a girl. Sadly, nobody ever got my joke.

My other pet peeve with my friends and nearly every other person with whom I spoke was their improper use of pronouns. I had no interest in a girl who misused her pronouns. It would make me cringe hearing it. I realized I could not say anything about this to anyone, but it truly annoyed me beyond belief. If I ever met a girl who was as beautiful as Hedy Lamarr or Rita Hayworth but misused her pronouns, I would be completely turned off.

Lu's sister, Nancy, was one of the worst offenders. She began every sentence with *Me*. It was always "Me and Mom are going downtown today" or "Me and Ed are going to the movies." She was so attractive, but the minute she opened her mouth, she sounded like an idiot. She graduated from Seton, too, but she apparently did not absorb anything the nuns taught her, particularly English.

I didn't mind the fellas massacring English because they were my buddies. I really hated it though, when they tried to sound intelligent, but got it all wrong. Irish was a master of misusing pronouns thinking he was so smart. He was the opposite of Nancy. Nancy was a *me* person, using the pronoun *me* in every part of the sentence. Irish, on the other hand, was an *I* person. He used *I* in every part of the sentence. What really irritated me the most was when he said, "Monty, let's keep this between you and I." It took all the restraint I possessed not to correct him.

After I was married and had five children many years later, I tried to teach my kids proper grammar, particularly in the use of pronouns. I was emphatic about not ending sentences with a preposition. I illuminated to my children repeatedly throughout many years at the dinner table the proper use of objective and subjective pronouns. It was simple, I explained an infinite number of times. The objective pronouns, such as *I, we, they, he* and *she*, were used in the subject part of a sentence. Subjective pronouns, such as *me, us, them, his* and *her*, were used in the predicate part of a sentence and as the objects of prepositions, as in *between you and me*. I admit that it was terribly rude of me to correct my children's grammar whenever they opened their mouths to tell a story at the dinner table, but at least three out of five of them learned acceptable grammar and the proper use of pronouns after my many years correcting them. Sadly, two of my children never seemed to absorb the finer points of grammar and they stopped telling stories all together at the dinner table to avoid being interrupted and corrected by their father. I was not certain if I failed or if they failed. Nevertheless, I tried my best

Lu, however, spoke beautifully from the day I met her. I loved listening to all her stories. I enjoyed looking at her even more. She was the full package. She was always so understanding, too. When I told her that I was going to enlist in the Marine Corps after graduation, she understood completely. She said she would miss me, but she knew all the boys were feeling very patriotic and wanting to join in the fight for their country. After it all went awry because my father wouldn't sign my enlistment papers, I told her I was going to go to school at College Park instead. She expressed to me that education was very important, too. She was working full time when I decided to attend the University of Maryland so when I came home on weekends, she said we could see each other.

Chapter Four

The I Love You

I started school in September. Nobody made a big deal about it, but to my knowledge, I was the first Culpepper ever to have attended college. My father was born in Chicago, Illinois. He quit school and went to work at the age of fifteen before joining the Navy at the age of eighteen. His father, my grandfather, who had previously lived with us, Leonard Culpepper, was born in Des Moines, Iowa. He was raised on a farm and had something like twelve brothers and sisters. I don't believe he ever received any formal education beyond grade school. He and my father were both lathers by profession. Neither of them ever graduated from high school or even attended high school, from my understanding. They both started working at an early age. My mother graduated from high school in Inverness, Scotland, but nobody in her family ever went to college either.

The problem with my going to college was that my heart was not really in it. I was homesick for one thing. I missed my friends, but mostly I missed Lu. I also did not see the point of attending school when I would probably be in the military within six months. Furthermore, I had no idea what my major should be, since I had no clue what I really wanted to be. The only certainty was that I would soon be in the war. After that, who knew how long that would be? I was also unable to return home every weekend due to the level of studying required for my classes. College was so much more in-depth than high school.

I signed up for a college algebra course, but it was by far my easiest class and the only subject that didn't require extensive preparation or studying. On the other hand, my English writing professor assigned two or three compositions a week. World history, beginning with the Roman Empire, required chapter reading assignments for every class. My other two classes, economics and accounting, were straightforward, but they required preparation for class. The professors called on everyone to answer questions from the assigned chapters we were required to read for these classes. I didn't want to be humiliated for not knowing any answers, so I read and studied every chapter they assigned. School required my full attention if I wanted to get decent grades, plus I really did not have enough money to take the bus home every weekend.

My father generously paid my tuition, room and board, and gave me money for books and incidentals. I only had a few extra dollars I had saved for transportation. I never had any kind of steady paying jobs in high school, but I did like to make a buck. I started selling newspapers when I was about ten years old. The largest number of papers I ever sold in one day was on May 7, 1937, the day after the Hindenburg disaster in New Jersey. Everybody was curious as to why the giant German Zeppelin burst into flames and crashed to the ground right before it was supposed to have landed. The funny thing was nobody really knew exactly what happened. The headline was great though, as was the accompanying picture of it bursting into flames as it neared the ground to land. I remember I made over two dollars that day selling papers after school. I had never made that kind of money before as a paperboy. The more papers I sold, the more money I got. Some days I was lucky to get ten cents, but usually I got two bits for the afternoon on an average day. Prior to going to college, I ordinarily utilized my own spending money. I rarely asked Pop for even a dime. I normally paid for my own candy from the time I was about ten. My favorite was chocolate-covered cherries. I paid my own way at the movies, too. As a boy, I never missed my favorite Saturday afternoon serial, *The Three Mesquiteers,* starring John Wayne, years before he became a big star.

A dime was a lot of money to a kid, particularly in 1937. I'm reminded of a day when I was maybe twelve years old and broke a ten-cent bottle of whiskey. Pop had come home from work one evening, and as usual, he took a nap. A couple of hours later, he got up and wanted a drink. When he realized he was out of booze, he summoned me and gave me a dime to go get him a bottle of whiskey. The liquor store was only about three or four blocks away around the corner on Aisquith Street. I cannot recall what brand of whiskey it was, but I knew it couldn't have been imported whiskey from a distillery in Scotland, not for a lousy dime. After purchasing the cheap whiskey, I departed the liquor store and walked up Aisquith Street toward home. I saw a black boy, maybe about my age, twelve or so, running like a deer down the sidewalk directly at me. Behind him were about eight or ten white kids, all around the same age, none of whom I knew or recognized though. I immediately thought that the black kid must have stolen something. Why else would they have been chasing him? As he rapidly approached, I instinctively grabbed the whiskey bottle from the brown paper bag and swung the bottle over his head, bouncing it rather hard off his skull. The glass bottle broke off at the neck leaving me holding the top part of the bottle in my fist. The fat part of the bottle crashed to the ground splashing the whiskey all over the sidewalk. The white boys sped by me in their pursuit without even looking at me or the broken bottle.

To my amazement, this black kid never even broke

stride. I mean I hit that kid with some real force. I played baseball and football and considered myself a fairly athletic young boy. I could hit and throw with some authority. I smacked that kid with a solid blow right on the top of his head with a whiskey bottle and it didn't faze him one bit. Luckily, I had another dime in my pocket. There was no way I could go back home without that whiskey and face my father. I went back to the liquor store to purchase another bottle.

The liquor store owner said to me, "We already did this just a few minutes ago, didn't we, kid?"

"Yeah, I drank the last one and I'm still thirsty," I responded sarcastically. The store owner frowned and shook his head. He took my last dime and gave me another bottle of the same cheap whiskey.

As I walked home that night, I thought about the valuable lesson I had learned. I was never a prejudiced person and I honestly thought that the reason the black boy was being pursued was because he had stolen something. I never thought for one second that he was being chased for any other reason. However, in later years, I thought it was likely he was being chased out of the white neighborhood. The city, after all, was segregated. The blacks largely lived in west Baltimore. I concluded from my experience breaking the whiskey bottle over that kid's head, which had no apparent effect on him, was that black guys had hard heads. The moral of the story was to never hit a black guy in the head, however racist that might sound. For the rest of my life, I possessed this valuable knowledge, not that I was ever in a situation again where I had to hit anyone, black or otherwise, in the head with a bottle or with anything else.

The best paying job I had in my youth was as a caddy at the Hillendale Country Club, located at the intersection of Hillen Road and Taylor Avenue, just a few miles from my house. Years later, in the 1950s, when I was married with kids, the country club closed. The city was expanding after the war. The members built another Hillendale Country Club in northern Baltimore County. I never played golf there, but it became one of the most prestigious clubs in the Baltimore area. I was paid a buck as a kid to carry the bag for eighteen holes at the old club on Hillen Road. Sometimes I got two bits extra, or even four bits, as a tip, depending on how generous or wealthy the golfer. Once, some rich golfer made his best score ever while I was on the bag, and he gave me a fin. I treated myself and all the fellas to ice cream sodas later that afternoon. I caddied quite a bit in the summer of 1942 for some extra cash. I spent most of it on dates with Lu, but I still had some left over for college.

After budgeting the extra spending money Pop had given me for school and with my caddy money, I calculated that I had enough cash left over for five roundtrip bus rides home on the weekends throughout the semester with just enough money remaining to take Lu out to the movies or dancing.

On October 12, 1942, I wrote my first letter to Lu from College Park. Before I left for school that fall, I told Lu in her parlor how much I loved her and how I thought of her constantly. We kissed passionately that night on her sofa in the parlor of her rowhouse on Biddle Street, taking advantage of some rare moments alone. It was usually like Grand Central Station at her house. Her sisters, brothers, aunts, uncles, and always somebody were continually passing through. I bribed little Charlie with the usual nickel to get rid of him that night and everybody else must have been out because we had some alone time for a change. Although I told Lu how much I loved her that night, she never said she loved me back.

Her response was, "I'm so fond of you, Monty."

The first weekend of October, I took a bus back to Baltimore after planning a date with Lu. She had not said she loved me, but she never went out with anyone else if she knew I was coming home. We took the trolley car downtown and went to the movies at the Hippodrome. We saw *Casablanca* with Humphrey Bogart and Ingrid Bergman. Lu and I loved the song in the movie, *As Time Goes By*. The lyrics were so prophetic, at least in my mind. I knew I loved Lu. I was never more certain of anything in my life.

"Lu," I asked with all sincerity, "could this be our song?"

"Yes, it's a beautiful song," she answered.

We took the trolley up Guilford Avenue which stopped a few blocks from Lu's house on Biddle Street. We sat on the couch in her parlor the rest of the evening, listening to the radio. I told her again how much I loved her as we occasionally kissed in between the traffic of her various family members passing through the parlor.

Charlie kept sneaking up on us behind the couch until Mrs. Flanagan yelled from the kitchen, "Charlie, get out of there and leave those two alone."

Charlie obeyed his mother and went elsewhere. I thought to myself, "Thank you, Mrs. Flanagan, you saved me a nickel." I did not get the response I wanted from Lu, though. We kissed and hugged on the couch that night, but she never returned the "I love you."

I repeated to her later in the evening that I loved her. She told me I was "getting a little mushy and silly."

After our date ended and I went home, I couldn't help feeling dejected. I loved her and nobody else. I kept thinking of the song, *As Time Goes By*, and how I proclaimed it to be our song. The lyrics stuck in my head. We were both wooing, but only one of us was saying I love you. I saw Lu again on Sunday afternoon. We went for a walk in Patterson Park and then made our way back to her house. We sat in the parlor listening to the radio. Everybody in her family seemed to be home. I think I said hello and chatted to every member of the family, including her Uncle Tom from next door. He drove a taxi just like Mr. Flanagan. They were both so congenial, you would have thought they were brothers, but Uncle Tom was Mr. Flanagan's brother-in-law. It was a wonderful two days I spent with Lu, but unfortunately, I had to leave at about eight o'clock Sunday evening to return to school at College Park. That Monday night in my dormitory room, I wrote Lu a serious letter about our relationship.

Lu Darling,

This may sound "mushy" and "silly" to you, but I am writing with all sincerity. I want you to write me and answer what I ask. You said not long ago that at first, you thought of me a great deal, but now – what? Let me know how you feel about me now. When you are in my arms, I imagine it's very easy to say things you don't really mean. That is why I want you to sit down and think before you write me. Take into consideration, how long you have known me, are you tired of me, do you still want to go around with me, everything?

I want you to do this because there is one thing missing between us. It's only the knowledge I do not have. I don't know where I stand. Am I but a good friend – what? Now that I am not with you, you can decide correctly. You evidently must know how I feel about you. It is obvious. To me, Darling, you are everything. I live and breathe you – night and day, sleep or awake, drunk or sober. Lu, Dear, I am getting so I do not like to be without you, and that is why I must know what I ask. I am sorry this letter is late, but I did not get here until four in the morning. The buses were late.

Loving you, Monty
P.S. - Please excuse the writing, for the desk hasn't two legs the same size.

About a week later, I received a letter from Lu. She proclaimed for the first time that she loved me, but at the same time, she explained that she did not want to be so serious. She said we had to be sensible, in light of the fact that the rest of the world was in so much turmoil. All our friends were going off to war and we were living in very uncertain times, she wrote. She elucidated that since we were both only seventeen, we should not rush into anything, but that she would still love to see me whenever I was home.

I took the bus home a couple of more times in November to include the long Thanksgiving weekend. Congress declared it a national holiday the previous year in 1941, so school was closed. I didn't see Lu on Thanksgiving. She had to work the day after, but I took her to the movies Friday night. Saturday night I took her dancing at the Alcazar. It was a grand time. I hated having to go back to College Park on Sunday.

I did not see her again until almost a month later when I took the bus back to Baltimore for the weekend. She told me she would try to change her plans whenever I came home. She spent many Saturday nights at the USO dancing with servicemen, but that weekend she spent with me, dancing at the Alcazar, catching a movie downtown, and strolling through Patterson Park Sunday afternoon. I left Sunday evening to catch the bus to College Park. I wrote her a letter immediately upon my arrival back at school on December 20, 1942. I was scheduled to take my final exams before the Christmas break.

Lu Darling,

It is now about 12:01 a.m. Monday morning and you can easily guess of whom and what I am thinking – you and the long Sunday night. Baby, I have really missed you. Being so far from you makes the days seem like years when they are not spent with you. This town is great, but it lacks one thing... you.

I will most likely leave Wednesday morning so I can arrive Wednesday afternoon to be ready to take you out that night. I would also like to inform you Christmas Eve is great for a certain two people to be together. I hope I need not have to tell you what two people (a light-haired fellow and a beautiful, darling brunette).

Loving you – always, Monty

I drew a little sketch of a Santa Claus at the bottom of the page with the caption, *I am dashing home for Christmas and you.*

I arrived home Wednesday night, December 23, 1942, and I couldn't wait to see Lu on Christmas Eve. I had a few days off for the Christmas break before having to go back to school on Monday for a short winter semester. When I got home, nobody at my house seemed to care I was there. I told Mom I was coming home Wednesday night, but she wasn't there when I arrived home. Pop was the only one in the house. He was listening to the radio and having a drink of whiskey. The only change in the house for the Christmas season was a small tree decorated in the corner of the parlor.

"Where's Mom and everybody?" I asked.

"I have no idea," Pop responded. I was pretty sure Pop was enjoying the solitude. I went upstairs to change my clothes and take a shower. I had a date with Lu to go dancing. I didn't really care that Mom, Margaret, and Edith were out, even though I told them I was coming home. All I really wanted was to be with Lucille anyway. As I left the house, Pop was still sitting in the parlor with the radio on.

"I'm going out, Pop," I said. "I have a date."

"Okay, Boy," Pop said in his typical introverted fashion. The man did not like to say much.

The next few days with Lu were simply wonderful. I took her out dancing at the Alcazar again, one of our favorite activities. We were becoming quite the dance team. It always felt so natural being with her. Our moves on the dance floor were always in sync. I could feel it in my bones that we were made for each other. We went ice skating in the afternoon on Christmas Eve in Patterson Park. I went to Lu's house again that night after we both had gone home to clean up and change our clothes before having dinner. Her house was in a whirlwind. People were coming and going all evening. The house was adorned with a beautifully decorated Christmas tree and wreaths were on every door. The plentiful pile of wrapped gifts under the tree added to the festive atmosphere. Mr. and Mrs. Flanagan seemed to be in an especially gay mood. I could feel the Christmas spirit at Lu's house. What a difference between her house and mine. Very little Christmas joy existed at my home. Sure, we exchanged gifts and Mom fixed a nice dinner, but the contrast in the atmosphere was as plain to see as the nose on your face. The reason was because the Flanagans had a strong belief in God and the Culpeppers did not.

The Flanagans were all devout Catholics. My family, on the other hand, didn't practice any religion. I wasn't really sure my mother and father even believed in God, since they never once talked about religion or God, at least not to me. They did take Margaret, Edith, and me to church when we were little, so I guess they must have believed in God at some point. We did celebrate

Christmas, of course, exchanging presents and gathering for dinner, but we didn't go to church. We didn't even say the blessing at Christmas dinner. I believed in God even though I didn't attend church. To me, it didn't make any sense as to why we were here if there wasn't some supreme being calling the shots. Otherwise, what the heck was it all about?

I went to dinner twice that Christmas Day in 1942. My mother cooked ham and we had dinner at one o'clock with just the immediate family. After dinner, Edith and Margaret left to go visit their boyfriends. I did the same as I was invited to dinner at five o'clock at Lu's house.

The dinner table at the Flanagan's house was at full capacity. Everyone squeezed in comfortably though. They lined up three tables so everyone would fit. Esther and Gordon were there with their three-year-old, Donny. They had recently moved into their own apartment, but I found out from Lu that Esther and Donny often came home to stay for short periods of time to get away from Gordon. Gordon apparently drank too much. I liked Gordon. He was a real regular guy. If he was a drunk, I never noticed it, although I had only seen him in passing. He looked sober to me that Christmas. Nancy and her boyfriend, Ed Stec, Charlie, Lu and me, and Lu's aunts and uncles from next door, the Harrises and the Digelmans, were all there too. John had joined the Navy the previous summer, so he was absent. Mr. Flanagan asked everyone to bow their heads for grace.

Mr. Flanagan recited the blessing, "Bless us, Oh Lord, for these Thy gifts which we are about to receive, from Thy bounty, through Christ Our Lord, Amen."

Everyone said in unison, "Amen."

Mr. Flanagan continued, "And Lord, please watch over John and all of our brave servicemen as we wait for their safe return from the war. Amen."

We all said again, "Amen." Lu glanced at me with a smile as we started to pass the plates. She knew the prayers were new to me. I had attended mass at St. John's Church with Lu a few times, but she knew my family was not religious and never said grace before eating.

Mrs. Flanagan was a far better cook than my mother. Mom's food was passable, but not delicious. Mrs. Flanagan cooked a twenty-pound turkey to perfection. The white meat was not all dried out like most turkey. It was moist and the gravy was scrumptious. I scooped up a mountain of mashed potatoes and poured the gravy over it like it was a volcano overflowing with lava. Mrs. Flanagan noticed and grinned at me with a look of approval. She also had string beans, cranberries, and sauerkraut, of all things. At my house, I was usually very picky about eating certain foods. It drove my mother crazy. I did not have that problem with Mrs. Flanagan's dinner. Everything was delicious and I ate large portions of each helping and then had seconds.

After dinner, Lu and I exchanged gifts. I gave her a pair of pewter earrings with little angels on them. I think she was quite pleased. She bought me a nice tie and a box of my favorite candy; chocolate-covered cherries with liquid centers. Lu knew me well and my finicky eating habits. I didn't like chocolate-covered cherries without the liquid center. I loved this girl for so many reasons. I think that was the nicest Christmas I ever had. I felt like I was on top of the world having all of Lu's attention directed at me.

We had another great date Saturday night, the day after Christmas, dancing at the Alcazar, followed by a trip to the late-night diner for some ice cream. I ordered my favorite, a chocolate ice cream soda. Lu had a chocolate ice cream sundae with marshmallow and chopped pecans on top. Afterward, we ended up back on the sofa in her parlor. Luckily, it was late, so nobody was around. Little Charlie had gone to bed hours ago. I didn't know if everyone else was already in bed or still out on the town. All I knew was that I finally had Lu to myself. Having her in my arms was all I wanted. Kissing her that night in the parlor filled my heart. I told her how much I loved her and wanted to be with her always.

Lu responded, "I love you too, Monty. You know how fond I am of you. Of all the boys in the neighborhood, I always liked you best. I'll tell you a little secret, Monty. I saw you when I was fourteen and thought you were so handsome. I've had a crush on you ever since." Lu paused for a few seconds, and then said very seriously, "But I think we should take things slowly."

"Anything you want, Lu. As long as I'm with you, that's all I want," I said.

"I just think it would be better to wait until after the war is over to get serious," Lu explained. "I think we're both too young right now."

"I can wait," I said. "I just want to see you and be with you."

"I want to be with you too, Monty," she said. "You know I've gone out with you every time you're home. I've even broken a couple of dates to accommodate you."

"Okay, Lu," I said. "You are always the sensible one."

"It's getting late," Lu said. "I don't want my mother or father catching us kissing. We better call it an evening."

"All right, Lu," I said. "I'll see you tomorrow. Thanks for a wonderful past few days. I've never been happier."

"Me, too, Monty," Lu said, as she walked me to the door and kissed me goodnight. "I have to get up for Mass tomorrow morning."

"I understand," I said. I walked the ten or so blocks home that night on cloud nine with the image of Lu's beautiful smiling face imprinted on my brain.

I never would have predicted that things would go so wrong between us in the next twenty-four hours. I telephoned Lu the next day, early Sunday afternoon, and told her I would come by her house to see her before catching the bus back to College Park in the evening. She said she would be home all afternoon and evening. At about four-thirty, I left my house and walked to her house. I guessed it took me all of ten minutes to get there. I felt a little extra pep in my step. As always, I couldn't wait to see her and hold her in my arms. The weather outside was beautiful for late December. It was a sunny day and about fifty degrees Fahrenheit.

As I approached 615 East Biddle Street, I could see Lu seated on the shiny marble doorsteps at her front door with her radiant, beaming smile and her wavy brown hair blowing in the breeze. The only trouble was she was not alone. No less than three fellas were there with her. Two of them were my supposed best friends, Rowley and Irish. Lu was sandwiched between them on the front steps. The third guy I had never seen before. He was standing there in his Marine's uniform.

"What the hell?" I thought.

The entire walk over to her house I was imagining myself in Lu's arms and kissing her on the couch in the parlor.

"Hey Monty!" Rowley said. "What's going on?"

"Not much at all," I responded glumly. "What goes on here?"

"We're just entertaining Lucille," Rowley replied.

"Hello, Monty," Lu said still smiling radiantly. "I'd like you to meet my friend, Gene Tress. He lives only about six blocks away from here off Guilford Avenue. He's in the Marines."

"I see," I said. "Hello, Gene, very nice to meet you. Hey Irish, what are you doing here?"

"Just enjoying my Sunday afternoon, that's all," Irish said in his inimitable annoying smart alec manner.

I was really trying to be pleasant, but inside I was so irritated I could have screamed. I just stood there like a dummy while the four of them continued their banter back and forth, telling stupid little jokes and talking about the unusual weather. Gene mentioned how much he loved dancing with Lu. Lu glanced at me with a very serious look after Gene's remark. I think she could see I was uncomfortable. Actually, I was feeling insanely jealous. I felt a flush across my face. I wondered if she could tell what I was thinking. I could barely stand it. The three of them flirting with her was enraging me. I was secretly wishing that I had an exterminator button in the palm of my hand.

"One, two, three," I imagined, would be all it took to make these three buttinskys disappear. It seemed like an eternity standing there. I didn't know how long it actually was. It felt as if time had stopped. It could have been five minutes or forty-five. I had no idea. I was seething. I felt like my insides were being torn apart. Finally, Gene said he had to go. I think Rowley and Irish sensed that I was upset. I didn't know how they couldn't have. They said their goodbyes, too, and left.

After they departed, Lu looked at me smiling, and asked, "Do you want to come in?" She acted as if nothing was wrong. I followed her inside.

Before we got out of the vestibule, I blurted out, "What were you doing with them?"

"What do you mean?" she asked curiously.

"I mean why were you spending all your time with them when you knew I was coming over?" I inquired more angrily.

"Monty, those boys just dropped by to be sociable," she said. "They're my friends."

"Really," I retorted. "It sounds to me as if you've got something going with that Gene fella."

"I don't like your tone, Monty," Lu said indignantly.

"My tone?" I countered. "How about you and all your boyfriends?"

"Monty," Lu continued. "You're going to have to get used to my seeing other boys. I told you before how I felt about you, but I'm not going to just sit home and be anti-social. Gene's from the neighborhood and I see him at the USO dances. He's a very nice boy. And Rowley and Irish are your friends, too. My crime here, Monty, is that I talked to three boys for an hour. They're my friends, two of whom I thought were your best friends! Honestly, Monty, I don't understand your attitude at all."

"Well, I'll tell you," I said rambling like a fool. "I thought we were exclusive and now I find out you have a boyfriend, and I can't even come over without finding three fellas fawning all over you. And you just eating it up. That's it, I'm done. I'll see you. We won't be going out together anymore, I guess."

"Fine," Lu replied, becoming increasingly more upset. "If that's the way you want it, then go home, I don't care. There are plenty of rational and less serious boys around."

"I think it's best," I said, not really knowing what I was saying at that point. My rage was almost like an out-of-body experience. I was mad as hell, but Lu was right - I was irrational. The damage was done, though. I acted like an ass, turned tail, and left.

I walked home that night almost crying. Why in the world did I act that way? I got home, packed my things, and headed for the bus station. I was miserable the entire bus ride to College Park and all the next day. I was so stupid to get so crazy jealous, but I just couldn't help myself. I really wanted Lu all to myself. I didn't go to classes the next day. Instead, I went to Washington to inquire about joining the Navy. I decided to write Lu a letter that night from my dorm room to explain my idiotic behavior.

December 28, 1942

Dear Lu,

I want you to know that when I left your house last night, I had a great lump in my throat. I have never felt so bad inside as I did then. On the bus, I felt something inside me was lost. I really know how much you mean to me now. Coming here on the bus in the past I was really happy and content thinking of you. However, last night I was actually unhappy and disgusted with myself. I just kept thinking of you never being with me again. It was sad. When I got down here, I thought of all the good times I had with you, similar to the bond of a teacher and pupil or of a mother and baby. I don't know whether you will think of these things or not, but I know I will never forget you or the times I spent with you. I did not go to any classes today, for I went to Washington to view the service situation. I am sure now I will be in the service by February if not before.

I want you also to know that 1942, the time I spent with you, was the happiest year I ever spent or ever hope, desire, or care to spend. Last night I thought a great deal, and I realized that I am the one who was the cause of all the petty arguments we've ever had. You are right and were always right. I have acted strangely and dumb. Your fellow must be one with far less faults than I have. I don't deserve you.

I have never met a girl as nice as you. Girls, as a rule, irritate me, with their walks and talks, but I could never say that about you. To me, you are one girl in a million – everything, pleasing in every respect. If I may quote, "There will never be another you." You may not believe this that I have written, but I grant you it is how I feel. I couldn't converse with anyone. You know these thoughts have just been lodging in my mind and I just had to write someone and there is no one but you to whom I can tell this. This letter probably won't mean anything to you, and you may even tear it up, but it makes me feel better just to be writing to you. It seems a long time since last night. I feel nothing matters now. Before, I busied myself so the time would pass swiftly, and I would be again with you. Now, however, I have nothing to look forward to. I deserve no pity for through my stupid thoughts of looking ahead and wondering, I ruined something beautiful – I have brought it upon myself. 'Tis true I am sorry. I have been a fool and I know it. However, I cannot expect you to forget or forgive, but I want you to know you are the girl that was meant for me. I must really love you. No other girl has ever made me feel or act as I have. Someday Santa Claus may bring you wrapped in cellophane down my chimney. That will be the happiest day of my life. Never change, Darling, you are perfect as you are.

If you have read this far and care for me even a little, send me that negative of you and me together – Please, Baby!

Loving you, Monty

I attended classes the next couple of days, but my heart was not in it. I left College Park on Wednesday night on the bus back to Baltimore. The next day was New Year's Eve. I felt awful, knowing I would most likely not be seeing Lu on yet another New Years' Eve. I called Rowley when I got home and asked him what he was doing. He said all the fellas were headed downtown to bring in the New Year. It would surely be the last time for maybe a long time before we could spend a night on the town together. Most of the fellas had some plan of signing up or at least getting drafted to do their part in the war. Of course, I told Rowley I would come too, but what I really wanted was to bring in the New Year with Lu. I couldn't bring myself to call her though. I was mortally embarrassed after last Sunday night, and she made it pretty clear that she didn't want to see me. I was such an oaf. Boy, I blew it with the best girl I ever knew. Tonight, I had decided, I was going to get plastered.

Sure enough, I went downtown with Rowley, Irish, Joe, Moe, and our friend, Harry Strawbridge. Harry attended Poly with me and Rowley. He was a very affable fellow and often accompanied us on a night out. Harry was about six feet three inches tall and very slender. The girls were attracted to Harry. It didn't hurt that he had movie star good looks as well. Part of the reason he didn't go out with the fellas regularly was he always had a date. I hadn't gone out with the fellas for quite some time either. Between being away at school and seeing Lu for most of 1942, I rarely saw the guys anymore, except for Rowley, who lived only two doors away from me. We did get together on many Saturday afternoons to play football or go ice skating. I liked all the fellas very much, but truth be told, I would trade all of their friendships to be exclusive with Lu. Irish and Moe each bought a bottle of whiskey. They generously shared their bottles with me, and I imbibed often that night. The fellas did a lot of talking about the war and enlisting.

"Monty, did you hear about Jack Burke?" Rowley asked me.

"No," I said. "What about him?"

"After he joined the Marines last August with Bill Cox, he did his basic training in Texas and then got shipped off to the South Pacific to Guadalcanal," Rowley explained.

"Yeah, so?" I asked.

"Well," Rowley continued. "He got killed."

"What?" I said in disbelief. "Jack got killed?"

"Yeah, the Marines are having a tough time on Guadalcanal," he continued. "I talked to Jack's younger brother, Mike. You know him. He's only a year younger than Jack. Anyhow, Mike said it's been a real bloody battle on this island, Guadalcanal, where Jack got killed. The Japs won't give up. Jack's battalion was sent in as part of reinforcements. He was evidently killed the second day after he arrived."

"Crap," I said, not knowing what else to say.

"I'm re-evaluating my options joining the service," Rowley said, unembarrassed by the meaning of his intentions. Clearly, he didn't want to die as Jack Burke did. I believed he no longer had any desire to become a Marine.

"I'm joining the Navy right after my birthday," Rowley continued. "I'm not waiting to get drafted."

"I'm considering the Navy, too," I said to Rowley. "My father will sign without blinking an eye if I decide on the Navy. He loved the Navy. It's the only subject about which I ever heard him utter more than three words. I think it would really please him if I followed in his footsteps."

Secretly, I shared the same beliefs as Rowley obviously did. Rowley didn't say it out loud, but I know he didn't want to end up fighting in some hot and humid jungle on an island nobody ever heard of and then get killed the second day after arriving like poor Jack Burke. Nevertheless, all of the fellas, including me, were all anxious to fight in the war. We continued drinking heavily throughout the rest of the night. By midnight, I was three sheets to the wind.

At some point following our discussion about

enlisting, I became unsure where we went or what we did the rest of the evening. I knew that when I woke up the next day at noon on New Year's Day, my head was splitting. I didn't even remember coming home or getting into bed. What a hangover! I had never drunk that much hard liquor before in my life. It was more than a headache. It felt more like influenza. At least I didn't believe I was really going to die from a hangover, but it sure felt like it. I stayed home all New Year's Day and night.

The following day, however, I began to feel much better. The weather was still quite mild for the middle of winter. The fellas and I played touch football at Clifton Park that Saturday afternoon. After we got done playing, Rowley pulled me aside.

"What's with you and Lucille Flanagan?" Rowley asked inquisitively.

"What do you mean?" I asked.

"She told me you guys had a little tiff and broke up," Rowley continued. "She said you were still friends though."

"Is that right?" I asked with a sardonic tone.

"Yeah, what happened?" Rowley inquired.

"I don't know," I said. "I guess I'm not the man of her dreams."

I was too embarrassed to tell Rowley about my petty fight with Lu that Sunday evening after he, Irish, and Gene left. It was too humiliating to admit to my best friend that my insane jealousy was the reason we were now only friends. I never told Rowley during all of 1942 while I was dating Lu that I was madly in love with her and that she dominated my every thought. I could never admit to him that I became possessive of her and could not stand the sight of her being with another boy, whether it was Rowley himself, Irish, Gene Tress, or anybody else. I wanted all her loving attention to be directed at me and to no one else. I had become irrational and stupid, but I could not reveal this to my best friend. He wouldn't understand, plus I would be ashamed to tell him.

After the rousing game of football, the fellas all decided to meet at the Alcazar later that evening. We all went home to get cleaned up first. Shortly after arriving at about nine o'clock, I immediately noticed Lu near the concession stand with her girlfriends. It was the usual group from Seton High, Jane Clark, Cuddles, Fran, and Elizabeth "Mike" Norris, plus another girl Lu worked with at the Curtis Bay Ordinance Depot, Netsy Mayfale. I glanced over at Lu. She gave me a smile, but like a dummy, I looked away and didn't acknowledge her. I was tired of playing the sap. She probably smiled at every guy who looked at her, I stupidly surmised, in my usual jealous tendencies.

I decided I wasn't going to be just another one of her admirers and get nothing in return from her except for a little smile once in a while. Why didn't she come over and talk to me? I asked her for a picture, and she still hadn't given it to me. Well, she gave me one picture of herself last week, but it wasn't the right one. She knew the one I wanted. I told her I wanted the negative and I would get a copy made of it. She probably had it on her right then, but she couldn't just stroll on over and give it to me. All I wanted was the negative. It would have been no trouble for her. Oh, the hell with it! She didn't love me. If she did, she wouldn't have given her attention to so many other guys. She didn't even care enough to walk a few steps and provide me with the stupid negative she promised. Didn't she know that the only thing I wanted now was a picture of her? At least I'd have some comfort looking at her in a photograph since I wouldn't be able to see her in person anymore. She obviously wasn't coming over to me, so I decided to get the hell out of there. I departed the Alcazar abruptly that night, making a beeline for the exit door. I didn't even say goodbye to the fellas.

I moped around the house the entire next day. I read a little bit, but my mind kept wandering. I couldn't focus on anything. I listened to some music on the radio, napped, and ate. Before I knew it, I had to catch the bus to College Park. The first thing I did after getting to my dorm room was to write another letter to Lu. I simply could not stop thinking about her. It was some kind of sickness of which I had no control over, so I composed the following.

January 3, 1943
Dear Lu

Well, Lu, another week has gone by, another bus ride has been taken, and another letter is written. That is, this is the second letter I have written since last Monday, December 28, 1942. I can't be sure you received the first letter, for I am still without the negative of a certain picture I wanted. I can't be angry about it though because if I remember correctly, in asking for the negative, I wrote "...and if you still think of me a little send me that negative." It's okay Lu, you did not think of me, consequently, I don't get the picture. Simple deduction of which I am the loser. Lu, I could never understand you, and I still can't. I shall never try to understand a girl again – it is humanly impossible to tell you how I feel about you. I would like to enlighten you on how things are going. School was fine, but it's over for me as of today. I am joining up within the week. All along, months ago, I felt I should be doing something for my country, serving. Now the time has come. I am going to enlist and do what I can. I don't feel like getting on a soapbox and shouting, but I do want to do something to help win this war.

You are probably wondering why I have left all the "Darlings" and "Lovelies" out of this letter. It's not that I don't think of you in these terms anymore because I do; you still mean as much to me as ever. It's just not my place to do it anymore. I can no longer be with you or take you out, due to my faults and errors, so I can't address you that way. You don't like every Tom, Dick, or Harry calling you Darling, so the same goes for Monty too. I know you want me to be sensible, and I am trying to be as you would like me to be.

I want to thank you for the smile you gave me Saturday night. You may not think so, but a smile makes me feel better. If you wanted to talk to me though, why didn't you speak first at the Alcazar that night? I was in Washington last week, and a few fellows and I had an artist sketch our profiles. The fellows thought mine turned out pretty good. The other boys sent their pictures home to their girls. I was a little sad thinking I did not have a girl anymore to send mine. Also, New Year's Eve seems to be the night I couldn't be where I wanted to be. Last Year's Eve and this Year's Eve I was not with you. I hope you had a good time; I was very pie-eyed, stinko, drunk. I was jolly and felt fine until the afternoon on New Year's Day. Afterward, Rowley was with me – he said you said we were friends. I guess you have always just classified me as a friend. I thought that you did not even consider me your friend – friends last – that's a good sign. If you like it that way, we are friends.

Your Chum, Monty.

Chapter Five

Aldine

I took the bus back to Baltimore from College Park on Thursday. It was official. I quit school and was ready for the next chapter in my life, the military. On Friday morning, I went downtown to the Navy Recruitment Office to pick up my enlistment forms. I had already spoken to Pop about my decision to enlist. I thought my parents would be upset that I quit school, but they didn't seem to care. Mom really didn't say anything about it one way or the other. She displayed a total indifference to my life-changing plans. I explained to both of them that I didn't feel right going to class when everyone I knew was joining up to fight in the war.

Pop said to me in his inimitable low-key style, "Boy, do what you think is right."

"You'll need to sign for me," I said to him.

"I'll sign," he responded. "As long as it's the Navy."

"It is," I replied.

Pop had made such a stink last August when I tried to join the Marines. At this point, I didn't really care what branch of the service it was. I had to admit, though, hearing about Jack being killed at Guadalcanal did not inspire me all that much in joining the Marines. I guess part of me wanted to please Pop, but I was ready to go. I was only going to join the Marines last summer with my friends because of all the hoopla graduating high school in the summer war class. I got a little caught up in the excitement of it all. However, after spending months away at college, I realized that it was my patriotic duty to join the military. I felt guilty attending classes. Besides, Rowley and Irish were joining the Navy as well. Rowley turned eighteen in January. Irish was already nineteen. Joe Albrecht joined the Army. He was nineteen, too. Joe said he hated the thought of being on a ship way out in the ocean, therefore, he was choosing the Army infantry. I didn't know the exact plans Moe or Harry had regarding the service. They never said much about it when the subject came up, which was quite often among the fellas. I figured they would eventually enlist, too. If not, they would certainly get drafted. I had been hearing about a number of guys from the neighborhood and the Tenth Ward being drafted.

The only friend I had who had a serious girlfriend was Joe. He had been dating Lu's good friend, Elizabeth "Mike" Norris from Seton. I envied Joe. Mike evidently told Joe she would wait for him. I wish I had that kind of relationship with Lu. When Rowley told me that Lu said she still considered me a friend, it really hurt. I would have given anything for Lu to have said she would wait for me. She was always the sensible one, though, always telling me we were both too young and that I was too serious.

Lu wrote two letters to me that January before I had to report for my Naval service. One arrived at my house. It had been delivered to my dorm room at College Park after I quit school but was then forwarded to my parents' house on Federal Street. The first letter was nice enough, explaining her usual reasons for us not getting too serious. The uncertainty of the war seemed to be her biggest argument. She at least said how fond of me she was and how much she enjoyed our time together. She filled the letter with the normal stuff she usually wrote about. For instance, she said a bug was going around her family and that both she and her father had been sick, but that everybody else was fine. She had gotten a raise at work. It was a very cordial letter, however, she made it plain that she would be writing to and seeing other boys, as well as attending USO dances in Baltimore and at Fort Meade.

I sent her a short letter explaining that she was right about everything, as usual, and that I was not good enough for her. I told her I was reporting for boot camp with the Navy on Monday, February 1, 1943. I provided her with my new address at the U.S. Naval Training Station in Bainbridge, Maryland. I told her how Rowley and Irish had already reported to basic training and that she must be broken-hearted that her boyfriends were leaving.

I reported on Monday at two o'clock in the afternoon at the Navy Recruiting Station downtown, marking my official first day of military service. A bus took the new recruits to boot camp in Bainbridge, Maryland, about forty-five miles northeast of the city, just beyond the Susquehanna River. It took about an hour and a half to get there.

The day I left for Bainbridge was anticlimactic. Nobody was home when I awakened at about eight-thirty that morning. I never knew where anybody was at my house. God only knew where Mom might have been. She had quite the social agenda. I did tell her the night before that I was leaving Monday afternoon. She always had someplace to be. Margaret and Edith were undoubtedly at work, as was Pop. I had hardly seen anybody that weekend. My sisters had steady boyfriends and were always out on the weekends. Pop typically spent Saturdays with his best friend, John, hanging out at John's barbershop, and on Sundays, Pop normally stayed home.

Rowley and Irish both joined the Navy in January and had reported to basic training. Irish had been at Bainbridge for two weeks already and I was not sure where Rowley had gone. I believed he was assigned to Newport, Rhode Island, for his training. I hadn't spoken to Lu for weeks and my only communication had been through the short letter I had written her. I wanted to say goodbye to her, but I assumed she probably didn't want to see me. As it turned out, I didn't say goodbye to anyone that day. I thought about heading over to Lu's house to say goodbye, but then I figured everyone would be at work. It was hard to get excited about joining the service when I got no send-off. I felt a bit down in the dumps leaving for the bus station. I felt so alone.

The bus arrived at the Bainbridge Naval Training Station in the early evening. I didn't have any time to feel sorry for myself once I got off the bus. The other new recruits and I were quickly herded into a building. Navy personnel were yelling orders at us every step of the way. First, we had to strip our clothes off, including our underwear. We packed our civilian clothes into boxes to be shipped back home. It was so embarrassing, standing there with no clothes on with a hundred other naked sailors. I was always on the modest side. I never even liked changing in the locker rooms at school. I was clearly the type of person who preferred privacy. I couldn't help but think at that brief moment that I had made a huge mistake. The other recruits and I stood there with our arms extended as Naval personnel piled new clothes into our arms. They never even asked us what size we wore, but everything seemed to end up fitting all right. I was just happy to finally get some clothes on.

We were then given our seabags. After filling the bags with a hammock and mattress, one pillow, two pillowcases and two blankets, every sailor stenciled his name on the side of the bag. We then marched off to our barracks. There, the Chief Petty Officer, or CPO, instructed us how to roll and fold everything to fit properly into the seabag, according to Navy regulations. In fact, every recruit was issued the Bluejacket's Manual, also known as the Navy Bible, which contained all a recruit would need to know to become a sailor and act like a sailor. I was issued my dog tags on the first day of boot camp. To my great surprise, my name was printed as MONTGOMERY ALDINE CULPEPPER, #258-58-67. Initially, I thought I should have advised the Navy of their error, but then I thought, what the hell, I hate my middle name anyhow. Aldine was no worse than Alpine, so I let it remain. From that day on, every U.S. Navy document pertaining to me from transfer orders and assignments to my eventual discharge papers, had my name appearing on them as Montgomery Aldine Culpepper.

"Up and at 'em," the CPO frequently yelled. His decrees always seemed to end in *'em*.

"This ain't your mother asking you; I'm telling you," he told us.

The CPO was almost humorous except the Navy was dead serious about discipline. The CPO never exhibited a hint that he possessed even the slightest sense of humor. Much of the CPO's screaming usually came in the middle of the night. Reveille was at four-thirty in the morning during boot camp. We had to be in the mess hall by five for chow. After breakfast, we had to fall in for calisthenics. We marched, hiked, marched again, sometimes with our rifles over our heads, and then ate again. They taught us to shoot, load shells into cannons and fire them, row a boat, scrub a deck, and clean our clothes. I believed that the most important thing they taught us was to swim. After all, we were eventually going to be on a ship in the middle of the ocean.

Luckily, I was already a strong swimmer. Some of the guys couldn't swim, and some had never even been in the water before. This didn't matter to the Navy. Those guys got thrown into the deep end of the pool just like everybody else. If you couldn't swim, you had better have learned fast. No recruits drowned, but a couple of them came fairly close to it before they were pulled out. For the life of me, I could never understand the logic of a fella enlisting in the Navy when he couldn't swim.

At the end of the first week of basic, I was flabbergasted I had received mail. And of all people, it was a letter from Lu. I was so pleased that she would write me. My mind raced about what she might have written. I was very excited to read it. My first thought was that she wanted to get back together with me. My wishful thinking was quickly dashed, though. Her letter turned out to be a real doozy. I'd never received anything quite like this letter in all my life. She really put me in my place. It nearly ruined me. It couldn't have come at a worse time. I was under a great deal of stress after embarking on such a life-changing event as joining the service.

To begin with, nobody seemed to give a damn that I had enlisted. I left home to join the Navy and there wasn't a single person in the entire city of Baltimore who said goodbye to me. Then, my welcome to the Navy was to strip naked and pack up my civilian clothes to be mailed back home with no explanation as to why my dirty clothes were in this box. What in the world would my mother think when she got that package? I could almost picture the horror and puzzlement on her face as she opened this parcel from the United States Navy and then retrieved my winter jacket, pants, dress shirt, filthy underwear, and smelly socks. She might think I died during my first week in the Navy. Then I had to spend the rest of the week getting up at the crack of dawn for calisthenics, going on endless hikes, training to do this, that, and the other all day, and eating shitty food every meal. The final insult at the end of the week was receiving the angriest letter ever from the prettiest, sweetest girl I ever knew. Lu wrote the following diatribe.

Monty,

I received both your letters and I suppose you received my first one which is a sort of contrast to this one. I'm doing well, but morale in the family, as well as nearly everyone's, is low because of this war. I'm over my cold, but Dad is not completely over his. My job at Curtis Bay could not be better. They are all so nice there and I even got a raise.

I'm going to say a lot that I was going to let go, but since you seem to want to know what the score is, maybe it's best to settle it, although it's hard to do in writing. If you aren't sure of the situation, you should be. After all, you created it, dating back to Sunday night, December 27th. And then that night at the Alcazar when you snubbed me! After that, I shouldn't even be writing to you and then you have the nerve to write that if I wanted to talk so much, why didn't I speak first. You didn't give me half a chance and you know it. In fact, you were practically standing right beside me, and then you disappeared. It did not make me feel so good. I'll tell you what I felt like doing – tapping you on the shoulder (with a sledgehammer) and asking you for that snapshot back I gave you previously, you ingrate. And now you keep nagging for a negative.

And I was not 'broken up' about Rowley's leaving, as you called it, and I took Irish's leaving as well as can be expected. I detect slight notes of sarcasm in your letters, too. I realize I took my time about answering you before, but why shouldn't I? You did not think enough of me to call me up before you left. Actions speak louder than words and then that letter you sent me was just a killer. Hello Chum? Say, friend, what kind of ignorance is that?

When I think of all these things, I write a cold impersonal letter. I hope this letter doesn't strike you as being harsh. I'm merely giving you an understanding since you seem to be so in the dark. Now I'll give you a chance to say something if you care to say anything.

Lu

Wow! I really blew it. She was absolutely within her rights to send me that letter. What a dunce I was. I was not exactly sure how to respond to her. She was obviously very irritated with me and for good reason. I tried not to be mean or sarcastic in my next letter. I wanted to maintain some kind of relationship with her, even if it was just for friendship, so I wrote her a nicer letter.

February 6, 1943
Dear Lucille,

Your letter was the first one I received since I have been here, and it surely made me feel good. About the change of heart – it was not my fault. A little birdie told me that you considered me just as a friend now – so. I thought you were the one that did not want to speak up at the Alcazar. I wanted to talk to you that night, but Rowley told me you considered me just as a friend, and I had more things to say to you than just friendly talk. I was really looking for you the last two Saturdays, but when I did not see you, I took it for granted the Marines had landed. Gene Tress, maybe? Rowley told me you weren't going to the Alcazar anymore.

If you really had wanted to tell me so much, I think you would have spoken first. I honestly wanted to see your mother and father before I left, for they are certainly swell folks for a girl to have. However, I barely had time to see my mother before I left, and my father and sisters hadn't come home from work yet and did not know I had gone. They did know I was going to leave one day that week, but they did not know just when. I assure you I did not miss seeing your folks because of their daughter. I can't say I don't care for her, for I do. I told you that Sunday night why I stopped going with you. It was not because I did not care for you. I have missed you plenty. Even from the first night to now I have wanted to call you and ask if we could get together again. By the way, what would you have said?

Don't say anything about hair because I don't have any. That is, I just about have two square inches of quarter-inch blades on top with nothing on the side.

I heard through the grapevine that your sister, Nancy, married Ed Stec. I would have liked to have been there. By the way, how are Esther, Donny, and Gordon? Have you heard from Rowley yet? I probably left before his card got to Baltimore. If you have his address, kindly send it to me.

I have been close to home it's true, but I still miss a few things. You know we have to wash our own clothes, make our beds, and clean the barracks.

I was sorry to hear you were sick, but I guess it did not affect your looks any. At least I hope it did not.

I remember when I used to go down your house during the day, and we did have a good time. We had plenty good times. Remember when you had poison ivy last summer?

I am sorry to hear your father has a cold, but I think he is in top shape; he will be over it soon. By the way, tell your father to think of me Saturday night by drinking a bottle of beer.

I did not get any card from Joe; I thought he had forgotten me. I'd appreciate it if you would see to it that I got his address. While you're at sending addresses, I'd like to have your brother, John's.

That's swell about your raise. It reminds me, we got a pay today. Ha! Ha! They call it a pay. One man handed us five dollars. A foot from him another man took it away and gave us a book, a tube of shaving cream, and three bucks change. When we got back to the barracks, our CPO calls for a dollar-ten from every made-man. I ended with a dollar-ninety.

You are right about your morale being down. I really feel sorry for everyone at home. Have you heard from Irish? He's here at Bainbridge somewhere, but I haven't seen him yet. I'll write you a sweet letter Monday, no kidding (That is, if this isn't sweet enough). Say hello to the family for me, and also ask your Aunt Nan to drink a beer for me. How is your Aunt Nan? And how is your Aunt Nellie? I remember her well, but I don't know if the name is Nellie or not. I do know, however, that she has a sweet niece named Lucille. Also, say hello to a nice little uncle of yours from next door. I don't know his name, but he strolled into the parlor one night. I always forget which one is Uncle Tom and which one is Uncle Frank. He must not smoke. I offered him a cigarette that night, but he refused. He was a nice fellow. Write soon, Lu, Baby, because I really like to hear from you. I still think you are the best-looking girl around, but… I would like to be top man, but you know how it is.

Love, Monty
P.S. - Say hello to Donny and Charlie.

I hoped my letter had just the right tone. I tried to keep things light and gay, but I still wanted her to know how crazy I was about her. I was on pins and needles waiting for her next letter. My goal was to deflect any anger she might have had toward me. I looked forward to her response.

My basic training was really getting monotonous. It was pretty much the same routine every day; reveille at an ungodly hour, chow, calisthenics, marching, hiking, swimming, firearms training, artillery training, cleaning, more marching, and more cleaning. The Navy had the cleanest kitchens and mess halls in the world; at least they did in Bainbridge, Maryland. I should know because I had K.P. duty continuously. It was mind-numbing work for a new recruit.

My only diversion from my dull existence was thinking of Lu. She still had not responded to my last letter, so what the hell, I wrote her another one.

February 14, 1943
Dear Lu,

I did not receive an answer to the letter I sent you Saturday, February 6, 1943. Did you get a letter from me? I would feel a little better if you did not get it. You know it is very sad when a sailor doesn't get his mail answered – especially when it is from certain people. I wish you would let me know what is going on. I have been worrying our mailman to death. He gives me mail from my family, then he wonders why I wait to find out if there is any more.

This is a ticklish situation. I don't know if I'm being foolish in writing this letter or not. I could be considered silly, writing to someone who won't answer.

I am taking it for granted someone is ill, you haven't had time or something! Is that so? Maybe your answer was lost. I hope that's the cause. I think I better wait before I write anymore. I don't want to write and say the same things twice unless it's necessary. I will, however, if the letter was lost.

There are no Valentine cards here so that is why you did not receive any! I can't say Happy Valentine's Day

since you know the position I'm in. I'll have to say, Will you be my Valentine?
Love, Monty
P.S. - I have been working on K.P. (Kitchen Patrol), mess cook; I get up at 4:30 now, go to work and get back to the barracks about 7:00 that evening. How about that? That last letter was long; drop a card or answer the last letter, please. Let me know something, I'm going dizzy.

Wouldn't you know it? I received a letter from Lu the very next morning after writing one the previous night. She was more cordial in her latest letter, but she made it obvious in the tone of her letter that we were now just friends. She admitted in this letter that she did in fact cry when Rowley said goodbye to her the day before he had to catch a train for his basic training. She saw him off, she said, since Penn Station was only a few blocks north of her house.

She wrote that she was feeling low in general since all her friends, including her own brother, were now in the war. She said it was all a bit overwhelming, but she was proud of everyone, too. It was apparently a mixed bag of emotions she was feeling. The message I got from her letter was that she was writing letters to all her friends in the service. She provided me with all the addresses I had asked for. Now that I got a better sense of our relationship and that she was seemingly no longer angry with me, I immediately shot off another letter to her.

February 15, 1943
Dear Lu,
I guess you have gotten the other letter by now so disregard it and forgive me for being impatient. I received your letter today, but you must admit you took your time about it. It's only evident how you feel about me now, so I guess I'll have to go back to "Dear Friend"

in my next letter. However, it's not agreeable with me. I think I understand the situation, but I am not sure. You certainly avoided something in your last letter. I came back from twelve hours work today (in the kitchen) to find your long last, gladly received letter. I enjoyed reading it, but in between the lines I could see you saying, "no mush." How about it?

Thanks a million for the addresses. I got Irish's letter, but I haven't seen him yet. Send me his barrack number, will you? I am sorry you were so broken up when Rowley caught his train. How did you take it when Irish departed? I felt pretty bad myself when Rowley left. You know I saw him at his house the day he left for his train. I had no idea you were going to be at the train station.

I imagine I'll really have to help (along with many other fellows) to keep up your morale now. I guess you were surely fed up during the past month – seeing me so much. I assure you I'm darn sorry I did not see you as much as you saw me. That's how it is when you're looking, you can't find. Give Charlie a nickel to hold him over 'til I see him – my very, very good friend, Charles, I mean. Also, pin a few medals on him for me.

I have been working so much I can't find time to hardly breathe so forgive this hurried letter. I only have 'til Wednesday on this job so until then.

As ever, Monty

The next evening, I received another letter from Lu. It seemed more than just a "friend" letter this time. In this latest letter, she wrote on the back of the envelope, *To My Favorite Sailor,* which really gave me hope. I was so excited that I wrote another letter to her that same night, my third letter in three days.

February 16, 1943
Dear Lucille,
There is no doubt in my mind that you think I'm crazy. Well, you aren't far wrong, I don't know what I'm doing. You probably don't know which letter is answering which. To inform you, I'm writing an answer to the letter that had a very nice saying on the envelope. It just came today at seven o'clock. I must admit this letter really hit the spot (the heart). It was quite different than the last. You need no alibi to write me, Baby; you are the one person I really desire to get mail from. Just at this moment, my CPO is telling our company what is wrong with it. I hate to say it, but we're out four towels. I had one towel missing. He certainly is giving us hell, too. I feel like a guilty criminal.

I hope you'll pardon the interruptions, Sweetie, but our barrack is really upset right now. I still haven't seen Irish yet, but I'm keeping my eye open. I can't say there isn't anyone here, for the place is clustered up with a hundred and sixteen fellows. We got a radio today; it's the first music I've heard in two weeks. They have played a few songs which bring back pleasant memories. Do you remember any special songs? I do and how! Darling, you must forgive me for not writing a long letter, but it is 8:15 p.m. and I must wash one sheet, two pairs of socks, one hat, one pillowcase, and one towel by 8:45 p.m. I'm not kidding either. I wish I were, though.

Love and Kisses, Monty

I did not receive another letter for the next five days. I wrote her on my birthday.
February 21, 1943
Dear Lucille,
I know you have a great deal of writing to do so you don't have to answer any of my letters if you prefer not

to. I still can't understand how you feel about me, so I'll stop fooling myself. I've been leading myself to believe I could see the day when I could take you in my arms again, but I'm finally getting the message where I know you wouldn't allow it. In your letter, you try to cheer up a lonely sailor by hinting you still care, but yet you don't actually say it. I guess there is no doubt in your mind how I feel about you. Well, you're right – "If I cared a little less and you cared a little bit more" – Oh, Baby. I can see you now saying, "Okay, he's a sailor now and at this moment he's getting serious just like all the rest of the boys." Well, you're not far wrong. There is an atmosphere here that surely sets you thinking of the ones you'd like to be with most.

It's a beautiful Sunday afternoon here – a perfect day for taking pictures. I have been thinking of the Sunday afternoons I spent with you taking pictures in Patterson Park and at Mother's Garden in Clifton Park. They are cherished memories now. There are many, many things about you I'll never forget. You asked me in your letter why I did not say goodbye to you before I left. If you haven't forgotten, I said goodbye one Sunday night. To be exact, it was Sunday night, December 27, 1942. I'll always remember because I made a grave error that night. Just brings something to mind to think about, "To err is human, to forgive is divine."

Well, Darling, I guess you're fed up with my mush by now, so I'll close. Definition: mush = outspokenness.

Love, Monty

P.S. - You'd Be So Nice To Come Home To (Remember that song on the radio in the parlor – I do and how!!!!)

No sooner did I drop this letter in the mail than a letter arrived from Lu, just in time for my birthday. She sent a birthday card with a letter enclosed. She said she hoped I was able to celebrate even though I was in boot camp. She told me how busy she was at work, but that it was also very fulfilling. She felt as if she was doing her part for the war effort, too. She was also extremely busy in her time away from work, writing letters to me, her brother, John, and to all her friends. She said it was almost like having a second job. Of course, Lu was still having a good time. She frequently attended USO dances in downtown Baltimore and at Fort Meade, too. The bus ride down to Fort Meade with all the girls was always a gay time, she wrote. She said it was too bad the bus full of girls could not make a trip to Bainbridge some Saturday night.

She got a bit serious in her letter by telling me she wanted to keep our written correspondence void of any of our personal business that previously transpired. Besides, she wrote, *we can discuss these matters better in person than in letters. Let's not dwell on the past. Rather, let's just dabble in being sweet to each other now and in the future. Don't make it so complicated! And for the record, I don't care for sarcasm.*

The best part of her letter was her proclamation that she looked forward to seeing me again when I got leave after basic training. She joked with me in her letter, too, by telling me she was going to call me Curly from now on. I had sent her a photograph in my last letter. Lu had always said how much she liked my thick, wavy brown hair. I was practically bald in the picture I sent her after my buzz cut, compliments of the United States Navy. She closed her letter with *What does 'TIFMBG' mean*?" I sent off another letter that evening.

February 22, 1943
Dear Lucille,
First of all, TIFMBG means "This is for my best girl."

I understand you have many things to do, so answer my letter when you can. Don't put yourself out on my account. I'm not being sarcastic, I mean it. When I was home, I neglected writing promptly to my friends, but now I know how they felt. I admit I was a bit sarcastic, but I'm sorry. You can see why, can't you? If you liked someone, I guess you wouldn't want to see them having a good time with your friends. To be true about it, I was just jealous because you hadn't missed my leaving. Well, let's not discuss sarcasm; I'm sorry now so let's forget it. We also shall forget this "business" as you call it and write swell letters to each other. I can see your point in not wanting to settle things in letters.

I was looking for you before I left, but you can see why I did not want to call up or go down your house. I wanted to meet you accidentally and start from there. I knew the situation was created by me and that's why I couldn't go down your house. It would have appeared I had made a fool of myself and then went crawling back.

I am very glad to hear you're having a lot of fun, for my sister, Margaret, said she needs me to keep up her morale. She said the 4-F's left are setting her crazy. You said you'd get a bus full of girls and come here. It's a swell thought, if only it could be possible. The fellows here would go crazy over an old washerwoman right now.

I'm not exactly worn to a frazzle yet, but I'm pretty worn. I suggest Rinso laundry detergent for washing clothes, for I've used it so much you can call me Rinsie. Say, watch that "Curly" stuff, will you? The hair is growing now. You'll have to change nicknames! I guess you've received the letter I wrote Sunday. Before I left, I wanted to get things settled too, but, as you said – I'm simple. I wish you would write those sweet letters you talked about. It would be nice. Thanks for the "Happy

Birthday." Guess what the boys did to me when they found out it was my birthday? Well, they raced me around the barracks, caught me, and put me under the cold shower, burrrr. It certainly made me feel good, physically as well as mentally.

I'll be home, Honey, but I don't know when. There's a rumor that twenty-eight of our company are leaving two weeks from today, but I don't know whether I'll be one of them or not. You see we have a hundred and twenty fellows in our company.

The parts of your letter were true but not harsh. I know I was not in the dark about the situation, that's true, but in the dark about how you felt about me. We are getting ready for bed now. Ha! Ha! It's nine o'clock. How about that? See you in my dreams.

Love, Monty
P.S. – "Baby, be mine."

I did not get a letter from Lu over the next three days, but that did not deter me from firing off another letter to her. I did nothing but think of her all week since my birthday. Her birthday card and letter really made my day perfect.

I yearned for the day I could get back home to her, so I wrote her yet again.

February 25, 1943
Dear Lu,
I am in favor of starting over again. It's evident now that we both feel the same way. Now all I have to do is think about coming home, and Baby, when I get out of here, I'm really going to do the town.

You know when we finish our training here, we get our nine days leave before we transfer. Well, Darling, when I get those nine free days – Wow!

Guess what, Lu? I received another haircut today. They took pity, however; they only shaved the sides.

Curly is alive and well!

At inspection the other day, the lieutenant told me to shave; consequently, I had to buy a razor.

The radio is playing at this very moment. The song is, "You can't say no to a Marine." How about that?

About morons, Darling, did you hear about the moron who took the train home from work? His wife made him take it back.

Did you hear about the moron who held the fountain pen up to his ear? He wanted to hear the Ink Spots sing.

Tell Charles I enjoyed his singing last year at the St. John's Talent Show, and I would really like to be able to see the show again this year. I am glad to hear you are doing a great deal of dancing for that makes enough dancing for both of us.

Guess what's playing on the radio now, "I don't get around much anymore." It's true now, but just wait until I get leave. I'm really feeling fine that we are back on the beam again for "There will never be another you."

Well, Lu, I am still washing clothes, but at present, I'm a little behind in my work. I must wash a bed sheet and those things are really difficult to keep clean. With all the dust and mud here, the sheets keep getting dirty. You keep dancing while I keep washing. We'll get along all right.

Boy, did we have a good dinner Sunday. I nearly dropped when I saw it. We had chicken for the main course, soup for the first, four side dishes, and ice cream for dessert. It's the first time I've had ice cream since I left. If they ever serve beer and sandwiches, they'll have to send me home in a pine box.

Until later, Hon,
Love, Monty
P.S. – "I Had the Craziest Dream Last Night"

I got no mail the next day, but it didn't stop me from

writing Lu again. I couldn't help myself but write to her every chance I could.

February 26, 1943
Dear Lu,

I'm sorry I forgot to thank you for your card, but the reason I did not was that I thought I had already. I got about seven cards and was happy to get them all. But yours really made me feel just a little bit happier than the rest.

I've finished my washing, and Honey, do I feel good that it's done now. It's snowing now and that brings an unpleasant thought to my mind. It reminds me of a Sunday night I was without you. Remember the weather that day? It was almost like springtime. Darling, your beau has a four-hour watch tomorrow morning. I'll have to get up at three o'clock in the morning.

My mother sent me a big box of candy and cakes for my birthday. It arrived a couple of days late, but it did not matter. Well, my friends gathered around my bunk, and we had a regular party with singing and everything – some fun!

I am surely a different fellow now that things are sewed up on both sides. My friends keep asking me why I'm so happy. When I get to see you, I have got something to tell you. It's about me. Don't get excited now, it has nothing to do between you and me. Sweetie, you can lay odds I'll never change my mind on how I feel about you.

There's a good picture show in camp tonight, but you might know, our company has to go to a first aid lecture.

By the way, Lu, how are your friends Jane and Cuds making out? Do they have any beaus to write letters or do you have the monopoly on that? Another thing, you never told me about which uncle or whoever he was I met in your parlor. Remember, I wrote and asked about who the nice fellow I had the conversation with was.

The fellows are getting ready to go to the lecture now, so until later.
Love, Monty
To see you but a moment would be heavenly.
These stirring words by Monty Culpepper.

I finally got another letter from Lu. It had been more than a week since receiving one. She always sent such cheerful letters. She and her girlfriends were making weekly bus trips now to Fort Meade to attend the USO dances. Those lucky soldiers! She did a lot for my ego by telling me that she knew a certain sailor who could dance circles around those soldiers at Meade. Boy did that make me feel good! Although Lu danced with, wrote to, and saw other boys, I always got the sense that I was her favorite. Maybe this was just my wishful thinking, but I was convinced I was the one for her and she was the one for me. Lu ended her letter with *I pray for you, my brother, and all the boys and their safe return home.* I fired off another letter.

March 3, 1943
Dear Lucille,
I am certainly glad to hear that you are enjoying yourself down Camp Meade. I wish the Navy would have girls sent up here. I haven't seen a live girl for a whole month now. Guess what? Our company graduates March 31st, but I may be home sooner. However, I can't depend on that. Baby, when I do get home. Wow!

Today, we received our last shots. When the doctor put that needle in my arm, I thought he was going to pull it out the other side. The injection today was for the prevention of yellow fever.

I finally saw Irish this week. He isn't in my regiment, but I went over to see him. It's so muddy where he is. I lost my overshoes and the left heel of my shoe. Irish looks pretty good. At least he can comb his hair – I still can't comb mine. Irish was wearing hip boots. Boy! He surely needs them, too. I told Irish where I bunk so we can get together again some time.

I have some unpleasant news for you. A fellow in a barrack near mine got disgusted and jumped out of a window. He broke his arm. It certainly was a strange thing to do. There are so many different types of guys here.

Our company has gotten a new commanding officer, and I mean he is really tough. For certain offenses, he promises seven days in the brig on bread and water. That reminds me, we had ice cream for lunch today. Also, my bunkmate received candy from his gal. Boy, I surely ate a lot of good things today! I received my identification card yesterday; you should see my picture. It's horrible. I look like a convict who needs a shave. Tomorrow morning, I'm supposed to report to the dentist again. We were on the rifle range Monday; Sweetie, I'm no sharpshooter, but I can hit the target. I received a passing score at least.

What do you think of the weather, Honey? Between the mud, the snow, and the rain, I'm driving myself crazy. Well, Honey, I'm getting ready to go to chow now. Did you know, Hon, that there are a great deal of hillbillies in the Navy? Every morning there is a great fight over the radio. Some fellows like swing, and some fellows like hillbilly music. I'll be glad to get back home to my own radio. Not a big fan of the hillbilly music.

Well, Darling, I'm really going to chow now.
Love, Monty
P.S. - I'm dying for a loving kiss and a big hug.

No letter arrived from Lu for the week, but that didn't stop me from rattling off another letter to her.

March 8, 1943
Dear Lucille,

I saw Irish again Sunday. We had a very interesting conversation. You might know the general topic was women. He said you might come here and see him next week. I don't know whether he was serious or just kidding. How about it?

About the fellow who jumped out of the window – he was crazy, insane, actually nuts. It reminds me of the lady on Federal Street a couple of blocks away from me and Rowley. She was a housewife with a couple of kids who hanged herself. I forget her name. The husband and two children moved away.

I'm very glad to hear you're praying for us. I'm doing a lot of praying myself. You know we go to church every Sunday. It's a must.

When I get home, you can bet your life I am going to eat gallons of ice cream. I'm going to drink a little something, too. Thursday night, I was on duty in the hospital during the blackout. Did you notice the stars that night? Baby, they had me in a trance.

I don't mind the interruptions, Lu, for I have a few – such as shaking the table, shoving my arm, everything. These sailors are regular cards. It was very nice of you to say that about Meade. You sweet thing, you. I can't wait to dance with you again. Irish showed me a letter where you mentioned Gene Tress. The Marine said he hadn't seen you for two whole weeks. Say, that's a shame - the poor boy. Don't worry about not seeing all your little pals. Just think, they will be home one at a time, and then you can have them all to yourself, one by one. I hope that I will be home when the other pals aren't, for I will need more time to spend with you. Remember you said it would take pages to write what we have to discuss? You know we all need an even chance with you, Baby.

Well, Sweetie, I'll have to get back to the hospital. Those poor boys need me, you know. I pack ice bags, hot water bottles, get drinks of water, raise and lower windows, everything. I'll be glad when this week of duty is over. It's almost time to go now, Honey, so I'll say, until later.
Gobs of love, Monty

I received a letter from Lu several days later. First, she wrote, *Irish is crazy. You should know by now that he's a kidder.* She said she told him that as much as she would like to visit, she hadn't the time. She did not mention Gene Tress by name, but she made it clear in her letter that she was writing to a lot of boys in the service, including her brother, John. She also told me how surprised she was that she owed income tax, but that was a predicament she quite enjoyed. Lu came from a poor family. She might have been making as much as her father made driving a cab. She wrote me about Rowley's older sister getting married and how funny it was that I had sent a frying pan as a wedding gift.

One of her best friends, Mike Norris, was going through a tough time. Her mother had some kind of blood disease and developed pneumonia. The doctors would not allow any visitors to her hospital room for fear of further infecting her mother's weakened state. Sadly, her mother passed away shortly thereafter. Neither Mike nor any members of her family were with her when she died. Mike's fiancé, Joe Albrecht, was stationed in Texas with the Army and they wouldn't give him leave since technically he wasn't family. It was a sad situation all the way around. On a lighter note, Lu said she had been drinking a lot of beer of late and believed she could drink me under the table. I wrote another letter to Lu.

March 11, 1943
Dear Lu,

Glad to see you are paying your income tax. Girls making plenty of money are my delight ---- only fooling Baby! When is the night Charlie sings? Thirty-five of our boys leave Wednesday, but I'm not one of them. However, more of our company leaves Saturday. I might be one of them, for the odds will be two to one. No kidding, I would really like to hear Charlie sing. You told me about Rowley's sister before, Honey, but that's all right. Big-hearted, am I not? About Irish, I go to see him on Sunday afternoons. Some fun, I'll say. All kidding aside, it's nice to talk to someone from home. You always think I'm serious, Baby, why? Remember you told me not to be so serious while I'm so young. I can't forget the advice you gave me. I'm a happy-go-lucky fellow who is always kidding. Nothing hurts or affects me anymore. My toes are all toughened. For example, I heard someone knows I write long letters. Do I worry what other people think or care? No, you see, I'm hard as nails. Some time ago I would have gotten excited for someone knowing to whom and how I write, but at present, it doesn't bother me.

Not serial now (get it, serial instead of serious!). Have you heard about the moron piano player who cut off his hands so he could play by ear? Or have you heard about the moron who held the fountain pen up to his ear so he could hear the Ink Spots sing? Uh-oh, I think I told you that one already.

I feel awfully sorry for Mike. Gee, I can just imagine how she feels. It's bad enough not seeing your mother when she's well, but when you can't see her when she's ill and then dying, that's really tough. The Army has no heart either. Joe should have been allowed to come home. I'll tell you about Rowley. I wrote him a card; he wrote me a card. I wrote him a letter, period. Have you heard from him? I'll skin him alive when I get a hold of him.

Guess what, Sweetie? I never told you my dog tag number. Just call me Mr. 258-58-67. That reminds me, Mister five by five married Missus four by four and they had one by one. Cute, huh? Well, Darling, I guess I'm boring you to death so until later.

Love and Kisses, Monty

P.S. – "My Sweet Embraceable You" is now being played on the radio. It reminds me of you. Do you remember "Come to Momma, Come to Momma, Dooooo?" I remember being with a certain beautiful girl in her parlor when that song came on the radio!

Another few days of monotony went by as I developed a bad cold and spent some time in sickbay. I wrote another letter to Lu.

March 13, 1943
Dear Lucille,

Since I've written you last, a little Nursie has held my hand. No kidding, I had a very bad cold, so I went to the sickbay. They had nurses, too. I only stayed there two days, so I did not worry my mom by telling her.

I've answered Joe's letter a great time ago, but I haven't heard a word from him yet. You probably know I'm an impatient fellow; so, if you write Joe, tell him to let those Texan girls alone long enough to write a friend a letter. I'm only kidding. I know Joe's faithful to Mike. You know some people wait so long to answer letters. Maybe they brood over them. I'll most likely take you up on that drinking stuff, but I guess I'll be under the table first from being out of practice. Again, I must say I'm not kidding.

You certainly are getting sharp as a tack, but don't get too sharp. I hope to get leave soon and to get back to

Baltimore to spend time with the only girl I ever think about. I have to go, Lu, for I just realized I have K.P. duty. If I'm late, I might end up in the brig! I don't think I'd get my mail in jail!

Lots of love sent your way, Monty

A couple of days later, I received a letter from Lu which really tickled me. She wrote *Dear Mr. 258-58-67*. I almost fell out of my chair laughing. The other sailors thought I was having a seizure. She wrote that she had written Joe Albrecht and told him to send a letter my way. She said Charlie's show was great. For a thirteen–year-old kid, he could really sing. He was following in his brother's footsteps, as well as his father's. Mr. Flanagan sang the Irish ballad, *I'll Take You Home Again, Kathleen*, all the time. Lu said that her father enjoyed singing, sort of the same as other people who enjoyed whistling. It was part of his being. I had heard him singing that song when I was at his house. He was quite good and always in tune. I loved music, but I couldn't carry a tune if my life depended on it.

Lu said John had gotten promoted. She was not sure of his rank. I was a little miffed when she told me Rowley wrote her and said he had little time to write because his training took up all his time. He had time to write Lu, but not his best friend. Rowley was so full of baloney, always was.

Lu sent me a bunch of moron jokes I had not heard yet. One was *There was a big moron and a little moron, sitting on a ledge. The big moron fell off. Why? Because the little moron was a little more on*. Another one was *Why do morons like lightning? They think someone is taking their picture*. My favorite was *Two morons are at the train station. The first moron asked the clerk, can I take this train to Chicago? No, the clerk responded. The second moron asked the clerk, can I?*

I wrote a letter to Lu that night, chuckling to myself about the moron jokes.

March 16, 1943

Lucille Darling,

First of all, let's not take me literally. Please resume calling me by name, not number. For your information, I am again sound in body and mind. I surely think we ought to be sent home though. Thank you for telling Joe what I said. Maybe now he will write. You can bet your life I know there is a war on. It's no easy life here, but who am I to complain or advertise? I'm glad to hear Charlie's show went off all right. I'm certainly sorry I missed it. I'll put a little light on the sentence that did not register. Someone told me that someone told that someone that I write long letters to you. Is that simple enough? If it isn't, I'll wait in line for three hours to get to the phone to explain it by voice.

Tell whoever wrote the jokes that I enjoyed them very much. Moron jokes are quite the thing here, so I'm gaining top honors repeating the ones you sent.

In referring to Rowley's training, I got the idea you think we have it easy here. I'm just as busy as Rowley, but I take time to write to my friends. Naturally, I should expect the same from Rowley. He's still my friend, I hope. You'd be impatient too if you've been waiting five weeks for an answer to your letter.

About the phrase "loving you to death," I noticed that it looked as though it was "loving you too death" but I did not think you would see it. However, I am loving you to death. I did not want to break down and tell you I'm driving myself crazy over you, but I am. Every song reminds me of you. When those slow, sentimental songs play, I get a hollow feeling in my stomach and think about you. At night when the stars begin to shine brightly,

I really long to be with you. I guess I better get back on the beam again now. I still have the feeling you don't think I'm your guy. I know how you feel about fellows in general. That is, from what you've said at times, I think I know how you feel.

Tell your mother "Happy Birthday" for me. You are a better singer than I, so be a Western Union and sing: Happy Birthday to you, Happy Birthday to you, Happy Birthday Mrs. Flanagan, Happy Birthday to you. Also, give your mother and dad congratulations and wish them many more anniversaries for me.

I won't be home Saturday, but I'll be home shortly. By the way, thirty-five fellows of our company leave for home tomorrow at eight o'clock. I'm glad to see John is advancing, but that isn't what I have to tell you when I get home. It's something else.

Say, Honey, you haven't told me what the F.A.S.S. part of S.W.A.B.K.F.A.S.S. means yet. How about writing the whole thing out for me in your next letter? If we keep this up, we'll both have codebooks. Wait a minute, it just came to me. Could it be – Sealed With A Big Kiss For A Special Sailor? Huh? Yes, I got it!

Well, Darling, I'll be out of ink soon.

Love, Monty

P.S. - How I'd love to be standing in your hallway right now, wow!

Chapter Six

Crab Cakes

The next three weeks went by so fast. I continued sending at least two letters per week to Lu. I was lucky to get one letter back from her in two weeks, but I didn't care. I knew she was busy working at her job at the Army Depot, helping her parents around the house, going to the USO dances and events, and writing letters to at least a half a dozen or more other servicemen. I didn't mind her writing other guys. I knew how nice it was to get a letter from home, especially from someone like Lucille.

When I found out I was getting liberty on Saturday and Sunday, April 3rd and 4th, I had to call her. This stupendous news couldn't wait to be sent by letter. I waited in line at the phone banks in the Administrative Building for almost two and a half hours. I must have smoked a half a pack of cigarettes standing in line waiting. When I told her I was coming home, she said she would reserve Saturday night and Sunday afternoon all for me. Well, I was over the moon, boy. After all this time, I was finally going to get to spend time with my one and only. I had so much to say to her, not over the telephone, but in person with my arms around her. She seemed very enthused about my coming, clearing her calendar just for me. I spent the rest of the week probably the happiest sailor on K.P. duty in the history of the United States Navy.

On Saturday morning, I took a train from Bainbridge at nine in the morning that arrived at Penn Station in Baltimore at ten forty-five. Penn Station was located on North Charles Street, less than a mile from my house on

Federal Street, so I walked home. Everybody was there when I arrived just after eleven. My parents came out from the kitchen and my sisters ran downstairs to greet me. They all seemed very excited to see me and they asked a million questions about boot camp. I was really very delighted at the reception I got. They all seemed genuinely happy to see me. We all ended up sitting at the kitchen table and Mom fixed me a roast beef sandwich on rye bread with a cold Coke to go with it. Everything was delicious. The chow at Bainbridge was rather bland. It was a lot like cafeteria food or meals from the automat.

"So, how's your training going, Boy?" Pop asked.

"It's not so bad, Pop," I responded, "But I've had it with the K.P. duty. I had no idea the Navy was so obsessed with cleanliness."

"Wait until you get on a ship," he said. "Every square inch is expected to be spic and span."

"Wonderful," I said sarcastically. "I have a lot to look forward to then."

"Aren't you almost finished your basic training?" Margaret asked.

"Yeah, I only have three more weeks," I said.

"Then where?" Edith chimed in.

"Not sure," I replied as I took another big bite out of my roast beef sandwich.

"You have no idea?" my mother asked skeptically.

"No, I don't," I said in between bites. "I'm hoping I get to stay at Bainbridge."

"I wouldn't count on it," Pop said.

"Why not?" I countered. "It's a huge training center. I heard a lot of guys who went through basic training there got to stay."

"Then don't tell anybody you want to stay there," Pop stated.

"What do you mean, Pop?" I asked.

"If the Navy knows what you want, then they sure as hell won't give it to you," he said.

"There's nobody to ask," I said. "It's just that some guys got to stay, that's all."

"Just don't count on it, Boy," Pop said. "Take it from me."

"Okay," I said, as I inhaled the rest of my sandwich. "Thanks, Mom. That sandwich was like a delicacy."

"You're welcome, Boy," she said. "Do you want anything else? I got some sugar cookies at the bakery, the kind you like."

"That sounds great," I responded. "It sure is swell to be home."

"Are you seeing Lucille, tonight?" Margaret inquired.

"Yes, I am," I answered with great enthusiasm.

"I'm making fried chicken and mashed potatoes for dinner," Mom added. "Are you going to want some of that before you go out tonight?"

"Oh, yes I am," I responded. "I wouldn't miss it."

"We'll be eating around five," she said. "You timed coming home perfectly. I was able to get the meat and vegetables we wanted with the ration book. The expiration date was yesterday, and I was lucky they had what I wanted."

"So, what's been going on around here?" I asked.

"Same old, same old," Mom said.

"Margaret, are you still going out with that Milton fellow?" I asked.

"Yes. In fact, we have a date tonight," she said.

"How about you, Edith?" I asked. "Still dating the same guy? What was his name?"

"Scott Crenshaw," she said. "We're going out tonight, too."

"Maybe I'll see you guys," I said. "Lucille and I are going to the Alcazar."

"No, I don't imagine you'll see us, then," Edith said. "We're not going dancing. We'll probably catch a movie."

"How about you, Margaret?" I inquired. "Where are you and Milton going?"

"We're not going dancing either," she said. "I think we're staying in tonight."

"I've been looking forward to a night on the town," I said.

"Wear your sailor uniform," Mom told me. "You look so handsome in it."

"I will," I said. "Thanks for the lunch, Mom. Everything really hit the spot. I'm looking forward to dinner. After two months at Bainbridge, I sure do appreciate home cooking."

"I know how picky you are, Boy," Mom retorted. "You look a bit skinnier than when we saw you last."

"The Navy training has got me on the go all the time," I said. "It's not like I'm not eating. I eat something at every chow time. I'm so hungry after all the work I do. I guess I'm burning off more than I eat. You'll have to fatten me up this weekend, Mom."

"I'll try," she said. "I take it you're seeing Lucille tomorrow, too."

"Yes, I am," I replied. "I think I'll see her after church tomorrow, so I probably won't be home for dinner."

"All right, then," she said. "You can just have another lunch like you had today before you go."

"That would be swell, Mom," I said. "Thanks!"

I had dinner at Mom's at about five-thirty. I gobbled up her fried chicken and ran upstairs to my room to get all spruced up for my date with Lucille. I had the whole night planned out. First, we would take in a movie at the Hippodrome Theatre on Eutaw Street at seven. The newspaper said a Jean Arthur and Joel McCrea movie, entitled *The More the Merrier*, was playing. Then, my plan was to go dancing at the Alcazar at about nine for two or three hours and spend the rest of the evening back at her house.

I walked to Lu's house and rang her front door at about six-thirty. Mrs. Flanagan answered the door.

"Oh, look who it is!" she exclaimed. "The handsome sailor has returned. I love seeing these men in uniform."

"Thank you, Mrs. Flanagan," I said. "How have you been?"

"We're just fine," she said. "You look a little thinner than when I saw you last."

"Yes, ma'am," I said. "The Navy doesn't give me a moment's rest. How is Mr. Flanagan?"

"Oh, he's fine," she said. "Where is he? John, get in here and say hello to Monty."

Mr. Flanagan entered the room and shook my hand. "You look very fit, Monty," he said. "The Navy's working you hard, I imagine."

"Yes, they are," I replied. "Thank you, sir. You're looking good yourself."

"You know my boy, John, got promoted already," Mr. Flanagan said proudly. "He's an officer."

"That's impressive," I said. "You should be proud."

Secretly I was thinking to myself if John was as big of an asshole as my CPO, yelling at a sailor every minute of the day and night.

"I am," Mr. Flanagan retorted. "I expect you'll be getting promoted soon, too, Monty."

"I don't know about that," I responded, rather embarrassingly. "I still have to get through basic."

"I know a fellow with your brains will go far," he said.

"Thank you, Mr. Flanagan," I responded. "So is John a Chief Petty Officer?"

"No, but he's a Petty Officer in charge of loading

bombs onto planes," Mr. Flanagan answered.

"Stop talking about the war," Mrs. Flanagan interrupted. "Come on in and have a seat. I'll tell Lucille you're here."

Mrs. Flanagan walked over to the foot of the steps and yelled, "Lucille, your date is here."

I could hear Lu respond from the second floor in a voice that sounded like it was very far away. She said, "Coming in just a minute, Mom."

Mr. and Mrs. Flanagan retreated into another room. I think they went into the kitchen. It sure felt great to be back in Lu's parlor. To think how many hours I spent in this room with Lu, talking and kissing, then talking some more, and then kissing some more. I couldn't believe that I was actually here again. I was a little nervous since the last two times I saw her I acted like a blockhead, first going into a jealous rage and then snubbing her. What a fool I was. I learned my lesson well though. I told myself that I had matured and could accept Lu dating other fellas while I was away. I was just lucky she was seeing me at all. I was bound and determined not to blow it now that I had this second chance.

As I sat there, lost in thought over my past transgressions, I heard footsteps coming down the stairs. I immediately jumped up from the sofa and turned to see the most beautiful sight. Lu entered the parlor with her gorgeous smile beaming, emphasizing the dimples in her cheeks to match the one on her adorable chin.

"Lu," I exclaimed. "You are a sight for sore eyes. I don't think I've ever seen anything so beautiful in all my life."

"Hello Monty," she said. "So good to see you. You look so handsome in your uniform, just like the picture you sent me."

I rushed over to give her a hug and kiss. She put her

arms around me and pressed her fingers into my back. I could have died and gone to heaven. We kissed with real passion. When I kissed her, I knew we were meant for each other. Nothing ever felt so right.

"Whew!" Lu exclaimed. "Let me catch my breath."

"You look as good as ever, Lu," I said. "Are you ready for a night out on the town?"

"Sure, Monty," she answered.

"Well, let's go then," I said. "The movie at the Hippodrome starts at seven. We'd better get going."

We walked a block and caught the trolley to get downtown. We arrived ten minutes early for the show. I ordered two buckets of popcorn with plenty of butter, and two Cokes, and we sat down in time for the newsreels. Unfortunately, the newsreels were all about the war. The Nazis were fighting in Russia, and the Japs were fighting to the death in the South Pacific. The newsreels always depicted America doing well in the war, but it was apparent that it was going to be a long, bloody, violent struggle against the Axis powers. The featured movie, *The More the Merrier*, was an amusing story of a girl, played by Jean Arthur, living in an apartment in Washington, D.C. Due to a housing shortage, she sublet her apartment to Charles Coburn, who in turn, sublet to Joel McCrea. Charles Coburn spent the entire movie playing Cupid in an effort to get Jean Arthur and Joel McCrea together. It was a cute movie and one that Lu and I both enjoyed.

Afterward, Lu and I caught the trolley to Mount Vernon. We arrived at the Alcazar ballroom at about nine. The swing band had the joint jumping. Everybody was jitterbugging on the dance floor as we walked through the front door. The place seemed to be energized. I sure felt like getting to it.

"How about it, Lu?" I asked not more than a few

seconds after walking through the door. "Wanna dance?"

"Sure," Lu said with a big smile on her face. "Why not?"

I took her by the hand and led her onto the dance floor. The band was playing *In the Mood*. They sounded exactly like Glenn Miller's version on the radio. I was in seventh heaven dancing with the girl I loved. We danced so well together, hitting every step perfectly with the beat of the music. We went together like two peas in a pod. When the song ended, I asked Lu, "Do you want to get a drink?"

"Sure, Monty, that would be fine," Lu responded. "I think we need a little break. That was a fast one, but fun!"

We were both a little out of breath. I ordered us each a Coke from the concession area.

"Here you, go," I said as I handed her a Coke.

"Thank you, Monty," she said.

"Here's looking at you, kid," I said as I raised my glass and took a sip.

"That's funny, Monty," Lu said. "I wish I were Ingrid Bergman."

"Lu, Baby," I said. "I'd take you over Ingrid Bergman any time."

"Oh, stop it, Monty," Lu said, laughing. "You've got it all over Humphrey Bogart, that's for certain. You look more like William Holden."

"No, I don't," I said, somewhat embarrassed. "I know one thing, though. If I were Rick and you were Ilsa, you wouldn't be getting on that plane with that stuffed shirt. You'd have stayed in Casablanca with me and Claude Rains."

"You're hilarious," Lu said. "Hey, are they playing *Begin the Beguine*? They are. I love that tune. Let's dance to that one, Monty."

"All right," I said, as I gulped down the rest of my

Coke. Lu took one sip more and put her unfinished Coke on a table. I grabbed her by the hand and pulled her close to me on the dance floor. I could have danced with her cheek to cheek all night. I loved the look of her, the touch of her, and the smell of her. I never wanted the night to end. We danced nearly every dance until about eleven o'clock.

I finally asked Lu, "Do you want to head back to your house?"

"Sure," Lu answered. "I'm pooped from all that dancing."

"So am I," I said. "But it sure was grand, wasn't it? I don't think I've ever had a better time dancing than with you."

"That's sweet, Monty," Lu said. "I had a wonderful time, too."

As we walked down the street, the wind picked up. Lu exclaimed, "Boy, the March winds have come late."

"I'll say," I responded. "Maybe all of this wind will dry up the mud at Bainbridge. That place is a mess. I hate walking across the base."

"You better be careful what you wish for," Lu said.

"What do you mean?" I asked.

"The wind is going to dry up the mud and the dirt will be blowing everywhere," she said. "You'll end up walking across the base in a dust storm."

"I never thought of that," I said.

Just then, we approached Lu's house. Mr. and Mrs. Flanagan and Tom and Nan were coming down the other end of Biddle Street as Lu and I arrived at her doorstep. We paused before entering to say hello.

"Hey, Mom and everybody," Lu said, as her parents and aunt and uncle came nearer. "Where were you guys?"

"We were at the saloon," Mrs. Flanagan answered. "Did you and Monty have a nice evening?"

"Yes, we did," Lu said. "We caught a movie and then went dancing at the Alcazar."

"Good evening, everybody," I chimed in. "I hope you've all had a pleasant evening."

"Oh yes, Monty," Mrs. Flanagan said. "Very nice."

"Yes, we threw back a couple of beers, Monty," Mr. Flanagan added.

"Good, sir," I said. "I hope you had one for me."

"Basic training almost over, Monty?" Mr. Flanagan asked.

"Just a couple of more weeks," I responded.

"That's grand," Mr. Flanagan said. "I'm proud of you boys."

"Thank you, sir," I responded. "I just wish they'd get me off K.P. duty, though."

"Maybe you're doing too good of a job," Mr. Flanagan said.

"I don't know about that," I said.

"If you don't clean up so well, maybe they might take you off it," he continued.

"Well, I'll tell ya, Mr. Flanagan," I said. "If I didn't clean up everything spic and span on K.P. duty, I'd only have to clean it again, and then they'd put me on K.P. forever."

"Is that right?" Mr. Flanagan asked curiously.

I knew Mr. Flanagan never served in the military and he had no clue how the military operated, but he was the nicest man. I really thought a lot of him.

"Hello Lucille," Uncle Tom said. "Hello, Monty."

"Hi, Uncle Tom and Aunt Nan," Lu said.

"Hello, Mr. Digelman," I said. "Hello, Mrs. Digelman."

"Hello, Lu and Monty," said Aunt Nan, who was a bit tipsy. "Good to see you youngsters having such a good time. Monty, you look so handsome in that uniform. Of course, you are handsome out of uniform, too. You and Lu make a beautiful couple."

"Thank you, Mrs. Digelman," I said.

"C'mon, Nan," Uncle Tom interrupted. "Let's get inside and get to bed. Good night, everybody."

Mr. and Mrs. Digelman entered their front door at 613 Biddle Street. Lu and I followed Mr. and Mrs. Flanagan inside their residence just a few feet away. Her parents said goodnight and Lu and I settled ourselves on the sofa after Lu turned on the radio. The Tommy Dorsey band was playing *Song of India,* and then they played *Boogie Woogie.*

"Hey, Lu," I said as the *Song of India* played on the radio. "Wouldn't this be a great song to dance to?"

"I love that tune," she answered. "Too bad Tommy Dorsey doesn't play at the Alcazar."

"Yeah, what a night that would be," I said. "We probably wouldn't be able to get in. Every jitterbugging couple in town would be there. Hey, your Uncle Tom and Aunt Nan certainly are a gay couple. They sure are fun. You have a great family, Lu. Your parents are swell, too."

"Thanks, Monty. I think so," Lu responded. "Hey, what did you want to tell me? You said in your letter you had something to tell me, but it was not about us."

"Well, it's not about us, exactly," I answered. "But it could affect us in a good way. I've heard a lot of rumors that after basic training, a lot of the recruits get to stay at Bainbridge to continue their training. If I get to stay, then I could come home at least one weekend a month or maybe more. Wouldn't that be great?"

"That would be great, Monty," Lu said enthusiastically. "When do you find out?"

"Probably in the next couple of weeks," I answered. "Both of my friends, Joe Cullen and Hank O'Neil, heard the same rumors."

"I hope it's true," Lu said. "Otherwise, I guess I may not see you for a while."

"I hope not, Lu," I said. "Seeing you is all I look forward to. It would be awful not to see you for too long a period of time."

"Won't you eventually be assigned to a ship?" Lu inquired. "My brother, John, was assigned to a ship not long after all of his training."

"I don't really know, to tell you the truth," I said. "I know eventually the odds are I'll go to sea. Hey, did I ever tell you about the guy in my barracks they call Tiny?"

"No, you've mentioned your friends, Joe and Hank, but I never heard you speak of Tiny," she said.

"Well, Tiny is this giant of a guy," I explained. "To tell you the truth, I don't even know his first name. His last name is Hinkle. He must be six feet four inches tall, and he weighs maybe two hundred and seventy-five pounds or more. The funny part about him is that he's the sweetest fella you'd ever want to meet. His personality is incongruous to his size. I've never seen him mad or upset about anything."

"That's funny," Lu said. "There's an officer at Fort Meade whose size makes him look scary, but he's one of the nicest people there."

"From your letters, it sounds as if everything is going very well with your job," I said.

"Yes," Lu replied. "I really love working there. The Colonel and the other officers in the front office are all so patient and kind. They seem to be happy with my work."

"That's fantastic, Lu," I said. "I'm really proud of you."

"Thanks, Monty," she said. I then moved in closer for a kiss. Lu put her arms around me, and we kissed. I felt a sense of euphoria.

I looked at her and said, "You're everything to me, Lu," before giving her a hug and another kiss.

"It's getting late, Monty," Lu said. "I have to get up for Mass tomorrow morning."

"All right," I said reluctantly. "Are we still on for tomorrow afternoon?"

"Yes," she said. "I look forward to it."

"I'll come around about two and we can take a walk in Patterson Park."

"That sounds great, Monty." Lu walked me to the door and kissed me goodnight. I walked home on cloud nine yet again. When I got home, I didn't see a single light on in the house. I tiptoed upstairs and went to bed with sweet dreams of my time with Lu.

I picked up Lu as planned the next day. She was waiting at the door and ready to go. She brought her camera to take some pictures. We hopped on a trolley car to get to the park, which was about two miles away. We had a great time just walking hand in hand through the park. We stopped at a secluded spot for some pictures. I took a couple of Lu, and she took some of me. We then went to the top of the Patterson Park Observatory, a pagoda-styled building on Hampstead Hill overlooking the rest of the park. It was a great view. We could see the kids playing, the swimming pool, which was empty since it was only about seventy-two degrees, the flower gardens, the tennis courts, which were crowded, and the many people just out walking or having a picnic. The day was very relaxing, and it was just perfect being with the girl I loved.

After walking around Patterson Park, I suggested to Lu, "How about getting something to eat? Are you hungry?"

"It's getting close to dinner time, isn't it?" Lu

responded. "I could stand a bite to eat. What time is it?"

"It's just after five," I said. "How about Haussner's? It's only a few blocks beyond the park on Eastern Avenue."

"Sounds like a plan," Lu said eagerly. "They serve the most delicious crab cakes in town."

"Okay, let's go," I said. "Crab cakes sound good to me."

We left the park and walked about five blocks down Eastern Avenue arriving at Haussner's Restaurant. We were seated right away.

"It's good to sit down," Lu said. "That was a bit of a walk."

"Yeah, after all that walking in the park, it is good to sit down," I said. "I worked up an appetite."

"Me, too," Lu said. "I'm going to have to go with the crab cakes, although everything here is good."

"I have to get the crab cakes," I exclaimed. "Who knows if I'll get transferred out of Bainbridge? I may not get back to Baltimore for a while. I hope not, but I may not be able to get a good crab cake again for quite some time. Who knows?"

"Better safe than sorry," Lu deadpanned. "Crab cakes it is." Lu then laughed in her inimitable sweet way.

Every time I was with Lu, it was wonderful. We enjoyed our delicious crab cakes and then we each had a slice of German chocolate cake for dessert. The experience eating at Haussner's that evening could only be described as a culinary delight. We took a series of trolley cars to get back to Lu's house. We spent the evening in her parlor on the sofa listening to the radio and chatting with her family members as they came and went. It was a gay evening and everyone in Lu's family was so pleasant and cordial. They all asked about my training and where my next assignment might be. Of course, I had no idea as yet, but I told everyone I was hoping my next assignment was at Bainbridge. Before long, the night had come to an end, and it was time for me to go.

"It's so late, Monty," Lu said with concern. "It's already twelve-thirty. What time do you have to be back at the base?"

"I have to be there for assembly at eight in the morning," I answered.

"Oh, Monty," Lu said. "You'll get in trouble if you're late, won't you? How will you get there on time?"

"Don't worry, Lu," I retorted. "I'll be on time. I'm gonna catch a train. I'll get there on time."

"It's so late, though," she said.

"I'll stay just a little bit longer," I told her. "I don't want to leave you." I wrapped my arms around her, and we sat there listening to the music on the radio for about twenty minutes more.

Lu finally said, "Monty, you're not going to make it to Bainbridge on time."

"Okay, Lu," I said. I then got up and Lu walked me to the door. "I love you, Lu. I can't wait to see you again."

"I can't wait to see you, too, Monty," Lu said. "I had a lovely time. Let me know when you're on leave again. I hope you get assigned to Bainbridge after basic training is over. That would be so convenient."

We kissed again and I hugged her tight. "See you soon, Lu, I hope," I said. I looked into her beautiful green eyes and said goodbye.

As I walked down Biddle Street, I glanced over my shoulder to see Lu at the door giving me a wave. I waved back and continued home. I felt a flicker of sadness come over me. I feared I would not see her again for a long time. The thought of my life without her frightened me. I had no such feeling concerning my mother or the rest of my family as I departed home later that night for the train station back to Bainbridge. It was Lu, and Lu alone, who was truly in my heart.

I returned to Bainbridge a little after dawn. I had time for breakfast before making it on time for assembly at eight. I slept less than two hours, but I was running on adrenaline at that point. I managed to get through the day. I immediately wrote Lu later that night.

April 5, 1943
Dear Lu,
First of all, you must excuse my writing in pencil, but as you know we aren't allowed out of the barracks to go to the canteen. Listen carefully, Darling. Bright and early this morning, I traveled up to the place where work details are given out. With good intentions, I signed up for work duty. About an hour later, I was assigned to the unloading of trains detail. When our detail arrived at the specified spot, thirty-five recruits were working diligently, consequently, we were relieved of all duties and returned to the barracks. How about that? The Navy must want me to take it easy. Having this time on my hands, I just had to write to the one I _____ (3 guesses).

I must admit I'm really tired now. Last night I left your house a little after one. By the time I ate and got to bed, it was two o'clock. My mother thought I was getting an early train, so she woke me at three-thirty. I was at the station at quarter after four, ready to catch the five-ten train. I got to Bainbridge at seven, ready for the eight o'clock muster. I'm a little early bird, aren't I?

Darling, leaving your house last night was really difficult. I had a lump in my throat large enough to sink a battleship.

Guess what, Lu? My friend, Joe Cullen, is being shipped out tomorrow.

Well, Baby, I want you to know I really miss you now. You're on my mind always --- every second. It's tough for me to say farewell for now so we'll say, 'until the next letter.'

Loving you, Monty

The next week went by with the usual daily routine of reveille, breakfast, assembly, marching, firearms training, swimming, ship duties, cannon and gunnery training, more marching, hiking, K.P. duty, guard duty, dinner, and back in the barracks to wash clothes or clean the barracks. The daily routine was getting monotonous, but worst of all, I was not getting any mail from Lu. I barely had time or the energy to write, but I was able to get three letters off the next two or three weeks, each one expressing my undying love for her.

April 11, 1943
Lu Darling,

I'm still here at Bainbridge and it is just starting to get unbearable. I've been on K.P. since Friday. I'm completely out of writing paper, ink, cigarettes, shaving cream, etc. Worse than that, we aren't allowed out of the barracks to buy anything. Just to write this letter, I borrowed a pen from Tiny, took some of Hank O'Neil's ink, and borrowed the writing paper from a fellow who just came in today.

In spite of all the difficulties, Honey, I think of you constantly. I miss you something terrible; I'll never forget how wonderful you were while I was on leave. Perhaps, Darling, I may get weekend liberty Saturday coming. If I do, I'll call you as soon as I get in town, and Precious, how about wearing your super black dress with your new black shoes? Don't think wrongly of me for saying what to wear, but I just think you look lovely in black. To be technical though, you always look lovely. Golly, but I miss you, Sweetie.

News Flash: Bainbridge mud has turned to sand. The

March winds have come late. You're right. Dust storms.

I wish you would write me here, Hon. Hearing from you would make me feel so much better. Have you received the other letter I wrote? Baby, at the present moment, I have the most longing desire to hold you in my arms. I'd give a million dollars to be sitting beside you on the sofa in the parlor. Have you heard from John? Does he like being an officer? Tell your father that Bainbridge has gotten out of control. I can't handle the place anymore. I hope everyone at 615 and 613 Biddle Street are all okay – the gay married couple (Tom and Nan), Charlie, your Mom and Dad, and the rest of your engaging family. Say hello to them all for me, Lu. By the way, give Aunt Nan a special big smile for me also. Darling, I would certainly like to have a nice, sweet picture of you for my new wallet. How about it, Honey-child?

Well, Gorgeous, let us both pray I get liberty this week, and say 'until Saturday.'

Loving you, Monty
You are to me – everything

I wrote another letter two days later.

April 13, 1943
My dearest dimpled Darling,

I am now sitting up in bed writing to you with my heart as the pen. All of my friends are on liberty in Baltimore at this very moment, but here I be. You know I'm on K.P. duty, therefore I'm not entitled to liberty today. Let me tell you about last night. As you know, I'm only supposed to work from 6 a.m. to 6 p.m., but last night, our Master of Arms was in a bad mood. He made up his mind to keep us in the mess hall until ten-thirty. We mopped the deck nine times. Naturally, I felt tired and sad last night, but tonight when I know my friends are so close to you and I'm so far, it makes me feel miserable. However, Darling, there is one consolation. After working so hard all week, it's only natural I'll be granted liberty Saturday and Sunday.

Adorable, there's a slim chance I may go to school here at Bainbridge and that means liberty every weeknight and every other weekend (Friday, 4 p.m. to Monday, 8 a.m.). However, the school here opens May 1st, and I would have to stay in the Office of the Guard until then. That would mean I would work my fingers to the bone, for as I have told you, Bainbridge has gotten out of my control. It would be well worth it just to be near you for a few months. Nothing is definite yet – just happy for gay dreams and rumors, but it's nice to think about it.

Precious, I miss you something simply sorrowful. I can't understand it. I missed you terribly before, but since that weekend, I can't help myself. I actually walk around in a daze at times. Fellows speak to me, but I don't hear them. I'm in a lovely world of my own. Have you the solution to my symptoms? No doubt the disease begins with the letter L, hey Doc?

Mail here must be misplaced, for I haven't received any of your letters yet. I certainly hope you are getting my mail. This is the third letter I've written since I've seen you. Well, Baby, it's tough sleeping these days, but I'll try again tonight. I'll most likely dream of you if I stop thinking of you long enough to sleep.

Love, Monty

P.S. - Leave Saturday and Sunday open (fingers crossed)

I found out on Friday of that week that I was getting leave on Saturday and Sunday. I happened to see Irish on the base that same day late in the afternoon as we both were heading to the mess hall for dinner. One could not miss Irish. He seemed to be the only sailor who had not gotten in shape in basic training. Every sailor there was fit as a fiddle with all of the calisthenics, marching, running, and hiking we did. I know I was in the best shape of my life, although I did not relish the extreme exercise regime. Somehow Irish maintained his slightly plump physique. Unfortunately, he also maintained his sarcastic, acid tongue. He started right in on me the second I saw him.

"Hey Irish," I yelled, as I ran to catch up with him. "How's it going?"

"How's it going?" he replied in his usual cynical tone. "I didn't get leave this weekend, that's how it's going."

"Sorry to hear that, old chum," I said rather sarcastically myself. "I'm heading to Baltimore tomorrow morning. I'm calling Lu tonight to set up our date."

"You'd better get in line, chum," he shot back. "You'll be lucky if she's home to answer the phone."

"What are you talking about?" I asked quizzically.

"I mean she's got a busier schedule than FDR, buddy boy," Irish said with his usual smugness. "You'll be lucky to catch her between dates with servicemen and USO dances."

"You're a bunch of baloney, as usual," I retorted. "I'll have you know I spent practically my entire leave with her just a few weeks ago."

"Must have been a hole in her schedule," he continued. "A bunch of fellas must have shipped out then."

"What the hell do you know anyway?" I said, getting a little angrier. "You're in the same boat I am. You're lucky to get out of here one weekend a month."

"Well, when I do get out of here, I try to see her and she's always busy," he said.

"Yeah, because she doesn't want to go out with you,"

I said. "Did you ever think of that?"

"She writes me all the time," Irish responded, slightly indignant. "We are very, very good friends and she tells me plenty in her letters and when I catch her at home. Don't kid yourself, Monty. This girl is quite popular with the servicemen and there are a couple of them she's very fond of."

"Oh, like Gene Tress," I said. "I know she writes Gene. He shipped out overseas. They don't see each other anymore."

"Yes, there's Gene the Marine and another fella she met at Fort Meade in the Army, Bob something or other. Plus, she meets a ton of other servicemen at the USO dances."

"You're forgetting about me," I said. "She's quite fond of me, too, and I don't mean just being fond of someone as a friend."

"Okay, okay, fine," Irish acknowledged. "She's mentioned you, if you want to know the truth. But I still say you've got to get in line."

"Maybe, but Lu and I have something special," I revealed, a little bit embarrassingly. I really did not like discussing the personal feelings I had about Lu with Irish, or anyone for that matter.

"Yeah, yeah, you're real special, Monty," Irish said with even more sarcasm than before. "Let's get something to eat for crying out loud!" We entered the mess hall and got our meals. We sat down at a table together to eat with no more discussion of Lu.

I called Lu that night to tell her I was coming home Saturday morning.

"Lu," I said. "I got leave and I'm coming home tomorrow morning. I was hoping we could spend some time together Saturday and Sunday night like we did before?"

Lu hesitated, but then said, "Sure, Monty, but I'll have to change my plans."

"Wonderful," I said. "I'll pick you up Saturday at about six-thirty or so. How about another movie and then dancing at the Alcazar?"

"I'd love that," she responded.

"Great, it's a date," I exclaimed. "I'll see you then, Lu."

"See you then, Monty," she said.

"Bye-bye," I said.

"Bye-bye, Monty," she said.

Wow! Take that, Irish. I wished I could have spoken to him that night to gloat, but he was in his barracks on the other side of camp.

I took the train home Saturday morning. I went through the same routine at my house with my family members asking where I was going to be assigned next. I told them I was hoping to stay at Bainbridge. My father told me again not to count on it. He said I couldn't depend on the Navy for anything but steady work. Nothing had changed in my family since my last leave. Pop was working hard during the week and hanging out with his best friend, John, at the barbershop on the weekends. Mom was spending more and more time with Jane, and my sisters were busy working and making time for their boyfriends.

I picked up Lu at around seven and we arrived downtown a little early for the movie. We walked arm in arm, looking in the store windows. All the shops closed at five. The movie started at seven forty-five. The picture was a war movie starring Humphrey Bogart, called *Sahara*. It was set in the desert of North Africa. Humphrey Bogart was an American tank commander separated from his division after a battle. His tank picked up several soldiers from various nations in their effort to rejoin their command. The story climaxed with Bogart and his men fighting and preventing a German Division from gaining access to a much-needed water hole in the desert. Although Bogart and the few men he had were successful against the German Division, nearly all of them perished in the fight against the Nazis. I thoroughly enjoyed the movie. It was exciting, the plot was very good, and the characters all seemed very real to me, plus there were many heroic characters. It made me feel patriotic, too.

As we left the theatre, I said, "I really liked the movie. It was very good."

To my surprise, Lu looked upset and said, "I didn't care for it."

"Why not?" I inquired intriguingly. "I thought it was very believable."

"That's why I didn't like it," she said. "I found it very upsetting, thinking about my brother, you, and all of our friends in the service possibly getting killed like that. It was a little too real for me."

"I'm sorry, Lu," I said. "It didn't even occur to me."

"It's fine, Monty," she said. "I just don't want to think about the war in those terms. It's too sad."

We walked down the street to catch the trolley car to Mount Vernon. We didn't say anything on the way. Lu looked as if she was in deep thought. I hoped the night had not been ruined. As we got off the trolley car and headed to the entrance of the Alcazar Ballroom, we could hear the band inside playing *Take the A Train* by Duke Ellington. I immediately made a joke and said, "It should be called *Take the Trolley Car*." Lu smiled and we went inside after paying for our tickets. Lu perked up once we got inside. The joint was really jumping as usual. I pulled Lu onto the dance floor right away. We jitterbugged to the end of *Take the A Train*.

If Lu was still upset about the war movie, she showed no sign of it on the dance floor or for the rest of the evening. We had another great night dancing to the fast ones, getting close on the slow tunes, and enjoying each other's company. It was the same as the last time. I hated for the night to end. We again headed for her house. This time though, we left the Alcazar later than the last time. It was about eleven-thirty. We were just having too much fun dancing together and neither of us was in a hurry to leave. Then, when we got outside, it was raining cats and dogs. We waited about fifteen minutes for the rain to subside. We finally walked home in a light rain.

When we arrived at Lu's home, it was very quiet, and the house was dark except for the light in the vestibule. We were not soaking wet, but we were definitely damp. Lu and I entered through the front door, and she flipped the light switch on in the parlor. She turned on the radio very low as it appeared everyone in the house was asleep.

"Wait here," she said. "Let me run upstairs and get some towels." She came back down the stairs a minute and a half later, threw me a towel, and then she ran back up the steps. I wiped myself off the best I could and sat down on the sofa. Five minutes later, Lu came down the steps and into the parlor. She had changed into some dry clothes and sat down beside me.

"You look refreshed," I said. I put my arm around her and snuggled up close to her.

"I think somebody's getting fresh," she said humorously. "And I think that someone is you."

I then kissed her and said, "Do you know I'm crazy about you?"

"Yes," she said. "I think I've been told that a time or two."

I leaned in to kiss her again, but this time more passionately. We were in full embrace on the couch with our lips locked. Thank goodness everybody in her house appeared to have gone to bed. Not a single light was seen in any window and not a sound was heard throughout the house except for the barely perceptible sound of an orchestra playing on the radio and the kissing sound of our wet lips pressed softly against one another.

"Whew," Lu exclaimed. "I need some air. I almost forgot; I have a picture for you. It's my Seton graduation picture from last year, but it's the only portrait I have. Let me go upstairs and get it."

The pitter-patter of Lu running up the steps and then back down after a short pause hopefully did not wake anybody up. She came back into the parlor proudly displaying the picture she had for me.

"Here it is," she said. "It's not exactly a pin-up poster of Betty Grable, but it's all I've got."

"Thanks, Lu," I said graciously. "It's perfect. You're every bit as adorable as Betty Grable."

"Oh, stop it," Lu said genuinely. "I'm no Betty Grable."

"I beg to differ," I shot back. "I feel as lucky as Harry James."

"Monty, you're a riot, you know that," she replied. "What am I going to do with you?"

"I'll tell what you can do, Lu," I said earnestly. "If I get shipped out and don't see you again before I leave, promise me you'll be the one waiting for me when I get home. I don't care if you go out with other fellas and dance with the boys at the USO dances, just so you'll be with me when I get back."

"I promise you, Monty," she said seriously. "I'll be here for you when you get back. I always make time for you, don't I?"

"Thank you, Lu," I said. "That's all I wanted to hear. And thanks for the picture. I can't wait to show the guys in the barracks that my girl is as good-looking as Betty Grable. And I can't wait to tell Irish what you said either."

"Why tell Irish?" Lu asked curiously. "Tell him what?"

"Irish is always razzing me about you," I explained. "That you don't have time for me, and you have other fellas and I have to get in line, things like that."

"Irish is silly," Lu said. "Of course, I always have time for you, Monty."

"I know that," I said confidently.

"At least it was nice of Irish not to come to my house those two nights last time you were home," Lu said.

I wasn't sure what Lu was talking about with regard to Irish not coming to her house, but I didn't like it. It sounded as if Irish was really trying to make time with Lu. Now I knew why he was telling me to get in line. He was the one at the end of the line. Irish was such a squirrel, a fat one at that. I didn't want to spoil the evening by fixating on Irish, so I said nothing more about him.

"It's so late, Monty," Lu said. "You're always here well past midnight. You need to get some rest for tomorrow. I bet they'll keep working you to the bone back at the base. Plus, it's still raining. I wish I could give you an umbrella, but if I give you Dad's or mine, we may not get it back for quite some time. I have a sinking feeling you won't get your wish to be assigned to Bainbridge."

"Probably not," I said, somewhat dejectedly. "That's more of a pipe dream."

"Hopefully, I'll see you soon," I said. "If not, I love you, Lu." I pulled her close to me and gave her another long, passionate kiss at her front doorway.

"Goodbye," I said as I left her house and started

slowly running down the street in the rain.

"Goodbye," Lu yelled, standing in the rain on the wet marble steps outside her front door. "Be careful."

I got home about ten or fifteen minutes later. My clothes were soaking wet. Even my underwear was saturated, not a good feeling. I removed my drenched clothes at the doorway and ran up to my bedroom in my sopping wet underwear. I set my alarm clock for four-thirty in the morning. Hopefully, my mother would not wake me up an hour earlier than necessary, as she had done on my previous trip home. Thankfully, she didn't.

I made it back to the barracks by seven, although it was still raining. I changed into a dry uniform, went to breakfast, and was on time for assembly at eight.

I had a very busy week and didn't have time to write a letter to Lu until Wednesday.

April 21, 1943

Greetings Sweetie,

I've been busy as a fiddler's elbow since I arrived. Monday and Tuesday I was back on K.P., but today I worked in the warehouse. Today is the first day I've gotten a chance to breathe, let alone write. Well, Darling, the latest rumor is that we get liberty from Friday to Monday. I surely hope that it is true, for Baby, I miss you constantly. However, we might also be shipped out before Friday, but I'm still hoping. I want you to know I had a swell time Sunday night, and the fellows who saw your picture think you're "all reete". Well, Gorgeous, this is just a little note to let you know you're always on my mind, and to let you know I arrived safely but wet Monday morning. I practically swam from the main gate to my barracks (1 mile). I'll be looking for Irish tomorrow to let him learn and understand the situation we have. Well, wovable woo (Lu), no use my saying any more just now when I hope to say it to you this weekend.

By the way, our Master of Arms isn't himself today – a great improvement. How about writing a few words, Precious, just to let me know you care?

    Loving you, Monty.
Oceans of love and a kiss on each wave

The weekend came and went, and no leave was granted, despite the rumors that we would. I ran into Irish again in the mess hall on the weekend. We talked only briefly, but I took great joy in telling him of my situation with Lu and that we had come to an understanding. The understanding was that she would make time for me when I was home. I could not have made my point any clearer to him, but Irish initially refused to believe it. He finally conceded my point as we departed.

He said grudgingly, "Well, Monty, if Lucille Flanagan has made you her number one priority, then good for you."

Irish was visibly annoyed. In my opinion, his anger was simply a result of envy and jealousy. Some friend he turned out to be.

Chapter Seven

The Ten Mile Hike

My military orders finally arrived on Monday, April 26th, to report to my new assignment at the University of Chicago in Chicago, Illinois, to attend the United States Navy Signalman School. My report date was Monday morning at eight o'clock on May 3, 1943. I was to leave by train for Chicago on April 28th and arrive on the 29th. At least I would get a few days to settle in before class started. I called Lu and Mom from Bainbridge to tell them where I was going and to let them know I would write them with my new address when I arrived.

    I had to admit that although I was disappointed at not getting assigned to Bainbridge, it felt exciting to be going to Chicago. It was the birthplace of my father, after all. His family moved to Baltimore when he was a little boy. I was not sure why they came to Baltimore; I assumed it was for better employment opportunities for my grandfather. Personally, I had never been out of the state of Maryland. Hell, I'd never even been outside of Baltimore City until I was twelve years old. The first time I saw a real cow was when my father and mother decided to take my sisters and me on a drive into the countryside in Baltimore County in the fall of 1937. The only bad thing about my new assignment in Chicago was that I had no idea when I might get home again. After the two-day ride on the train, I arrived in Chicago and finally settled into my dorm room. Following some confusion on the Navy's part regarding which residential building the new arrivals were to be assigned, I ultimately received my permanent room assignment.

    I wrote the following letter to Lucille as soon as

I got settled.
April 30, 1943
Lu Darling,

I am in Chicago now and the place seems all right at present. The Navy has practically taken everything over at this university. In the building where I am living, there is a swimming pool and a library (lounging room). I mean it is certainly comfortable here. You should see the hall in which we dine. Bread, butter, coffee, milk, sugar, and dessert are kept on the tables, and there are attendants to keep the plates and pitchers filled. What service! I can't understand it. I left Bainbridge at 2:30 p.m. on Wednesday and arrived in Chicago at 9:30 a.m. on Thursday. The views from the train through the countryside were swell. The hills of Pennsylvania aren't too bad for sightseeing, and Indiana's plains don't harm the eyes. As for Ohio, I was asleep when we traveled through there. The trip was a grand one. Card games were numerous, but there was only one crap game. You're right – I participated. Imagine, I actually won nine dollars. The Navy treated us to two meals on the train – dinner and breakfast. I had roast duck for dinner, and Baby was it good.

I guess Chicago will be a fine place to dwell, but as for now, I wouldn't know. We new fellows won't rate liberty until Saturday, May 8, 1943. Lu, do you remember what you wanted me to promise you the last time we spoke on the telephone before I left Bainbridge? I guess you don't recall, but you wanted me to inform you of what goes on here. Well, Darling, I miss you so terribly much that I'd cut my right arm off and send it to you if you wanted it. At Bainbridge, missing you was not too bad, for I knew I could look forward to seeing you soon, but now being so far away, I'm dying a slow death. Gorgeous, the fellows in school here are entitled to every weekend liberty, providing they keep up with their studies. The liberty starts on Saturdays at 2 p.m. and ends on Sunday at 1 a.m. Then it begins again Sunday at 8 a.m. before ending at 9:30 p.m. Sunday night. That means I'll spend wonderful Sunday nights in my bunk dreaming of you.

Next week, when I take a look at the town, I'll write a nice long letter to let you know what Chicago and its people are like. As for now, all I can say is that I miss you very, very much and I'd gladly give up everything here to spend a few days with you. I don't have enough stationery to begin to tell you how much I love you. I guess you're wondering why I haven't written sooner. Well! I've been moved about quite a bit and I couldn't put my correct address down until now.

By the way, Darling, how did the pictures you took that Sunday afternoon at Patterson Park turn out? If they are all right, please send me a set. Well, Lu, how and where is Rowley? I guess you know about Irish. He got transferred to Norfolk, Virginia. I ran into him at Bainbridge right before I left. He got his orders the same time I got mine. Also, would you mind sending me their addresses? I want to know what you meant by saying "It was nice of Irish not to come down to your house those two nights I was home." Well, Love, I surely must say farewell until later, so give my regards to your mother and father. Say hello to Mr. and Mrs. Flanagan (your swell parents) and tell Esther I think you should have been in the Easter parade. She would have been crowned Queen provided you weren't in it, Dear. Tell Charlie to take care of the girls in Baltimore while I'm away.

Love, Monty
Please write very soon.

I missed being so far away from Baltimore but being at

this school did not even compare to Bainbridge. Basic training had not only been monotonous and irritating, but our CPO and our Master of Arms at Bainbridge were real sons of bitches. I spent half my time at Bainbridge on K.P. duty. If I had my way, I would never clean up another kitchen for the rest of my life. At least the training classes in Chicago required having some level of real intelligence. I assumed my assignment as a signalman came about because I did well on the battery of tests we were required to take during basic training. The environment at the university was like night and day compared to Bainbridge.

The University of Chicago was a place of higher learning, despite the fact that the United States Navy had the run of the place. The academic atmosphere at the university was a far cry from the rigid setting at the Bainbridge Naval Training Station. In fact, the feeling at this school was that we were more like college students attending the various classes each day rather than sailors being ordered around by officers. About one hundred and fifty students in total were attending the Signalman School. They broke us into five groups of thirty. The curriculum required us to attend five classes each day Monday through Friday, except Tuesday mornings. Attending school here was a much more laid-back atmosphere, barring Tuesday mornings.

Each Tuesday morning, we were required to go on a ten-mile hike, all one hundred and fifty sailors, before going back to class in the afternoon. It was quite chaotic in the locker room getting ready for the hikes. On my second day of class, Tuesday, May 4th, I ate breakfast with two sailors who were considerably older than me. I guessed that they were about twenty-five years old. Their names were Harry Davenport and Charlie Kazinski. Charlie was from the Bronx in New York and Harry was from Queens. Both were veterans, each having served in the Navy for over three years. They had passed the required tests and were assigned to Signalman School. Their previous assignment had been as Seamen First Class aboard the battleship, the *U.S.S. Colorado*.

On December 7th, eight of the nine battleships assigned to the United States Pacific Fleet were moored at Pearl Harbor. The ninth, the *U.S.S. Colorado,* was the only battleship not there. Harry and Charlie were lucky to have been aboard while it was docked at the Puget Sound Naval Yard being overhauled when the attack occurred at Pearl Harbor. The *U.S.S. Colorado* remained off the west coast of the United States after being repaired, patrolling throughout the summer of 1942. Then, in the fall of 1942, their ship sailed back to Pearl Harbor before going on patrol in the South Pacific near the Fiji Islands in a defensive posture against the enemy. Harry and Charlie were assigned aboard the *U.S.S. Colorado* until they got transferred to Chicago to attend Signalman School.

Harry and Charlie, in my estimation, seemed to be very savvy individuals. I could relate to their description of the boredom they suffered being at sea for so long. The opportunity to attend Signalman School was merely a way to get off the ship for a while. They were assigned as gunners on twenty-millimeter cannons on the *U.S.S. Colorado*. They explained to me how they had befriended a signalman on their ship. They watched and studied him and the other signalmen as they performed their duties. Harry and Charlie subsequently learned Morse code, which their friend had advised was essential in becoming a signalman. A signalman's job was just a matter of using the Morse code with flags and searchlights. Harry and Charlie had gained a vast knowledge regarding the work of a signalman while assigned to their ship.

Basically, Naval signalmen were responsible for

transmitting, receiving, encoding, decoding, and distributing messages by different visual transmission systems. These systems involved flag semaphore, flashing searchlight signaling, and flag hoist signaling, all of which utilized Morse code. Flag semaphore was a system of sending messages by holding the arms of two flags or poles in certain positions. In a nutshell, signalmen were responsible for visual communications. When ships were under radio silence, all ship-to-ship communications in sight were performed by signalmen. If not signaling with flags, flashing the signal searchlight was used. Messages were sent by opening and shutting a lens on the searchlight which represented dots and dashes of the Morse code.

Signalmen also used flag hoist signaling by hoisting flags on halyards, which are lines running from the yardarm of the mast down to the signal bridge. They had to know what each flag and pennant represented, and the meaning of standard flag hoist combinations. When not signaling, signalmen were on the alert for signals from other vessels and aircraft, all the while keeping a sharp lookout for enemy aircraft and ships. They also had to know about storm warnings, distress signals, emergency signals, and signals to lifeboats and aircraft.

I was immediately impressed with Harry and Charlie. They were not only extremely knowledgeable about the Navy and its use of signalmen, but they possessed a certain degree of rare intelligence, which I could only describe as "street smart," except I imagined it might more appropriately be called "Navy smart." As I sat there eating my fried eggs, bacon, and toast, absorbing the wisdom of Harry and Charlie, and enjoying their company immensely, Harry brought up the subject of the ten-mile hike which we were scheduled to participate in after breakfast.

"Hey, Monty," Harry said. "You're not going on that hike, are you?"

"I was planning to go," I said rather puzzled at his question. "We're supposed to report at eight o'clock in the locker room by the gymnasium, aren't we?"

"We ain't goin' on no hike," Charlie said.

"What do you mean?" I asked. "We have to go. Won't we get into trouble if we don't?"

"Not if we don't get caught," Charlie responded with a real shit-ass grin plastered on his face, the sight of which I found extremely off-putting.

"How are we gonna do that?" I inquired.

"I figure it's going to be complete chaos with a hundred and fifty sailors getting ready for a hike," Harry chimed in. "They're taking roll call in the locker room. By the time everybody gets out the door, we'll hang back and hide inside the lockers. When they come trickling in two or three hours later, we'll get undressed and hit the showers like we just finished."

"I don't know," I said doubtfully. "That sounds kind of risky. I don't want to get kicked out of school here. This place is pretty nice."

"Listen, Monty," Harry said. "Do you really want to go on a ten-mile hike after breakfast?"

"Not really," I said, rather sheepishly.

"Neither do I," Harry continued. "Let me explain something to you, Monty, about the Navy. Charlie and myself have been in for three years and he'll back me up on this, won't you Charlie?"

"What he says," Charlie answered, looking straight at me, speaking in his full Bronx accent. "We been in for *tree* years and we knows what we're talking about."

"This outfit is full of the biggest saps I've ever seen," Harry explained. "Did you ever notice when the CPO asks for volunteers, and all these dopey sailors raise their hands like they think they're gettin' a date with Rita Hayworth or something? They're all suckers, Monty. They don't even know what they're volunteering for and they're all such stupid eager beavers. They could be volunteering to scrub the decks of the ship, or to go on K.P. duty, or to jump overboard for all they know. They could be raising their goddamn hand for a suicide mission, yet they enthusiastically volunteer every time like they're trying to impress Admiral goddamn Halsey for Christ's sake. All a bunch of suckers, I tell ya. So, I've got two words of advice for you to follow in this man's Navy, Monty, never volunteer."

"I gotcha," I said, quite impressed with his forceful and convincing outlook and opinion.

"So, we ain't gonna run with all the suckers after breakfast," Charlie said, backing up Harry's assertion, almost threatening in his tone.

"It's practically foolproof," Harry said. "Believe me, nobody's gonna miss us."

"All right, I'm in," I said more confidently. "Why the hell not?"

"That a boy!" Harry said approvingly. "Just follow my lead, kid."

"Okay," I said.

I was really impressed with the confidence they exhibited, particularly Harry. Harry was a bit more eloquent than Charlie, even in his slightly crude way. Charlie was a bit scary. He didn't retain the charm that Harry possessed. I had to admire their point of view; however cynical it might have been. Nevertheless, I was worried about getting caught. I certainly didn't want to get expelled from Signalman School. The last thing I really wanted to do after breakfast, though, was to go on a run, especially for ten miles. I figured that these two fellas were wrought with experience, and it seemed to me as if they had dabbled in this type of thing before. I surmised that they surely must have hidden in lockers on previous occasions to avoid strenuous activity and knew exactly what they were doing. I convinced myself that following their lead and getting away with this would be a cinch.

After breakfast, the three of us, not the *tree* of us, went back to our dorm rooms to change into our gray sweatsuits. We agreed to meet at the entrance door to the locker room by the gymnasium. The scene was exactly as Harry had described it. It was bedlam. One hundred and fifty sailors were signing in and then making their way to the other side of the locker room to the door leading outside. Many of the sailors were already spilling into the grassy area outside.

The CPO was outside screaming at the boys to stretch their legs. Sailors were pouring out there steadily. The scene resembled preparations for a track meet at the Olympic trials or something. The massive crowd of men was out there pulling their ankles up to their hips, touching their toes, and even lying on the ground in all kinds of contorted positions. Harry, Charlie, and I, of course, had no intention of stretching, let alone going outside. We signed in nearly last and then got behind the last bunch of sailors making their way to the exit. Except instead of following them out the door, we took a quick right down a row of lockers where we couldn't be seen. We opened the tall metal locker doors and each shimmied into a separate locker pulling the door shut as quietly as possible behind us. We probably hid there for about ten minutes or so, but it felt like an eternity to me. I was still terrified of getting caught. Harry exited his locker first.

"The coast is clear," he announced. Charlie and I then followed.

It was a bit eerie in the locker room. I felt like a

hardened criminal.

"What do we do now?" I asked nervously.

"Relax, Monty," Harry answered with a smile. "We make ourselves at home like Goldilocks until the hundred and fifty bears return."

"Funny, Harry," Charlie said. "More like a hundred and fifty saps, I'd say."

"Yeah, but what'll we do for two hours?" I asked with earnestness.

"I've got dice," Harry said with a grin. He pulled two dice from the pocket of his sweatpants.

"And I've got this, too." He displayed his money clip from the other pocket. "Did you boys bring some dough?"

"Yeah, I got some dough on me," I answered. No sailor risked leaving his money clip in a dorm room. I carried my money clip with me everywhere, as did most sailors.

"I've got a few bucks," Charlie said.

"Good," Harry said with a certain degree of glee. "Let's get down to business then."

I was quite pleased to be playing craps. It seemed my entire life, no matter where I was or what I was doing, I was in constant search of a crap game. I think it was my love of mathematics that drew me to shooting craps, and, of course, betting on it. The time passed quickly as I played my favorite game in the locker room that Tuesday morning, as it did every Tuesday morning for the next three months. For you see, Harry, Charlie, and I never did participate in the Tuesday morning ten-mile hike. In fact, I not only never went running or on a hike for the remainder of the entire war, but I never even went on as much as a jog for the rest of my natural-born life.

I was about forty dollars ahead when we heard some clamoring outside the locker room door.

"Hey, I think they're back," I said, quickly retrieving my last bet off the floor. "Let's hit the showers, fast!"

"Yeah," Charlie said, ripping off his sweats as fast as he could.

All three of us disrobed and shoved our clothing into lockers adjacent to the shower. As the sailors returned, they immediately started entering the shower area. The second they entered, the three of us departed, recovered our sweatsuits from the lockers, and got the hell out of there. We returned to our rooms, later went to lunch, and arrived at class at one o'clock. This routine continued every Tuesday without a hitch.

I received my first letter from Lu in Chicago on May 4, 1943. She said she had written me a previous letter, but I never received it. She wrote on the envelope, *A Kiss FMHT*. It took me a while, but I deciphered her message. Boy did that really make my day. I was not completely pleased when she told me that she accompanied a boy to his prom. The Colonel where she worked had a son who needed a date to prom. The school was somewhere south of Baltimore where the Colonel lived. I imagined the kid didn't know anybody, since his father just transferred the year before to Curtis Bay. I was sure it was all very innocent.

Lu provided me with Irish's address. He somehow got transferred to some cushy administrative duty in Virginia Beach. She received a letter from Rowley who apparently wrote a very long letter. Lu was not specific about what he said, only referring to it as *his life story,* whatever that meant. Then she implied she was thinking of leaving her job because some superior yelled at her, but I couldn't believe she would quit such a great job. She later said she was getting promoted so I wasn't sure. I wrote back to her the very next day.

May 5, 1943
Dear Lu,
I wouldn't claim to be intelligent or above average but was the kiss on the envelope "For My Heart Throb?" Well, Darling, if I'm correct about the translation, it's just sweet as sugar cane. This letter I am now answering is dated May 3, 1943. I wonder what happened to the letter you wrote Monday. I'm certainly glad you had a fine time at the prom. I would surely like to have seen you decked out in your evening gown. By the way, you did not tie a bender on? I get the idea you are quitting your job – quoting from your last letter, "the nicest little girl" is leaving the depot, her boss yelled at her once too often so she's going to take her business elsewhere. Now you explain it to me, Darling. I concepted the "nicest little girl" to be you.

It's surely nice to hear Irish has the situation in Virginia Beach well under control. He really is the little surprise package. You can take that literally.

I guess it's only natural you'll be quite busy for about a week now. Oh well! I can look forward to the day I get my chance to be with you. I won't tell any life story just because you asked me if I've written Rowley, but just tell me where you get that stuff. Also, for your information, I've written Rowley and I'm anxiously awaiting his answer.

Forgive me, Sweet. Gorgeous, I see you are hep to the mello Navy slang. I guess you know I'd like to be putty in your hands at this very moment. You know it's a liberty night, and here I be restricted.

Gobs of Love, Monty

I received a letter from Lu on May 16th. The tone of the letter, in my biased opinion, was one of heartfelt love. She repeated that she longed to be with me and how she missed me so much that it hurt her inside. She had told me these same things when we were together in Baltimore following my basic training at Bainbridge. I felt on top of the world that entire weekend and I could feel it in my soul she felt the same way. I loved her so much it hurt me too. Lu had so much love to give, and I was tickled pink she was sending it my way. In the words of the late, great baseball legend, Lou Gehrig, I considered myself the luckiest guy on the face of the earth, minus the fatal disease, of course.

She wrote me with a great deal of pride and admiration about her brother, John, who was attending training in Newport, Rhode Island, at the Naval Training School. Lu told me of her promotion from the secretary in the front office to the position of office administrator. She had previously written implying she was not very happy in her job, but the situation must have improved there. She ended this particular letter with a charming secret code, as she did on most letters, as well as a not-so-subtle lipstick imprint of her kiss. I loved it. Her lovely letters and our continued separation made me crave her even more. I wrote right back.

May 17, 1943

Lu Darling,

Your wonderful letter arrived today. I know exactly what sort of a mood you were in when you wrote it. Baby, when you're in that mood, you're tops. That first night I came home from boot camp, you were feeling as such. You are still the best girl in the world without being in that mood. However, Gorgeous, I would have given a million dollars to have been with you at the time you wrote that letter. I must really break down to tell you how I feel Lambie Pie, these three weeks away from you have seemed actually like three years. I'm missing you every second. I'm getting to a point where I can't stand it away from you. I surely must be in love. What do you think?

I'm certainly glad to hear that John is situated and that he likes Rhode Island. I must also extend congratulations to the secretary who got the boss' job. All kidding aside, Lu, I think it's swell. You're not only the most beautiful girl in Baltimore, but you're the most intelligent and progressive one. I guess I'll have to become an Admiral, no less. You can bet your life I'm absorbing the opportunities at the USO, but I'm not overdoing it.

Well, Sweetie, I ordered a large picture of myself. It won't be ready for about ten days, but rest assured you'll receive it as quickly as possible. I hope I'm not overstepping the boundaries in taking it for granted you'll want of me mug.

When I get home, I may be a Chicago square, but I'll still be capable of holding you in my arms to stroll slowly upon a soft cloud. Well, Precious, forgive me if I seem to be brief, but I don't have much time. I'll be home just as soon as it's humanly possible. I hope that'll be in a week or two. I really truly liked the way your ending of the letter was made. Technically, I kissed you tonight.

Loving you, Monty
P.S. - Regards to the Flanagan Family

On May 25th and 26th, I received two letters from Lu. She wrote with her usual positive and upbeat manner, but not exactly like her last letter. This letter lacked the affection toward me I sensed from her previous correspondence. In fact, she went so far as to tell me how busy she was attending USO dances and dating servicemen. Holy crap! Last week, I apparently fell into a false sense of security in thinking she was all mine. I just didn't know anymore. At least she said she was attending church during the week as well as on Sundays. I gained some solace from this fact. Surely, she wasn't meeting more boys at church, or maybe she was. How would I know a thousand miles away stuck here at Signalman School?

She indicated that the priest was holding nightly prayer services and speaking about our American boys going off to war. Lu advised that she gained comfort in listening to his words. Lu was a devout Catholic and lived her life following the church's teachings. I admired her so much. I wasn't as good of a Christian as Lu, but she certainly inspired me to do better. She had such a good heart. I always thought of myself as a decent person, but I had my vices and flaws. I was not the most forgiving person, and I would have to admit that I have wished a few people in my time to have dropped dead. I always admired the Catholic Church, particularly the Sacrament of Penance. I relished the thought of going to confession and being given a clean slate. If I ever married Lucille, I would surely convert.

Lu was corresponding with my old buddy, Joe Albrecht, presumably because he was going with Lu's best girlfriend. He was my friend first, but I never got one letter from him. Lu said he was assigned to the Fort Greely Army Base in Alaska. I knew the Japs attacked the Aleutian Islands, but I didn't know if Joe was in the fighting or not. He wouldn't have been allowed to tell Lu one way or the other.

According to her letters, Lu's work sounded as if it was going fine, as was everything else in her life. The Captain at the Curtis Bay Army Depot drove Lu around in his new convertible which Lu said was loads of fun. Strangely though, she asked me about her weight. It was not about her gaining weight, but about her being too thin. This was a real switch for a girl, being worried about getting too thin. I knew Lu was one of a kind.

Apparently, some idiot officer told her she looked too skinny. Jesus, she was built great, like a brick shithouse, as we used to say in the old neighborhood. The good news, at least, was that nobody told her she was getting fat. I never knew any girl on the planet who could take that comment in stride. Maybe the officer was trying to ingratiate himself with her by taking this approach. At any rate, it was a stupid remark.

Lu sealed the letter and wrote on the outside envelope, *S.W.A.B.K.*, easily decoded as *Sealed With A Big Kiss*. Her silly little codes and remarks made me feel like a million bucks. Her letters were always so uplifting, even if she was dating half of the Army's Seventh Division. I trusted her completely, though. I knew she was a good girl. I wrote her right back.

May 25, 1943
Lu Darling,
I only have a few minutes until taps so I'll write what I can tonight and then continue tomorrow. I'm simply stupefied over the fact that I received a letter both today and yesterday. You're really burning on the front burner now. I've just come from the phone booths. I guess you're already aware of that though. Darling, I'm sorry, but I should have known you were at those talks by your priest. Well! When I find another open phone booth and more change, I'll call you again. In answer to your first letter, I'm sorry Friday was such a dreary day in Baltimore, but it was also very unsatisfactory in Chicago.

Saturday night, I went to see "The More the Merrier" again, starring Jean Arthur, Joel McCrea, and Charles Coburn. Remember it? It certainly was good, but it filled my heart with sorrow and a longing to be in your parlor with you in my arms.

I'm just as sorry about my error in time in accordance with the transfer as you are. However, I feel sure that I'll be in Philadelphia attending Villanova University within the next few weeks. I sent you the group picture of our company, but I won't receive the other pictures until Saturday, so be patient, Gorgeous. Sweetie, I know you have me sewed up, but the situation is – have I got you all sewed up? Sporting about Baltimore, one is apt to forget one. Don't take me wrong, Darling, I enjoy hearing you're going to dances, etc., but dates and such make cause for me to think. Or did I say worry?

Should you gain weight? I don't know. However, you'll be interested to know I now weigh 165 pounds. Getting plump, aren't I? I'm contented in hearing you're riding in a Captain's convertible, but don't let me hear about your riding in a Lieutenant's car. Some of the girls about the college have solid old convertibles to sport the sailors about, but I haven't gotten around to meeting these babes as yet. Personally, I'm not going to either. I take it Joe Albrecht's in Alaska. How is he making out in the Army? That is, is he a corporal or what?

About your getting to work so late, I guess it's okay now since you're the boss and not the secretary. Guess what, Lu, I actually sleep to 7 a.m. nowadays. There is only one disadvantage I have though; I miss chow every morning. I really love sleep, don't I? I'm glad you like my letters, but in order for me to write more, you must write more. Darling, I only wish I were Superman, I'd end this war and...

About the rain, it's rained in Chicago so much since I've been here, the papers here say that a record has been made in rain which was only equaled sixty years ago. Well, Cutie, taps have been sounded so I'll have to call a stand-still until tomorrow. Remember the song we heard on the radio with those lyrics? "I want to go to sleep so I can dream of you."

Love and Kisses, make no misses, Gee, I wish you

were my Mrs. S.W.A.B.K.
Love, Monty

I woke up the next morning and composed another letter to Lu before heading to breakfast.
May 26, 1943, 6:30 a.m.
Good morning, Darling,
I did not sleep very well last night. In fact, I barely slept at all. I really did a great deal of thinking last night. Yes! It was about you. If I wrote anything last night that seems to be out of bounds, just ignore, for it was a dreamy-eyed boy thinking you were all mine. I guess you don't remember, but about a month ago, I was out with you on a Sunday night – splendid time too. Then, the next week on the telephone you said just as cool as ice – "Oh, I went out with Irish last Monday!" Well, Sweetie, you might not know, but it broke my heart up into wittle bits. Now, don't take me wrong, I know we aren't engaged or that we never even went steady, so I can't say one single word about it. I know you're the best girl in town so who am I to be jealous? Well, Baby, Hon, enough of that, back to the bright side.
I got your letters and this morning's writing is in answer to your second sugar report. I am going to call you, Darling, but give me another chance. I've already made two honest tries. Besides, the booths are so crowded, a fellow has to man-handle a few sailors to get a chance to use a phone. Darling, I know every single minute I've been away from you, and I'm doing my best to come home. It won't be long now.
Love and Kisses, Monty
P.S. – Honey, I'd love to get lost with you.

Later, I went across campus from my dormitory to the Navy's phone booths, specifically constructed for the overflow of sailors attending the university. The booths were always crowded, but on this Friday night, I lucked out and found an empty booth right off. Everybody must have gone into the city early to start their weekend leave. I was even more fortunate to catch Lu at home. When I called the previous weeks, I always seemed to have missed her. She was always out somewhere, at a USO dance, with her girlfriends, at church, on a date, you name it. This girl was always busy as she was extremely popular. The phone rang and a woman answered.

"Hello," she said. I recognized her voice right away. It was Lu's mother.

"Hello, Mrs. Flanagan," I said. "This is Monty Culpepper calling from Chicago. I was hoping to catch Lu at home."

"Hello, Monty," Mrs. Flanagan responded. "I'll get her for you right away, Monty." I heard Mrs. Flanagan yelling upstairs. "Lucille, Monty Culpepper is calling from Chicago long distance. Get down here right away."

After only about a half a minute, I heard the loveliest voice in the world.

"Monty?" Lu inquired. "Is that you?"

"Yes, Lu," I answered excitedly. "It's Monty! How are you?"

"I'm doing fine, Monty," she said. "How are you and how is Chicago? It's been so long since we've spoken."

"I know," I said. "I've been trying to reach you, but the phone booths here are usually so busy. The couple times I did call I missed you."

"I'm sorry about that Monty," she said. "Mom told me you called a couple of weeks ago. I was so disappointed I missed you. I've been so busy. How is it going there?"

"It's going all right," I said. "I'm learning a lot here. The scuttlebutt is that we're getting transferred to Philadelphia for more training when class ends here in

August. I'm hoping I'll be able to take a train to Baltimore to see you for a day."

"Oh, I'd love that, Monty," Lu said. "I've missed you terribly."

"Me, too," I responded. "Especially the evenings we spent together in your parlor."

"I loved all our times together, Monty," Lu continued. "I really hope you get back home soon. I'll make sure we spend every minute of the day together."

"That would be swell, Lu," I said. "How is work going?"

"Well, it's okay, I guess," she said. "This new promotion has a lot more responsibilities for me now. I can't say I'm enjoying it as much as when I was just the secretary. I'm really not sure about it now. I wouldn't mind quitting."

"I'm sure things will improve as you get used to it," I responded, trying to be positive. "How is the family?"

"Everybody here is doing great," she answered. "Mom and Dad are heading down to the saloon for some beer. Esther is taking Donny out with a girlfriend to dinner. I haven't seen Nancy since I got home from work. I don't know what she's doing."

"How is little Donny?" I inquired.

"Oh, he's getting to be a precocious little fellow," she answered. "He keeps coming into my bedroom when I'm changing and says how pretty I am. I guess you might say it's flattering, but from a four-year-old, it's also a bit embarrassing."

"That's funny," I said. "How's his dad doing?"

"Gordon's okay, I imagine," Lu answered. "He's still out in San Diego, but Esther said he has no idea where the Navy is sending him next."

"I really like Gordon," I told Lu. "He's a solid guy."

"Yes, he is nice," Lu said. "I hate to go, Monty, but I

only got home from work fifteen minutes ago and I have a date with Jerry tonight. I have to get ready, or I'll be late."

"Oh, okay," I said, hiding my extreme jealousy. Lu had mentioned dating Jerry in letters. He was an Army lieutenant. Secretly, I was hoping he would get shipped off to North Africa immediately. No such luck, I guess.

"I understand," I said, lying through my teeth. "You have a great time Lu and I hope to see you soon. I'll let you know as soon as I hear anything concrete about Philadelphia. I can't wait to see you again."

"Me too," she said. "I'll write you. Take care of yourself, Monty."

"Bye," I said.

"Bye-bye," she said and hung up.

Talking to Lu made my entire night, except for the fact that she had a date. I had to accept the reality that Lu was dating other fellas, no matter how distasteful it was to me. To hell with that asshole, Jerry. I still felt fortunate to have caught her at home on a Friday night. I loved that girl so much. I wrote Lu a very nice letter a couple of days later, void of any bitterness or resentment toward that no-good son of a bitch, Jerry.

May 28, 1943

Lu Darling,

Here I am on Sunday night without you again. I'm telling you it's getting unbearable. Honey, I miss you something awful. You know, of course, I have liberty today, but you might know, it's raining so it's only natural I'm writing to my best gal. I'm still existing over the fact that I actually heard your voice. Payday is Friday so I'll most likely call you to let you know my status here. Have you received my company's picture? Baby, that's really a pip. I sent the other picture today, but Sweetie, forgive me for I couldn't get a frame anywhere.

You really have the excitement on Biddle Street. I certainly hope you're in top shape for handling matters. By the way, Jerry must surely be an all-right fellow. I know how Donny is – ah, yes – but maybe he has reached the stage where one begins to appreciate the feminine sex. Hey, what's this? Are you really going to quit your job? Well, if you are, here's wishing you luck in finding a better one. About Philadelphia, I'm hoping and praying the final dope is published tomorrow. Last night, Lu, was beautiful. Yes! Stars, moon, and a cool mellow breeze were all in full bloom. Sweetie, if you had only been here. I took a stroll through the park by the lake, and on every bench for a mile there were couples solidly caressing. Was in a mood to have you in my arms... OOOOH!

Baby, writing this is giving me the same torture I experienced last night. You know what they say, Lu, "Absence makes the heart grow fonder." Well, Precious, I believe that completely now. Honestly, I never felt this way before in my life. Darling, if you are missing me half as much as I'm missing you, I feel for you because I surely miss you. Remember, I'm anxiously awaiting your sugar report.

Love, and more love, Monty

I received another letter from Lu a few days later. She said that she and her girlfriends had gone to Ocean City, Maryland, for the weekend. Ocean City was a favorite vacation spot not only with Lu but with thousands of other Baltimoreans. She described the beautiful weather and the activity in her neighborhood on Biddle Street. She said that her neighbors were outside on their doorsteps nearly every evening, talking about the war and about their sons and brothers who were serving. Some construction or repair work on the rooftops was also going on, she said. Lu went to the Hippodrome Theatre prior to her Ocean City trip and saw Woody Herman. He had a big hit a few years ago called the *Woodchopper's Ball*. Lu always sent such upbeat letters that were so enjoyable to read. This letter, however, contained so many coded messages that I was lost. I couldn't decipher anything. I wrote her a few days later to respond to her most recent letter.

June 5, 1943
Lu Darling,
I would have written sooner, but I thought perhaps you would probably still be away. Well, I take it you had the "Pippest time" – I surely hope so. Lu, I must admit I'm quite rusty on my chemistry; therefore, you'll have to inform me about the translation of C6 H4<CO/SO2.NH. Also, W.W.A.P. S.W.A.K. I.L.T.S. W.G.T. A.I.D.M.Y. was rather difficult to concept. I may be wrong, but could this be correct – "Written with all priority, sealed with a kiss, I love the sailor with good taste, and I do mean you."

I see grand old Biddle Street is still as exciting as ever, but please be careful walking about – something or somebody may fall on you. Sleep still seems to agree with you, but I'm well aware of that, aren't I? Talking about theatres, the ones here are really on the beam. Since I've been here, I've seen Jimmy Dorsey, Louie Prima, Les Brown, Sammy Kaye, and scores of others. Chicago's jumping, I can tell you. Oh! But you would have to see the lake in the moonlight to really appreciate it.

Well, I see all the fellows are all reet. By the way, I wouldn't be overstepping the bounds to ask any of the boys about how I'm making out, would I?

I imagine you're really sunburned now – a solid tan I'd hope. For your information, I'm sunburned as a fresh red apple. My nose is peeling, but it isn't as red as W.C. Fields' as yet.

Oh, you wanted to know what M.A. stands for. You surely seem to go for the Navy in a big way, so I'll tell you. M.A. stands for "Master of Arms." I can't tell you what the rest of the fellows call an M.A., for I don't use that language in mixed company. M.A.s keep order in the mess hall, barracks, etc. Your Morse code was sweet, but the vertical line separates each letter while two vertical lines separate each word. Well, Baby, I want you to know I miss you more than ever now. I'll be here for about seven more weeks after which I don't expect to get any leave. Usually, after the course here, seventy-two hours is given. If I got that, which is doubtful, I still couldn't get home and back very well. However, I can always wish for delayed orders or nine days.

Well, Sweet, I must get to bed now so just keep smiling. Give my best regards to your family and when you talk to Rowley, ask him if he knows I'm still alive. I answered his letter about nine weeks ago. I was thinking of calling you tonight, Lu, but the booths were very crowded, and I couldn't get enough change. At least I had the thought, Precious.

Good night, Love, Monty

I got an unusual letter from Lu today. She attached a note to an old letter. She said her friend, Gloria, a secretary at the Curtis Bay Army Depot found a letter on Lu's desk amid some papers. Lu said that she thought she had mailed it, but it apparently got lost in the shuffle. Lu was friendly with Gloria, but her best friend at work was a girl her age, named Netsy Mayfale. The two became fast friends and often went to the USO dances together and double-dated. Her latest letter was written about the time she went to the prom with the son of the officer with whom she worked. Lu further indicated in this letter what I had already known; Lu was quite the social butterfly. I

responded to her with the following letter.
June 26, 1943
Dear Lu,

Surprisingly enough, I received the long, lost mystery letter today. It may be a bit late but thank Gloria for looking out for my interests. You said you were going to tell me all about the prom, but from my recent letters received all I've gotten is, "I had a pip time." Tell me, did you tie a bender on? Stay up all night? Go to the bandbox? What? I understand you're really stepping out – good girl. How is the Arundel Boat Club? Solid, I hope. Well, I see Joe is a P.F.C. He's really doing all reet in the Army. Alas! I see Irish is in Boston. I take it that's better than an isle in the Pacific. By the way, how's Rowley? You know I must keep tabs on all my boys. I admit I'm gaining weight, but I want you to know that I also high jumped five feet today. That isn't high, only to an amateur.

Oh! About the sleep, we have a new M.A. who sees to it that all the fellows arise bright and early at five-thirty. You can bet your sweet life I get up too, for there is an "or else" – five days in the brig on bread and water. It's very awkward answering that delayed letter, for you probably don't recall everything. However, you wanted a little light on this subject – "Darling, I only wish I were Superman. I'd end this war and ..." Well! All I can say is that I would want to do certain things after this war, but it's only obvious people will be changed, situations will be changed, new acquaintances will and most likely already have been made which will naturally change relationships. However, I'm confident I'll never meet another you. I couldn't conceive of another person filling the place in my heart that is yours. Consequently, if everything is the same the "..." will be done, not written or said.

To enlighten you, I'll now answer the last letter I've received. Oh! Oh! Oh! The opening of your letter was really in rare form. Don't get the idea I dislike it, being referred to as "The Most Handsome Signalman in Chicago," but I was thinking if any of the fellows saw this, they would probably rib me to death. No doubt, you know the pictures of me you have are a little better looking than what "me true mug really looks like." In fact, the advertisement of the studio stated they would clean your hat, wash your teeth, give you a shave, and even make a movie star out of Quasimodo.

I see you went swimming Sunday, well, anytime you need a fellow to strangle, just call on me. I've been swimming here quite a bit, but it's not what it should be – no women. Just to help you along with the Morse code. I'll enclose the alphabet. It's easier that way. I'll also enclose the poem and give up shorthand as a bad case. Besides, why should I learn it when a solid job like you could be on my lap getting all the work done. I simply can't wait to see you in your bathing suit. You surely must send me a picture, but quick. By the way, while glancing through a magazine, I came across this picture (enclosed). On the first look, I thought it looked like you. That is, as you would have looked in those styles or press and hairdo.

Well, Precious Lambie-Pie, I'll have to close for now. Bye, Sweet!

Love, Monty

P.S. – "A pretty girl is like a melody" being beneath the picture was quite a coincidence, was it not?

Poem: The planners and schemers and dreamers
Have fashioned a world bright and new;
Gleaming towers of steel and concrete
Are Pushing the stars from the blue.
But in all their mast'ry of myst'ries

In seeking the good and the true;
They have not devised a scheme nor dream
To improve on my love for you.
Morse code:

· —	A	— ·	N
— · · ·	B	— — —	O
— · — ·	C	· — — ·	P
— · ·	D	— — · —	Q
·	E	· — ·	R
· · — ·	F	· · ·	S
— — ·	G	—	T
· · · ·	H	· · —	U
· ·	I	· · · —	V
· — — —	J	· — —	W
— · —	K	— · · —	X
· — · ·	L	— · — —	Y
— —	M	— — · ·	Z

I read this recently, what do you think? A sailor's wife was gasping her last breath on her death bed. She said, "Steve, I want you to know I've been unfaithful."

"I know," Steve said. "Why do you think I poisoned you?"

A couple of weeks later, I called Lu on the telephone and caught her at home.

"Hello," Lu said, as she answered the telephone.

"Lu, is that you?" I asked.

"Monty!" she answered excitedly. "Where are you?"

"I'm still in Chicago," I said. "I'm so happy to hear your voice. I haven't had a chance to write. They've been keeping us so busy here. How are you, Sweetie?"

"I'm fine, Monty," Lu responded. "You wouldn't believe it, but I just returned from Ocean City. Cuddy and Mike and a few other girls and I went down for a couple of days. It was a grand time. The weather was beautiful, and the water was warm."

"Lu, I'm just delighted hearing your voice," I said exuberantly. "I think of you all of the time."

"You do?" Lu said. "I don't know. You're getting to be a worldly fellow. There's got to be a lot of girls in a big city like Chicago."

"None as sweet as you, Lu," I said. "I can't wait for this training to be finished. I'm praying that I get leave to come home to see you."

"I hope so," Lu said. "I've missed you terribly, Monty. It would be so nice to spend time together."

"I'm counting on it, Lu," I exclaimed. "I better get going. I'm out of change and I'm getting dirty looks from the sailors in line behind me. I love you and miss you, Lu."

"Love you, too," Lu responded. "Take care of yourself, Monty."

"I will," I said. "Goodbye, Lu."

"Goodbye, Monty," Lu said.

A few days later, I received a package from Lu. It was a box of delicious Dolle's Saltwater Taffy from Ocean City, Maryland. I wrote her immediately.

July 13, 1943

Dear Lu,

First of all, I want to thank you for the candy. You could have knocked me over with a feather, I was so surprised. Baby, you can't imagine what it means to me to know you were thinking of me in Ocean City. I also received your card and letter. You were right about the first paragraph; I've been negligent writing to you. However, I want you to know I haven't been making excuses for not writing, I've just been stating facts. You would be surprised to know how many times I've tried to write you a letter but couldn't for reasons impossible to control.

Darling, when I spoke to you on the telephone the other night I could have floated in thin air. I was so happy and contented I was awake half the night just smiling. Sweetie, if you continue these sweet acts of loveliness, I'll be pure putty and you'll be the mason. I'm certainly glad you enjoyed your stay in Ocean City. I guess you're a mellow brown baby after absorbing all that sun. By the way, thanks for the information regarding your previous letter. I haven't looked up saccharin as yet, but if a dusty part of me brain is correct, saccharin is several hundred times as sweet as sugar. All I can say, Baby, is that you're original as well as tremendous.

Darling, I'm anxiously awaiting the pictures you've promised so don't disappoint me. It's been so long since I've seen you. I must have something to keep my heart beating regularly. Well, I'm surely glad to see the fellows wondering or not about their competitor being on the beam or off. Darling, on the phone, you seemed to doubt whether I felt the same or not. Well, I'll tell you, I've loved you from the very first time I saw you and I guess I'll always love you. However, I'm not in a position to be the right guy. Baby, I'm the side which is doubtful or may I even say doubtful. Hopeful is a more appropriate word. You never seem to answer these delicate parts of my letters, so I'll stop and save the paper. Give my regards

to the family and take it easy at the office.
Love, Monty

I received yet another letter from Lu. She had gone to Ocean City again with her girlfriends. She had also been going to the pool frequently in Baltimore and said she was learning to dive. We had gone swimming together the previous summer and she was quite amazed by my high diving skills. I was very capable of an impressive swan dive, as well as a pretty good jackknife. Lu seemed excited about the possibility of my coming to Baltimore after Signalman School ended. She sent me a beautiful, colorized picture of herself, looking every bit like a movie star. She had it done at a portrait studio. She and her family seemed to have been making the best of things despite the war. Her parents often had friends and relatives over for get-togethers. I wrote her yet another loving letter.

July 31, 1943
Lu Darling,
According to you Baby, I'll be home in three more weeks. I surely hope we aren't kidding ourselves for I am practically existing over the fact that I'll be seeing you in less than a month. Sweet, I repeat, you'll be such an excellent diver that I won't even be able to be seen near the water with you. All kidding aside, I'm wild about your advancement in the art of diving. Last Friday must have been a gay night for family and friends. I only wish I could have been there. It also reminds me I haven't touched the firewater here for quite a while. Baby, you're not in a bathing suit, but oh my you'd drive the little boys wild. Honestly, the picture was grand, but oh! It makes me miss you so. Guess what? Fred Waring is dedicating his program on the fourth of August to our little establishment here. Baby, do me a favor. The next time

you write Rowley, ask him if he answered my last letter. Well, Angel, I must end for now not because I've run out of words but because time is so short until I have to hit the hay. I must say again – what a picture! Yipe! You know Darling, you're oh so - yum yum.

Give the family my love and say hello to the fellows when you write them.

Love, Monty

Lu wrote me another beautiful letter. She described how much she enjoyed relaxing in the evenings after work listening to the Fred Waring radio program. She especially enjoyed listening with her parents. She loved her mother and father so much. Her parents loved Lu dearly, too, especially Mr. Flanagan. Lu's near-death experience as a child must have been a jolt to Mr. Flanagan. Luckily, Lu only lost hearing in her right ear as a result of her illness. I always made sure I whispered my sweet nothings into her left ear.

She really loved the musical numbers on the Fred Waring show. His band played all the favorite songs of the day. She took great pleasure in spending time with her mom and dad. She idolized her dad. He really was a genuinely nice fellow and very pleasant. I never saw him lose his temper or even appear moody. He and Lu had very similar sunny dispositions. Lu said she always thought of me during the commercials on the program. The sponsor was Chesterfield cigarettes. She seemed very anxious for me to come home and was actually counting the days until the end of my training in Chicago. She hoped I would be granted leave, and of course, this was my fervent wish, too.

She communicated a funny story about Irish going swimming with her when he went home on leave. He was apparently in Newfoundland and flew to Boston on a clipper before going home to Baltimore. I was a little put off at first that she and Irish spent time together until she told me what happened. Apparently, when they went swimming, Lu wanted to show off to Irish her recent diving ability.

After her dive, stupid Irish made one of his typical sarcastic remarks saying to Lu, "You're no Esther Williams."

Wrong thing for you to have said, Irish. Lu was a very sensitive soul and did not like sarcasm. Luckily for me, she thought Irish was being a horse's ass. Of course, those were not Lu's words. She would never use that kind of language in a million years, but she was not happy with Irish. It served him right, I thought. Who the hell did he think he was, trying to move in on my girl? Lu liked him, but honestly, what did she possibly see in him? He was not good-looking at all. I would more aptly describe him as goofy looking, not the least bit handsome.

Irish gave me a pain if anyone wanted to know the truth of the matter. And that damn Rowley, my supposed best friend, wrote Lu all the time. He only wrote me once in a blue moon. What the hell? I really started to dislike these guys for trying to move in on my girl. Irish, Rowley, and that Gene Tress, all of them, writing Lu and getting dates with her. To be honest, I had a hard time understanding the correspondence with Joe Albrecht, too. He was supposed to be engaged to Mike Norris. And now, it looked like some Army Lieutenant Jerry something or other was getting time with Lu. From the sound of her letters, she seemed to really like Jerry. The whole situation was getting to be a goddamn national emergency.

There was absolutely nothing I could do about it, being stuck in Chicago studying to become a lowly signalman. I knew where signalmen went after training, too, out to sea. My future had already been ordained. I would be assigned to some goddamn ship signaling other goddamn ships out in the middle of the goddamn ocean. I feared I had moved right to the end of the line with Lu. Maybe I needed to become an officer to win her exclusive affection. I wanted to get back to Baltimore to Lu to show her how much I loved her and to make her realize that I was the guy for her, not these other numbskulls.

I wrote her another letter immediately, but I faked my feelings toward the other fellas. I figured, however, that I had better remind her who her favorite fellow was.

August 9, 1943
Dear Lu,
I just received your letter today. You seemed to have forgotten that D-1 should appear on the address. I'm only suggesting you put it on the next letter so I will receive it a lot sooner. Our letters seem to be far apart in arriving so anything to help speed delivery I would appreciate.

I'm certainly glad you liked Fred Waring's program. On the brighter side, I'm simply thrilled that you'll take off a few days to spend with me. If and how I get home, it will be in about ten days for probably only a day. I can't be sure, but I'm surely hoping.

Give Esther my love and wish her a speedy sound recovery from her pneumonia. Speaking of the Miller family, how is my fine friend, Donny?

Well, it's nice to know your friends are getting home. By the way, how is Irish? Irish was certainly determined to get home, wasn't he? I think that was grand – flying the clipper from Newfoundland to Boston. It must have been a sensation reaching Baltimore after traveling all that way. Maybe Irish was kidding you about your diving, Lu. What do you think? Irish is a swell fellow, Lu. I do think he would kid you. I haven't seen Irish for quite a while now. Perhaps he may get home again for a day when I do. We could all have a fine day at the beach. Rowley should be getting home soon. Wouldn't that be a surprise if we all got home at the same time? We would all spend Sunday afternoon together – just like old times. However, Joe and Tress would have to make it complete.

Now, when I think about all those fellows, it makes me just a bit homesick. It's strange when you think of the fellows before the war and then realize where they are now. We were so close together before, getting dates with the same girls, going out together, and even having a few arguments, but now it's so different with the miles between us. Well, as soon as we finish this war, we'll take up where we left off.

I can understand your desire for your rider to get a convertible, Lu. Your suitors could find competition in a convertible, if there were any nice fellows home with enough gas to drive a convertible. However, I don't think the boys in the service have to worry about their girls going out with civilians. From what I hear, the masculine population is practically all absorbed by the armed service. There is the fear that the girlfriends might fall for another serviceman, though. A great many fellows have their worries, but do I? No! It's always been the same with me. I feel the same about you, yet I never seem to be right in on the old beam. You're tops with me, and you know it by now or at least you should know it. There are so many things unexplained. It's difficult to understand so we'll forget it.

Forgive me, Lu, I'm off my orbit. I'll most likely be seeing you very soon so we'll have a very good heart to heart talk then. I'm not sure, but in ten days I should be home.

Love and pinches, Monty

Chapter Eight

SPAM

In the middle of August, after I received another letter from Lu, I found out that I was getting shipped out after training ended in Chicago. I was to be assigned to the *U.S.S. Detroit*; a cruiser docked in San Francisco. I still was not sure if I would be getting leave. I just had to get back to Baltimore to see Lu. I had no idea how long I would be at sea. The thought of it distressed me terribly. The week before training ended on August 20, 1943, however, we were told ten-day passes would be awarded at the conclusion of classes. My orders revealed a report date to San Francisco of September 1, 1943. I immediately made travel plans that included a trip to Baltimore first. I called Lu to give her the good news. Luckily, I caught her at home.

"Lu, is that you?" I gleefully asked when she answered the phone.

"Yes, this is she," she answered. "Monty! Is that you?"

"It sure is, Baby, and I've received ten days leave," I said even more enthusiastically than before. "I'm coming home."

"That's wonderful, Monty," Lu said. "I can't wait to see you."

"Me too, Lu," I said excitedly. "I'm catching a train tomorrow. It doesn't leave until three o'clock in the afternoon, so I won't get into New York until Sunday morning at eight. I should be in Baltimore by Sunday afternoon. That'll leave us the rest of the day to spend together and a couple more days before I have to leave for San Francisco."

"That's great, Monty," Lu said. "We can spend Sunday together, but remember Monty, I have to work all week."

"Can't you take off?" I asked.

"Well, I might be able to get a day off, but I can't take any more days off on such short notice."

"All right," I said. "I understand. I just want to see you as much as possible. I don't know when we'll have this chance again."

"I know, Monty," Lu said. "I can't wait to see you. We can go out in the evenings after I get off from work."

"That'll be grand, Lu," I said. "It's been too long. I've been waiting for this day for months. You don't even know."

"Well, call me Sunday when you get home, and we'll spend the day together," she reiterated.

"That sounds wonderful, Lu," I said. "Until then. Goodbye."

"Goodbye, Monty," she said.

Boy, I felt as if I were on top of the world. I couldn't believe I was finally going to see my girl again. I then telephoned my mother.

"Hello!" my mother said.

"Hi Mom, it's Boy," I said.

"Boy, where are you?" Mom asked.

"I'm in Chicago, Mom," I answered. "My training's ending this week and I'm coming home for a few days."

"Well, that's fine, Boy," she said. "When should we expect you?"

"I'm catching a train tomorrow afternoon to New York. Then I'm taking a train from New York to Baltimore on Sunday so I should be in Penn Station and home by early Sunday afternoon."

"We'll look forward to seeing you then, Boy," Mom said. "I'll fix you a big dinner Sunday. What would you like?"

"That's all right, Mom," I responded. "Don't bother to make anything special. I've already made plans to go out with Lu in the afternoon. I'll just grab a sandwich or something when I get home."

"Okay, Boy, suit yourself," she said. "It'll be less trouble for me."

"Thanks, Mom," I said. "Tell Pop, Margaret, and Edith I can't wait to see them."

"I will, Boy, but I don't know what the girls are doing Sunday," she explained. "Your father and I will be home, but they might have plans."

"Okay, Mom," I said. "Just be sure to tell them I'm looking forward to seeing everybody again. I have to report to San Francisco on the first of September, which is why I can only come home for a few days."

"I'll tell them, Boy," she said. "We'll see you then."

"Okay, bye Mom."

"Goodbye, Boy."

I was so excited to be getting home to see the folks and my sisters, but nothing compared to the thrill of seeing Lu again. The train from Chicago departed right on time and it arrived in New York just before eight on Sunday morning. I slept fairly well through the night, even though I didn't have a sleeping berth. I managed to get on an eight-thirty train to Baltimore which arrived at Penn Station at twelve-thirty. I walked through my front door before one in the afternoon.

I had the greatest next few days of my life. I spent every available minute with Lu, dancing at the Alcazar, going to movies, sitting in her parlor, listening to the radio, conversing with her family members, talking to her, and best of all, stealing kisses from her. Lu told me in no uncertain terms that she loved me. We didn't discuss our future exactly, but it was clearly a mutual understanding that I was her number one guy and that we would get married after the war.

She said to me on my last night in her parlor on Tuesday night, "Monty, I will always make time for you, no matter what. The other boys I'm seeing, dancing with, and corresponding with, don't mean to me what you mean to me."

"You have no idea how much you mean to me, Lu," I replied. "You're all I ever think about, Lu. I love you so much."

"I love you, too, Monty," she said.

Those words from Lu made my heart melt. Having to leave her after that was as painful as anything I ever had to do. The long train ride I embarked on the next day to San Francisco was a miserable journey. The thought of not seeing Lu again for what I knew was going to be a very long time troubled me deeply. I spent four days on the train, and I never felt so lonesome in my entire life. I felt relieved to finally report to the base in San Francisco at Treasure Island. I sent off a telegram to Lu upon my arrival to let her know I had made it safely. After a few days on Treasure Island, we were told we were going out for gunnery practice, but instead, they took us to board our ship and we didn't come back to port for months.

Boarding the *U.S.S. Detroit* for the first time was exhilarating. I was ready to do my job as a signalman and fight the war, albeit in my own small way. My sense of pride as an American and as a sailor reached its peak that day. It did not take long, however, for reality to set in. For the life of a sailor on board a ship was certainly no picnic indeed. The first reality check was the sight of my bunk. The sleeping arrangements at first glance seemed utterly absurd. They remained that way at every subsequent glance, too, because they were, in fact, ridiculous. My living space consisted of a top bunk with two bunks below me. The ceiling was only a few inches above my head, so I had to be careful not to jump up out of bed for fear of cracking my head on the overhead. It was easy to make friends considering the tight quarters. The fellow to my right in the top bunk, Buck, formerly a watchmaker before enlisting, was a married man from California. We quickly became friends, but rarely ever saw each other due to our different work schedules.

My life as a signalman on the ship was all about getting enough sleep for my shifts. This was all but impossible. The shift was four hours on and eight hours off, but it was not really because they put us on what they called dog watches. A watch was four hours long. From midnight until four in the morning was a watch. I thought, oh boy, that will be great. If I worked from midnight to four in the morning, I would be off every day until noon. The Navy, however, did not make it that simple. Somehow, they figured that rather than having a four in the afternoon until eight at night four-hour watch, they would have what was called a dog watch. So, for example, if I had the midnight to four in the morning watch, then I would be off from four to noon. I would be off for eight hours, but the next watch was a dog watch so I would be on from noon to four. Instead of then getting off for eight hours from four to midnight, they only gave us off from four to eight, and then we had to go on watch from eight to midnight. At least I got to go to bed from midnight to eight the next morning. In that one day, however, I would be on watch for twelve hours. The days when I had the midnight to four watch were the toughest, but they only happened every third day.

I thought the midnight to four watch would be great at first because I thought I could get some sleep from four to noon. I determined very quickly though that this was not the case. We would get to our bunks at four in the morning, but then at six-thirty, they would blow general quarters. They sounded a bugle alarm for general quarters, and everybody had to man their stations. Occasionally, general quarters sounded at other times when they sighted the enemy, or they read a blip on the radar and thought it was the enemy. My station was the twenty-millimeter cannon if I was not on watch. I was the relief gunner, so I had to be in place in case the regular gunner got killed. During my time on the ship, however, the twenty-millimeter cannon was never fired. We dropped depth charges and fired torpedoes, but our ship was never under immediate attack, and I never saw the enemy.

Fifteen destroyers and three cruisers were in the fleet, the *U.S.S. Detroit* being one of the three cruisers. Our ship was designated as an anti-submarine ship equipped with new radar equipment. They would see submarines on the radar and go into the area and drop depth charges, hopefully to blow them up. Before I was on board, the *U.S.S. Detroit*, as part of the fleet, had gone to the Aleutian Islands off the Alaskan coast. The Japanese held several of the islands and the fleet bombed them for four or five days. The Americans then went ashore, but the Japs were all gone. They slipped out at night. However, the remnants of the Jap force were still there. Their planes remained and they left behind two-man subs and even one-man subs. Can you imagine getting into a sub that was only big enough to hold you and a torpedo? The fleet chased them back toward Japan and its territorial waters. Radar was a new thing. The Navy would get a blip on the screen and then the fleet went after them.

During my time on the ship, the first torpedo I ever saw was fired by one of our own destroyers that almost hit our ship. The *U.S.S. Detroit* was hit one time from a depth charge from one of our own destroyers. It put a big hole in the port side. The United States Navy had a lot of accidents like that. All these ships maneuvered by flag hoist because a five-hundred-foot ship did not turn on a dime. It took a great big radius for a ship to turn. They turned in columns usually. There was normally a ship five hundred yards ahead and a ship five hundred yards behind. To make these turns, one had to be an expert seaman. The officer of the day gave all the commands. If he cut it too short, the ship would ride up on the fantail of the ship in front, which was not good. If he took it too wide, the ship would get out of line and might run into the destroyers or other ships nearby. They did this maneuvering by flag hoist. They would run up a flag that represented T and one that represented nine. This signal meant that the ships would turn ninety degrees together. After the admiral of one ship ordered the signalmen to put all the flags down, then all the ships involved turned at the same time.

We learned all of this in Signalman School and all the officers learned it in Annapolis at the Naval Academy. It worked very well. But then they had flashing lights, too. They were always communicating with the other ships. The ships were going up and down in the ocean waves and they had steering control. They communicated by flashing lights because the Japs had these listening devices for radio. We were close to Japan. After leaving the Aleutian Islands, the fleet went to the Andreanof Islands off the west coast of Alaska. The fleet was part of an effort to block the Jap Navy from coming across the Pacific Ocean to the west coast of the United States. We spent many days maneuvering and patrolling these waters.

If I was on the bridge on watch from midnight to four, I would get back in bed at ten of four, and then they would get us up for breakfast at six anyway, so while I was having breakfast, they sounded the alarm for general quarters. Then at six-thirty, as I said, I would be back up on the twenty-millimeter cannon as the relief gunner. The regular gunner was on it, and I would be waiting for whatever was going to happen, if they spotted Japanese planes or whatever. Most of the time it was just a drill. If they did spot any planes, they never came our way so there was nothing to shoot. Usually, I was up there until about nine in the morning before they sounded retreat, and everybody could get back to what they were doing.

I finally found some time to write Lu a letter after almost three weeks of getting adjusted to the hectic life aboard the ship.

September 22, 1943
Lu Darling,

The censorship doesn't permit me to express my doings as vividly as I would like, but I shall endeavor to do my best. In other words, I can't brag as to where I've been or am at present. However, I think it is permissible to let you know I am now "salty." Besides the dominating fact is that I miss you very much. After the wonderful leave we spent together, being without you is even more difficult. Darling, you can't imagine how much better I feel now that we are on a smooth course again. It may be that true love never runs smooth, but I'm happy ours is running smoothly, for the "knocks" haven't been and won't ever do us any good.

Well, here I am, but where seems to be a military secret, consequently that's not a topic for discussion. You may be interested to know that I'm in good physical shape, but getting a haircut seems to be a problem. Tell your father I'm in great shape for a violin, for my hair is so long it tickles my back at night. Now, I would like to know if Gordon has been home. Does he look good and where is he at present? Nosey fellow, aren't I? Another question, how is Nancy?

Oh yes, Sweet, the next time you go up to the corner, look at a bottle of beer and think of me. I surely would enjoy a night there now. Give the family my regards and say hello to Aunt Nan and Aunt Nell for me. Tell me if you have heard from any of the fellows and send me Joe's address. Lu, Gorgeous, number your letters as I am doing. In that way, we can keep track of the correspondence accurately. "Wait for me, Mary Lucille?"

Loving you, Monty

I found out some very interesting information from the sailor in the bunk below me, George Dixon. George joined the Navy in early 1941 before the war started. He was on the *U.S.S. Detroit* when it was docked at Pearl Harbor on December 7, 1941. George told me that the *U.S.S. Detroit* got underway and was only one of three ships able to get out of the harbor during the Japanese attack. The ship set up anti-aircraft fire and was responsible for downing one of the attacking Japanese aircraft.

"I was on the ship when we were docked at Pearl," George said. "Many other sailors aboard ship now were at Pearl Harbor, too. It was pandemonium that day. We were sandwiched between two other ships in the harbor which were both hit by the Japs. Somehow or another we managed to get out of that hellhole without getting hit. The gunners were so wound up and excited that they spun those twenty-millimeter cannons around so fast that they would go all the way around and strafe their own ship. They later put stops on them so they wouldn't do that again. Only one sailor from our ship was injured on December 7th. In fact, we've had no casualties in 1942 or 1943, not even during the bombing of the Aleutian

Islands by the fleet earlier in the year in August, just weeks before you came on board, Monty."

A few days later when I had a break, I wrote Lu another letter.

September 27, 1943
My dearest Darling,
Here is that little missing you sailor again writing to make sure you receive a letter. Just in case you did not or haven't received the first letter, this is the second in the series since I saw you last. It's evident you received the telegram I sent from my last home. The reason I did not write from there was due to the fact that I had been put on mess cook duty which commences at 4:30 a.m. and expires at 6 p.m. Also, the Navy did not keep me there very long. You understand the predicament I was in, don't you Gorgeous? By the way, Precious, I am anxiously awaiting a word from you.

Guess what, Hon? I broke my watch about three weeks ago, so I put it away until enough money accumulates in my account to pay for its repair. Today, however, I was talking to my bunkmate, Buck, who mentioned the fact he knew a bit about watches. He's a watchmaker from California, a married man, too. Naturally, I presented my watch to him who surprisingly enough put it into top shape condition. It's uncanny. What'd you think? On the beach, a watchmaker would most likely have charged me a mint to have it repaired, but this fellow wouldn't take a dime, for he said it was not an expensive job.

Darling, I have your picture before me. It reminds me of the day we shared down the shore. It's the photo taken in Ocean City – solid – is all I have to say.

I was in my bunk last night thinking of you. And what did they play on the radio but "A Pretty Girl is a Melody." Remember that song? Baby, you'll never know how much I miss you. Every small word or song, day or night, reminds me of you. For instance, it's two minutes past eight, Sunday night. Now just where would I be if I were home?

Well, Sweet, it's time to say – until tomorrow. Give my regards to the family. Say hello to Fran for me and double your fist, smile, and tap on the arm lightly the guy who works up the drug store.

Loving you – Monty

When I was off watch, I was not allowed to lie down during the daytime. My biggest concern aboard ship was to get enough sleep. The only time the Navy would let me sleep was after dinner in the evening and before six in the morning. If I wasn't on watch, I could sleep during those hours. It was complete madness. The worst day was when we started at midnight. Also, there was minimal recreation during time off.

As a signalman, I stood on the bridge. There were no lights. It was pitch black. I was there as a lookout. Five guys were up there at one time. One side was always windy, known as the windward side. Only one signalman was on the windward side. It was terrible over there. The four other guys would be on the other side. We would change every half hour. Every night we were on watch. No signals were sent at night in order not to alert the enemy of our position.

If a sailor fell asleep on his watch, we were told he would be shot. I fell asleep several times on watch while standing up. Actually, I was leaning against the shield for the twenty-millimeter cannon which was at an angle. It was at a perfect incline of about thirty degrees off the vertical, ideal for leaning back and falling asleep. With the crazy shifts that were in place, we didn't get much sleep, so it was very easy to nod off. Of course, I had a helmet on and all my gear, but it was pitch black. The ship was normally rolling and rocking. If there was moonlight, then I could see, but I often fell asleep.

An officer came up one night while I was on watch. I heard this far-away voice, "Are you asleep? Are you asleep?" I opened my eyes, and the officer was nose to nose with me. The officer again screamed in my face, "Are you sleeping?"

"Of course, I'm not sleeping," I yelled back at him. "I'm answering your question, aren't I?" I had no idea how long he had been there. The officer could have been there for three days for all I knew.

"Do you know you could be shot for falling asleep on watch?" the officer said, continuing to scream in my face.

"I'm not sleeping, I'm awake," I reiterated. Guys often fell asleep on watch because we didn't have any time to sleep. I figured it out, if I slept every moment that I could, to get down to my bunk and actually sleep, I would only have had enough time to get maybe five hours of sleep a day.

Within the week, I found time to write Lu yet another letter. She was on my mind every minute of every day. I longed for nothing more than to get a letter from her.

October 2, 1943

Lu – Gorgeous,

I surely hope you receive one of these letters for I haven't received mail from anyone as yet. However, I know it must be due to my moving around so much lately. After being subjected to the rocking and rolling of the sea, I finally went ashore here at _____ blank _____ (CENSORED). I took a short jaunt in a truck, well after banging and bouncing about in that truck, I felt worse than I had ever felt at sea during any weather. However, the solid soil felt perfectly fine under my feet and the smell of the earth was a good change for me.

Well, Sweetie, I'll have to "cast off" now. Give my

regards to the Flanagan clan and write soon, Darling. I could tell you so many things of interest, but circumstances don't permit me. However, I can still tell you the same three little words of eight little letters – I Love you.

Yours, Monty

Funny, the first night I was on watch, the supervisor of the watch, a Signalman Third-Class Petty Officer, liked me immediately for some reason. He picked me to leave watch at three-thirty to go below deck and wake up the five guys that were to replace us at four for the next watch. These guys were spread out all over the ship. The supervisor told me all the compartments they were in. The reason they were spread all over the ship was in case the ship was torpedoed. If the signalmen and radiomen all slept in the same place, the whole communications division might be killed in an attack. I had a terrible time finding these guys. The sleeping areas had three tiers of bunks about eighteen inches apart. I initially thought this assignment was great, getting to leave a half an hour early. The supervisor instructed me of a sure way to wake up somebody. The way the supervisor told me to wake these guys up was to light a cigarette, shake them, and as soon as they woke up, which was usually with a lot of grumbling, put the cigarette in their mouth. Incidentally, everybody smoked.

"You better get up now, you're smoking," I would tell them. This worked fine with the first four guys, but the last guy, who I had seen around the ship, was the toughest guy I had ever seen in my life with muscles all over him. I shook him very lightly.

"Ooooohhh, come on, get up, get up," I said to him ever so nicely. "It's twenty-five until four." This monster of a guy was grumbling and grousing so I lit a cigarette and put it in his mouth, as I had done with the others.

"You've got a cigarette in your mouth now, are you awake?" I asked him. The guy growled again so I left.

I had to admit I was a little scared of him. After all, I was just a skinny eighteen-year-old kid, and this guy was Mr. Atlas. I was also dead tired myself. I went back to my bunk and went to sleep. By breakfast, I had forgotten all about my encounter with the sleeping giant. The same tough muscular guy I left in bed hours before with a cigarette in his mouth grabbed me later at the chow hall, lifting me right off my feet. In fact, he had both of his massive fists gripping the front of my uniform, pulling me close to his face.

"Wake me up harder," he growled. "I caught a lot of hell for not getting up. They sent somebody else down to get me."

"I lit you a cigarette, I lit you a cigarette," I said excitedly in an unusually high-pitched voice.

"Well, it went out," he said, continuing to give me hell.

The next time, I did everything I could to get this guy out of bed. "Come on, get up, get up, get up," I pleaded.

The big guy rolled over and made some unintelligible noise.

"You're on watch, you have to get up," I yelled as I shook him violently. The scary sailor just laid in his bunk dead to the world. Finally, after my continued persistence, the muscular ape suddenly jumped out of his bed and lifted me off the deck again by my shirt. He stared at me for a few seconds as I was now at eye level with him. He had an angry look on his face like he wanted to kill me. He then dropped me abruptly, realizing he had to get on watch.

"I don't want that job anymore," I later told the supervisor.

"But you get off a half-hour early," he said.

"I don't care, I don't care, I don't want that job anymore," I said emphatically.

"Okay," he replied. "I'll get somebody else."

When I had some rare downtime, I wrote Lu again.

October 4, 1943

Lu Darling,

As yet, I am still without word from anyone, but my hopes are still as high as ever. The object of this letter is to inform you that wart you thought so irritating and ugly is gone. I had it burned off a few days ago and it has finished healing, leaving but a smooth part of my forehead. I surely hope you are pleased. Guess you know it was done all for you. Yes, I'll take that medal – thank you.

Hon, this very moment, a fellow who came aboard with me is upchucking. It's disgusting, but he will have to clean it up. Some of the "salts" find it very amusing, but I can't imagine seasickness would be very amusing. As for me, I've been anticipating seasickness all this time, but nothing has happened as yet, so I'll just consider myself immune to it. From what my friend has gone through, I'm just thankful I haven't been sick.

Today is Tuesday, but very often I know not what day it is. Every day seems just the same as the next. Being like that, there is one great advantage, there isn't any blue Monday. Being aboard this ship isn't bad but being away from you, Darling, is "bad and that ain't good." Movies are shown twice a day. Not up-to-date shows, of course, but the idea of going to a show makes a fellow feel as though someone was doing something for his benefit. Surprisingly enough, there is a soda fountain here that sells ice cream as well as Coca-Cola --- genuine Coke, but there's no mixer to make a proper ice cream soda. However, you undoubtedly will be interested in the fact that I bought an entire box of Wrigley's gum yesterday for the reasonable fee of sixty cents. I wanted to send it to you for our upcoming anniversary this January, but much to my disappointment I was told the transaction couldn't be arranged. The next time I arrive in Baltimore, I will make up for all the celebrations I've missed by having one glorious time. You will be my partner of course, won't you?

Gorgeous, last night a song was played during which I wish you could have been in my arms. The song was called "Let there be you… da da da… let there be me." I'm not certain about the title, but that's how it began. To me, it was out of this world. What do you think about it?

I listened to a very weird story last night on the radio. It was called "Suspense." You did not hear it perchance? Living aboard here is all right now that I'm settled and familiar with the surroundings. In fact, I have actually found time to read and enjoy myself. The call for chow was just piped down so I'll have to cease for the present. Speaking of Navy terms, Sweet, I know you like to learn them, so I'll write you every new one I learn. First of all, a "gizmo" is a thing. That is, if you can't recall the technical name of something at present, you simply call it a gizmo. Well, Gorgeous, I'm being patient waiting to hear from you.

Loving You, Monty

Another week went by, and I finally got a letter from Lu after our ship went into a port. I was not even sure where we were. I believed it was some island off Alaska, maybe the Aleutian Islands. It was damn cold, I knew that. I was initially excited because we were supposed to do four hours on a watch and then get sixteen hours off while in port. Sadly, we were there for two days and all we did was load food and ammunition. Everybody loaded, every last one of the five hundred sailors on board. A chain of guys walked down a gangplank, picked up crates, and carried them to the galley. Some of the crates were filled with quart-sized cans of fruit cocktail. We picked up one hundred cases of fruit cocktail and only twelve made it to the galley. Can you imagine that? Eighty-eight cases filled with six quarts in each case, five hundred and twenty-eight cans, were pilfered. As much as I liked fruit cocktail, I didn't take any, but some months later, I was leaning back on the twenty-millimeter cannon on watch, my favorite place, when another sailor, a gunner's mate, asked, "Hey mate, do you want some fruit cocktail?"

"I'd love some," I said. He proceeded to hand me an open quart can with no spoon.

"How are you supposed to eat this?" I asked.

"Like this," he said as he put his big, grubby hand in the can and ate some out of his hand. I was repulsed and didn't enjoy that fruit cocktail as I should have after seeing his disgusting hand in the jar. Nevertheless, things like getting fruit cocktail were actually a delight, just to break up the monotony. My intense craving, however, after months at sea was for a chocolate ice cream soda. I tried to make one myself on the ship. I bought the ice cream and Coca-Cola, but it didn't work without a soda fountain mixer, which the ship's soda fountain lacked. It was a big disappointment.

Of course, the older guys wanted a beer or any kind of alcohol. Now and again, we went to some sandbar off Alaska. Honestly, I never knew where the hell we were. We went for supplies quite frequently it seemed, and it would always be some tiny little island, a speck on the ocean filled with all kinds of supplies. Sometimes they couldn't dock our big cruiser, so they would anchor out a few hundred yards and take these little liberty boats to go ashore. They would have everything. One time the sailors went ashore, and they found crates of Ballantine Ale. This stuff had the highest alcohol content of any beer in the world I was told. These guys would drink themselves into oblivion. It was though they were unleashed. We had to carry them back to the ship. It was wild sometimes.

Our cruiser was always going after submarines. Sometimes they would find them, drop depth charges, and you would see them bubble up. I went to a reunion about forty years later and I found out that a sailor from our ship had fallen overboard. A man overboard was considered a man lost. The Navy wouldn't turn around and pick him up. The guy at the reunion said that the ship behind us picked him up though. The Navy's rationale was that they couldn't risk everybody on the ship for one sailor. I had always thought we were so close to Japan because we were always chasing submarines. The sailor at the reunion confirmed it. He said we were very close to Japan to lure out their fleet and aircraft carriers, since the Japs apparently would not leave the territorial waters of Japan as the war went on.

After getting Lu's letter while we were in port, I wrote her back. We corresponded throughout my assignment on the ship. I wrote her letter after letter. My relationship with Lu was the only thing keeping me sane. I wrote her at least once and sometimes twice every week.

October 12, 1943

Lu Darling,

Yesterday, everyone received a letter except me. Naturally, you can imagine how I felt. The tide changed today, however, and I was the only fellow in our outfit to receive a letter. You can't imagine how I felt today. I was floating around the ship, not walking. I'm sure you understand that while we're out to sea no mail is received. Consequently, when we enter some barren port (this one) we all expect our mail.

Those big hugs you are issuing are being engrained in my memory so that I'll have an accurate account of just how many to collect when I return. Also, I am storing away many of my own to issue for the time we've been apart. I can just imagine the gay occasion when we are together again – Yipe! Loveable. By the way, along with the haircut I just got, I tried to grow a beard. It's hopeless. I let it grow for about two or three weeks. The only result was a six o'clock shadow. I gave up. Now you may call me "Singing Sam – the Shaving Man."

Signaling is very interesting. Strange as it may seem, I enjoy working on the bridge. Perhaps it's due to the fact I'm always handling the first-hand news about the ship.

It's great to see Gordon got a leave. I guess Esther really enjoyed being with him those eight days. "Absence makes the heart grow fonder." Listen, Gorgeous, all sailors look good. I'm sorry I missed seeing you run up Greenmount Avenue; I'd have given anything to have seen that. Just kidding, Darling. You're beautiful with your hair up, down, or in a net, with or without shoes, in the morning or at night, raining or in the sun – all the time.

Lu, Hon, I will approve of your every second habit. In fact, I'm an old participant of that habit myself – thinking of you.

Regarding the beer, I think I told you that I had gotten two bottles when I went ashore here. They did not have chocolate ice cream sodas! Oh! I knew Nancy was going to be a momma that night Aunt Nan and Nell were whispering with you, then saying something and grinning, I put two and two together and got one – a bouncing baby girl we hope. Thanks a million for the addresses. I'll write the fellows tonight. However, I wonder what happened to the twelve-page letter Rowley wrote and forgot to mail. Remember?

Sweet, if you aren't the actress in the Tenth Ward, I don't know who is. I feel confident in stating – "You'll mow 'em down." The only thing that irks me is that you have these productions while I'm away. This is the second one I'll miss. The songs are soft, solid, and sentimental. That's the way I like them. I'm sure it will be a swell show. Perhaps I may get leave by opening night. When is it? No use my extending wishes that it will be successful. St. John's always puts on a great show, but with you participating, Hon, it will be colossal.

Lucille, you did not surprise me too much about Nancy getting married. In fact, I'm expecting to obtain a brother-in-law soon. Edith is getting married. If possible, I hope to be home for the affair for I can just picture the reception – Wow! Let's be presumptuous and make a date for then, okay?

Hon, my friends simply are going wild over the picture you sent me taken in Atlantic City.

There is no doubt in my mind that you must be dancing yourself to a frazzle knowing just how people of other states dance. I haven't danced with any girls in California. I was not there long enough to catch my breath.

Well, it's about time your rider got back on the beam. Let's not have any more trouble with him. He doesn't sound very reliable. I can't stand having my baby put to inconveniences. Oh! By the way, reveille is at 6:30 here, breakfast at 7, work at 8; it's almost like the office. Signalmen stand watches though - four hours on - eight hours off.

Hon, if you keep raking in the money, you'll have a house on the hill. A bond a month is wonderful; it surely makes my bond a "tri-month" look sick. Darling, you know I'm not after your money – or am I?

Oh! You must know the song being played on the radio

at this very moment. It's "My Sweet Embraceable You." Of course, you remember the time, place, and session connected with that sweet little ditty. I'm glad your mother likes my letter writing, but I'm equally glad you did not read the entire letter. Not that I wouldn't shout from the highest housetop my love for you, but some things must be kept personal.

Tan or no, you will keep the eyes of fellows at the USO popping. However, a little song I heard ensures me of the situation at home – "they're either too old or too young."

Everyone seems to be having children nowadays. I guess you're aware of the fact that my old schoolmate from your neighborhood, Richard Wallace, is the proud father of a bouncing baby boy. The Army shipped him over to North Africa. Well, Darling, I learned some more Navy slang. Going ashore isn't referred to as such anymore. It is now expressed as going on the beach. I'll be thinking of you, Hon, and I'll be coming home one day.

Loving you, Monty

Lu's letters finally started arriving regularly. Initially, they were just a little slow making their way onto the ship. Her letters were always entertaining and provided me with a glimpse of life back home, normalcy in the real world, her world. She always had some cute way of referring to me. Lately, it was M.C., or Master of Ceremonies, indicating I was her number one guy. Being M.C. was great for my ego. By the way, I had my own little code words. Armstrong was my way of telling her how sweet I could be to her. Armstrong soap was a popular brand at the time advertised as possessing a very sweet smell.

October 20, 1943
Greetings Gate,
Alas, the #2 letter has arrived unharmed and just in time. The true story is that little #2 drifted into the 4th Division while I'm in the C Division. To eliminate that happening again, feast your lovely eyes upon the return address on the envelope now.

M.C. only wished he could be present to dish out the Armstrong. Having you in my arms again is another of my ever-longing desires. Baby, ever so often I shut my eyes and imagine I'm in that solid hallway with you. It's a wonderful feeling, but when I open my eyes again – what a disappointment.

Don't let the mail business upset you, Sweetie. You're perfectly right, wacky it is. Thanks a million for sending Rowley my address. I'm getting rather impatient waiting to hear from him.

I can just see the Flanagan home with all its wonderful people. However, I would much rather be there even helping your dad than here. Darling, I'm glad you are writing, but I don't think you'll be having any troubles. At least let's hope so. I would like to have joined you at the Navy-Cornell game after which we would have visited the saloon and then spent a lovely remainder of the evening on the parlor couch.

I'm certainly glad to see your brother is progressing in the Navy. No doubt, you're wondering what my delay in advancement is. All I can say is that – I'll surprise you one of these days.

At the rate you are going with the car situation, I'll be expecting you at the station next time waiting to drive me home. All kidding aside, you have all my wishes of making a success "behind the wheel."

Dove, for your information, I got a haircut today. I wouldn't like to say it was short but distinguishing me

from a Nazi spy will be very difficult. By the way, the haircut was gotten at the request of our Chief. Before condemning me, I had a special reason for wanting a bit of hair on my head. I'll enlighten you when I see you again.
Love, Monty

Lu should have figured it out on her own that I loved her running her fingers through my thick, wavy hair, inasmuch as she did so while sitting in her parlor on many a night. Her latest letter was full of more funny stories, the latest family news, and her jokes of my advancement in the Navy. Plus, she gave me a heads up in her letter of a package that was on its way. It arrived two days later. The envelope had a picture of a joker from a deck of cards with a sexy pin-up girl painted on it. Two decks of cards, one for Old Maid, and one for Pinochle were enclosed. Every playing card in both decks had a pin-up girl on it.

October 20, 1943
Dear Lu,

That admiral stuff really is to my liking, but let's just hope I become Seaman First Class shortly. Darling, I hate to admit it but I'm afraid the girls are correct about the MMM – Tuckus. It is slightly more than a shadow I'd say. I am happy to be your number one guy, or as you put it "MMM - My Main Man." With regard to my weight and my shrinking backside, Darling, it may interest you to know MMM is gaining quite a bit lately. First, I put it on, and then I work it off. Monotonous. If you ever care to work off a few excess pounds, just obtain a scraper and chipping hammer and commence chipping paint. That is what I've been doing for the last couple of days. Don't let me confuse you; that isn't one of the Signalman duties, but it just so happened it had to be done. It did not discourage me; it returned me into condition – I hope.

Darling, you're wonderful. You seem to be a mind-reader knowing when I'll be inquisitive and just what songs I remember. You can bet your right eye "I'd like to get cuddly." Sweetie, I remember the last time I was home very well. I only exist on its memory, but the thought that I'll be home again with you really keeps me going. Always, I'm thinking and dreaming of a future with you, where we'll go, when, what I'll say, how I'll say it. Baby, it's always you.

Please give Esther my love and tell her I hope she does fine working at the Crown Cork and Seal Company in Highlandtown. The beer drinkers of the world will appreciate those Baltimore bottle caps. However, if you told her not to follow my example it will have a good effect. Jobs and I ----- Ohhhhh!

I hate to say this about the two little card games I got in the mail today. I was not too alarmed when I saw the envelope, but a few fellows who were with me at the time just about split their sides. I really appreciate the thought, Precious, but honestly, Sweetie, I haven't played Old Maid since I was a kid and I've never played Pinochle. The joke was cute, Hon, but the cards are not my style. I'd be embarrassed to play with those cards. Don't misunderstand, Darling, I still love you.

I see your point in not wanting to go to the Alcazar. Remembering those gay times there is swell, but I can well imagine how it would be without the same atmosphere and people. You and I were in every sort of mood there and I agree everything ended okay which is very, very good.

Washing your hair on Saturday night is gruesome, Hon. It seems I simply must get home soon to eliminate that. Drying your hair is a pleasant job now that I am experienced. Well, Lamb-a-kins, it is now Friday at 8

p.m. so I have to be content to "hit the sack."
Love and pinches, Monty
P.S. - It seems every time I write you the song is played which is playing now, "A pretty girl is like a melody."

Lu indicated that my letters were arriving back home now at a fast and furious pace, so I wrote her yet another.
October 24, 1943
Hello Darling,
It thrills me to know you are receiving my letters so rapidly and it surprises me to get yours so swiftly. Number five arrived today thus casting me back into a splendidly happy mood.

My mother told me about the party and you're wanting to come. Incidentally, she mentioned that all the fellows present anxiously offered to go down to get you. Like that? It's nice to know my girl is popular; makes me feel like expanding me little chest.

About seeing a movie with you, Hon, is a thought which I hope comes true shortly. The shows shown aboard here are old shows I've either seen or missed when I was a youngster not attending movies. They are shown in the gun room, which is usually crowded. The film is made in sections of small reels. Naturally, when the narrative reaches an interesting or exciting part the reel ends and for a period of a few minutes you sit anxiously awaiting the operator to change reels in order for the picture to continue, however, much to my delight, this happens only about five times. Not complaining, just describing. I'm thankful we even have movies. I would have liked to have been with you when the moon was shining so brightly. Being "romantical" is the berries. Rest assured, Darling, I will talk your left ear off when I see you the next time. However, I'm sure a session will take place which requires sweet words in a soft tone. What say, Hon?

I'm glad to see Esther donating her blood, no doubt, she must be in fine physical shape. Her back doesn't trouble her anymore, I hope.

Eating again, Hon, what about your MMM? It stands to reason I missed you while you were gone, but where did you ever dig up the addressing word "smoke?" For a second, it appeared to be "snake." I was really relieved upon examining closer. Your living on a budget impresses me. It may prove profitable to you later, OOOPS! Do you know how much I've spent in the last five or six weeks? I spent exactly ten dollars. Don't grasp the idea I'm being a miser. I've been liberal with the cash on luxuries and necessities, but there isn't anywhere to spend it.

"More than anything in the world," if you like it, must be destined for the top. We have plenty of music here, Hon. The ship has a phonograph set with scores of records. Also, all the command performances, radio shows, and ball games are short waved here. It's good they are too, for it's about the only pleasure enjoyed except reading. Well, Gorgeous, this is Sunday afternoon, so I'll read the papers now, but oh how I wish I were reclining in your parlor's soft chair reading them. Give my regards to the family and goodbye until later, Hon.

Love, Monty

The grind of going on watch was getting to me. Monotony had become my enemy on the ship; however, the high point was the midnight rations. On the midnight to four watch, someone was sent to the galley to get a hot loaf of freshly baked bread and a can of SPAM. I loved SPAM. I had never had SPAM before entering the service. Most guys hated it or got sick of it, but it was like a delicacy to me. I didn't know why, but I just loved the stuff, especially on warm, fresh-baked bread. I ate SPAM sandwiches for the rest of my life after being introduced to it in the Navy. The other signalmen on watch made me the official sandwich maker because we had five guys, and I could make ten sandwiches with the SPAM and the loaf of bread. I would cut the loaf into twenty perfect slices and divide up the SPAM evenly, which the other guys apparently couldn't do, so they made me the official sandwich maker. Plus, it broke up the night quite nicely.

I always thought SPAM got a bad rap. I read all about SPAM in a magazine story sometime later. Apparently, the first can of SPAM was made in 1937 by George A. Hormel and Company in Austin, Minnesota. A French chef working for Hormel came up with the original recipe using otherwise wasted pork shoulder meat. It was packaged in a distinctively shaped can, to ensure that a slice of the meat would fit on a piece of bread, very ingenious I thought. It was opened with a key attached to the top of the can. You just turned the key and peeled the tin back. I preferred opening it with the key, as opposed to the tab you pull to get the top off, which they later developed.

SPAM apparently became quite popular before the war, but I never had it before then. I guess my mother was not impressed with it because she never bought it. By 1944, most of Hormel's business was supplying the American military with SPAM, as well as other generic lunch meat. Many soldiers equated SPAM with other canned lunch meats, consequently, many soldiers developed an intense dislike for SPAM, mistaking the original recipe with the other generic lunch meats they produced, which contained no ham and higher amounts of salt. In 1966, former President Dwight D. Eisenhower sent a congratulatory letter to the Hormel Company in commemoration of their seventy-fifth year in business. In this letter, Eisenhower wrote, "During World War II, of course, I ate my share of SPAM... as former Commander in Chief, I believe I can officially forgive you your only sin: sending us so much of it." I was not in agreement with Eisenhower. I couldn't get enough of it.

Between watches, I sent Lu another letter.

October 31, 1943
Lu Darling,

It grieves me to know you did not have your picture taken while with Esther and Donny. You are not camera-shy, are you? Seriously, I wish you would have had a photo taken. You know I like to have as many pictures of you as possible. However, at present, the pose of you at Ocean City seems to be "driving all the little boys wild" including me. The air raid you mentioned reminds me of the times the fellows and I spent lightless evenings in your ever-pleasant parlor. Keith's Roof is a place where I have never trod, but since the social register has been changed, I am looking forward to spending an evening there. I guess you know I'm pleased to know the male population is low. The fewer fellows in Baltimore, the happier I feel. Selfish, am I not? No! Just in love.

Early dates are more than agreeable with me. On my next leave, I'll be at your house so often you'll think I'm a permanent fixture.

Being that you liked gizmo so much, the Naval slang expression for the word candy is "porky bate."

I am still feeling as well as ever, but I had a few teeth filled. Incidentally, it is an experience I won't forget. We were at sea which made the little operation seem uncanny to me. Irish wrote me a very interesting letter which I received yesterday. He and I expect to get together in Frisco someday. I am still awaiting that long letter

Rowley forgot to mail. Remember, Hon? That seems to be all for now, Gorgeous, so we'll say goodbye until later.
Love, Monty
P.S. - Give my regards to family

When I first went to sea, they had these wooden tables that were on the ceiling, commonly known as the overhead. The mess cooks would lower them down when we got ready to eat. It was cafeteria style so sailors would go through the line first, and then sit at these wooden tables that had this little edge around them so their trays wouldn't slide off. They would go through the line, get the tray, put their food on it, and sit on the bench attached to the table. I sat at a table by myself initially because I didn't know anybody. The ship was always rolling sideways it seemed. I had to hold my left hand on the tray to prevent it from sliding over to the other side. When another sailor would sit at the other side, the table was only big enough to hold two trays. His tray would hold mine in.

A big salt sat down at the table next to me one day and I looked out of the corner of my eye to see how he was going to eat. He pulled out a knife and pierced it into the table to keep his tray from sliding. Wow, I thought, what a good idea in order to eat with both hands. I had no knife, so I wrote my mother to send me one. She sent me my old Boy Scout knife. I used it not only to keep my tray from sliding, but also to cut the bread on watch.

And yet again, I wrote Lu.
November 2, 1943
Lu, Darling,
Your sweet little letters both came on the same day. I'm glad to know you're receiving my letters so swiftly, but I know this one must have been delayed as I am aware of the fact that when we are at sea, no mail is sent

out. That is only natural. There isn't anything known as a mail buddy or anywhere you can deposit the outgoing mail. Well, that being the case, I usually write after we're in port or write them while at sea and take them to be mailed when I anticipate our anchoring.

About your boss, what was the matter with him? Did he acquire some defect? Just what happened? The postcard is enclosed, but I know why you desire it.

Another thing – what puzzles me is just how "Doc" obtained my address. He was a very good friend of mine, but not that good. It was not I who gave him my address. For your information, he was the fellow who accompanied me on the journey back to Chicago at the end of the summer. You remember him at the station, don't you? Speaking of that particular night, Hon, I want you to know I often see you standing there in the moonlight like a spotlight shining on you. Beautiful, you were dressed in a blue checked suit-like frock with the gay little fringe on it. Baby, how I miss you!

It surely pleases me to learn rank and position doesn't mean anything to you, for it seems to me I shall be a Seaman Second Class for quite some time. It isn't that I'm no longer ambitious, but my traits of initiative and perseverance have been exhausted. Undoubtedly, you know the expression, "It's not what you know, it's who you know." Well, take heed, Lassie, it's correct.

Yes, it's true I've been to California, but I want to visit the state again after the war. If our little road remains smooth, we could even make the trip together. What say?

Give Mr. Green my regards, Hon. Strangely enough, I would enjoy knowing our friend, Major Green. Mentioning Gloria before, I was only joking. I certainly hope I don't need her or anyone else's assistance. By the way, express my regards to the girls – MaryJane, Cuddles, and Fran, the girl that talks so fast, and the other girls. I hope you are all getting along fine.

The next leave I receive I plan to take the afternoon off so you can accumulate your driving hours. I'm sure John Battaglia won't mind lending you the car and I'd be delighted.

That haircut was the first since leave and until now it has been the last. The Arundel Boat Club always appealed to me. I would appreciate making my debut one day with you introducing me there and to all of the other gay circles in town whenever I see you again.

Honey/Baby, where did you ever pick up the Navy slang about the sack? Beyond a doubt, you're becoming an old salt. I hope I'm not kidding myself by believing you receive these little tidbits from brother John, Irish, and Rowley. I'm sorry, it slipped my mind about the USO, it's only obvious that's where you obtained Navy slang.

Well, Gorgeous, I wish I could say I'm going to hit the sack, but I have the 8 to 12 watch.

Love, Monty

P.S. - You're right, I'm out of writing paper. Today is Saturday, I think. Hu Hu, that's right. It is Saturday. Just think how grand it would be dressing now in preparation for a night at the Alcazar with all the same boys and girls there.

Two weeks later, I wrote to Lu in response to her letter about the goings-on in Baltimore. I continued writing letter after letter to her.

November 15, 1943
Lu Darling,
Culpepper is still the same fellow, being physically well and still content, but I personally believe the lad is in love. What is your opinion? You may think the left-hand corner of this letter is corny with my sketches of a young

sailor in love, but please notice the stationery. It is old so to relieve the monotony of receiving "University of Chicago" paper, the picture was added. How I would really enjoy getting on the beam again. And you? Would you care to climb on with me?

About the play at St. John's Church, I'm not only crossing my fingers, but I'll even cross my eyes. However, with you in the production, Hon, there is no doubt in my mind that it will be a success. I will be thinking about you on the 17th. Let's "Wow" the Tenth Ward, what say?

My sister, Edith's, wedding ceremony, will most likely take place without me. I'm not pleased about it, you might know, but I understand the situation. It seems as though I'm in the habit of missing weddings. Let's hope I don't miss one particular wedding though. In fact, I have a great desire to be one of the major participants someday!

You will have to introduce me to the USO when I return. I would like to have seen you and Mike in formal attire. I know Joe Albrecht would have loved to have seen his future bride all dolled up. I know I would have loved to have seen you, Lu. I'll bet you looked like the Queen at the May Parade in the Tenth Ward. Solid – no doubt.

And Lu, you drinking? It must have been quite a sight to see your downing a shot. I'm surely glad you are enjoying the correspondence, but we must not get too pleased. We have been progressing the "Rocky Road" all too smoothly. It must be the understanding we have. We are defying that statement – "True love never runs smooth."

About the beard, I'll be truthful. Noticing all the beards about, I decided I would grow one. After a month, I had nothing to show but a five o'clock shadow. Consequently, I shaved it off. I then proceeded with a mustache. It was not exactly successful, but it could be seen. What with trimming it and the accumulation of the morning cereal milk in it, I decided I would remain a clean-shaven fellow.

Tell your sister, Esther, I'll be looking for our fellow sailor, Gordon. If I ever get back to the States and discover him, we'll have a bit of brew together. Esther is a lucky woman. That Gordon is all right!

Rowley never writes me, I know, but tell him he is forgiven in your next letter to him. Please ask him to remember his old, best friend, at least.

The song playing this very moment explains precisely how I feel "There will never be another you." You are such a great girl, Lu, for giving blood. You undoubtedly must be sweet with Type A blood. I guess you know I have the ever-common Type O. Sorry to hear about your Uncle Tom's appendicitis. He will probably be even healthier now than he ever was. At least I hope so.

Well, Gorgeous, I have the watch from 8 to 12 so I'll say goodnight. Here's looking up your old address!!!!

Love, Monty

P.S. - "Good-Nights" now are much different than at home, aren't they?

I received a parcel from Lu packed with puzzle books and a checkers game. I didn't have the heart or even know how to tell Lu, especially since I recently told her I didn't want her risqué pin-up girl card games, but checkers and puzzle books were not my thing. I occasionally enjoyed a crossword puzzle, but puzzles generally did not interest me. When I told my bunkmate about my predicament, he immediately suggested that I give them to him as he loved playing checkers and solving puzzles. "I'm your out," he said. After two weeks, I fired off another letter to Lu.

November 30, 1943
Dearest Lu,
I'm grieved to say I can't save those games you gave me, but thanks for the checkers and the puzzle books. A young fellow became attached to them, so thinking you wouldn't mind, I let him have them. I really appreciated your sending them, Hon, but chess is the game I chance to play.

Forgive me for saying any harsh words or implying anything about your weight in my previous letters. You know as well as I do that, as you are, you're lovely. Without a doubt, the play you were in at St. John's must have been superb. I am eagerly anxious to view the reenactment you said you'd do for me. About our future date, whenever that may occur, you are perfectly correct in that I will do all the talking. All narrating can be left to me. I'll relate my every experience to you, even the ones I've already written to you about.

The fellows are certainly enjoying playing checkers, especially on a new board. That is why I presented the game to them. Incidentally, they extend their heartfelt thanks to you. I know you'll be surprised to learn that Bingo is even played and strangely enough, practically everyone participates. However, it is played on a profit-paying basis.

Lu, Hon, the expression "Here's looking up your old address" which concluded my last letter was merely used as such. I had no idea you would take it so seriously or be offended by it. Have you lost your sense of humor? I have noticed the saying used frequently and I actually paused to think before writing it. I can see how it might be construed as something off color. I apologize. However, you can rest assured I'll never again write anything which may be misinterpreted.

It's been so long since we've been bowling together, I

can't recall your scores. No doubt though you surely must be good with the experience you've been getting in these leagues. Do you remember the last time we were bowling? The party consisted of you, a girl whose name escapes me, Rowley, and me. Do you remember the occasion? Being how that I had just met you recently, there was a gay affair between the fellows wondering who was with whom.

About the females, I haven't seen any in so long a time, I've nearly forgotten what they look like. My only relation with women is when I look at the pictures I have of you. In fact, even the girls, my friends, with whom I had been corresponding, have ceased writing because I neglected seeing them while home on leave. That fishing line I had the girls on seems to have unwound – no mermaid either.

On the brighter side, I, too, had an examination for Seaman First Class. Judging from the length of the test, I would say not many fellows passed it. All I need to do now is to wait for the results. Let's hope that they prove satisfactory. Well, Lovely, I'll bid pardon until later.

Loving you, Monty

P.S. - I miss you, Darling.

I received a letter from Lu the day after her parcel arrived with the games. Lu's biggest news was that her sister, Esther, was finally getting out of the doldrums. She apparently had been quite lonely since Gordon joined the Navy. Gordon, I imagined, felt the same way. I was fairly certain, however, that my darling Lu rarely got down in the dumps. She was the most fun-loving person I had ever come across. She was not only dancing with the soldiers at the USO, but now she was participating in ping pong tournaments with them. The highlight of my Navy life during the previous week was getting promoted to Seaman First Class in which I made a lousy extra twelve dollars a month. I really had it made now, making a whopping sixty-six clams each month with free room and board. If only I had something to spend my newfound riches on.

And yet another letter from a lonely sailor to his beloved Lu was composed. I was so lonely without her.

December 1, 1943

Hi Beautiful,

What is this? I cried when I read you had been doing housework. On second thought, though, I was very pleased. Do you know why? Don't get peeved, but how is your cooking? I'm serious, Hon. That ping pong contest you competed in at Fort Meade must have been quite the berries. Maybe I've been missing something by avoiding the USO. It sounds like so much fun. I hope you are correct in your assumption about my returning home soon. I would be thrilled just to set my foot on the soil of the great US of A, let alone set foot in the halls of a USO. Being away has changed my attitude toward the little things in life. When I get home again, my appreciation for those little things will be very much increased. Just to lie on the green grass under a giant tree will be wonderful. I'm most in favor of your eyelash wish coming true. 'Twould be grand to never leave you again.

I'm very glad Esther is rosy again. I know she was upset about Gordon joining the Navy, but we all feel compelled to do our part, I guess. I'm sure little Donny misses his daddy. Please say hello for me to Esther and also give my regards to your friend, Fran, and the rest of the girls. Now that your "poor ole" civilian morale is at stake, I must become friendlier with my friend. You are without a doubt my best friend in this world. Your morale is more important to me than anything. Honestly, Hon, I'll do my best to write more often, but the odds are great.

It's difficult just to write you and Mom. My time is very limited between working my shifts, eating, and finding time to sleep. It's a real grind here. I am beat all the time.

Well, Gorgeous, you've noticed by my address that I have finally advanced a tiny step in this Navy. Yes, I am now a Seaman First Class. It certainly sounds good, and it also causes my pay to be increased somewhat. Well, Honey, the advancement gave an enormous uplift to my morale. According to the custom, I passed out cigars today. Now I know how a newborn father feels. Incidentally, it's rather swell passing cigars out. Lu, Hon, I stood in the line to get a haircut yesterday for all of a half an hour, but to no avail. Chow began and haircuts ceased. I try, don't I? The lights are about to go out, Darling, so I'll say goodnight, Honey.

Love, Monty

My monotonous life aboard ship was alleviated to some extent when I was assigned an additional duty, which made me feel important. When I was off watch, it became my responsibility to update the signal book, a giant book about eighteen inches thick. If our ship ran across another ship in the middle of the Pacific Ocean, we would send them a question by flag hoist that asked them to identify themselves. They would have to give us the allied signal for the day. If it was the correct signal, we would say it was okay and go on our merry way. If they didn't know the signal, then they were the enemy. It was my job on the bridge to record these instances in the signal book. I enjoyed the extra duty and felt I was performing a very critical role. I still found some free time to write Lu.

December 3, 1943
Darling,
Your package arrived today, and I acted like a kid opening his gifts on Xmas morning. I had been expecting

a package from my mother, so I was pleasingly surprised to find your card. Well, my going about the ship with a smile from ear to ear was the result. You could not have made me happier. The sweets were devoured by me and my friends approvingly. They were really delicious. "Casey's Gardens" undoubtedly must be a swell place for candy. I only wish I could have been as lucky as the school children you and the girls from Fort Meade visited. You surely must save a little act for me to view. I hope you will don your paraphernalia for me when I get home. I bet you were the most adorable elf on the planet. The Major must have stuffed his Santa outfit with a pillow. I don't picture an officer that high in rank as being naturally fat. I can imagine, however, your sister, Esther, at the USO with the Army personnel. You are right, it must have been a scream. I cannot imagine her conversing with any sergeants. She would surely get the best of them, being how she's the original Sarg!

Speaking of sisters, my sister's wedding will take place tomorrow, and I'm certain I won't be able to be present for the ceremony. I feel bad not being there. I hope you have a good time without me. It was swell of my sister to invite you. My family really likes you, Lu. Well, your old buddy Gene Tress must have changed, you never spoke of him like that before. I can't say that I'm completely unhappy that you're not writing him any longer.

By the way, the appropriate name for you is "Miss Lucky." It sounds as if you made a killing at the St. John's Christmas Bazaar. Let's see, you won a dollar at Bingo, a cake for a penny on the carnival wheel, and $10 from the raffle.

Well, I'm sorry to learn you lost your compact at Keith's Roof. I guess you had one too many beers! Just kidding!

I was reading a magazine the other day when I came upon an article which did much damage to my morale. The column was entitled "Bedeviled Baltimore" and contained a poem entitled "Beloved Baltimore, MD." It is as follows:
Baltimore Oh Baltimore, you moth-eaten town,
Your brick rowhouses should all be torn down.
Your winters are cold and your summers are hot,
The air is so foul with mildew and rot.
The land of bad colds and sore throat and flu,
Of stiffing, aching muscles and pneumonia too.
You're a blight on the landscape, the nation's eyesore,
Your people are dull-witted and gad, what a bore!
The home of white steps and bumpy thoroughfares,
With your rough-riding streetcars and ten-cent fares.
You live among filth and you don't mind the rats,
They thrive on that filth and the scariest of cats!
You don't speak English, you speak Baltimorese,
And the stench of the Bay certainly does not please.
You make us pay double for all you can sell
But after the war you can all go to hell.
And when you reach Hades and Satan greets you,
You'll feel right at home, he's from here too
Yes Baltimore, Oh Baltimore, it isn't all gravy,
To be planted on your doorstep by the Army or Navy.
The WMC and the draft Boards too,
Have frozen us here and we're stuck with you.
The worst of it is you think you are swell,
You think you are perfect and that gripes like hell.
You're dead and rotten, you think you're alive,
You think you're a place, instead you're a dive.
You're not worth this paper, you're not worth this ink
You can take it from us, Baltimore – YOU STINK!!
How about that? No doubt you can imagine the ribbing I received as a result of this publication. The only

defense I could render was that of the Baltimoreans who complained to the Baltimore Evening Sun. They replied thusly:

Stranger, Oh Stranger, you low down bum,
I would sure like to see the town from where you come from.

I certainly hope your rendezvous with the dentist proved satisfactory. Donny's screams weren't heard here. He must have survived the tonsillitis operation without pain.

Say hello to everyone for me, Darling.
Love, Monty

It was getting close to Christmas, but I couldn't shop for any presents for Lu or my family. It was such a weird feeling being stuck aboard ship during the Christmas season. My entertainment for the week, sadly, was getting a haircut.

On the positive side, I received a letter and a package of homemade chocolate chip cookies from Lu. No sailor could have received a better surprise. Unfortunately, when I opened the package, I suddenly became the most popular sailor. My bunkmates helped me devour the cookies in short order. Lu attended my sister, Edith's wedding, which sounded as if it was a swell affair. Lu's description of it actually depressed me, since I was not there to celebrate with her and my family. Apparently, I missed my father dancing and being romantic with my mother. I would have given anything to have seen that. I'm not sure if I ever saw Pop really letting go and enjoying himself. Missing the wedding was just another nail in the coffin for the worst Christmas I ever had. Of course, Lu reported on her activities at work and home. She never ceased to amaze me with the level of activity in her life. I was also not surprised to hear the news that

Gordon was finally assigned to a ship and out at sea. I fired off the following letter to Lu, trying my best to stay cheerful.

December 20, 1943
Greetings Gorgeous,
Your letter took fourteen days to arrive, but it was worth waiting for. I am certainly glad you liked my little sketch of "Louie and the Gob." More will follow, I assure you. Just to be in the States would please me, Hon. A phone conversation with you would be super. Let us both pray that it will be days we are to count and not months before I see you again.

Quite a sight I was with the hairy face. It was difficult to distinguish the difference between the werewolf and me. However, now it would be proper to call me Singing Sam, the Barbasol Man. In fact, I visited the barber yesterday. I made a mistake while there though. Proceeding with the operation on my head, the scissor man said, "Do you care to have any taken off the top, sailor?" Well, truthfully, my locks were not very long, but I murmured casually, "You may trim a little off the top." Yipe! His definition of the word trim and mine just did not coincide. I wouldn't care to exaggerate, but my ears appear as though they were lowered two or three inches. As for the hair on top, it was so well trimmed it now stands as straight as a forest of young spruce. Consoling me, my friends told me although I may be taken as Pro-Nazi, the haircut gives me the characteristic of being clean-cut and neat. I'm satisfied though, for there aren't any people here who are impressed by long, combed hair.

If Gordon's ship ever comes to this part of the world, I'll put every effort forth in order to see him. However, no corner saloons are available for afternoon chatting, as if we would chat if there were.

Precious, the experience you are obtaining is much to

my liking. What with taking care of children, house cleaning, and cooking, you are becoming very domestic and nubile. Be calm, Darling, I'm just kidding. Donny is certainly an independent fellow, isn't he? Tell him he better take care of you when he accompanies you to the theatre. It seems as though I better come home to do the escorting. Your case of the grippe was only "libble" I hope. In the pink again, I am waiting to hear. I can imagine how you felt missing Thanksgiving dinner, Darling. As for me, I must have eaten enough turkey for three people. The meal was the best I've had since entering the Navy, so I took advantage of it.

The wedding hasn't been described by the family as yet. You have been the first to supply the details. Writing Edith, I told her not to feel too bad about my not being at the affair, for she and I could make up for the mishap at my ceremony – if and when. I can just picture the reception from what you have related. Dad and his sister can be a panic when they get together. As for Daddy's turning Romeo though, I'm speechless. Also, dancing is news to me. Dad must really have had a swell time. My knowing he enjoyed himself so much makes me feel good.

Darling, work and you are on such good terms it is almost unbelievable. I can hardly understand. Please make it a point to give me the lowdown, Hon. Again, when I become "Joe Civilian" I want to find a job where I am contented. While going to school, I was actually glad and anxious to get up in the morning to get to school. I want to find a job that causes me to behave as such.

I have received the sweet array of cookies. They were swell, Hon. That saying about the best way to a man's heart is via his stomach, in my estimation, is absolutely correct. When I found your card that day, I had the greatest sensation to give you an enormous hug. I'm looking forward to the holiday season you and I spend together, Darling. Missing so many together, we have a great deal to make up for. Please say hello to MaryJane for me. Well, Lambie, my pen has grown tired, but my love for you is still aflame.

Missing you, Monty, Goodnight.

After a depressing Christmas and an anticlimactic New Year's Eve aboard the *U.S.S. Detroit,* I was more homesick than ever, not necessarily for my own family, but more to be home spending all my time with Lu. I would have given my right arm to have spent the holidays with my beloved Lucille.

We patrolled God knows where in the Pacific Ocean for weeks on end before finally going into port on some tiny island after the New Year. Fortunately, a small gift shop was in the town. It wasn't really a town, more like a couple of small buildings at a crossroad. Nevertheless, I was finally able to buy a belated Christmas present for Lu, a pin, and a pair of earrings, which I mailed immediately. Later, I wrote Lu another letter.

January 5, 1944

Darling,

I am now answering your fifteenth letter since being aboard ship. However, I haven't the letter anymore. Receiving a letter both from you and my mother, I read and put them in my portfolio of writing equipment. Well, some nefarious person grew very fond of my stationery, for the "crums" took the folder, letters, and everything. Along with his loot, this blankety-blank got my small black address book. Yes, I am not at all happy over this change of possession. Christmas is over so now it can be told. I assure you no one on board was missed. Dinner consisted mainly of turkey, ham, stuffing, and mashed potatoes covered with a blanket of delicious hot gravy.

All this was supported by soft rolls, celery, green peas, olives, and tomato juice. To end it all we had numerous desserts. Ice cream, fruit cocktail, and fruit cake were served. You are correct; we did have coffee finally.

Oh! By the way, I now know to what use the Red Cross donations are put. Along with the meal, some boxes were given out containing cigarettes, candy, and a small gift, usually a tobacco pouch or a handkerchief. In addition, each fellow was given a navy blue, hand-knit woolen sleeveless sweater. The particular sweater I received was knitted by a Red Cross lass in St. Paul, Minnesota.

Well, Hon, I guess you are aware of what month it is, but you must recall a special memory about it. That's right, it was two years ago that we first danced together at the Alcazar and began dating. The 3rd marked another year gone by happily together. Together may seem odd for I haven't been with you for any great length of time this past year, but you have been in my mind and my heart constantly. I wish I could be with you so we could celebrate, and I really mean celebrate.

For a moment, you frightened me by saying "were two swell years," but as I continued reading, life revived in my heart again and as you probably know I feel very much better. Honey, ease your pretty little head, I have gotten a haircut. I know you love my thick wavy hair. Oh, I have received another small promotion. Along with my other duties, I am now required to keep the corrections up to date in the various publications on the bridge. In the other direction though, I have been ousted from my bunk. Originally, it was not mine anyway. Now I am a real sailor, for I've been sleeping in a hammock for the last week. Actually, it is just as well as a bunk except for a bit of dripping water. Yes, it seems as though every time I climb into my little nest, condensation takes place resulting in dripping from the overhead (ceiling).

Well, Sweet, chow has just been sounded. Consequently, I'm about to fill that vacancy.
Loving you, Monty.
P.S. - You know that fellow everyone admires so much --- the bugler. Well, he really happens to be a friend of mine. Even the fellow who wakes the bugler is a chum of mine. Uncanny, isn't it? Reminds me of that Irving Berlin song, "Oh how I hate to get up in the morning," and something about murdering the *bugler!*

Life aboard the *U.S.S. Detroit* was really starting to get to me. I thought being on the ship was great for the first month or so, blue skies and big sunsets, but you never saw any land. From the ship to the horizon was twelve miles. That was the limit of your vision. You couldn't see anything but water from any direction. That was no fun after a few months. And the food started running down. In the beginning, we had great food. All kinds of steaks, mashed potatoes, and vegetables were served, but then after a while, it was just stew and soups.

However, on Wednesdays and Saturdays, the bakers made sugar doughnuts for breakfast. Man, they were so good, but they also had beans for breakfast. Whoever heard of beans and sugar doughnuts for breakfast? What a horrible combination. I didn't like beans at all so I would always trade my beans for a sugar doughnut. They served two doughnuts to each sailor. I always took the beans because I always ran across somebody who would trade his doughnut for a pile of beans.

The only thing keeping me sane aboard the ship was my correspondence with Lu. Yet another letter was written.

January 16, 1944
Hello Hon,
Actually, this letter is the twentieth, but your

seventeenth one arrived without its companion, number sixteen, so I am waiting for the sixteenth letter to come in order to answer it with my twenty-first. Complicated, isn't it? You did write number sixteen, did you not? I hope!

I am glad you are keeping calm, for this war is keeping me calm. Honey, I admit my hair was short, but it doesn't even compare to its condition that day in Bainbridge. Since I wrote that letter, my hair has grown long again. The truth of the matter is that I need a haircut again. About our rapid writing system, I will say nothing. I might speak too soon. Just tell Esther she has my sympathy about her job at the Crown. I'm sorry it was not all that it was cracked up to be. I can imagine that working in a factory making bottle caps is not very exciting. What you said about "first place in line" is much more than satisfactory. I could not be happier than to be your number one in line. You had better obtain more ice for the stowage of those hugs, they are multiplying.

I wish the censor would permit my informing you of our sunrise. About conditions here, a book could be written. Honestly, your mornings would appear sick in comparison. You are certainly the soothsayer; I was wondering what you had done New Year's Eve. I would like to have seen your formal attire. I really must be truthful; I did not quite hear your voice wishing me a Happy New Year at twelve, but thanks anyhow. Also, I hit the sack early on the Eve so arising early, I wished yours bright and early on the first. What's this about Army men? Let's see if we can't have Navy fellows the next time. I assure you the gobs won't prove to be perfect bores. Just joking Hon, doggies are all right, but Marines are absolutely "verboten."

By the way, I neglected to tell you. Every time some

fellow does some task badly, walks aft in a forward passageway, or anything which is wrong, the common saying to him is "gwan you Marine." Also, if one rushes to the washroom to give himself a lick and a promise, he always states that he is off to take a Marine bath. How about that? I imagine Tress would enjoy hearing that. Darling, no, no, no, he wouldn't, and it did not make me feel bad telling me about how much you would like to see me. About the Congressman from our Baltimore District you met, you may pass on to him what sailors think of Marines.

To console you, I am saving my money like a miser so that I'll be able to fly home if and when I see the shores of California again. Judging from your New Year's Eve Charles Club incident drinking champagne and getting kissed at midnight from your date, I assume my little baby is getting to be a big girl now. Yes, that was a joke --- corn. Seriously though, I hope you will send me the picture that night we danced together at the Alcazar on my last leave. Heaven was surely crowded, for I was there too.

A few days ago, I heard the song, "Have you met Olivia, solid chick Olivia." Well, if you have forgotten the connection, I'll refresh your memory. We sang that ditty while we were on the straw ride to Ocean City. Remember? The song brought back all those beautiful memories of a grand time. That is, we did have a swell time after you and I were straightened out. Ocean City has not seen the last of us, I hope. Well, Darling, that's all from this end for a while, 'cepting I miss you more each day.

Love, Monty

P.S. - I have just finished reading a book, a hilarious book. I have finished reading it, but every so often, just anywhere, I'll burst into laughter thinking about it!

My thoughts were consumed with the lovely girl from Baltimore Maryland, but it was with a sense of dread waiting for Lu's next letter. I hadn't received a letter from her in three weeks. During this period of time, one of my bunkmates received a "Dear John" letter from his fiancée. He was devastated. He evidently had proposed to her the previous summer before shipping out. She wrote him that she had met someone else and that they were through. His nightmare had been my greatest fear all along - a "Dear Monty" letter. Lu already knew loads of other guys and dated them frequently. She could have been falling for one of them. After all, the adage "out of sight, out of mind" fit the bill perfectly for poor old me. She might have already been dating her true love and dumped me for him. I was just waiting for the other shoe to drop, so to speak.

Coincidently, Margaret had written that week to tell me Milton had proposed to her while he was on leave from the Army.

When a letter from Lu finally arrived, I was a nervous wreck opening it. I was convinced she had gotten engaged to someone else. Thankfully, she gave no indication in her letter that it was over between us. In fact, it was a typical letter from Lu, describing her life back home and keeping me abreast of the news about family and friends. I wrote her as if everything was fine. I never divulged to her my deep-seated fears and insecurities.

January 21, 1944
Lu Darling,
The U.S. Mail must have employed that pony express system again for your sixteenth message rode that 26-day passage. It must have been the overland route through El Paso, Texas. Seriously though, I'm glad our numerical

setup is straightened again. John was surely lucky Christmas. Milton was just as fortunate for he received a 48-hour liberty which proved satisfactory. He and Margaret are now engaged. It pleases me to know you liked the pin and earrings, but I only wish I could have presented them. Santa Claus did not miss Donny in the least. However, in one way, it was good that I was not home for Christmas. I could just see Donny crying for his pool table and my not giving it to him. If the table is still in one piece when I see you again, you and I will have a contest. We may allow Donny to play if he's good. What say?

I remember your singing in the choir last year; it was grand. Do you recall my meeting your dad and you as you were turning the corner at Chase and Valley Streets? Vividly, I can recollect your walking arm in arm with your father. I crossed the street to meet you. Remember? You may be a teetotaler, Darling, but I could easily blackmail you. At a particular party while I was on leave, a very lovely young lady of whom I am closely acquainted passed her teetotaler stage. Something tells me I am a bad influence. Honey, of the Flanagan-Culpepper duet, you are still the star. My singing is strictly reserved for park nights on the bridge without an audience. Honestly, missing those commando tactics in the Flanagan manor grieved me mercilessly. Donny, Charlie, and I will open a second front on my return. Yum! Yum! I surely liked that paragraph. I can't say I heard the noise of that Flanagan Christmas day battle, but I can surely visualize the charges and retreats of John, Charlie, Don, and your father.

I shall describe my surroundings at present. I am no longer sleeping in a hammock but am back in my bunk. The sailor whose bunk they said was his got transferred so I got my bunk back. Feeling like a bird, I am perched on the top bunk of a layer of three. Measuring the distance between my head and the overhead (ceiling), I have found it to be exactly four inches. At the level of my nose runs three 4-inch diameter steam pipes on which now is situated a can of peanuts, yours and Mom's letters, cigarettes, ashtray (on top of the peanut can), and someone's shoes. To my right, just barely three-fourths of an inch is a friend of mine "Buck." I think I told you about Buck before. He is a Californian whose first name is Elwin, but we both prefer "Buck" which was pierced from his last name, Buchholz. He was married the last time the ship was in the States. I keep telling him he has been actually only married for six days, but he claims it has been six months. His reply is that I haven't been going with you the last year then, since we have only been together 18 short days. Naturally, I must discontinue my antagonizing from thereon. Well, Precious, I could rattle on for hours, but I must save some for the next time.

Until then, Love, Monty

After months on the ship, the routine became grossly monotonous for me. My only real distraction was receiving letters from Lu and writing back to her. My daily schedule, however, was pretty much the same day in and day out. Thankfully, the Navy was always soliciting for sailors for something, assignment to a PT boat or aboard a submarine, for example, and each day they would advertise on the ship's bulletin board. I applied for many of these things, anything to get off the ship, which I had grown to loathe. I was bored mostly and wanted desperately to do something different, anything!

The Navy also advertised for Navy pilots, listing all the necessary requirements, which I didn't even bother to read. I applied to be a pilot. Another fellow and I put in for it together, but he never told me, or maybe he had not read the requirements either, that we would be expected to take a battery of tests. The Navy gave us no advance warning about when these tests were to be given. We never saw anything on the bulletin board about it. At any rate, I had no idea the Navy would require me to take tests to be a pilot. Honestly, I just applied for anything that might get me off the ship. However, I never put in for the vacancies on submarines or PT boats. I was tired of being at sea and I wanted at the very least to get back to the mainland, preferably to the east coast, to be close to home and Lucille.

I was very fortunate though when I did get called in to take the tests to become a pilot some months later. Ordinarily, my appearance was less than what it could be. I rarely shaved or got a haircut. Apparently, when out at sea during wartime, the United States Navy didn't enforce strict discipline regarding a sailor's appearance, at least on the *U.S.S. Detroit*. Many sailors often didn't adhere to regulations and would get away with minor infractions for the most part. I saw some sailors who were actually wearing red sweaters, and they were never put on report by the officers, to my knowledge. They let their hair grow and they didn't always shave. I was no different, but I just happened to wake up this one particular morning feeling very uncomfortable, so first off, I shaved. Then I went down to get my haircut. I sat on a bucket and paid the barber a quarter, the best quarter I ever spent, it turned out. I got all cleaned up, put on a pressed uniform, and then by dumb luck, I heard my name called over the public address system on the ship to report immediately to the wardroom. I had no idea why. I had completely forgotten about applying to be a Navy pilot.

When I arrived at the wardroom, I looked sharp. The officers there administered me an oral examination as part of the tests required. They asked me a lot of things I had learned in high school, and they were amazed I knew the answers. The tests involved a lot of stuff concerning descriptive and analytical geometry, trigonometry, and even calculus. I told them I had attended the Baltimore Polytechnic Institute which was strictly a technical engineering high school. They were impressed by that, plus it just so happened that I got all spiffed up that day and looked like every sailor should have looked but did not. The officers loved my appearance, even if it was completely serendipitous on my part.

The officers were not only very impressed by my clean, sharp appearance, but more so, I was sure, by my vast knowledge of mathematics. I had, as you might recall, never missed an answer on any test in my high school geometry class, despite my bullshit ninety-nine percent final grade. I wished my teacher had been there in the wardroom that day to witness me answering one hundred percent of the geometry questions correctly. Sure, nobody was perfect, I got it, but sometimes things went oh so perfectly. In the words of the great Jackie Gleason, "How sweet it is!" That was a perfect day for me on the ship, plus I now had the knowledge I was finally getting off the ship, although it was not official yet. A month or so later, I finally received my United States Air Force Cadet appointment from the Navy to become a pilot. They only selected two guys from the Seventh Fleet, me and another sailor, but not the fellow from my ship with whom I applied.

It took a couple of more months for me to receive my transfer orders from the time I took the oral test. By that time, I had been on the ship for more than six months. I was ready to go. I had been able to break up the tedium to some extent. I wrote letters to Lu, my family, and my friends, of course. I also found time to read, and I even found a guy to play chess with, but you had to find these things to offset the boredom. In the beginning, it was tough being on the ship, but I survived. I just knew I needed to do something different, and this was my chance. The ultimate goal was to fly for the United States Navy. I found the prospect of that very satisfying and fulfilling. I felt a real sense of pride and patriotism. I knew Lu would be proud of me, too. She constantly talked about her brother, John, and how well he was doing in the Navy. He had already been promoted to an Aviation Ordnanceman Petty Officer First Class, in charge of ensuring planes were loaded with their payload prior to take-off. He was transferred in early 1944 and assigned to a brand-new aircraft carrier, the *U.S.S. Franklin*.

A couple of months after I passed the pilot's test, another ship happened to hit us. We were loading fuel while in port in the Aleutian Islands from a Russian tanker that tore off one of our gun turrets. The *U.S.S. Detroit* was subsequently required to sail into port at Bremerton, Washington, for repairs. When we got back to port in Washington, they were going to transfer me off the ship to report to San Diego before going to Philadelphia to attend Villanova University. In peacetime, you needed two years of college to be a pilot. They waived this requirement when the war broke out, however, by the time I qualified, they had plenty of pilots, so they reinstituted the college requirement. I was confident in my academic abilities, and I had no qualms about attending college again. Before joining the service, my heart hadn't really been in it when I was at the University of Maryland, but now I had more purpose in attending college with the United States Navy. I was off to Villanova to start my education, but I had to report to San Diego first, I thought.

I asked my Chief Petty Officer, Jules Yoman, before we docked in Bremerton, "Do I have to be in San Diego three days after we dock?"

"No, not necessarily," Chief Yoman said.

"I live in Baltimore, you know," I said. "I was hoping to try to get home before reporting to Villanova."

"Oh, you have to go all the way across the country and back," he said. "I'll just change your orders, so you'll have to report to Bainbridge, Maryland instead of San Diego."

"Thank you, Chief," I said. "You're the tops."

"Think nothing of it, Culpepper," he said. "It just makes more sense. Good luck to you, Seaman. I hope you get some time at home." Although I would never see the Chief again, I would always remember this favor and what a good fellow he was.

Chapter Nine

Madeline Bennett

I caught a train out of Bremerton, Washington, but it ended up taking me six days to get across country by train and reporting to Bainbridge. When I arrived, it didn't appear that I would be getting leave after all before reporting to Villanova. It was frustrating, since I was in such close proximity to Baltimore. I could have taken a train to get home from Bainbridge in less than a couple of hours. It was hectic reporting in at Bainbridge. I didn't even have enough time to write Lu for another two days.

February 22, 1944
Lu Darling,
I have been here exactly two days. The first night I arrived at 11:15, just 45 minutes before the deadline. As you might know, my seabag hadn't arrived, so I was without a sack. There were plenty of bunks, but mattresses were scarce. The fellow in charge told me to sleep on the springs, for I was to be awakened at 6:00 a.m. Taking his advice, I put my collar up using my hat as a pillow and went to sleep. At 3:30 a.m., I woke up shaking all over with frost on my toes. There was not any heat in the barracks. The washroom had wooden benches and radiators with steam, so I curled around a radiator on a bench to sleep for the rest of the night. Last night's conditions improved though. Mattresses had been given to everyone. Blankets were rare so only a few were fortunate. No, I was unlucky. Missing a blanket, I slept between the mattresses with my peacoat as an added protection to the cold. I slept like a lamb, for I did not wake up until 7 a.m. Yes, I missed breakfast. Tonight will be even better, for my seabag arrived bringing my

blankets.

Well, Lu, Gorgeous, no liberty is being granted so I won't be getting home just yet. I have been assigned to Villanova though, which is situated just outside Philadelphia. I surely enjoy going to Pennsylvania, for I'll be but just a few steps from you, Precious. Classes are to convene on March 1st. These fellows will be leaving every day according to how far they are to travel. On account of this liberty not being given, the officers will call upon a fellow to be transferred at any time. Honey, I miss you already. Well, Baby-duck, we can look forward to a summer together. I can just picture my meeting you in Ocean City for a weekend. I think I'll be here for a week or so. I'll be waiting to hear from you.

Loving you, Monty

P.S. - Give my regards to Mr. and Mrs. Flanagan, Ed and Nancy, Esther and Don, Charlie, and Aunt Nan and Uncle Tom.

I was granted no leave to go home and was deeply disappointed. I was required to report directly to Villanova University. Upon my arrival there, I was kept extremely busy. I wrote Lu that I had arrived.

March 5, 1944
Lu Darling,
Your letter has not arrived as yet, but that isn't why I haven't written. Getting settled, obtaining books, and taking examinations have kept me quite busy. The arrangement here really pleases me. Two fellows are assigned to a room that is complete with desks, beds, closets, lamps, and other necessities. It surely is homey living in a room like this. My roommate's a grand fellow who was previously a First-Class Signalman. However, he was reduced, as I was, to the rate of Apprentice Seaman. We get along fine. By the way, this is an all-boys

school. Strangely enough, remember our comparison of schools, this is a Catholic college with priests doing all the teaching.

School commences at 8:30 a.m. and ceases at 5 p.m. From 8 p.m. to 10 p.m., there is a compulsory study period. Every weekend except this one a student is entitled to liberty, providing his studies are up to par. However, liberty is limited to a fifty-mile radius of Villanova. Baltimore is over a hundred miles away, but a special pass can be obtained once a month. We have a PAS station phone down the hall so I will be calling you quite a bit. I miss you, Hon. Tell me the time you finish supper, so I'll know when to call. Incidentally, the number here is BRYN MAWR 9149, in case.

While in Bainbridge, I had nothing whatsoever to do for nine days. I just lay around reading, tearing my hair out, and missing you terribly. I read "A Tree Grows in Brooklyn" knowing you read it. I just kept picturing your reading certain parts. I could see you at times, and then again, I was wondering what you were thinking here and there.

Darling, I love you. Lu, I'll call you Friday. It has been snowing the last few days. The place looks swell. Snow is everywhere making everything look so bright and clean. Well, Sweetness, I'll knock off for now. Waiting to hear from you,

Love, Monty

P.S. - Give my regards to the family. This is my last scrap of Chicago writing paper (that the dirty thief missed). To be exact, it is my last scrap of any kind of writing paper. Be (writing) seeing you on the new stationery.

My time at Villanova was extremely busy with class and studying. I stopped writing Lu as a result, but I began calling her routinely every weekend since I couldn't get leave for the entire weekend. The curfew on campus for all sailors was at midnight each night, including weekends. It was impossible to catch a train to Baltimore in the morning and be back by midnight. Even if I tried, the first train left at ten-forty-five from Philadelphia on Saturday mornings. It took almost two hours and then the last train out of Baltimore was at seven at night. I would only have had a few hours in the afternoon to spend with Lu. I could not very well go home and not visit my parents and sisters, too. It would have been far too hectic of a day. I told Lu I hoped I would get a ten-day pass after the three-month semester.

I ended up getting that leave in late May. Lu and I spent nearly every day together. I was so much in love with her, and we both knew that we would get married after the war was over, although we never really spoke of it. Our feelings for each other were so strong that it was an unspoken understanding. When I returned to Villanova University in June for the beginning of the summer semester, it was with a great deal of melancholy. I would not get leave again for almost another three months. I was doing extremely well at school since I had no distractions. I really put my nose to the grindstone as far as my academics were concerned. I was quite competitive, too. I always enjoyed trying to get the top grade in the class or at least trying to get close. My military academic career was rolling right along. I finished the summer semester and went home to see Lu for another ten days before returning to Philadelphia. I finished my third semester at Villanova in late October 1944, but I received no leave after my final semester.

After completing my studies at Villanova University, the Navy sent me directly to Brown University in Providence, Rhode Island, to continue my education. I really had to pinch myself. I never would have imagined attending such a prestigious school as Brown. In my wildest dreams, who would have thought that a poor kid from Baltimore like myself would be attending an Ivy League school? This was incredible to me. I continued calling Lu every week. She was disappointed that I couldn't come home to see her, as was I, but we still maintained constant communication. Our relationship was strong, even though Lu continued to date other servicemen. I was beyond thrilled upon my arrival at Brown. I enjoyed my time at Villanova University very much, however, it didn't compare to Brown. Villanova was a beautiful campus, about ten or twelve miles from the middle of Philadelphia, although I didn't care for the city of Philadelphia. I preferred my hometown of Baltimore. Too bad the Navy didn't have their V-12 Navy College Training Program at Johns Hopkins or the University of Maryland.

The V-12 Navy training normally concluded with sailors becoming commissioned officers at the end of four years of college, but my pilot training required only two years of college. They had these mini-semesters which were less than three months long, so it took three mini-semesters to complete a year of college. I completed a year at Villanova and now I had to complete a second year at Brown before I could become a pilot. I was told that 125,000 sailors were attending classes and lectures at well over a hundred colleges and universities across the country. Most of these sailors never got their commissions to become officers or even completed their training to become pilots due to the war ending. Some even returned after the war ended to earn their degrees from the colleges where they were previously stationed. Even the Army had its own program to produce officers, which had 200,000 soldiers studying at colleges all over the country.

I fell in love with Brown University, maybe because it was one of the first universities founded in the United States, but also because it had the oldest engineering program of any university in the Ivy League. Villanova was a good school, but it had no engineering program. Brown was more suited to my strengths. With my aptitude for mathematics, I was destined to become an engineer, and Brown University was the place to accomplish this. The campus was a beautiful place with most of its buildings dating back to the nineteenth century. It was located on the east side of the city of Providence. Providence was more like a large town than a city. It was nothing like Baltimore, even though it was the most populous city in Rhode Island. It was much quainter than Baltimore and far less busy.

Providence was also much older than Baltimore City. It was founded in 1636. The city was very modern with major manufacturers and large companies based in or near Providence, making it one of the richest cities in America. Some of the companies included Brown & Sharpe, which made tools; Babcock & Wilson, which manufactured steam boilers; the Grinnell Corporation, which made gas mains; the Gorham Manufacturing Company, which made sterling and silver-plate; the Nicholson File Company, and the famous Fruit of the Loom clothing company. I loved my hometown, but Providence was a much prettier town than Baltimore, and the Brown University campus bowled me over with its beauty, old buildings, long history, and prestige.

I began going out more on weekends to parties and dances. The engineering courses I was taking were coming much easier to me than my classes had at Villanova which were more along the lines of general studies, encompassing history, literature, and English, all of which required a lot more studying and writing. My nights and weekends at Villanova occupied my time with studying and completing term papers to keep up with the classes. My courses at Brown University largely involved mathematics and engineering, which came so naturally to me that studying was kept at a minimum. I had so much more free time that I suddenly became a social animal, hanging out with the other sailors, and attending parties and USO dances. I danced with a lot of girls while at Brown, more so than any other place I had been. I enjoyed myself immensely, but none of the girls attracted me in any romantic way, at least initially.

I became a bit depressed when I found out in December none of the sailors would be given leave over the Christmas break. We only had a couple of days off from school. Christmas was on Monday, and we had to be back in class on Wednesday. The schedule was the same the following week for New Year's Day. All the sailors were off from school, but we were restricted to campus and the city of Providence. I would have had plenty of time to take a train to Baltimore and get back in time when classes resumed, but the fellas from the west coast would never have made it there and back in time. I guess the Navy figured it was not fair to give the east coast guys leave and not the west coast guys, so nobody got it. The same thing happened every time a new semester started. We usually had a few days off between semesters, but leave was restricted to Providence. It was a shame because I would have had plenty of time to get to Baltimore and back.

While at Brown University, I met a girl who I dated for several months. She was the daughter of one of my professors. Her name was Madeline Bennett. Professor Bennett was a brilliant professor who seemed to be a really good guy. He taught calculus and an engineering class. Madeline was his only daughter. I met her through one of my friends from class, Fred Baker. Fred's girlfriend, Shirley, had a small party one Saturday night at her apartment in Providence. Fred approached me after class on Friday, December 15th. I remembered the exact date because Christmas was on a Monday, ten days later. Fred ran up to me very anxiously following our last class, which happened to be Calculus with Professor Bennett.

"Hey Monty," he said. "What are you doing tomorrow night?"

"Nothing," I responded.

"Well," he said. "You've met my girlfriend, Shirley, right?"

"Yes," I replied. "A few times, she's a nice gal."

"Shirley's having what you might call a cocktail party tomorrow night," he continued. "It's at her apartment in town. I asked Charlie down the hall from me in the dorm to come and he's bringing a girl. The trouble is, Shirley asked a girlfriend to come. I asked Frank from class to come, too, and he said he'd come with a date. Now I know you have a girlfriend back home and all, but I was hoping you'd come so her girlfriend isn't the odd man out, you know what I mean? It's not like a date or anything. It's just so we'll have four on four. How about it?"

"Sure, I'll come," I said. "What time and where?"

"It's at seven tomorrow night," he said, looking relieved. "Don't worry, I'll meet you at your dorm tomorrow at six-forty and we'll go together. Shirley's apartment is within walking distance. Don't eat dinner. Shirley's fixing a bunch of hors d'oeuvres. You'll love her chip and dip and her Italian meatballs. Those meatballs are to die for."

"Okay, sounds like a date, Fred," I stated. "I'll be there with bells on, and I'll consider it my dinner."

Fred came by the next night promptly at six-forty. I was dressed in my navy blue Navy dress uniform, as was Fred. We looked very smart. We arrived at Shirley's apartment at about five until seven. Shirley, an attractive brunette wearing an apron over a lavender dress, answered the door. She was mixing something up in a bowl with a large spoon when the door opened.

"Hi Fred," she said enthusiastically as she kissed him. "Come on in and make yourselves at home." Charlie and Frank were already there sitting on the couch with their dates. Shirley made her way back into the kitchen.

"Hey Charlie, hey Frank," Fred said as we entered the living room.

"Hello, fellas," I said.

"Hello, Fred, hello, Monty," Charlie said.

"Hello gents," Frank said. "Let me introduce you to my date, Miss Marlene Huber. "Marlene, these are my classmates, Swabby Fred Baker, you've met, and Swabby First Class Montgomery Culpepper."

"Call me Monty," I responded. "Pleased to meet you, Marlene."

"Monty, this is my date, Norma," Charlie said. "Fred, you know Norma."

"Nice meeting you, Norma," I said.

"Hey Monty," Fred said. "How about a beer?"

"Sounds fine," I shot back.

Fred disappeared into the kitchen. I stood there awkwardly with the two couples in the living room. They sat back down on the couch and continued whatever chit-chat we interrupted. The radio was on softly with some big band music playing. Charlie and Frank were yucking it up with their dates reminiscing about their time together the previous weekend, dancing at the Biltmore Hotel ballroom in downtown Providence.

"Do you like dancing?" Marlene asked me, politely

trying to include me in the conversation.

"Yes," I said. "I've been known to cut a rug or two in my day." Just then, thankfully, Fred and Shirley and an attractive girl with dirty blonde hair emerged from the kitchen with plates of food and drinks. Fred handed me a bottle of beer.

"Thanks," I said.

"Monty," Fred said. "This is Madeline Bennett, your date for the evening."

"Hello, Madeline," I said. "The pleasure is all mine."

"Hello, Monty," Madeline said. "Nice to meet you."

"Did I not tell you he was a handsome devil?" Fred asked.

"He is at that," Madeline responded. "I love those blue eyes!"

"Stop it before I start blushing," I said. "Let's sit down, Madeline."

We all started eating and drinking and before long, I was seated on the floor, eating meatballs at the edge of Madeline's seat, finishing off my third bottle of beer.

"So, what do you do, Madeline?" I asked, trying to make small talk.

"I'm finishing up my first semester here at Brown," she said.

"You're kidding," I retorted.

"No, I'm not," Madeline said. "Does that surprise you?"

"Not at all," I said. "I mean, Fred said your father was Professor Bennett."

"Don't you approve of girls going to college?" Madeline asked.

"I approve whole-heartedly," I replied ardently. "It's just that where I'm from, not many girls go to college."

"Where are you from?" she inquired. "Don't they believe girls should attend college where you're from?"

"I'm from Baltimore," I nervously answered. "It's not a matter of approving or disapproving; I just don't know any girls from my neighborhood who went to college. For that matter, I don't know any fellas who went until the war came along. I'm the first person in my family, male or female, ever to attend college. I think it's swell you're going to Brown."

"Well, thank you, Monty," she said. "I was afraid I might be dealing with a Neanderthal man there for a minute."

"Oh, no," I said. "I'm a firm believer in education and progress."

"That's good to hear," she said. "You certainly don't look like a Neanderthal man. I'd say you're more along the lines of a Dana Andrews."

"Now c'mon, let's not go there again," I said laughing.

Madeline was probably the first girl, other than Lucille, I ever talked to at length who did not get on my nerves. Madeline was very articulate, and she had brains, in spades. She was not quite as adorable as Lu, but she was attractive, taller than Lu, and well built. She was terribly engaging, and I enjoyed her company very much that evening. I did not really expect that we would be going out again together. I thanked her for a lovely evening and went on my way. Later that week after class, Fred approached me and asked me if I wanted to go to the Biltmore Hotel Friday night with the same four couples to go dancing. Of course, I said sure. Madeline and I had a terrific time dancing. We were not quite the perfect fit on the dance floor as Lu and I were, but we had not stepped on each other's feet either. The slow dances together were very nice. I felt a bit romantic with Madeline cheek to cheek with her. At the end of the night, Shirley suggested that everybody stop over at her apartment for a nightcap. It was on the way back to our dormitories anyway and it was within walking distance, so I figured why not. Madeline and I ended up seated on the floor, leaning against the living room sofa. After a few sips of my beer and before I knew it, Madeline and I were necking full throttle.

I had danced with a lot of girls, and I had kissed a few goodnight since going with Lu, but this was the first girl where we were both getting carried away. I liked Madeline and I could sure tell she liked me too. All four couples were smooching in various parts of Shirley's apartment early into Saturday morning. It was approaching one in the morning, and we were an hour past the midnight curfew. When we realized the time, we made our quick goodbyes. We would have to be very careful not to get caught sneaking back into our dormitory.

Upon leaving, Madeline asked me, "What are you doing for Christmas?"

"Not a thing," I answered. "Except going to dinner at the cafeteria. The Navy's preparing a special Christmas dinner with all the fixings, since they're not giving us leave to go home. We have to be back in class two days after Christmas."

"Yes, I know," Madeline said. "I'm a student too, remember? Dad must be back in class, too. Why don't you come to my house for Christmas dinner? It's just me and my mother and father."

"Are you sure it's all right?" I responded. "I don't want to intrude."

"My parents would be happy to have you," she said. "And I would be most grateful if you came."

"If you think it's not an imposition, then I'd be glad to come," I said.

"Dinner's at two," she said.

"Where do you live?" I asked.

"Oh, it's right off campus," she said. "16 University Parkway. It's an old Victorian home. Get there a little early."

"All right, Madeline, I will," I said. "I had a very nice time this evening. Why don't I just walk you home and you can show me where you live?"

"That would be fine," she responded. "It's only a couple blocks from here."

Madeline and I walked home arm and arm. I couldn't help but feel guilty like I was cheating on Lu. But then, on the other hand, I felt as though I was getting even a bit. Lu had other boyfriends besides me. I always believed that I was the most important one to her, but the fact remained that she had other relationships and I had no idea how emotionally involved she might have been with those other fellas. I was by no means emotionally involved with Madeline, but I enjoyed her company, and she was easy on the eyes. Besides, I was lonely for female companionship. It was true that all I ever did was think about Lu, but I knew I wouldn't see her again probably until summer. I kissed Madeline goodnight, despite my guilty conscience, and told her I would see her on Christmas. I then walked two or three blocks more and snuck into my dormitory unnoticed.

I continued dating Madeline during my tenure at Brown, but my heart still belonged to Lucille. I rarely went out with Madeline alone. We occasionally went to the movies, but for the most part, we usually went dancing with Fred and Shirley, and Frank and Marlene. Charlie would sometimes join the group if he had a date. Charlie never dated any one girl for very long. His motto was 'variety is the spice of life'. Another reason I didn't want to get too serious with Madeline, besides my enduring love for Lu, was because I knew I would be completing my two years of college by summer. The

Navy had plans for me to attend flight school.

The events in the spring of 1945 indicated that Germany would be defeated. The Allies were closing in on Hitler in Berlin, the Americans and British from the west, and the Russian Army from the east. Hitler finally killed himself in his Berlin bunker on April 30, 1945. On May 7, 1945, the Allies accepted Nazi Germany's unconditional surrender of its armed forces. The following day was celebrated across America and around the world as Victory in Europe or V.E. Day. It was on a Tuesday, and I had class. Of course, all the sailors attending Brown were ecstatic about the news, but we didn't really ever expect to be fighting the Nazis. The United States Navy was playing a major role in the Pacific in defeating the Japs. The majority of sailors I knew at school had seen action in the Pacific and we all expected to be going back there. We all also knew that although the Nazis were viewed as pure evil, their armies tended to surrender in great numbers when defeated. The Japanese, on the other hand, fought fanatically in every battle and by most accounts, to nearly the last man.

General Douglas MacArthur returned to the Philippines in October 1944, but the Japanese kept fighting there until the war ended. Then, the United States attacked Iwo Jima in February 1945 with a force of 70,000, but at a cost of 7,000 dead Marines and another 20,000 wounded after five weeks of some of the bloodiest fighting of the war. Reports indicated that only about 200 Jap soldiers survived out of the 21,000 who were occupying the island.

On April 1, 1945, Easter Sunday, the Battle of Okinawa began and surpassed Iwo Jima as the bloodiest battle in the Pacific, lasting more than three months. More than 180,000 United States Army and Marine Corps troops carried out the largest amphibian assault in the Pacific to date on an island occupied by an estimated 130,000 Japanese soldiers. This battle was the first time that the Japanese soldiers were defending on their own soil. Only 7,000 Japanese troops eventually surrendered. The United States military lost 12,500 men in the long and ferocious battle for the island and more than 35,000 were wounded. The Navy's Fifth Fleet had thirty-six sunken ships during the battle and 368 damaged ships from more than 2,000 Japanese kamikaze attacks. Almost 10,000 United States sailors were killed, drowned, or wounded in the battle for Okinawa.

Of significance to me personally was the fact that the Navy lost 763 planes during the three-month blood bath on Okinawa. Although this did not deter me from my goal of becoming a pilot, it gave me pause. If the United States continued fighting north toward the Japanese mainland, there was no telling how many American troops would be needed to defeat Japan. The general consensus among my sailor friends at Brown, as well as the opinions of my civilian friends and family, was that the Japs would fight to the bitter end before surrendering. The war against Japan was in no way, shape, or form winding down. Most everyone, including myself, believed we would win eventually, but how long would it take and at what cost?

In June, I left Brown University after completing my third mini-semester. I had gone out with Madeline and the gang the weekend before leaving. We spent our typical night out dancing and then going back to Shirley's apartment for drinks. Madeline and I had a short conversation about our relationship, and she was surprisingly very understanding about my ambivalence. She might have been just trying to save face.

"Madeline," I said. "I want you to know that I've had a swell time with you the last six months. It's been grand.

I'll miss you."

"I'll miss you, too," Madeline responded. "I've grown very fond of you. I know my parents will miss seeing you. My father always spoke very highly of you."

"Tell them goodbye for me, will you?" I asked. "I only have a day after final exams to get my things together and head to Chapel Hill for the start of my pilot training. I don't even get leave to go home. I have to take the train straight to North Carolina. It stinks that the train actually stops in Baltimore, and I can't even get off to visit my family. It's been ages since I've been home."

"That's too bad," she said. "I hope you get back to Rhode Island someday."

"Maybe after the war," I responded. "I'd sure like to finish at Brown and get my degree."

"I'll be here," Madeline said. "I'm going to miss you terribly, Monty. I haven't even looked at another man since we've been going out."

"I like you a lot, Madeline," I said. "I can't get serious though. I don't know where I might be after I become a pilot in the fall. I'm sure I'll be sent back to the Pacific."

"Let's stay in touch, shall we?" Madeline asked.

"Sure," I answered. "I'll let you know my address at Chapel Hill."

I walked Madeline home for the last time. We kissed and departed. I never saw her again. I had intended to write her, but it was an eventful summer and I never got around to it.

Chapter Ten

Where's All My Stuff?

I arrived at the University of North Carolina campus a week and a half later. I called my mother and Lu from Brown prior to my departure explaining to them both where I was going. After settling in my dormitory and starting flight school, I found that I had little free time. During the last week of July, the Navy flew me and my classmates to upstate New York for our first actual in-flight training with an instructor. The Navy had a slew of Piper Cubs at the base in New York. We stayed there for two weeks, where we received eighty hours of flight training. I was quite confident in my abilities to take off and land. We did not get any combat flight maneuver training or anything like that. It was just the basics. We were not instrument-trained and were not ready by any means to fly Navy combat fighters or other Navy planes, but it was a great experience, and I took to it like riding a bicycle. It came very easy to me, and I was extremely confident in my ability to fly a plane.

When we went back to Chapel Hill to continue our classroom training, it was Monday, August 6, 1945. After classes ended for the day, we heard the news over the radio that evening regarding the atomic bomb dropped on Hiroshima, Japan. We didn't understand the vast destruction it had caused, nor could we comprehend it. We listened to President Harry S. Truman on the radio the next day calling for Japan's surrender, warning them to "expect a rain of ruin from the air, the like of which has never been seen on this earth." The reaction amongst ourselves was that the war might end before we finished our pilot training. Three days later, another atomic bomb was dropped on Nagasaki, Japan, obliterating yet another Japanese city and killing tens of thousands more people in an instant. We continued with our pilot training, but we knew the war was over.

On August 15, 1945, after the Soviet Union entered the war against Japan, Emperor Hirohito announced the surrender of Japan. I never really understood why the Japs didn't surrender immediately after the first atomic bomb. It took them almost another week after the second bomb was dropped to accept surrender. Talk about fanatical. I always thought they should have dropped the bomb on top of Mount Fuji, near Tokyo. I believed that the Japanese leaders would have surrendered in two seconds had they seen the highest mountain in Japan leveled to rubble, plus, countless innocent lives would have been saved. At any rate, I believed President Truman made the right decision. An invasion of Japan and the cost of American lives, as well as Japanese, would have been even more catastrophic. It was estimated that an attack on the Japanese mainland might have cost a quarter of a million American deaths with a total of one million casualties, dragging the war on to the end of 1946 or beyond.

Of course, I was happy the war was over, and I could go home, but part of me was disappointed at not completing my pilot training. I was honorably discharged from the United States Navy on August 31, 1945, but I enlisted in the United States Marine Corps Reserve upon leaving, a decision that almost changed my life in the years to come. The Japanese signed the formal surrender on September 2, 1945, aboard the *U.S.S. Missouri* in Tokyo Bay, the same day I arrived back home in Baltimore. I had telephoned my mother and Lu prior to my departure from Chapel Hill. After taking the train to Baltimore and hoofing it from Penn Station to Federal

Street, I walked through the front door and dropped my seabag in the parlor.

"Mom, Dad, Margaret," I yelled. "I'm home."

"Boy!" Mom responded as she came out of the kitchen. "We didn't think you'd get home until this evening."

"Yeah, I got out on an early train," I said.

"Hey, Boy, how are you?" Pop asked as he entered the parlor from the stairs. Margaret was right behind him.

"I'm great, Pop," I said. "It's good to be back home."

Margaret ran past Pop, giving me a huge hug and a kiss. Margaret always showed me physical affection, unlike Mom and Pop.

"Welcome home, Boy!" Margaret exclaimed. "It's so good to see you. You look great in your uniform and you're so fit. I think you filled out a bit."

"Thanks, Margaret," I said. "You look swell, too. How's Milton? When's the Army letting him come home?"

"He's fine," she replied. "At least that's what he said in his last letter. I don't understand why they have to keep him over there all this time. I thought we beat the Nazis."

"Yeah, I guess they need to keep the peace with those Hitler youth, I don't know," I said.

"He said he should be home soon, hopefully before Christmas," she responded.

"When's the wedding?" I asked.

"Milton said we could get married as soon as he returned," Margaret answered optimistically. "How about you and Lucille?"

"No plans as yet," I told Margaret. "We'll see."

"Aren't you going to see her today?" Mom interjected.

"Yeah, she knows I got home today," I responded. "I'm seeing her this evening."

"How about some lunch?" Mom asked. "You must be

hungry."

"That would be great," I said. "A sandwich would be nice. I'll put my bag in my room."

"We've got some fresh Vienna bread we picked up especially for you at the bakery this morning," Mom said. "And I have some ham and potato chips."

"Sounds good, Mom," I said as I went upstairs to my room. I noticed my bedroom looked somewhat barren. The few knickknacks I had on my dresser were gone and nothing was in my closet. All my clothes were gone, including my shoes. My baseball glove was missing, as were my bow and arrows I had when I was on the Poly Archery team. Upon further investigation, I found my entire dresser where my underwear, socks, and shirts had formerly been, was empty, too.

"What the hell?" I said out loud as I made my way downstairs. "Hey, Mom! Where's all my stuff?"

"I gave all your things away, Boy," my mother said rather nonchalantly.

"You did what?" I asked incredulously.

"I gave your clothes and things to charity," she said.

"Why in God's name would you do that?" I asked exasperated.

"Well, you sent your dirty clothes home from boot camp," she responded rather lamely.

"So?" I asked. "That was two and a half years ago. I came home a few times after that, and my clothes were still here."

"You haven't been home for a long time now," she continued. "You've been away at sea, in Philadelphia, Providence, and then in North Carolina. I thought you had all the clothes you needed."

"Jesus Christ, Mom, did you think I was never coming home?" I asked in total disbelief.

"I don't know, Boy," she said, unfazed. "Come eat

your sandwich. Do you want a Coke?"

"Yes," I said as I sat down to eat my lunch.

Pop had gone back upstairs and didn't even come down for lunch. At least Margaret joined me for lunch, but she had also gone back upstairs and missed my conversation with Mom about my clothes. I didn't bring up the subject again as I had no desire to spoil my homecoming, although it was completely ruined for me. I couldn't believe that my mother thought I was never coming home again. I was absolutely floored by her actions and disillusioned. That woman was a complete nut.

"Edith said to tell you she couldn't come over today," Mom said.

"You haven't even seen Edith's new baby, Joey," Margaret chimed in. "You're an uncle now, Boy!"

"I know," I said. "I haven't even met the father. I was so disappointed not being able to attend the wedding last year."

"You should have been there, Boy," Mom said. "We all had the greatest time. It was a beautiful wedding and reception."

"I would have loved to have been there, Mom, but the Navy wouldn't give me leave and take me into port," I said sarcastically.

"It was a fun time," Margaret added. "I was sorry you and Milton weren't there."

"It was nice of you to invite Lucille," I said. "She wrote me and told me what a good time everyone had. Hey, that reminds me, I better call her. Thanks for lunch, Mom. I probably won't be home for dinner. I expect I'll be at Lu's house this evening."

I was chomping at the bit to see Lu and to take her in my arms and kiss her. I hadn't seen her for over a year. I telephoned Lu and she was thrilled I had gotten home early. Lu invited me for dinner at her house at five. I walked on cloud nine the entire way to her house. It was like an old familiar stroll through the neighborhood of my youth making my way to 615 East Biddle Street again. It felt as if nothing had changed, as if there had been no war and I was never away. I rang the doorbell and the most beautiful sight I had ever seen answered the door, Lu. All I could see was her gorgeous, exuberant smile beaming at me as she threw her arms around my neck and gave me the most welcoming hug I had ever gotten or would ever get for the remainder of my life.

"Welcome home, Monty," Lu said. "I've waited for this moment for so long. I've said so many prayers for you, and my brother, and all the other boys from the neighborhood."

"It's great to be back, Lu, believe me," I said. "I've done nothing but think about coming home to you, Gorgeous. You're more beautiful than ever."

"Come on in!" Lu exclaimed. "Everybody's here to see you. Mom and Dad have been asking about you all day and when you're coming. Mom made a ham and potatoes and string beans."

"Mom! Dad!" Lu yelled. "Look who's here. It's Monty!"

Mr. and Mrs. Flanagan came out from the kitchen.

"Hello, Monty," Mrs. Flanagan said. "You always look so handsome in your sailor uniform."

"Good to see you, Mrs. Flanagan," I said. "It's good to be back home."

"Hi, Monty," Mr. Flanagan said shaking my hand. "Welcome back."

Just then, Charlie ran down the steps. I almost didn't recognize him. He was fifteen now and had his growth spurt.

"Hi, Monty," Charlie said. "Glad to see you again."

"Hey Charlie," I said. "I think you grew a foot since I last saw you."

"I see you have those bars on your uniform," Mr. Flanagan said. "Did you make officer when you became a pilot?"

"No sir, I didn't," I responded. "In fact, I didn't get to become a pilot. As soon as the Japs surrendered, they discontinued classes and gave us discharges."

"What are those bars, then?" Mr. Flanagan asked. "You look like an officer in that uniform."

"No, I'm still only a Seaman First Class," I replied. "Actually, I'm nothing now. The Navy gave me my final monthly paycheck before I left, a measly sixty-six dollars, plus they gave me thirty bucks in travel expenses to get back home. I'm only wearing my uniform now because I have no civilian clothes."

"Did you grow out of 'em?" Mrs. Flanagan inquired.

"Not quite," I said embarrassingly. "It's a whole other story." I didn't really want to explain how my mother gave my clothes away because she evidently thought I would never return from the war.

"John makes a hundred-fourteen dollars a month," Mr. Flanagan said, with a bit of braggadocio. "Of course, he got promoted to a Petty Officer, an Aviation Ordnanceman First Class, I think they called it. He had something to do with making sure planes were loaded with bombs before taking off from the aircraft carrier."

"Yeah, I know. Lucille told me," I said.

"Our boy, John, was a hero," Mr. Flanagan continued. "The Navy awarded him the Bronze Star for his heroic and meritorious deeds aboard his ship, the *U.S.S. Franklin*. At least, that's what it said in the letter that went along with his medal."

"Yes, you must be very proud of your son," I said. Secretly, I was a little jealous that Mr. Goody Two-Shoes ended up a hero and made almost twice my pay. If the war had lasted a little longer and I had finished my pilot's training, I would have been promoted and maybe gotten a medal, too.

A Jap kamikaze plane hit the *U.S.S. Franklin*," Charlie added. "Eight hundred sailors got killed and more than four hundred more were wounded."

"Yeah, your sister told me all about it after it happened last March," I said. "I didn't know there were that many casualties though."

"John saved dozens of sailors who were injured and would have drowned," Mrs. Flanagan said proudly. "They described it all in the newspaper and it said how John received the Bronze Star for saving all those sailors. John always was a strong swimmer."

"I saved the newspaper article," Charlie interjected.

"John's in Honolulu right now," Mr. Flanagan said. "We got a picture of him this summer posing with a hula girl. I expect he'll be getting sent home soon. How was it you got home so quickly, Monty? I just heard on the radio earlier today that the formal surrender was signed by the Japanese and General MacArthur aboard a ship in Tokyo Bay this very day."

"I don't know, Mr. Flanagan," I said. "I guess they figured they had no use for any more pilots so why keep us around."

"Well, we're all glad to see you back, safe and sound," he said. "And I know Lucille is delighted to see you and to have you back home."

Just then, Lu's sister, Nancy, came down the steps from upstairs holding her one-and-a-half-year-old. Damn if he was not a brute. I hadn't met his father, Ed Stec, yet. They got married while I was away. Ed was in the Army and was still in Germany.

"Hi, Nancy," I said. "You're looking swell. I guess

this is Michael, the newest addition to the family, huh? He's a healthy-looking little fellow, isn't he?"

"Yeah, he's a handful," Nancy said. "Good to have you back, Monty. You look so handsome in that uniform."

As Nancy and Michael entered the parlor, Esther and Donny came in the front door. Esther hadn't changed a bit. She was still her same old self, a true force of nature, always full of piss and vinegar. Donny was six years old and unrecognizable.

"Hi Esther," I said.

"Oh, hey there, Monty," Esther responded. "Welcome home."

"How's Gordon?" I asked Esther. "I was always disappointed he and I never crossed paths in the Navy. When's he coming home?"

"I don't know," she said, sounding somewhat exasperated. "His ship is supposedly headed back to San Francisco, so hopefully, he'll be home soon."

Lu's aunts and uncles, Tom and Nan, and Frank and Nellie, from next door, were right behind Esther. We all exchanged pleasantries, and everyone welcomed me home as we all marched into the dining room for supper. At the dinner table, everybody talked about how horrible the war was and how happy they were now that it had ended. Lu was especially loquacious.

"I don't know what I'm going to do with all my free time now that the war is over," Lu said. "I was the letter writer for the family. I wrote to all my friends who went into the service, including my brother."

"You were a regular pen pal to everybody," Esther said.

"We live in a wonderful neighborhood," Lu said.

"We really do," Nancy added.

"It's nice how everybody went to the same school and

you girls know everybody," Mrs. Flanagan said.

"Sadly, a lot of the servicemen that were killed I knew very well," Lu said solemnly. "We knew their whole families. Two of my girlfriends' brothers were killed. Every night I scanned the newspapers for names of people I knew who were killed."

"Let's just thank the Lord that it's all over and the boys can return home safely," Mrs. Flanagan said.

"Did I ever tell what happened to me on the day the war ended?" Lu asked everyone.

"No, Hon," Nancy answered. "What happened?"

"Well, on the fifteenth last month, when they announced that Japan surrendered, before the formal surrender today, I was on a bus downtown to shop for a new purse. We heard these shouts, 'The war is over. The war is over.' So, the bus driver stopped. Everybody jumped off the bus and joined the throngs in the street. Of course, all the girls were kissing the servicemen. A soldier in uniform was on the sidewalk, a total stranger, and he hugged and kissed me. It was really a fun thing; a joyous occasion and the war was over. Everybody was so ecstatic."

"That's extraordinary," Mr. Flanagan said. "I saw pictures in the newspaper of people in New York City celebrating similarly."

"It's wonderful," Mrs. Flanagan said. "I just pray that the rest of the boys get home safely. I want to see my boy, John, Gordon, and Ed back with their families."

"I'm sure they'll be returning in due time," Mr. Flanagan added. "There's nobody left to fight. They won't keep those millions of boys in the service for long. There's no need for them."

Lu and I spent the rest of the evening listening to the radio and talking in the parlor. We spoke for hours about our friends, our future, and the good times ahead. Lu really surprised me when she said, "I told my mother I thought I'd be getting married soon." She was finally committed to me, and only me.

We had seen each other on every leave I had during the war, which was normally a few times a year, except for the last year when I was at Brown. We had always liked each other a lot. It was no secret that I loved her madly. She had occasionally told me she loved me, but I was never sure I was the one, considering she was close with a couple of other boys in the service, including Gene Tress, the Marine she dated, and a couple of soldiers she met at Fort Meade and at USO dances with whom she corresponded. We were both very young when the war began, but now we were older and more mature. It had been an unspoken understanding that we would finally get married when the war was over, at least as far as I was concerned. I was thrilled at the thought of marrying Lu. She was indeed the only girl I ever loved or wanted. I couldn't live without her before the war or now that it was over. Only, I wasn't in a huge hurry to get married.

Honestly, after leaving the service, I really didn't want to do a damn thing but relax. My immediate ambition was to do nothing.

I was so pleased with the reception I was given by Lu's family. My own family's greeting, apart from Margaret's, seemed to pale by comparison. Hell, my father had virtually nothing to say to me, and my crazy mother thought I was never returning. I would never get over that she gave away my clothes and all my things. My childhood baseball glove was even gone, for crying out loud.

Lu and I began going out with each other exclusively from the day I got home. We did all the same things we had always done together; dancing, going to the movies, walking through the park, spending time in her parlor listening to the radio, going to the beach in Ocean City in September while it was still warm, ice skating later in the fall when it got colder, and strolling around together downtown. Lu was still working full-time at the Curtis Bay Army Depot. I didn't want to work, at least not for a while. Nevertheless, I proposed to her on Christmas Eve. Lu was over the moon. She loved the diamond ring I bought for her at the Carl J. Doederlein Company, a jewelry store downtown on Saratoga Street. It cost me all the savings I had from my time in the Navy. She immediately began making plans for a June wedding.

"Lu," I told her. "I'm not sure I want to get married in June."

"What do you mean?" she retorted. "Don't you want to get married?"

"Yes, of course I do," I responded. "I love you and there's nothing I want more than to spend my life with you, but I'd like to finish school at Brown and get my degree."

"Why does it have to be at Brown?" Lu asked.

"Because it's a great school and they offer engineering degrees," I said. "I only need two years to get my B.S. and it's paid for by the G.I. bill."

"But when will we get married?" she logically inquired.

"After I finish," I answered. "I might be able to go during the summer and maybe finish up in a year and a half. With you working, we could save a lot of money before we get married and start a family. I'd be able to get a good-paying job as an engineer after graduating from an Ivy League school. This is a great opportunity for me for a top education and possibly a great career."

"Yes," Lu said. "But that's a long time to wait."

"I think it would be for the best," I explained. "It won't be like when I was in the Navy, and I couldn't get leave. I'll be back for a week at spring break and a couple of weeks between each semester. We can spend plenty of time together. You can take your vacation when I come home, and we'll spend every minute together. I really think it'll be the best way to go for our future."

"Well, all right," Lu said. "If you really think it's for the best, but I'm not sure I like it."

At the end of January, Lu accompanied me to Penn Station where I was to catch the train for Providence, Rhode Island, to begin the spring semester at Brown. Lu went absolutely to pieces at the train station. She quickly became emotional and began sobbing uncontrollably.

"Oh, Monty," Lu cried. "I'm going to miss you so much."

"I'll miss you too," I responded. "But I'll be back. We'll still see each other."

"But Monty," Lu said. "It's like you're going off to war again. We won't see each other for such a long period of time. We waited so long to be together and now you're leaving again."

It broke my heart to see her crying in my arms. I knew then how much she really loved me. She couldn't live without me, just as I couldn't live without her during all the time I was away in the service. How could I possibly leave her now? I loved her too much.

"Okay, Lu," I said. "I'm not going. We'll get married in June as you planned."

"Oh, thank you," Lu said, still crying. "I love you so much."

"I love you too, Lu," I said. "More than anything."

Chapter Eleven

Thank You Notes

Lu spent the next few months planning our wedding ceremony to be held at St. John's Church the following June. I agreed to convert to Catholicism, although I had always intended to do so. I got a job as an artist at a greeting card company. I sketched little scenarios to match the short, clever greetings appearing in the cards. It was very tough working as an artist because I had to please the supervisor and his particular tastes. He literally sent me back to the drawing board ten times daily. It was not as if he hated my work, but he always had some suggestions. I was at the mercy of his personal preferences. It could get very frustrating, but I needed the money.

    After marrying, we planned on living on the third floor on Biddle Street, where Esther, Gordon, and Donny had lived. Gordon returned from the war in November and resumed his job as a guard at the city jail. I always got along swell with Gordon. He was a man's man, no bullshit about him whatsoever. However, he and Esther had a volatile relationship. Gordon tended to drink a lot and he and Esther often went at it. Esther was a tough cookie herself, but she and Donny had been returning to her parents' house periodically over the last few years to get away from Gordon. Apparently, Gordon became violent when he drank and at times, it proved too much for even Esther to handle. They always seemed to reconcile, though, and she would always go back to him.

    Our wedding was much more enjoyable than I anticipated. I had no qualms about marrying Lu and spending the rest of my life with her. This was my dream.

However, I was not keen on a large wedding and being the center of attention. The whole idea of it made me very uncomfortable. Lu was so happy about the entire affair that I never complained about anything. Everybody we knew, it seemed, was in the wedding party. My best man was my buddy, Rowley, and the ushers were my other good friends, Irish Clark, Harry Strawbridge, Joe Albrecht, and Lu's brother, John. Lu's maid of honor was her best friend from work, Netsy Mayfale. Her bridesmaids were her friend, Elizabeth "Mike" Norris, her cousin Frances Harris, her sisters, Nancy and Esther, and the flower girl was her second cousin, Elenora Smith. Lu wanted more of her friends in the wedding, but Mrs. Flanagan invited Lu's cousin, Francis, to be a bridesmaid without consulting Lu.

The St. John's Church altar was loaded with flowers, mostly tiger lilies, daisies, and baby's breath. The church was full, with over two hundred and fifty guests. I was very impressed with how the church looked and how many friends and family attended. Lu's father was only a cab driver and had little money. He had a friend who loaned him a limousine so Lu and I could be chauffeured to the reception. Mr. Flanagan was very active in politics and the Democratic Party in the Tenth Ward. As a result, the Democratic Party's headquarters in the ward was used for our reception at a minimum cost, I presumed. The venue was not large, but it was an adequate hall for a reception. No sit-down dinner was served, but they had beer and hors d'oeuvres and plenty of room for dancing. They had no live band, but big band music was played over the public address system from a radio station.

A table was set up near the entrance with a beautiful wedding cake on it, and an area to leave wedding gifts. It was a very nice affair and very festive. I am sure it didn't set Mr. Flanagan back too much money, for which I was grateful. He worked hard for the little money he made, and he was about the nicest fellow you would ever want to meet. He loved Lucille so much and wanted her to have the happiest day he could manage, and I think he accomplished just that. Lu was overjoyed with her wedding. After the reception, the limousine driver took us to Penn Station. We spent our wedding night in a berth on the train on our way to our honeymoon destination, Miami Beach, Florida. We had the greatest week of our lives in Miami Beach and really started our marriage out on a high note of marital bliss.

When we returned from our honeymoon, however, we moved in with the Flanagans on the third floor. The only downside to our return involved a debacle concerning our wedding presents. Mrs. Flanagan took it upon herself, more than likely to be helpful, to open every gift before we returned. The dozens of gifts, including cash, were lined up in the Flanagan's parlor.

"Mom," Lu yelled when she saw the room full of gifts. "Why did you open all our gifts?"

"I thought you'd be tired after your honeymoon, Hon," she replied.

"Where are all the cards?" Lu asked her mother. "How am I supposed to know who gave me which gift?"

"I saved all the cards," Mrs. Flanagan replied with some degree of confidence. "They're over there on the table."

"But Mom," Lu said as she picked up some of the cards. "This doesn't tell me what they gave. And you've got this cash all in one envelope. I don't even know who gave us cash."

"I didn't even think about that," Mrs. Flanagan said.

"Mom, I intended to send thank you notes to everyone who gave us a wedding gift," Lu said, somewhat exasperated, but not wanting to offend her mother.

"You don't have to worry about that," Mrs. Flanagan retorted. "When I got married, I didn't send any thank you notes for our gifts. We just thanked everyone at our reception for coming. People are supposed to bring gifts. It won't matter."

Lu didn't say anything more about the matter to her mother that night or ever again. Her mother just didn't get it, I guess, or she really didn't think it was important to write thank you notes. Lu, however, was very upset about it. She not only wanted to thank those who gave her a gift, but she very much wished to know who gave her each gift.

In August, we vacationed in Ocean City for a few days with our old friend, Irish, and his new wife, Irene, who went by "Toodles." The first thing I asked her was, "Why do they call you Toodles?"

She responded, "Well, when I was a little girl, I loved noodles, but for some reason, I always asked my mother for toodles, instead of pronouncing it noodles. My father thought this was hilarious and started calling me Toodles. It stuck!"

"I like it," I told her. "It's cute."

Now Toodles was anything but cute. She was a gangly-looking gal with big hips and a long nose. She had a no-nonsense type of personality, but she was nice enough. We got along fine with her, and she and Irish became good friends of ours for the remainder of our lives. She was two years older than Irish. Irish met her the previous summer before the war ended. They got married at the Baltimore City Hall in the fall with little fanfare. I didn't even know he was married until right before Christmas when I ran into him downtown.

We had a nice time at the beach. Lu and I had a very loving and respectful relationship, plus we had only been married for two months. Irish and Toodles, on the other hand, didn't seem to have a similar relationship. Irish was his usual sarcastic self and Toodles generally gave it right back to him. They were not exactly the Bickersons, but they never let each other get the best of the other. Deep down, though, I could see that they had affection for one another. They were just two outgoing people with large personalities who spoke their minds in their unique cynical natures. Irish and Toodles stayed our lifelong friends. They always took great interest in our children since they never had any children of their own.

Lu continued working at the Curtis Bay Ordinance Depot during the entire first year of our marriage. I quit my job as an illustrator by the end of the year with the greeting card company as it not only didn't pay well, but the situation with the supervisor was irritating. Lu realized she was pregnant after the start of the New Year, so I got a job with the Stebbons Construction Company as a lather, of all things. My Pop was instrumental in getting me the job. He was a prominent member of the Baltimore Lathers Union and had a lot of pull around town. The illustrator's job was not hard work, but I needed to make more money with the prospect of a baby coming. Our expenses were low, living with the Flanagans, but we really needed to get our own apartment, not only for more room but for privacy as well.

We found a nice two-bedroom apartment in the northern part of the city. We had a daughter, Julia, in September, and then Lu got pregnant again within a few months. Our second daughter, Jacqueline, was born one year and two days to the day after Julia. I was killing myself working as a lather. I never understood how my father and my grandfather worked as lathers their entire lives. I had gotten myself in fairly good shape over the last two years, though. I appreciated and understood why my father was the most fit and muscular fifty-five-year-old man I had ever come across. Except for wearing a hearing aid and having a few wrinkles, he showed no signs of aging. His loss of hearing was a direct result of his deep-sea diving activities in the Navy. His stomach was as flat and tight as any twenty-five-year-old, probably more so. We were the same size, but I was certain he could have licked me in a fight. I never forgot the right cross I witnessed as a boy. The man was a rough customer.

In any event, when I got hired in 1948 as a draftsman at the Glenn L. Martin Company in Middle River outside the city, I was thrilled beyond belief. I was finally making decent money. We were outgrowing our two-bedroom apartment with the two babies, so we purchased a two-story rowhouse on Belgian Avenue in the north central part of the city. Money was tight with all the expenses related not only to owning a house, but also in raising a family. I bought a car to get to work. No trolleys or buses went out to Middle River. I purchased appliances for the house, a refrigerator, a dishwasher, and a washer and dryer. We needed baby clothes, a crib, a stroller, and formula. I drove a taxi at night and on the weekends to make ends meet.

Luckily, my career at the Glenn L. Martin Company took off. I started as a draftsman but was soon promoted to Senior Technical Illustrator. The company was growing rapidly as the defense industry exploded after World War II with the advent of the Cold War. By 1952, I was promoted again to the Senior Engineer Group, Mechanical Design Division. As part of my duties, I wrote final testing reports for the Air Force's Design Engineering Inspection of the B-57, a twinjet tactical bomber and reconnaissance aircraft. I also worked on Martin's projects developing the Mace and Titan missile underground bases. The Mace missile was a tactical surface-launch missile that could be launched from a mobile trailer or an underground bunker. The Titan missile was an intercontinental ballistic missile launched from deep beneath the ground in super-hardened silos of concrete and steel. The silos were required to be lifted to the surface for launch. The site-lift configuration was primarily what my group at Martin's worked on. My job was more fun than actual work. I was finally working as a mechanical engineer and utilizing all my mathematical skills which provided me with a great deal of self-satisfaction. I really loved Martin's and working with a team of engineers to perfect weapons needed to protect our country.

Chapter Twelve

Get Her Mother to Watch Them

After the war ended and I was discharged from the Navy, I signed up with the United States Marine Corps Reserves. I did so with the feeling that this was part of my patriotic duty. However, I was single at the time. After I got married and we had our first child, Lu began nagging me to get out of the Marine Reserves.

"Monty," she said. "What if you get called up to serve again?"

"Then I'll have to go," I replied.

"What would I do, Monty?" Lu pleaded.

"What do you mean?" I responded, having never really thought about it before.

"Well, for one thing, I'd be here alone with a baby," Lu explained. "I can't really get out. I don't drive. Money might be a problem since I no longer work and your pay from the military wouldn't even cover our monthly mortgage."

"Yeah, I guess you're right, Lu," I said. "I'll get out of it."

Almost three years went by, and Lu brought it up periodically, but I never followed through with my promise. Then finally, Lu became adamant about it.

"Monty," she said. "You have got to get out of the Marine Reserves now. If there's a war, you're going to get called up. You can't leave your wife and two daughters and go off to war at this stage in our lives. You need to go downtown to the Navy Recruiting Station or wherever you need to go and get out."

"Okay, Lu," I said. "I'll do it."

"Promise me, Monty," she pleaded.

"All right, all right," I responded. "I promise. I'll take care of it tomorrow."

I was discharged from the United States Marine Corps Reserves on June 21, 1950. The Korean War began on June 25, 1950, after the North Koreans invaded South Korea. Within three days, North Korea captured the capital city of Seoul and moved toward the southern tip of the Korean peninsula. Lu could not resist the "I told you so."

"Did you see the news, Monty?" Lu gloated.

"I know, Lu," I said sheepishly. "You called it."

"President Truman is calling up reservists," she continued. "That would have been you and I don't know what I would have done being left home with two little babies."

"Lu, your timing was impeccable, I have to admit," I said.

Honestly, I was relieved that I had been discharged. It was dumb luck that I got out just days before the war started. On September 15, 1950, the First Marine Division invaded Korea at Inchon. By September 28, 1950, the Marines took back the city of Seoul and drove the North Koreans north of the 38th parallel. From August 1950 to July 1953, more than 130,000 Marine Reservists served on active duty. During the entirety of the war, over 4,200 Marines were killed, and 28,000 plus were wounded. Every third aviation combat mission during the entirety of the war was flown by either a Navy or Marine Reservist. Ted Williams, the great Boston Red Sox baseball player, was one of those guys. He was called up in the middle of his legendary career to serve as a Marine combat aviator in 1952 and 1953, flying 39 combat missions. Lu repeated time and again for the remainder of our lives how she prevented me from fighting in the Korean War.

"Monty, you would have left me a widow with two daughters if I hadn't told you to get out of the Marine Reserves," she would often tell me.

I had to admit that she had done me a favor. It reminded me of the advice I had gotten from the two salty sailors at Signalman School in Chicago to never volunteer. However, I always felt a little envious of Ted Williams. The truth was, I would have loved to have flown a jet. I had no idea if the Navy would have allowed me to finish my pilot training had I been called to active duty again, but I wondered. Lu was right, though, as she always was. She was a very practical and wise person.

However, after the war, I was inspired to get my pilot's license. I was inspired to do a lot of things. I decided to attend night school at Loyola College in Baltimore to get my degree. I also began playing a lot of golf and joined the Martin's Wednesday night golf league at Mount Pleasant Golf Course. On Saturday mornings, I played with a group of guys at Clifton Park Golf Course. I had great fun playing and enjoyed the camaraderie. On Wednesday evenings, the play was particularly slow. We waited at least five minutes or more on every shot. One evening, I was waiting in the twelfth fairway to hit my second shot to the green when the group behind us drove off the twelfth tee before we hit. The ball landed not more than three feet from me. I instinctively dropped to the ground as if I had been hit with the ball. I laid there for a solid minute. The guys in my group thought it was the funniest thing they had ever seen. As a result of all my extracurricular activities, I stopped driving a taxicab, but I was still barely making ends meet. I was forced to find another job which took up less time. I was able to obtain a position with the Baltimore City Adult Education Program teaching mathematics a couple of evenings per week.

In 1954, Lu got pregnant again with our third child. After the birth of our son, an incident occurred involving my mother which would change my relationship with my family for years to come. My mother continued to favor my sisters and their children over my family. This was no surprise to me, as this was her modus operandi since I was a boy. I was used to it. I didn't mind keeping her and my sister at arm's length. I never had to worry about anybody popping in unexpectedly, which was the way I wanted it. I rarely saw them, only occasionally at family parties. When my daughters had a birthday, I would invite them to the house, and I would see them on Christmas and Thanksgiving. I probably saw them only once a month or even every other month, which was fine with me.

I asked my mother if she would watch Julia and Jackie while Lu recovered for a week in the hospital after giving birth. I figured I would ask my mother since she was only fifty-two years old, while Lu's mother was sixty-one years old, overweight, and maybe not up to taking care of a six and seven-year-old. Julia and Jackie were a bit rambunctious. Lu and I were not strict disciplinarians. I generally left the child-rearing to Lu, who was far too nice. When they were toddlers, Lu disciplined them by constantly telling them no and patting their bottoms ever so lightly. Since then, however, we definitely took a laissez-faire approach in raising the children. For the most part, I did not like a lot of noise so I would yell at them occasionally to keep them quiet. I could tell they were afraid of me, and they always ceased their riotous conduct at my command, but they never received any kind of real punishment for their bad behavior. I would have to admit that they were wild little girls with way too much energy, often running around the house and climbing over the furniture with impunity. Nonetheless, they were sweet-natured and never seemed to operate with any malicious intent.

My mother seemed more than happy to help us out when I asked her. Within two days, though, she was singing a different tune. I arrived home from work the second night and my mother was furious. I could see it in her face immediately. She was scowling and her countenance seemed to be twisted. My mother never looked uglier to me.

"Mom, what's wrong?" I asked. I took my coat off and walked into the living room.

"I've had it with those two brats," she said rather nastily.

"What happened?" I inquired.

"Those kids are brats and don't listen," she said, sounding exasperated. "I can't take any more of this."

"C'mon Mom," I said. "It can't be that bad. They can be a handful sometimes. They're very high-spirited, but I'll talk to them."

"They're impossible," she responded with her face still contorted. "I'm done. Why don't you get *her* mother to watch them?"

"Okay, Mom," I retorted, now getting angry myself. "I'll do that. Sorry you can't watch your own grandchildren for a few days."

"No, I can't," she said. "Not those two wild little Indians!" She got her coat from the living room closet and stormed out of the house.

"Well, the hell with her," I thought to myself. I was furious. I went upstairs to see where Julia and Jackie were. I found them in their bedroom happily playing with their dolls. They apparently had not heard anything their grandmother said, luckily.

"Is everything all right?" I asked the girls.

"Yes, Daddy," they answered.

"Did everything go okay with your grandmother today?" I inquired.

"Yes," they both said again.

I never knew exactly what happened that day, but my mother incensed me, not only because she obviously didn't like my girls, but because of the way she told me to get Lu's mother to watch them. I called Mrs. Flanagan and told her my mother could no longer watch the children. Mrs. Flanagan didn't hesitate for a second to help and came over that very evening. Mrs. Flanagan was such a sweet and kind person. She showed so much love for my children, in contrast to my mother, who showed none. Julia and Jackie were thrilled when I told them Mom-Mom was coming over in place of my mother, Grandmom. They knew who loved them. They might have been wild little Indians, but they weren't stupid. I told Lu what happened after she got out of the hospital. My mother told me she was "done" - well, I was finished with her. I had no contact with her for five years, and consequently, I didn't see my father or my sisters and their families for all that time either.

In 1955, Lu's favorite aunt died, Catherine Flynn, nee McCusker. Her Aunt Cate, as she was called, was actually Lu's great aunt, the eldest sister of Mr. Flanagan's mother, MaryJane McCusker Flanagan. Mr. Flanagan was the only one of her nieces or nephews who Aunt Cate would have anything to do with, and she absolutely adored her grand-niece, Lucille. Aunt Cate had been a widow for over thirty years. She was married to William F. Flynn, a former Boxing Commissioner for the State of Maryland and later the superintendent of the Baltimore Life Insurance Company. In 1928, five years after her husband's death, she began working as a clipping clerk, serving four Baltimore mayors and keeping them up to date about what newspapers were saying about them until her retirement in 1953. She dropped over dead of a heart attack at the age of seventy-nine. We attended the funeral, but only the Flanagan family was there. Neither Mr. Flanagan's three sisters, Marie, Nan, and Nellie, nor his brother, Charles, nor any of their family members attended. I asked Mr. Flanagan why none of them came to the funeral.

"Well, the family had a bit of a squabble before the war," Mr. Flanagan said, somewhat hesitantly. "My Aunt Margaret died in 1938. She was a widow with no children and left an estate of $30,000. Aunt Cate was named administrator of the estate. Initially, it was believed that Aunt Margaret had no will, in which case, the surviving relatives would benefit. Somehow it was determined that Aunt Cate would receive a third of the estate, and the nieces and nephews would receive two-thirds of the estate. But then Aunt Cate produced an eighteen-word will signed by Aunt Margaret which left the entire estate to Aunt Cate. My family didn't believe it."

"What made them think Margaret had no will?" I asked curiously.

"I don't know," Mr. Flanagan continued. "I didn't think anything of it when Aunt Cate said she did in fact have a will, but all of my siblings and the nieces and nephews on the McCusker side of the family decided to sue Aunt Cate over the authenticity of the will. You can imagine the hubbub this caused. I wanted nothing to do with it."

"How come?" I asked.

"I didn't doubt the authenticity of the will," Mr. Flanagan said resolutely. "I just figured Aunt Margaret must have signed it. I never thought Aunt Cate would try to cheat her entire family. She was not that type of person. She was a tough, straightforward woman, but she was no cheat. I never knew her to lie."

"So, what happened?" I asked.

"Well, they took her to court, and they lost," Mr. Flanagan explained. "They brought in a handwriting expert to testify, and he said it was Aunt Margaret's signature, so the court ruled in Aunt Cate's favor. Understandably, she never spoke to any of her nieces or nephews again, except for me, of course. She was so angry with the family that a week after the verdict, she had her husband's remains moved from the McCusker/Flanagan family burial site at New Cathedral Cemetery to another plot on the other side of the graveyard. She never said it, but I knew she appreciated the fact that I was not part of the lawsuit. I knew my mother's sister was no thief. The entire incident was so ridiculous. Greed can be a terrible thing. It's a deadly sin, the Bible says. Aunt Cate was always crazy about Lucille, too. Nothing ever changed."

"I've heard Lu speak highly of her," I said. "I recall she always remembered Lu's birthday."

"Yes, she did," Mr. Flanagan said. "And she was always generous with her gifts."

"Yeah, come to think of it," I said. "I recollect Aunt Cate at our wedding. She gave us sterling silver salt and pepper shakers, I think. She asked Lu afterward how she liked them."

A few days later after the execution of her will, Lu received Aunt Cate's diamond earrings. Lu was touched by Aunt Cate's gesture. Lu would wear them for the rest of her life with pride and with love, in memory of her favorite aunt. Twenty years later when it was in vogue for women to get their ears pierced, Lu said she never would, partly because she thought it was slightly barbaric, but more so because Aunt Cate's diamond earrings were clip-ons. I couldn't help but think that Lu was rewarded with Aunt Cate's diamonds not only because of her father's loyalty, but because she possessed the same sweet disposition as her father. I did not think I ever met a kinder, more affable, and congenial man than Mr. Flanagan, and fortunately for me, he produced a lovely daughter with the same traits. Presumably, Aunt Cate recognized how special they were, too.

As the years passed by, I was a busy man. I continued working at Martin's in a very fulfilling career. I wouldn't even qualify it as work because it was so exciting. I purchased a Piper Cub single-engine plane for $3,000 in 1956 with three other pilots. I continued attending night school at Loyola College and Lu and I were raising a family. We threw a big party for Lu's parents' fortieth wedding anniversary in the club basement I built in our home on Belgian Avenue. It was a wonderful celebration. Then, in February 1959, Lu gave birth to a beautiful, red-haired, baby girl. She was the prettiest baby I had ever seen in my life. Life was good, but I began feeling a bit melancholy about my separation from family.

My parents had moved from Federal Street to a house just off Northern Parkway, only a couple of miles from our house on Belgian Avenue. I started driving by their house when I was in the neighborhood. One Saturday afternoon, I saw my Pop walking up the street on the sidewalk. I pulled my car up to the curb next to him.

"Hey, Pop!" I yelled out the car window. It was the first time I had seen him or spoken to him in five years.

"Hi, Boy," he said as he walked over to the car and leaned into the passenger window.

"How are you, Pop?" I asked.

"I'm fine, Boy," he answered.

"How's Mom?" I inquired.

"She's fine," he said. "All right then, I'm heading up to the store. Good seeing you, Boy." Pop then headed up the street.

"Goodbye, Pop," I said as he walked away. This was not the reunion I had imagined. It was rather abrupt. Frankly, I got the distinct impression that Pop didn't give two shits that he hadn't seen me for five years. Still, I felt the need to reconcile with my parents. I really wanted my mother to see our new baby daughter, too, who looked like a wee Scottish lass with her red hair. Mom and her four sisters all had red hair. I called Mom that evening.

"Hello, Mom," I said when she answered the phone. "It's Boy. How have you been?"

"I'm good, Boy," she said. "It's good to hear from you. It's been a while."

"I thought we might come over for a visit, Mom," I said. "Lu had another baby, a beautiful, red-haired, little girl. She looks just like a little Scottish girl."

"That'll be fine, Boy," she said. "Margaret and Edith are coming over tomorrow afternoon. Why don't you come? I'm sure they'd all like to see you again."

"All right, Mom," I said. "We'd love to come. We'll see you then."

After hanging up the telephone, I couldn't shake the fact that my mother, although cordial, was not exactly enthusiastic about me and my family reuniting with her. Her attitude was slightly better than Pop's apparent indifference earlier in the afternoon, however, she didn't even acknowledge my remarks about my daughter and her red hair. It reminded me of an incident in my childhood when I was about ten years old. I was in the neighborhood playing with the other kids when a girl called me a dirty Scotsman. I shot right back at her, "Well, you're a dirty bastard."

The brat girl ran home and told her mother what I called her, who, in turn, complained to my mother. I thought my mother would be on my side since I defended the family heritage, but I was mistaken.

"What are you doing cursing at little girls?" my mother asked.

"Mom," I explained. "She called me a dirty Scotsman."

"I don't care," she shot back. "You watch your filthy mouth." She then whacked me right upside the head, and it hurt. I never felt as if my mother was on my side.

Five years earlier during our falling out when she told me to get Lu's mother to babysit the girls, I thought I was finished with Mom. I would never forget her abhorrent behavior that evening. Still, I didn't want to take my grudge to the grave. Furthermore, I wished for my children to know their grandparents, aunts and uncles, and cousins, on my side of the family. My pride played a part in this reconciliation, too. I had a very strong desire for everybody to see my beautiful baby girl. She was a little, red-headed angel, the prettiest baby on earth. This was my unbiased opinion, but anybody with eyes could see it!

Chapter Thirteen

Humphrey Bogart Lapels

We began visiting my parents and my sisters and their families regularly again. My mother liked to have everyone over on Sunday afternoons, so we began dropping by every few weeks. It was ordinarily a pleasant time. Pop would generally be watching a baseball game on the television with the volume turned down. He was completely deaf by this time. He wore a hearing aid, but he still could hear very little. My children would greet Pop, yelling "Hello, Grandpop" as we made our way to the kitchen. Pop would nod to the children and wave, and then shake my hand. Mom was usually in the kitchen. We always sat around the kitchen table talking. The children normally stayed briefly before going down to the basement to get a kickball to play with outside. My sisters and their husbands would often be there.

It was always very congenial, but Mom was still as unpredictable as ever. She was almost totally deaf, too, but she was too vain to wear a hearing aid. Consequently, she never really heard an entire conversation. The family would usually be discussing some topic at the kitchen table and Mom would only be able to follow part of the conversation, due to her limited hearing. Then, without fail, Mom would suddenly combust and begin a tirade, screaming at everyone. It was very disconcerting, particularly since no one ever knew what precipitated her outbursts. Every incident was nearly identical. She always believed we were talking about her disparagingly, no matter what the subject was.

One Sunday afternoon in her kitchen following some innocuous conversation, she screamed, "I never said that."

"We weren't talking about you, Mom," I told her.

"You were, too," she said emphatically. "I'm not going to stand for it, either. This is my house, and I won't be talked about like that in my own house."

"Mom, we weren't saying anything about you," I said.

"Yes, you were," she reiterated. "I heard you."

She often made our visit so tense that we would have to find an excuse to leave early. I tried to be nice. I didn't want to have another falling out with the family, so I put up with her insanity. We visited regularly, despite her erratic behavior. She began giving the children birthday and Christmas presents. A card with five dollars arrived on every child's birthday and she would give them another five dollars each at Christmas. The kids loved it and it seemed very generous until my daughter told me what her cousin received for her birthday. Deborah, Margaret's oldest daughter, told Jackie that she received a leather purse from her grandmother for Christmas worth a hundred dollars. Nothing had changed since my childhood, but I just sucked it up. It was annoying, though, witnessing Mom now playing favorites with grandchildren.

I graduated from Loyola College in 1960 and Lu threw a big party at the house. My side of the family attended, and it seemed as though we were one big, happy family, but I knew better. We outgrew our rowhouse on Belgian Avenue and moved to the suburbs of Baltimore in August 1961. I bought an $18,000 brick rancher on a third of an acre on Penn Avenue in Perry Hall, a bedroom community in Baltimore County, approximately twelve miles from downtown Baltimore, and only about three miles from work at Martin's in Middle River. In retrospect, I should have purchased a larger house. It only had three bedrooms. We put the boy in the smallest bedroom and the three girls shared the other. It was a little tight. Immediately after moving in, Lu became pregnant.

"Monty," she said. "I can't believe I'm pregnant."

"You're kidding," I answered.

"No, I'm not," she said with consternation. "We don't have enough room, Monty, and now we'll never be able to go away together like we had always planned."

"Don't worry, Lu," I said. "We'll get away someday together."

Lu and I had never gone anywhere alone together since our honeymoon. Julia and Jackie were just now getting to be teenagers and we thought we would be able to travel in a few years and leave the smallest one, Kelly, home with Julia and Jackie. Now with another little one on the way, our travel plans would be delayed for years.

"Maybe I could throw myself down the stairs," Lu joked.

"Very funny, Lu," I said.

"I love the children," she said. "But we never get to go anywhere and be alone."

"Someday, Lu," I told her. "Someday."

Lu's father died the next year. Lu was devastated. Mr. Flanagan had smoked his entire adult life. He began having shortness of breath just before Christmas. He finally went to the doctor after the New Year and was diagnosed with lung cancer. The cancer was too far along and there was nothing they could do. Sometimes one lung could be removed to save the patient, but Mr. Flanagan had it in both lungs. He deteriorated quickly and died on March 27th. The funeral was April 1st. Lu went into labor the morning of the first. She missed her father's funeral, and we had our fifth child, a boy, at 11:17 p.m. on April Fool's Day. It was a cruel joke for Lu, giving birth the same day her beloved father was buried.

The joke was on the baby, too. Aunt Esther and Aunt Nancy unwittingly played an April Fool's joke on him every year after wishing him a happy birthday, except it wasn't funny.

"Happy birthday, sweetheart," both Esther and Nancy would say, quickly followed by "Can you believe Dad's been dead for ten years?" decimating any birthday celebratory feeling. This exact scenario literally repeated itself for thirty years.

We had intended to name the baby, Barry, but Lu said she wanted to name him after her father, John Robert Flanagan. I said all right, but ultimately, we would be naming him after her brother, too, who was John Robert Flanagan, Jr. This did not sit well with me.

The truth was, I never really respected John, with the exception of his heroics during the war. After the war, John attended college on the G.I. bill and obtained his degree in physical education. Now I thought his choice of a college major was so dumb. John then opted to become a World Book Encyclopedia salesman as his profession; even dumber, I thought. He married a sweet girl named Reba from North Carolina he met after the war, and they had two kids, Kathy and Mark. We saw them at family functions, but our families were never that close. Of course, Lu loved her brother very much and thought the world of him. He was not a bad guy, but I just couldn't stand him. He always greeted you with a big, phony, "Hey, how ya doin' Monty? You're looking good. Are you working out?"

I guess most people liked him and enjoyed his good-natured manner, but he got on my nerves. I found him completely insincere. At any rate, I was not about to name my kid John Robert. I changed it to John James when I filled out the paperwork at the hospital. Lu stayed in bed at the hospital after the birth for about a week.

When she saw the baby's identification tag on his wrist with his full name, she was flabbergasted.

"Monty, why is it John James instead of John Robert?" Lu asked.

"I just went with the first name, Lu," I answered. "I didn't know you wanted the middle name, too. I thought John James rolled off the tongue much better."

"But Monty," she said with some disappointment. "I wanted to name him after Dad."

"I'm sorry, Lu," I said, rather disingenuously. "Basically, he's still named after your father. I thought it was just the first name."

I never told Lu the real reason I couldn't name my son fully after her father. I would have if it wasn't for her brother being a junior and having the same name. I had absolutely nothing against her father. He was a prince of a guy, but I wasn't about to name him after her brother. It was never going to happen.

Life flew by at lightning speed. Lu and I remained extremely busy raising our five children. I built a club basement in the new house on Penn Avenue, complete with a bar suitable for family parties. I continued to play golf Wednesday evenings in the work league and on Saturday mornings. I flew my airplane on Sunday afternoons, often taking the children for a plane ride, although not all of them at once, since the plane was too small. Lu, however, soon grew tired of the plane rides.

"Monty, I want you to sell your share of the plane," she said one day out of the blue.

"What do you mean?" I shot back in complete surprise.

"I mean I don't want to end up a widow with five children," she said emphatically. "You've got to sell it; it's making me a wreck thinking about it."

I didn't argue with her. I could see she was upset. Lu

had always been very understanding, patient, and indulgent when it came to my various interests and endeavors.

"Okay, I guess I could sell my share of the plane, Lu," I said. "It shouldn't be difficult. I'll just let the other three guys know. Don't worry about it."

"Oh, thank you, Monty," Lu said, apparently relieved. "That's a load off my mind."

I knew Lu was a chronic worrier. I'm sure my flying a plane caused her unnecessary anxiety. I still loved Lu more than anything and genuinely wanted her to be happy. I missed flying after I sold my share of the plane, but it had been getting costly to maintain anyway, even though I shared the expenses. Money was always tight, especially with five children to feed and clothe. It seemed every time I started to save some cash; a big expense always came up or another child came along. When I first got married, I had all kinds of expenses. It took years to pay off a new refrigerator, a washer and dryer, a dishwasher, and a car. I thought I was ahead of the game, but then a few years passed by, and I had the same expenses all over again. I guess I never really figured I'd have to keep replacing these items every five or ten years.

In 1964, the Glenn L. Martin Company decided it was transferring my workgroup to their new facility in Orlando, Florida. I was thrilled at the prospect of this move. My job there as a mechanical engineer had been a dream job. I loved going to work. Martin's continued developing missiles for the military. The defense industry was booming, and the Martin Company had its large share of government and military contracts. I routinely traveled to Colorado and California where the company tested rockets. I had worked there for sixteen years and was making $14,000 per year. I was not rich by any means, but I was doing very well. The house I purchased in 1961 cost only $18,000 and my mortgage rate was only four percent. I knew Lu would not be happy about my transfer, but I was certain she would understand that we had to go for the sake of my career and our livelihood. When I got home that evening, I broke the news to her.

"Lu," I yelled as I walked through the door. "I've got some big news."

"What?" she responded from down the hall in the bedroom. "I'm in here."

As I walked down the hall into the bedroom, she greeted me with a kiss and then asked, "What's the big news? Are you getting promoted?"

"Not promoted yet," I said enthusiastically. "Transferred."

"Transferred?" Lu asked bewildered. "Transferred where?"

"To Orlando, Florida," I replied. "My group is getting transferred to the new facility there."

Lu's face just dropped, and she stared off in shock. Then, she looked as if she might start to cry.

"I can't leave my family," she said.

"We have to, Lu," I said. "Otherwise, I'll lose my job."

"I'm not leaving Baltimore, and my mother, and my sisters and brothers," she said. "This is our home and my whole family lives here."

"But Lu, you don't understand," I said, pleading to her. "I'd have to give up my job and my career if I don't go. I have to go."

"You can't do this to the children, again, Monty," Lu continued. "We just moved less than three years ago. They had to leave their friends on Belgian Avenue and leave their school at Blessed Sacrament."

"They adjusted fine," I said. "They made new friends and they like Perry Hall. They'll make new friends in

Orlando."

"Julia graduates next year, and Jackie the year after that," she said. "They've made too many friends and they both have steady boyfriends. They'll be devastated if they have to leave. You can get another job."

"Lu, it's not just a job," I said desperately. "I've worked at Martin's for sixteen years. This is my career. Hell, I started out as a draftsman and now I'm working as a mechanical engineer in a group that's developing rockets for the United States government. It's important work and I get a great deal of satisfaction from it. On top of that, it's actually very stimulating going to work. I enjoy it. I like the people with whom I work, and I love the camaraderie there. All of these people are transferring to Orlando to continue our work and I want to be a part of it."

"Well, you can't," she said adamantly. "Because I'm not going, and neither are the children." Lu then began to sob.

"Don't cry, Lu," I implored, as I put my arms around her.

"I can't help it," she said, continuing to cry. "I don't want to uproot our family and leave Baltimore. I don't want to leave my family. This is our home, and I don't want to go to Florida. We may as well be going to China. I can't leave my mother and my sisters."

"All right, all right," I said, exasperated. "I'll have to find another job here, I guess. But I hope I can find something fast. We have bills to pay, you know. We have a mortgage to pay and car payments, and bills I can barely pay as it is. I'm thirty-nine years old. It's not exactly a good time to be jumping ship and starting over."

"Oh, thank you, Monty," Lu said, still with tears in her eyes. "You're smart and experienced. You could get a job anywhere."

"I hope so, Lu," I said rather dejectedly. "I just want to keep you happy, Lu. I love you."

"I love you, too," Lu said.

I was very worried about securing another job. I immediately applied to the United States Army for a civilian job as a mechanical engineer at the Letterkenny Army Depot in Chambersburg, Pennsylvania. I was laid off within three months at Martin's after not transferring to Orlando. Luckily, I got the position at Letterkenny. The good news was that I made about the same salary and was able to pay my mortgage and other bills. The bad news was that the commute was two and a half hours each way from Perry Hall to Chambersburg. Five hours a day on the road proved to be too much. After a few months, I applied as a mechanical engineer to work for the United States Air Force in Silver Spring, Maryland. I got the job, but I still had another hellacious commute. It took me an hour to an hour and a half each way, depending on the traffic.

I suggested to Lu that we move to Colombia, Maryland, a new planned community in Howard County, which would have shortened my commute to about a half-hour or so, but Lu was having none of it. She made it clear that she didn't want to move. Any move away from Baltimore or the Baltimore suburbs was like moving to another planet as far as Lu was concerned. After two and a half years of driving to Silver Spring, I couldn't stand the commute any longer and I landed a job with Westinghouse in Baltimore.

At about this same time, my oldest daughter, Julia, who was only two years out of high school, became pregnant. She was still going with her high school boyfriend, Frank Graham, who was attending Frostburg State College in western Maryland. Julia had been a bit wild through high school and had only been an average student. She landed a good job after graduating as a customer service representative at the Chesapeake and Potomac Telephone Company in Baltimore. Frank Graham always seemed to be a punk to me, slicking back his black hair, and driving a revved-up, red, Chevy convertible. He fancied himself as a bit of a hotshot and really thought he was something cool. Julia apparently thought so too.

Julia told her mother that Frank had said nothing to her about getting married when she told him she was pregnant. At any rate, we contacted his parents and urged them to talk to their son about marrying our daughter to provide her baby with a legal father. The Grahams agreed and said they would contact their son who was away at college in Frostburg. He had apparently told them nothing of his situation. The Grahams called us the following day and informed us that their son agreed to marry Julia. I wasted no time in contacting our pastor at St. Joseph's Catholic Church to arrange Julia's marriage. The pastor was surprisingly cooperative regarding the urgency of the situation. I don't think this was his first rodeo so to speak. They got married in the small chapel at the rear of the church. Only the immediate families and a few of their friends attended. The reception was held at Velleggia's Restaurant in Little Italy in Baltimore. Julia moved in with Frank in an off-campus apartment in Frostburg, Maryland.

Three months later, Julia telephoned her mother from Frostburg and told her she was coming home.

"Hello, Mom," Julia said crying on the phone.

"What's the matter?" Lu asked her.

"I have to get away from Frank," Julia responded, still sobbing. "He threw me down last night."

"What?" Lu said, startled by these remarks. "You're

five months pregnant. What does he think he's doing? He'll hurt you and the baby."

"Mom," Julia continued. "He has an awful temper."

"Has he done this before?" Lu inquired.

"Well, yeah," Julia said hesitantly. "He's pushed me down before, but he always pushed me onto the bed. Last night, I bounced off the bed and onto the floor. It really frightened me that it might hurt the baby. It really jarred me."

"Oh, Julia," Lu said frantically. "You need to come home at once."

"I know," Julia said. "But how am I going to get out of here? I don't have a car."

"You need to get to the bus station," Lu explained. "Pack up all your things and leave there immediately. Call me from the bus station and let me know when the bus will get into Baltimore. Your father and I will pick you up tonight."

"All right, Mom," Julia said. "I'll pack up my suitcase and I'll call you in a bit. The bus station isn't far."

We picked up Julia that evening. Julia became hysterical in the car as I was driving her home.

"I think I've made a big mistake," she said, crying like a baby. "I shouldn't have left him."

"Julia," Lu calmly explained. "You did the right thing. He's going to hurt you and the baby. Think of the welfare of your child. It's unconscionable that he would shove a pregnant woman to the floor."

"He didn't mean it," Julia said defensively. "He meant to push me onto the bed."

"Julia, the very thought that he would lose his temper and physically assault you and the baby is criminal," Lu said.

"You should swear out a complaint with the police and have him arrested," I chimed in.

"I know one thing," Lu said. "You're not going back to him. You're not going to jeopardize yourself and your baby's health and safety. This is not right."

"But Mom," Julia pleaded. "He just lost his temper. I don't think he meant to hurt us."

"It doesn't matter," Lu said unwaveringly. "I witnessed this same thing with my oldest sister, Esther. She and Gordon had so many terrible fights, and he would hit her. She would come home with little Donny and then go back to Gordon, and the same thing would happen all over again. It happened repeatedly, she and Donny running home to my parents' house to get away from Gordon, and then going back to him. I won't have it. He's never going to change, and I won't have you spending your whole life leaving him and then going back for more abuse. I've seen too much of this kind of thing before. You are not going to be Esther and Gordon."

"Oh, Mom," Julia cried. "I'm sorry."

"Don't you worry," Lu responded. "It's not your fault. He's not going to hurt you or our grandchild ever again."

Frank called Julia two nights later and said he was sorry. He told Julia that she and the baby were not leaving him. When she told Frank it was over, he said, "We'll see about that."

Frank showed up at our house at the end of the week shortly after dinner. Julia was in her room at the end of the hall. My youngest boy, John, was playing in the basement with his G.I. Joes. Jackie, Michael, and Kelly, luckily, were out. Frank showed up at the front door, banging it violently with his fist. I opened the front door and he immediately barged into the house.

"I want to see Julia," he demanded, as he tried to get past me.

"She doesn't want to see you," I said sternly, as he

began pushing me backward through the living room.

"I'm taking her back to Frostburg with me," he fired back.

"No, you're not," I said, as he continued to back me up down the hall. The basement door was open, and I saw John playing with his toys at the bottom of the steps. As I glanced away, Frank cold-cocked me. I felt the hard sting of his punch over my left eye, and I instinctively put up my dukes to defend myself and block any other punches to my face.

Frank was screaming by this time, "Julia, get out here, I'm taking you home."

I finally stood my ground halfway down the hall, after shaking the cobwebs from my head following his punch to my face. I gave him a couple of left jabs that did not land, but my right cross to his jaw landed and stopped him in his tracks. He threw a couple of more weak punches back, but my arms blocked them. Julia was behind me in her bedroom, screaming and crying hysterically.

He abruptly turned around and said, "Screw it. Stay here then."

Frank briskly walked out of the house and drove away. We never saw him again. Julia filed for divorce and had the baby in September. Our first grandchild was a beautiful red-haired little fella. Frank never paid alimony or child support and subsequently never laid eyes on his son. That was fine with all of us. He was an unstable nut. I had to take off work a couple of days to allow the black eye he gave me to heal. I always thought that it would have been nearly impossible to have a relationship with him if he had reconciled with Julia. After all, he gave me a black eye and I smashed him in the jaw. Not easy to forget.

The new baby was more like our sixth child. Julia

went back to work full time at the telephone company and Lu more or less raised him. However, the difference was that this kid basically had two mothers. He got everything he wanted and was really spoiled rotten, unlike the other five kids. We were never strict disciplinarians, but we raised them in the Catholic Church and taught them right from wrong. They were never without, but anything special that they wanted usually had to wait for their birthday or Christmas. The grandson typically got whatever he wanted whenever he wanted. He just had to work on Julia to get it. Julia, without fail, always said no initially to his demands, but then caved every single time after about two weeks of his crying and nagging. It was really a pitiful routine that continued through his teenage years. Our twelve-hundred-fifty square foot, three-bedroom home, was far too small for eight people. I built a bedroom for Michael and John in the basement so that Julia and the new baby could have a room and Jackie and Kelly could share a room.

The late 1960s were very eventful in our family. I was finally happy again working, but then after three years at Westinghouse, I got laid off. My brother-in-law, Milton Shelby, was the President of the Western Electric Company in Baltimore and he landed me a job at Chesapeake and Potomac Telephone Company in 1970 when I was forty-five years old. Western Electric was closely tied to the telephone company since Western Electric provided all the materials and labor for the installation of telephone cables across the region. I was eventually put in charge of the construction of the telephone switching buildings needed in every community. I was never really accepted at the telephone company by the management, since everybody knew Milton was my brother-in-law.

Most of the other engineers had worked there for twenty years or more before being promoted to the first level of management, which I was appointed to from the start. My boss, a horse's ass named Rickle, hated me from the outset for this reason. In fact, I was never promoted past the first level of management in my eighteen years working there. It was annoying working for a guy who resented me, and who was also not very bright. Whenever I went on vacation, I noticed that my files had been rifled through, which really irritated me. I finally organized my files by Morse code, which nobody in the office was apparently familiar with, since Rickle complained every time I returned from vacation.

"What's with your files, Culpepper?" he griped. "What the hell is with the dots and dashes? We couldn't make heads or tails of how you organize them."

"I have my own system," I answered.

"Well, we can't find a damn thing when you're gone," he retorted angrily.

I couldn't have been more pleased with myself. I hated that rotten cocksucker with a passion. He did nothing but try to make my life miserable, all out of spite. Why did people have to be such colossal assholes? I hated to be un-Christian, but I sincerely hoped Rickle would die of cancer. If I had that exterminator button in the palm of my hand, Rickle would be gone forever. I never got promoted, but luckily, Rickle eventually transferred to another group and my job became much more tolerable.

We saw a lot of Esther and Gordon in the late 1960s. Despite all of Gordon's faults, he was truly a good fella and he and Esther loved our children. Lu and I made them godparents to Kelly, and they gave her a lot of special attention, sometimes too much. When Kelly was about eight years old, their German Shepherd, Sarge, nipped at Kelly. Gordon, being half drunk, as he was most of the time, went for his rifle and was going to shoot the dog. Esther and I dissuaded him, and he put the gun away, but sadly, he was fully prepared to take the dog out in the backyard and shoot it. Regardless of his erratic behavior, Gordon possessed a heart of gold. Sure, he drank, gambled, fought with Esther, and could go off the handle easily, such as with the dog incident, but he always meant well. I never knew what exactly went on between him and Esther, especially in their younger days when Esther was running home to her parents, but I didn't judge him for that. Esther was a dynamo anyway, so whatever went on with them in the past, I figured they forgave each other. He taught my six-year-old son how to shoot craps on one visit, which I didn't mind at all. I just liked the guy.

Sadly, in 1969, Gordon suffered a heart attack. The doctors said he could no longer work, so he retired from his job as a guard at the Baltimore City jail after almost twenty-five years. The last time I ever saw Gordon, he poured out his guts to me.

"Monty," Gordon said. "I'm so down from this heart attack. I can't do anything. The doctor just wants me to rest. He told me I can't work; I can't drink, I can't smoke. I don't know what to do with myself. I have nothing to live for."

"Don't say that Gordon," I said, not knowing really what to say. "Things will get better."

"I don't think so, Monty," Gordon said with complete hopelessness. "They can't do anything for me. The doctor doesn't want me to do a goddamn thing for fear I might have another heart attack."

I felt so bad for Gordon. Everything he said was true. In those days, doctors didn't routinely perform quadruple by-pass surgery or put stents in arteries, as they do nowadays. When somebody suffered a heart attack back then, the prescription was rest with instructions not to exert yourself. Typically, the patient invariably suffered another heart attack, proving to be fatal. Gordon was no dummy. He knew he was a ticking time bomb sitting around waiting to explode. When the news came a few weeks later that Gordon went into his kitchen at three in the morning, put a .30-30 rifle in his mouth, and blew his brains out all over the kitchen ceiling, it was really not a total surprise to me. I thought it was slightly inconsiderate to Esther, though, who found him in the middle of the night in the kitchen with half his head splattered on the ceiling. She was a resilient person, but that had to be traumatic, even for her. Nancy's son, Michael, a former Marine and one tough hombre himself, cleaned up Gordon's brains off the ceiling and walls. Gordon's viewing at the funeral home was the first closed casket funeral I had ever attended, for good reason.

About a year and a half later, Esther held her own engagement party at her house. Esther and Gordon's best friends were George and Myrna Blockson. Myrna died in a car accident six months after Gordon died. They believed maybe she had a stroke because she ran her car off the road and crashed after rolling her car over several times. No other cars were near her. At any rate, Esther and George apparently consoled each other and soon married. Lu's entire family attended the party, and everyone was happy for the engaged couple. As I was leaving, I made a joke to Lu's brother, John. He was wearing an overcoat with very large lapels.

I jokingly took hold of his lapels and said, "Hey, these are just the kind of lapels Humphrey Bogart might grab a hold of in one of his movies."

John reacted very aggressively and rather strangely, I might add, contorting his body into a weird jujitsu stance, then putting his hands and elbows together between my arms, and violently flinging his hands and arms outwardly, breaking my grip on his lapels.

"Hiya," he yelled, as he completed his defensive move like some kind of cartoonish, crazed, karate fighter.

At first, I thought it was a joke, but then I could see that John's adrenalin was pumping and he was ready to fight me, remaining in an aggressive stance with his hands up.

"What the hell's wrong with you?" I asked, not really expecting a response. "You're out of your goddamn mind."

I turned around and walked away, leaving him standing there like a frozen middle-aged Bruce Lee. Sadly, nobody witnessed this bizarre event. Lu was saying her goodbyes to her relatives.

I grabbed her and said, "Let's go." When we got into the car, I told her what happened.

"I don't believe it," she said. "Why would he act like that?"

"I don't know," I said. "Maybe he forgot about wanting to become a priest or maybe selling World Book Encyclopedias is getting to him. But I know one thing, the hell with him."

I spent the next ten years avoiding John. If Lu's family was having a party and John was supposed to be there, we made an excuse not to attend. I did attend Esther and George's wedding. John was there, but I didn't talk to him. Lu's sister, Nancy, married for the third time in 1972. I attended her wedding, too, but avoided that nut, John. Nancy's first husband, Ed Stec, died in 1959 of cancer. Lu and I had gone to the hospital to visit Ed before he died, and we inadvertently passed right by him in the hallway. Ed Stec had been a well-built, good-looking guy, but his cancer ravaged him to the point of being unrecognizable. Nancy married again a couple of years later to Ben Renner, but the marriage didn't last. Ben got kicked by a horse before they separated, and then sadly, he died of a blood clot shortly before their divorce was final. Nancy's third husband, Dean Smith, was a Baltimore City Police Department detective who had a great sense of humor and was always the life of the party.

Lu and I socialized weekly with Esther and George, and Nancy and Dean, over the next twenty years. We all belonged to the St. John's Old Timers Club and attended nearly all of their functions. We enjoyed seeing our childhood friends from the Tenth Ward on a regular basis. It was very nostalgic and reminded us of the good old days when we were growing up in Baltimore City. We vacationed in Ocean City, Maryland with the Old Timers Club every summer. Everybody from the Old Timers Club stayed at the Commander Hotel. Toodles and Irish were always there too, as well as Franny Driscoll, Joe and Mike Albrecht, and many other friends from our youth. Esther's husband, George, was a Shriner at the Boumi Temple, and we attended all their functions and dances. The Shriners founded the original Shriner's Hospital in Shreveport, Louisiana, and eventually expanded to over twenty hospitals nationwide.

George's Shriner friends, Dick and Norma Enberg, and Charles and Dorothy Routsen, became our friends. Charles was an interesting fellow, having spent two and a half years in a Nazi prison camp during World War II. Charles really had a thing for Lu, but I didn't mind. Lu loved his attention, and it was expressed in a very respectful way. Charles obviously recognized her sweetness, plus she was still so cute, even as she aged. We began going on vacations with Esther and George, and Nancy and Dean, and their friends, including to Hawaii, Las Vegas, the Bahamas, and Ireland. We had Julia at home to keep an eye on John and Kelly. Jackie married a law school student in 1970 and Michael graduated from high school in 1972.

I had taken the family on vacations to Ocean City, Maryland, and Atlantic City, New Jersey, in the late 1960s. In 1970, Lu and I took Michael, Kelly, and John to Miami Beach, Florida, and stayed with Lu's Aunt Rose and Uncle Lou who retired there years earlier. The last family vacation we took with the children was to Disney World in 1973, but it was just John, Kelly, Julia, her son, Ty, Lu, and I. Lu and I never got to go anywhere alone for twenty years, so when the kids were old enough, we left them home so we could have some time to ourselves with our friends.

Nancy's husband, Dean, would get drunk at nearly every party, but never in an intolerable way. He normally got a funny grin on his flushed face for the evening and stated something so utterly ridiculous that it was comical. His sense of humor was unique. He didn't tell typical jokes, act stupid, or ever be obnoxious.

He would generally suddenly rise from the table, for instance, and say, "Let's make a toast to Menachem and Anwar," referring to the former leaders of Israel and Egypt, Menachem Begin and Anwar Sadat. He found humor in simple things. Dean's demeanor was always the same. One had the sense he was always thinking of something outrageous to say. I thought he was humorous, and he had this happy-go-lucky attitude, but I always believed Dean was not a man of good character. Dean told me many stories of his time as a Baltimore cop which disappointed me. He admitted to taking bribes and beating the hell out of suspects.

When Dean began dating Nancy, his first wife was home, dying of cancer. No one knew what kind of relationship he had with his first wife, but it certainly seemed in bad taste to date another woman while his wife was dying. Sadly, twenty-five years later, Nancy suffered a heart attack and became an invalid. Dean didn't hesitate for a minute to put her in a nursing home. He immediately started dating another woman while Nancy was dying. I hoped his new girlfriend stayed healthy. You didn't want to get sick with Dean around. I never saw Dean again after Nancy died in 1995. Esther told me she never saw him again either.

My father died in 1972 of lung cancer. My sisters and I threw a big fiftieth wedding anniversary for my parents the year before he died. Pop got lung cancer, which was not surprising since he smoked for over sixty years. Lu and I visited him the night before he succumbed to his cancer. He was in his own bed at home. A neighbor from across the street who was a nurse was helping him. He looked like a skeleton, and he was obviously in severe pain. I couldn't communicate with him that evening due to his deteriorating condition. After he died, the nurse told me he screamed out a woman's name, Joan, the moment before he died. Nobody ever heard of Joan. Luckily, Mom wasn't in the room when he passed. She was never told anything about his dying utterance.

When Pop died, my nephew and my brother-in-law pretty much raided his house for his belongings. While I was mourning his death at the funeral home, they were ransacking his house, taking his tools, clothes, and whatever else they could lay their greedy little hands on. My goofy mother probably told them to help themselves. I really only wanted two items, my grandfather's lucky five-dollar gold piece, and his .45 caliber automatic pistol from World War I. After the funeral, they held a wake at the house serving food.

"Mom," I asked. "Where's Pop's .45 pistol? I'd like to have it."

"I don't know," she said. "You can look around for

it."

"Okay," I said. "I'll look in your bedroom if you don't mind."

"Go ahead," she said. "Milton and Joey have already been in there."

"What?" I asked. "What were they doing in there?"

"The same as you, I suppose," she said unfazed.

"I'm his son, Mom," I said, getting angrier by the second.

"Well, Joey's his grandson," she shot back.

"Jesus Christ," I muttered under my breath.

I entered my parents' bedroom, and initially thought I was too late. I could see in the closet at a quick glance that they had already rifled through his clothes. I investigated the now sparse closet bereft of his clothes and found no sign of the pistol. I noticed a woman's hatbox on the shelf, however, underneath a blanket. To my surprise, the box didn't contain a woman's hat, but my father's 1920s era fedora hat. I was so pleased to find something so personal of my father's. My brother-in-law and nephew were apparently not very thorough in their search. I figured this was probably going to be the only remembrance of him I would have. Nevertheless, I searched his dresser hoping to find the pistol and the five-dollar coin.

To my amazement, in the back of his underwear drawer, I found a small tan box. I opened it anxiously to find my grandfather's lucky gold piece. I was thrilled with this discovery, although it was not for any greedy reason. I had heard about this lucky coin throughout my childhood. I wanted the coin purely for sentimental reasons and for the purpose of handing it down to my son. The last thing I wanted was for it to be in the hands of my nephew or brother-in-law. The thought of it in their covetous hands made me angry. I was so relieved to have found it. They obviously missed it because there was no sign of the .45 pistol. I went down into the basement to look around in the hopes the pistol might have been there, but I couldn't find it. Nearly all his tools were gone, though, I noticed. The goddamn vultures!

Within five years, Mom was diagnosed with Alzheimer's disease. She and Jane came to visit us on Penn Avenue fairly regularly after Pop died. However, by about 1977, she was greeting my daughters by the wrong names. She called one, Hildegard, and the other, Veronica, possibly girls she had known from Inverness. I had never known any women Mom associated with by these names. Ironically, Mom only remembered my name, the one person in the family she seemed to like the least. She knew I was Boy, but I'm not sure she knew I was her son.

"Lu," I said. "How is it that my mother doesn't know who the hell anybody is, but she calls me Boy, the one person in the family she seemed to have liked the least? It's really kind of humorous when you think about it."

"Monty, you know how nobody in the world ever forgets names like Hitler and Mussolini? Well, it's the same," Lu explained in a deadpan manner.

Mom lived for another eleven years, but she ended up dying in a nursing home with the brain of an infant baby. I hated to admit it, but I never shed a tear for my mother, nor for my father for that matter, when they passed away. I felt bad about them dying, naturally, but for some reason, I wasn't very emotional about it.

Chapter Fourteen

All Organisms Die

In 1978, life began to take some bumpy roads for me and Lu. Early in the year, Lu began feeling very sick and she couldn't shake it. She experienced a prolonged malaise having very little energy. She finally visited the doctor where a blood test revealed she had leukemia. Initially, I urged the doctor not to divulge his diagnosis to her. Lu was an extreme worrier. However, she had to be told because the cancerous white blood cells had gathered in her spleen which the doctor determined had to be removed. The operation proved to be successful. I was never sure what function the spleen had. It was apparently some kind of filter for the blood. Luckily, a person could apparently live without a spleen. The doctor advised that the liver took over for the spleen. Lu was then prescribed chemo pills. The disease caused her to become anemic, too, as she also didn't have enough red blood cells. Her immune system became very weak due to a lack of good white blood cells required to fight off germs and infections. I sat the children down together at the kitchen table to explain their mother's condition while Lu was in the hospital recovering from her spleen surgery.

"Kids," I said. "Your mother has leukemia, which means her white blood cell count, which is part of your immune system, is off. Leukemia produces bad white blood cells that decrease the body's ability to fight any kind of infection. Mom is going to take chemo pills that kill the bad white blood cells. The doctor said this should work."

None of the children said a word. I could see the

worried looks on their faces. I didn't want to alarm them, but I also wanted them to know what happened to her. The truth was that leukemia produced cancerous white blood cells, but I didn't want to use that word. Lu told me to instruct the children not to tell anyone of her condition. Lu didn't even want to tell her brothers and sisters. She told them she was anemic and had to have her spleen removed. She said nothing of the leukemia. Lu was emphatic that she didn't want anyone to know.

"Your mother told me to tell you not to tell a soul about her condition," I continued telling the children. "The thing is, your mother doesn't want anyone, and I mean anyone, to know that she has leukemia. Your mother and I have discussed it and it's nobody's business."

"I don't understand," Kelly said. "Why is that such an awful thing for people to know?"

"Because people gossip," I explained. "The last thing your mother wants is for people to see her and start talking about her. You see, it's only human nature for people to point and whisper, saying, oh, look, there's Lu Culpepper, you know she has leukemia. So don't say a word about it to anyone. If anybody asks, you can tell them she had her spleen out and that she's anemic, but don't say anything to anybody about the leukemia."

"Is she going to be all right?" Michael asked, very concerned.

"Of course, she is," I said. "These chemo pills are supposed to kill off the bad white blood cells. The only problem is that it kills good white blood cells too, so it affects her immune system. She could be very susceptible to getting sick or even getting pneumonia, but she'll be all right."

I seemed to have calmed their fears for the time being. Lu came home from the hospital and didn't seem sick at all. She got right back into her normal life. The only problem was that six months later, I got colon cancer. I could hardly believe it.

Prior to my diagnosis and eventual surgery, I had gone to a local general physician in Perry Hall for help, as I was having difficulty with my bowel movements. The quack merely gave me constipation pills. Of course, the pills weren't working because I had a giant tumor in my colon. When I went to a different doctor, he scheduled the appropriate tests that concluded that I had a malignant tumor requiring immediate surgery. I would never forget the sickening feeling that came over me after getting the news from the doctor.

As I walked through the front door to my house, Lu ran out of the kitchen and immediately asked, "How did it go with the doctor?"

"Not good," I responded solemnly.

"What is it, Monty?" she asked nervously. There was no mistaking the look of despondency on my face.

"It's horrible," I said, shaking my head, as I was still in disbelief.

"Oh, my Lord," she said. "What's the matter?"

"I have cancer," I said bluntly. "There's a large tumor blocking my colon. It's the size of a softball, the doctor said."

"What?" my wife cried, as she placed her hands on her face with a confused and shocked look.

"The doctor said I needed immediate surgery," I said. "I'll have to wear a bag."

"Oh, my Lord, Monty," my wife said, tearing up.

"I know, I can hardly believe it myself," I said to her. "If this isn't the biggest kick in the gut I've ever had. I feel absolutely sick. Well, the hell with this, I'm not doing it."

"What do you mean?" my wife asked incredulously.

"I mean I'm not going through with this operation," I shot back resolutely. "I'd have to wear a colostomy bag for the rest of my life. I'm not going to do it. I'd rather be dead."

"Well, you have to do it, Monty," my wife said in a most serious tone, fighting back her tears. "The alternative is far worse."

"No, I don't care," I said, even more frustrated. By this time, I had walked down the hallway and into my bedroom. I was standing in front of my bureau where I usually put my wallet, watch, keys, and rings. However, I could not seem to do anything. I just stood there with my head hanging down, leaning on the bureau as if it were holding me up. My wife followed me down the hallway to the door of our bedroom pleading with me and becoming increasingly more upset.

"Monty," she said, crying. "I love you and the children love you. You have to have the operation."

"I can't do it," I said.

"Listen, Monty," she said very empathetically. "I understand it sounds awful, but I won't love you any less. I just want you here with me and the children. We need you and love you. You'll have a long life ahead of you with people who love you. You can cope with it. I know you can. You're tough, Monty. I've never known you to back down from anything. Now, c'mon Hon, you can do this, I know you can. And it won't make any difference to me or the kids. We'll love you no matter what."

"I know," I said after staring at the floor for several minutes. I exhaled a huge breath and then looked up at her. "But we can't tell a soul outside the immediate family. It's just like you having leukemia. You need to tell the children that they are not to tell anyone, and I mean nobody. The last thing I want is for everybody to know I'm wearing a bag. And that includes your family, too. I know exactly what people would say. Every time somebody saw me, they'd be whispering behind my back, oh, look, there goes Monty Culpepper, you know he wears a colostomy bag. The children need to understand that. They can't tell a soul."

"Don't worry, Monty," she responded. "I'll make sure the kids don't tell anyone. They understood about my leukemia."

"Good," I said. "The doctor was confident that the cancer was concentrated in the tumor and that having the colostomy and removing my lower intestine should get all the cancer. Of course, if he's wrong, then it's a moot point regarding keeping it a secret."

"What do you mean?" my wife asked.

"I mean if the doctor's wrong, I'll be dead," I responded.

"Oh, don't say that, Monty," she said. "You'll be okay, won't you?"

"I'll be alright," I said, as I took her in my arms, now trying my best to allay her fears. I actually was optimistic about the success of the operation, based upon what the doctor told me. It was the goddamn bag that was bothering me. The very thought of it repulsed me.

I went ahead with the operation which proved to be a complete success, but it was a cross to bear for the rest of my life, defecating into a plastic bag from my abdomen. Can you imagine? I never got used to it.

I finally quit smoking at the age of fifty-three after contracting the colon cancer. I never had another cigarette following my colostomy, but the urge never ceased. In the hospital room after my surgery, I simulated smoking with small pencils, the kind they handed out at the golf courses. Luckily, the doctors saved my life by completely removing the tumor blocking my colon. The procedure required removing more than three feet of my intestine. The downside was that I had to wear the damn colostomy bag for the rest of my life. This was quite the challenge for a somewhat fastidious person like me.

A few years later, Lu's brother, John, also got colon cancer. It allowed me the opportunity to reach out to him after years of being estranged to offer my help to him to get through it. We never became great friends, but at least we let go of the past. We bonded in sharing the same disease. We had different ideas, however, in dealing with it day to day. I wore the colostomy bag and changed it two or three times a day as it filled up. John chose a different method. He preferred the option of cleaning out his system every morning. This required him to place a plastic tube into the hole of his abdomen and flush water into it like an enema. The idea was to clean out all the fecal material in his abdomen at the start of the day. I tried doing this once, but it was a filthy, disgusting mess flushing out all your crap for the day through a plastic tube. It was something I couldn't stomach. John liked the idea of not having to deal with it the rest of the day. He still wore his bag just in case.

I never got used to dealing with it, but what was I to do? For the most part, it was manageable, but it could become embarrassing at times. Sometimes it really reeked. Basically, it smelled like I shit my pants when the bag filled up. I had no control over it whatsoever. A couple of times, I was playing golf and the bag overflowed. The only thing I could do was go into the woods and take a golf towel to clean myself up. It was a humiliating experience with no bathroom nearby. My youngest son was playing golf with me. I hated for him to see me in that condition, but he was a good kid, and he never said a word about it.

I first took my sons out to play golf with me in 1973. It was Lu's idea. I loved the children and played with them when they were little. I tried my best to spend as much time with them as I could. I was interested in their studies and their activities. However, I was always busy. In the 1950s, I went to night school to get my degree. I played golf and flew my airplane. In the 1960s, I spent a lot of time at my jobs and traveling for work. I also went back to night school for my master's, which I obtained at Johns Hopkins University in 1967. I earned a master's degree in Liberal Arts, something I was particularly proud of inasmuch as I was a mechanical engineer. I hated that the majority of engineers with whom I worked over the years only excelled in mathematics. Most of them massacred the English language. I thought it was important to be a well-rounded individual.

I also attended night school taking engineering classes in order to become a "Professional Engineer." By the early 1970s, while working at Chesapeake and Potomac Telephone, I passed the necessary exams to become a Professional Engineer. Part of my motivation might possibly have been to satisfy my ego, but it became very important for me to be able to put "P.E." after my name on my company business cards. I got great satisfaction from this achievement in my chosen vocation. I likened it to an accountant striving to be a Certified Public Accountant or a lawyer passing the bar exam.

Nothing was more important to me than education, not only for myself but for my children as well. I was very disappointed when my daughter, Jackie, decided to get married immediately after graduating from college. I believed that she was limiting her potential by marrying so young. Then in 1983, when my son told me he was getting married, I couldn't believe it. I loved Lu so much, more than anything, but getting married and having children at such a young age was detrimental to my education and career. I passed up an Ivy League education at Brown University because of marriage. Then, Lu's refusal to transfer to Orlando ended my dream job at the Glenn L. Martin Company. I was laid off shortly thereafter and my rising career was over. I loved Lu and never did anything to make her unhappy, but I knew that marriage and family limited my prospects.

John was an intelligent young man who excelled in school and sports, and his potential was unlimited. The only thing to limit him, I believed, was marriage. He proved me wrong four years later when he became an FBI agent. His wife didn't hesitate for a minute in quitting her job as a high school history teacher, leaving her family behind in Baltimore, and following John to Orlando, Florida, ironically, for his career. I really missed John, though, when he left. We had been playing golf nearly every weekend together for almost fifteen years since we first played at his mother's suggestion. Lu rued the day she ever had the idea of taking the boys with me to play golf, not realizing that we would make golf a priority for the rest of our lives. Lu grew to abhor golf, as it became her rival. My oldest son only played that one time. He found no enjoyment in it and never played again. It might have had something to do with his baby brother, John, beating him.

Lu battled her leukemia bravely for fourteen years. For the most part, she led a normal life except for the fact that she took chemo pills daily and had a low threshold for sickness. Due to her condition, she suffered pneumonia practically every year and was hospitalized each time. On occasion, she looked like death warmed over in her hospital bed. I was often very concerned. Fortunately, Lu recovered from her bouts of pneumonia. I was always optimistic, especially since she pulled through each time. However, in 1992, Lu's health started to deteriorate rapidly. She developed a fever blister, a condition which she suffered from her entire life, but this one would not go away. This was a killer of a fever blister. It bled constantly and formed a giant scab covering her entire lower lip and part of her chin. She became embarrassed just going to the grocery store. She said people were staring. She began to lose weight, but her stomach was distended. The doctor said that the cancerous white blood cells were gathering in her liver, as they had fourteen years ago in her spleen. However, they couldn't remove her liver. Lu knew she was dying.

"Monty," Lu pleaded in early 1992. "Make sure my funeral is a full Catholic mass."

"Oh, Lu," I responded. "Don't talk about that. You're going to be fine."

"Monty," she continued. "I want a full mass at my funeral."

"Lu," I said. "You're going to be okay. You're not going anywhere."

Sadly, Lu became obsessed with this. She was very depressed and felt poorly. She knew she was getting worse. Then in late April, she developed another pneumonia and was hospitalized. I was still optimistic that she would pull through, as she had always done before. I must have been in denial. I knew I couldn't live without her. My son transferred with the FBI from Orlando to Washington, D.C. at the beginning of May 1992. His mother was released from the hospital the week before he moved back. She was home in her nightgown, but she was pulling around her IV. She was very thin and weak. She was also very disheartened. Even when her old friend, Toodles, visited, Lu couldn't muster up any enthusiasm or hide her deteriorating condition. She didn't smile once and said very little. Lu had lost her zest for life. She felt too poorly. Her old vivacious, endearing personality was squashed by the cancer inside her.

I hadn't told my son about Lu's worsening condition because I didn't want to worry him. He had too much on his mind with his transfer. When he got home, I told him how she had been in the hospital for her pneumonia. Lu asked John's wife, Shirley, to make sure she would have a full Catholic mass at her funeral because I wouldn't listen to her.

"Mom, you're going to get better," Shirley responded.

"That's exactly what Monty keeps saying," Lu said with deep frustration. "Now promise me you'll make sure I have a full Catholic mass at my funeral."

"I promise, Mom," Shirley said reluctantly. "I'll make sure you have a full Catholic mass. Don't worry."

"Thank you," Lu said. "That's all I want."

By the end of May, Lu was back in the hospital. At first, she seemed to rally. Her brother, John, and his wife, Reba, came to visit her in the hospital on Friday evening. Lu projected the most energy and personality I had seen from her in over a month. She seemed like her old charming, loveable self, but it was short-lived. On Saturday, Kelly and her husband and three small children visited. Lu was sociable but not as vibrant as the previous day. She was much more subdued. Kelly became alarmed when she told Kelly she saw bugs on the wall. Kelly told her nothing was on the walls. The following day, her condition worsened, and she went into a coma. John and Shirley visited on Sunday, but Lu never awakened. I told John she was just tired and was sleeping. The nurse brought in an oxygen apparatus and laid it on the bed prior to their departure.

"What's that for?" John inquired worriedly.

"It's to give her oxygen," I said nonchalantly. "She needs it because of her pneumonia."

"Is Mom going to be okay?" John asked.

"Yes," I answered optimistically. "She's just tired

from the pneumonia and will need a little oxygen to help her along. She'll be fine."

"I hope so," John said. "I'm so disappointed I couldn't tell Mom that I won my flight in the club championship this weekend at the golf club. Do you remember how she always told me to quit golf when she saw me upset over losing a golf tournament?"

"Yes," I said. "She hated to see you unhappy. You'll get a chance to tell her later when she's feeling better."

"Okay," John said. "Let me know how she's doing."

"I will," I said. "You guys give my love to the babies and don't worry. She'll be fine."

I did actually think she would be fine, too. Through the years, I witnessed Lu many, many times appear to be at death's door, and she always recovered. I was hopeful even though I knew it was much worse this time. She recovered from numerous bouts with pneumonia, but this was the first time the doctor had said that cancerous white blood cells were gathering in her liver and distending her stomach. I wondered why she wasn't allowed to get a bone marrow transplant or more intensive chemotherapy, but the fact of the matter was that her cancer had become too far advanced and there was nothing they could do. She was dying and she knew it, but I didn't want to believe it.

The nurse put her on oxygen that evening, and she never woke up. On Monday at about five o'clock in the afternoon, per the instruction of the nurse, I called all the children to come to the hospital to see their mother. She was not expected to live much longer. My three daughters, two sons, and I gathered around Lu's bed. I was holding her hand on one side of the bed and John was holding her hand on the other side. The girls were whimpering as they stood close to her bed. Lu's eyes suddenly opened.

The girls screamed, "Mom, Mom!" Everyone got excited at Lu's apparent lucidity, however, this lasted just momentarily.

"Dad, she stopped breathing," John said as he looked across the bed at me. He then shut her eyes.

The girls began crying hysterically realizing that their mother was gone. I left the room to retrieve the nurse. The nurse checked Lu's vital signs and confirmed that she was dead. I felt some comfort in believing that Lu opened her eyes one last time in order to say goodbye. I felt her presence lingering above the bed after she opened her eyes. John came home with me that night. As we walked through the front door, we both broke down, cried, and hugged each other in the living room.

"I can't believe she's gone," John said.

"I know," I said. "You can take comfort though in that you and Shirley have the same love for each other that your mother and I had."

Later that night, I had the most vivid dream of my life of Lu flying across the sky on a cloud like an angel, but without wings. She flew through the window and said to me, "I'm at peace, Monty. Everything is going to be okay."

The days that followed were surreal. John accompanied me to the Schimunek Funeral Home in Perry Hall to pick out a casket.

"This casket is very popular," the funeral director said as he showed us an ornate wood-finished casket with carvings of Jesus and the cross and the Holy Mary on it.

"No, my wife wouldn't like that," I responded without hesitation. "She was very religious and a devout Catholic, but that one would be too ostentatious for her."

"How about this one?" the funeral director asked pointing to a silver metal casket with nothing on it. "Of course, all of the caskets are guaranteed to be water-tight and include a cement underground vault where no water will leak in."

"That one will be fine," I answered, secretly thinking what the hell difference it would make if water seeped into the casket of a decaying corpse six feet underground.

At the viewings, everybody kept telling me how good Lu looked. My daughter picked out a new blue dress she purchased just last year, and her hair was done up as if she had just returned from the beauty parlor. People were being thoughtful and nice, but they really didn't know what to say. Lu looked fine in her casket, but I knew it wasn't her lying there. It was just her shell. Her soul was gone.

The funeral went well. The priest conducting the funeral mass at St. Joseph's Church was my favorite priest of all time. He was one of only a handful of Catholic priests in the world who was actually married with children. He had previously been an Episcopalian priest who converted to Catholicism. The Catholic Church allowed him to become a Catholic priest even though he was married with a family. He was a great speaker, and he never referred to notes, as most priests did. During his homilies at Mass, he stepped out from behind the lectern and spoke to the congregation at the front of the altar. I always thought his homilies to be more poignant than the other priests' sermons, maybe because he was more like everybody else in the congregation. He did not disappoint and spoke beautifully at Lu's funeral mass. I kept it together quite well until the choir began singing *How Great Thou Art* and then *Amazing Grace,* which reduced me to tears.

At the wake at our house, I was disturbed by the whole party atmosphere, the drinking, and the laughter. I was in no mood for it. I could not fathom how anybody could be laughing at a time like this. I was feeling the lowest I ever felt, and for the life of me, I could not comprehend why people were having such a good time only one hour after my beloved wife had been buried.

Then, my sister-in-law came upstairs from the basement and asked me, "Where's Mr. Flanagan's framed portrait that was hanging in the basement?" I could only assume that she wanted it.

"Lu gave that to Reba years ago," I responded, secretly disgusted by her inquiry.

Lu was always her father's favorite. After her mother died, Lu ended up with the earliest known picture of her father, a large professionally made photograph in an approximately two-foot-long, oval-shaped frame, taken in the early 1900s when he was about twenty. Lu gave the picture away a couple of years before merely because her other sister-in-law, Reba, asked for it. Lu did this because she was the sweetest, most generous, and unselfish person I ever knew. She truly never wanted anyone to be unhappy. This incident brought back the unpleasant memory when my father died, and my brother-in-law and nephew rummaged through his things.

I couldn't bear any more of the wake and went outside to sit on the front steps. I was sitting there in my own thoughts, basically trying not to cry when a neighbor down the street walked toward me. I hadn't seen him at the funeral, but I thought it was at least nice of him to come see me and to give his condolences. However, his idea of condolences was in stark contrast to mine. His only remarks to me concerning Lu's death were, "We're all just organisms, and all organisms die."

I could only look at him with what felt like the most disgusted expression on my face I had ever had in my entire life. I said nothing and he walked away. Wow, I thought the atmosphere at the wake was unbearable. I didn't think it could have gotten any worse than the people inside my house, but I was wrong. My neighbor's comment took the cake. I never really understood how stupid and ignorant people could be. So many people apparently possessed no self-awareness. How could a person not have realized that their words could have such a profoundly hurtful impact?

My children tried to include me in everything that summer following Lu's death. I attended their Fourth of July party, the grandkids' birthday parties, and I even went to Ocean City for a few days to vacation with them, but it just wasn't the same anymore. Lu's absence at every family function was a huge and obvious void. She was the glue that kept everything together. I was so lost after Lu's passing, and I didn't want to socialize without her. I declined all invitations from Lu's sisters to events and basically just withdrew from life.

I still played golf and saw my children and the grandkids, but I did so less and less as the years passed by. I didn't like being alone in the house without Lu, so I started taking road trips. I still enjoyed gambling and golfing because I could do these activities alone. I drove all over the country. Once I drove to Connecticut to go to an Indian gambling casino called Foxwoods. I drove through the Southwest sightseeing and then went to Las Vegas for a few days. Another time I drove to Shreveport, Louisiana, and gambled on a riverboat casino on the Red River. I frequented Atlantic City, too, and I played golf all the time, usually by myself. I wished I could have written letters to Lu as I did in the good old days.

Chapter Fifteen

The Cuckoo's Nest

In the summer of 1996, I found myself worrying about my health. I coughed up phlegm every morning, as I had for the last twenty years, the result of smoking two packs of Chesterfields with no filters for thirty-seven years. The doctor told me I had the first stage of emphysema. The years of smoking had burned the cilia hairs in my esophagus, causing my hacking, but it wouldn't get any worse, the doctor said, because I no longer smoked. I also had an enlarged prostate, causing me problems with urinating, but the doctor said it wasn't cancerous. However, by 1996, I was convinced these things were going to kill me. I was also forgetting a lot of facts. My mind had been like a steel trap my entire life and now I was forgetting even how old my children were. I could no longer remember their years of birth, which previously had been a strong point with my memory. I remembered dates, for some reason, more than anything else.

After Lu died in 1992, I normally went to dinner at John and Shirley's home in Crofton, Maryland, on Thursday nights. Shirley cooked many of the same meals Lu cooked for me, pot roast, spaghetti and meatballs, steak and mashed potatoes, chicken rice soup, fried chicken and noodles, and other delicious meals. I enjoyed playing with their children and watching *Seinfeld* on television later in the evening. I called Shirley one Thursday afternoon in May 1997 to inform her I wasn't coming.

"Hi Shirley," I said. "I'm not going to make it for dinner this evening."

"Oh, no," Shirley responded. "John's coming home

today. He's been out of town on business all week. He'll miss seeing you."

"Well," I continued. "I can't see anyone. My health is so bad, and I've been a terrible father."

"What?" Shirley asked incredulously. "What's wrong?"

"I'm a terrible person," I continued. "I can't see anyone."

"What are you talking about, Dad?" Shirley asked. "You're not a bad person."

"You don't know, Hon," I explained. "I've not led a good life."

"Of course, you've led a good life, Dad," Shirley said. "You're a wonderful father-in-law and a terrific grandfather to my children."

"I can't come, Hon," I told her. "Tell John I'm sorry."

When John got home from the airport shortly before dinner, Shirley confronted him and told him of his father's odd behavior.

"John," she said anxiously. "Something is wrong with your father. He acted so strangely on the phone when he canceled for dinner tonight. I'm so worried about him."

"I'll call him," John said.

"He's not making much sense," Shirley warned. "It's very concerning."

"Dad," John said. "This is John. Shirley said she talked to you earlier, and you said you weren't coming for dinner. Is everything all right?"

"I can't come," I explained. "My health is very poor, and I've led a terrible life."

"No, you haven't, Dad," John said. "You're a good man."

"No, I'm not," I further explained. "I've been an awful husband and father. I'm not going to live long because my health is deteriorating."

"Dad, you're wrong," John said forcefully. "I'll tell you what. I'm going to come up and see you right now."

"No, that won't be necessary," I insisted.

"Yes, it is," John said. "I'll be there in about forty-five minutes."

John arrived at my house less than an hour later. I was sitting at the kitchen table drinking coffee.

"Dad, what's going on?" John questioned. "You don't sound like yourself."

"John, I have to tell you," I explained. "I'm a terrible person and I've led an awful life."

"No, you haven't, Dad," John shot back. "You've led a great life."

"No, I've been a bad father and husband," I said.

"Dad, you've been a great father, a loving husband, and wonderful family man your whole life," John countered.

"Do you know that I gambled away more than $10,000?" I told him.

"Yeah, but Dad, that was over a period of over twenty years," John clarified. "I know you've been flying up to Atlantic City for free on gambling junkets for twenty years and you keep meticulous details on your winnings and losses."

"I squandered so much money gambling," I said, convinced of what I was stating.

"Dad, if you lost $10,000 in twenty years, then you probably only lost $500 a year," John explained. "I went with you many times to shoot craps. You were a very conservative bettor always trying out one of your systems."

"No, I was reckless," I insisted.

"That is one of your hobbies," John said. "You enjoy yourself just like you enjoy golf. You spend way more money on golf every year than $500 to shoot craps. It was worth $500 a year for the enjoyment you got out of it."

"I didn't give enough to the Church either," I told him.

"Yes, you did, Dad!" John retorted. "You go to church every week and put an envelope in the collection basket. I've seen you. You're wrong!"

"I didn't give enough," I continued. "I should have given more."

"Dad, you gave plenty," John refuted. "I know you did. I witnessed it. I've gone to church with you. Remember how we always attended seven o'clock mass Sunday mornings before heading to Clifton Park to play golf? We never missed mass and you put an envelope in the collection basket every time."

"I'm not healthy either," I told him. "I'm dying of emphysema."

"No, you're not, Dad," John said. "I've played golf with you and spent a lot of time with you. You have no trouble breathing."

"I can't catch my breath, lately," I said. "I'm dying."

"You're okay, Dad," he asserted. "You haven't smoked for twenty years. You have a touch of emphysema, that's all. You told me before how the cilia in your esophagus was damaged from smoking, but the doctor told you it wouldn't get any worse since you no longer smoked. It only affects you in the mornings when you have trouble coughing up phlegm. You're not dying from emphysema."

"I'm a selfish person," I maintained. "I've led a horrible life and I was a terrible provider for the family. I'll tell you another thing. I never volunteered."

"Yes, you did, Dad," John contended. "I remember you were a member of the Knights of Columbus at St. Joseph's."

"I was a member, but I never once volunteered for anything," I said forcefully. "I only attended the meetings. I joined when I first moved to Perry Hall just to meet people. I never volunteered for a damn thing."

"You volunteered to serve in the Navy in World War II," John retorted. "What was that? I'd call that volunteering."

"No, once I got in, I didn't volunteer for anything," I insisted.

"You took tests to be an officer and a pilot," John explained. "I'd call that going above and beyond the call of duty, volunteering to do more."

"I just wanted to get off that damn ship," I said. "I've been a terrible person, an awful father, and a worse husband. I've lived a very bad life."

"Dad, I hate to say this, but you're sick," John said. "You need to get some help. Something is seriously wrong. You're not yourself. The things you are saying are wrong and completely irrational. I'm worried about you. You need to go to the hospital."

"I'm not going to the hospital," I said unequivocally.

"I'm afraid you're going to have to," John said. "I'm going home tonight, but I'll be back for you in the morning. Try to get a good night's sleep and don't think about all of this."

John returned in the morning to take me to the hospital.

"I'm not going to the hospital," I told him as he came into the house.

"Yes, you are, Dad," John said.

"No, I'm not going," I said adamantly. "I don't want to go to the hospital."

"Dad," John said very calmly. "I have my handcuffs in the car. If you don't cooperate, I'm getting my handcuffs and I'll cuff you and hogtie you to get you to the hospital if I have to. Now you don't want me to do that, do you? We can do this nicely or we can do it the hard way.

What's it going to be? Now let's go."

I knew John was dead serious and he meant what he said. He was a very determined person, downright hardheaded most of the time, as a matter of fact. I knew I would lose this fight. John was still a relatively young man, very muscular and fit, and a trained FBI agent. I really didn't want to go, but what else could I do?

"All right, all right," I said reluctantly. "I'll go. No need for any of that."

"Good," John said. "Let's go."

We got into the car and proceeded to St. Joseph's Hospital in Towson, Maryland. After John explained to the Emergency Room doctor why he had brought me there, a psychiatrist was called to meet us. Honestly, I wasn't sure exactly what was going on. John told the doctor that I was irrational and not myself. It was true. I felt tortured inside. I believed with all my heart that I had lived a horrible and unworthy life. I was convinced that I had done everything wrong and was a complete failure. Hell, these people didn't know my life.

"So, what seems to be the problem?" the psychiatrist asked me.

"I'm all right," I told him. "You wouldn't understand. I've lived a terrible life, that's all."

"Are you feeling down?" he asked.

"Yes," I said. "I'm not a good person and I've been an abysmal father and husband."

"Are you having any suicidal thoughts?" the doctor asked.

"I'm very tormented," I responded, not wanting to reveal that I was in fact having suicidal thoughts. I was quite beside myself. I couldn't shake my anguish and I believed that my only relief would be death, but I didn't divulge my true feelings to the doctor.

"How are you tormented?" the doctor asked.

"I told you," I responded. "I've led an awful life."

"In what way have you led an awful life?" the doctor asked.

"I've been a selfish man," I explained. "I wasn't a good husband or provider for my family. I gambled away $10,000. I didn't give enough to the Catholic Church. I only thought about myself my entire life. And my biggest sin was that I never volunteered."

"Are you sure you're not having any suicidal thoughts?" the doctor asked again.

"It doesn't matter," I answered. "I'm dying of emphysema."

The doctor then walked across the room to speak to John.

"I believe your father is suffering from clinical depression," the doctor explained. "It might be caused by a chemical imbalance in his brain due to old age. I cannot say with any certainty as to the cause, but it is quite common among the elderly. He has two options. We could admit him to the Psychiatric Ward here at St. Joseph's and provide him with anti-depressant drugs intravenously, but there is no guarantee we could reverse his condition. The other option is electroshock therapy. I know this sounds radical, but the latter has proved to be very effective in combatting his type of depression and irrational thought."

"Do you mean electroshock therapy like in the movie, *One Flew Over the Cuckoo's Nest*?" John inquired.

"The therapy depicted in that movie dated to the 1950s," the doctor said. "The technology has advanced dramatically. The idea is that the electroshocks cause a mini-seizure in the patient which has the effect of reversing clinical depression such as what your father is experiencing."

"What is your recommendation?" John asked the

doctor.

"I would recommend the electroshock therapy," the doctor said. "We don't offer this at St. Joseph's, but across the street at Shepherd Pratt Hospital, which treats mental illness exclusively, they offer it. As I said, I think this treatment would be most effective in reversing your father's condition."

John admitted me into Shepherd Pratt Hospital. As I entered, the place was full of mental patients screaming, and acting nuts, quite frankly. It was disturbing. It really was the cuckoo's nest. I felt as though I didn't belong there. I really wasn't entirely sure what was going on. I spent three weeks in this insane asylum and received electroshock treatments twice per week. After getting my brain zapped, I improved, and the thoughts I had regarding my judgment on my life as being appalling disappeared. The trouble wasn't so much that I didn't have bad thoughts about myself any longer, but that I didn't have any thoughts about it at all.

After my three-week stay in the nuthouse, John picked me up and took me home. On the drive back to my house, he made reference to the irrational thoughts I was having prior to my admittance to the hospital. I really wasn't sure what he was talking about. I felt like my personality and once sharp intellect had been diminished after leaving Shepherd Pratt. I only knew that I was ready to go home and start playing golf again. My life slowly got back to normal, resuming my previous routine, playing golf every day, visiting family, eating out, and attending church every Sunday. However, after about a year and a half, my feelings of leading an inadequate and awful life consumed me again. I had been seeing a psychiatrist in the town of Bel Air, twelve miles north of Perry Hall, after my release from Shepherd Pratt, but I stopped seeing her after about a year or so. She had prescribed me anti-depressant pills, but I stopped taking them. My thoughts about my failure in life returned and began to torment me again. It became unbearable. It was like living in purgatory. I came to the dark realization that the only way to stop these demons inside of me was to end my life.

On one cold Saturday night during the fall of 1998, I was in constant agony suffering from my guilt. As I sat in the dining room, I was tortured by my memories of my failed and dreadful life. I felt complete and total despair. I was hunched over with my head in my lap and my hands wrapped around my head. I tried to rub my bad thoughts out of my head, but they just wouldn't go away. My daughter, Julia, was on her way out the door for a date with her long-time boyfriend. I couldn't hide my tortured state of mind. I was suffering and filled with torment. Julia headed out the door oblivious to my agitated state. Her only concern was making her date. She didn't seem to care in the least about me.

I sat there for a long time and then finally went downstairs into the back part of the basement behind the clubroom and the boys' old bedroom. It was the part of the basement where the washer and dryer, the furnace, the sump pump, and my workbench with all my tools were located. I could picture Lu doing the laundry while I made some repair at my workbench. I had been quite the handyman. I then retrieved a metal wire from my toolbox. I fastened the wire securely in the rafters. I climbed onto a footstool and wrapped the wire firmly around my larynx. My final thought was that I should have volunteered.

About the Author

I was born in Baltimore, Maryland. I graduated from Towson State University with Magna Cum Laude honors in 1984. I worked my entire career for the Federal Bureau of Investigation (FBI), from 1984 to 2012, transferring several times to assignments in Florida, Louisiana, Pennsylvania, Oklahoma, and Washington, D.C.

I have been married to my wife, Cindy, since 1984, and have two grown children, Ethan and Mary, and an adorable granddaughter, Lucy. I retired to Waynesboro, Pennsylvania, where I play golf several times per week. I enjoy spending time with Cindy and the family. I also enjoy playing the trombone, hiking, watching old movies, and listening to music, particularly anything by Elvis Presley or Dean Martin. My favorite travel destination is the Highlands of Scotland, the ancestral home of my paternal grandmother. I love golfing on Scottish links courses, hiking mountains, visiting my Chisholm relatives, and taking in the beautiful scenery of the Highlands.

I like to read as much as I like to write. I gravitate toward biographies and American history. This is my third book. I published a novel in December 2016, entitled *L'Archevêque,* based on the true story of a French fur trader in the 1700s, my direct ancestor, Paul L'Archevêque, also known as Paul Larsh.

In October 2017, I published a detailed memoir of my career, entitled *The FBI – They Eat Their Young*. The book disclosed fascinating details of the inner workings of the FBI, as well as exposing a dark side of the FBI executive management.

Club Charles, Baltimore, Maryland, circa 1943.

www.blossomspringpublishing.com

CPSIA information can be obtained
at www.ICGtesting.com
Printed in the USA
LVHW041541220623
750504LV00001B/93